THE SCOTTISH RUIN KEEPER

A Historical Novel

DEB HOSEY WHITE

the three
tomatoes
The Three Tomatoes Book Publishing

Published: February 2025

ISBN: 979-8-9916508-5-4
Library of Congress Control Number: 2024923707

For information address:
The Three Tomatoes Book Publishing
6 Soundview Rd.
Glen Cove, NY 11542

Cover design: David Stewart White
Interior design: Susan Herbst

Dedication

"Is it done yet?"

The Scottish Ruin Keeper is dedicated to
my late nephew Jimmy Kauffman who made me
promise I would finish writing this book.

"Destruction of Elgin Cathedral" Thomas Allom - Scotland: illustrated in a series of views taken expressly for this work by Messrs. T. Allom, W.H. Bartlett, and H. M'Culloch (London 1835-1838)

PROLOGUE

JUNE 1390 –
THE WOLF AND THE DEVIL

Midsummer twilight settled like a shroud over the cathedral town of Elgin, Scotland. The night was warm, and the hour was late. All was calm and silent. Not even a dog stirred in the streets. Inside the cathedral, the last vesper hymn had died away. None were awake save for a few souls kneeling before the Virgin's shrine, quietly offering up prayers of penitence. It was a nightly ritual that had not changed in one hundred and sixty-six years. But this was not to be another peaceful night in Elgin.

The new moon shed no light upon the approaching danger, but a rumble of fast-moving horses began to awaken the town. Only the bravest in Elgin opened their shutters to peek outside. What they saw made them tremble in terror. The jangling harnesses and clanking weapons confirmed all fears. These were neither peaceful gypsies nor tinkers passing through town. The unfamiliar men-at-arms looked eerily like the Horsemen of the Apocalypse.

Although he was the son of royalty, Alexander Stewart was widely known to be the notorious Wolf of Badenoch. He had ridden into Elgin to seek revenge for his excommunication from the Church. Elgin's Gothic cathedral was his target. The town's peace-loving citizens were simply in his way.

Merchants, tradesmen, and poorer townsfolk shrank back within their homes, praying the invaders might pass them by. Those last moments of calm were quickly replaced by shrieks of despair. Men, women, and helpless children spilled out into the night, fleeing the town in a terrified mass.

Intense flames pierced the sky, and the vault of heaven began to redden. Elgin was in chaos. Screams and shouts rang out. "Fire! Fire! Murder! Fire!" No one dared to stop. The growing crowd pressed onward, too frightened to look back until they reached the woods outside of town.

The exhausted survivors collapsed upon the forest floor. A few brave souls crept to the edge of the trees to witness the destruction unfolding in Elgin. The church of St. Giles, the hospital of the Maison Dieu, and the college were all in flames. But those fires paled against the conflagration engulfing Elgin's cathedral. An inferno raged high within its walls, illuminating the tracery of Gothic windows and towers. The terrified people of Elgin cried out in dismay. But their cries were lost among the earsplitting sounds of the cathedral's roof and timbers collapsing in flames.

Alexander Stewart had come to Elgin to wreak vengeance on the Church. And to this day some still say the Devil himself rode with the Wolf of Badenoch on that fateful summer night.

SPRING 1824 - A PIECE OF THE PAST

Will was searching for a hiding place.

In a game of All Hide, the rules frequently changed at the

whims of older boys. But Will wanted to do something he had never done before—hide and not be found. Or at least not found first, which was his usual fate.

The cathedral ruin was a rocky playground with plenty of hiding places. Will slipped away quickly from the voices of playmates and cousins. His smallness let him squeeze past rubble piles and broken walls that others would struggle to navigate.

Pausing to catch his breath, Will noticed a tiny shaft of light piercing the gloom. It illuminated a trail of dancing dust motes and lit the nose of a sleeping stone man. Will ran his fingers over the cool face. He felt the carved eyes but could not see them. His hand slid down a smooth fold and touched the intertwined stone fingers. The pinpoint of light assured him that what he touched was real. He thought he saw other stone men sleeping in the shadows beyond.

Will heard someone calling his name. He crouched down low. The light shaft shifted. It fell upon the wing of a tiny carved creature half-buried in the rubble beside him. A feathery wing took Will's breath away. Before the magical piece of stone could disappear, or fly away, or change into ruined rock—before the sliver of light moved again and the little carving was lost to him forever—Will scooped it into his hand and sunk it deep into his pocket. Right next to a bit of oatcake he had tucked away for later. His belly gurgled.

"Will! Come out, Will!" Many boys were calling now. Suddenly what Will had seen in the darkness was unimportant compared to winning the game. Following the voices, he squeezed through tighter and tighter spaces until at last he stumbled into the ruin's open yard.

"There you are!" The boys ran to greet him. An older cousin draped his arm over Will's small shoulders. "We thought we'd lost you, Will. Why didn't you answer when we called?"

"Where were you for so long?" The others wanted to know.

"Hiding." Will grinned and shoved a hand into his pocket. "Did I win?"

I

CHANGES AND WISHES

Will's father and grandfathers were stonecutters.

That was the trade of his Clachan ancestors. It was meant to be his trade, as well. As far back as anyone remembered, the stonemasons of Elgin quarried the ruin to build new structures in Moray. But that changed when Elgin's town council gated and locked the six-hundred-year-old ruin. Allegedly the locks were intended to stop townsfolk from dumping rubbish there.

John Shanks was appointed keeper of the ruin. His responsibilities included historic preservation of the site. Shanks had the fiscal backing of Isaac Forsyth, Elgin's distinguished patron and scholar. Although Shanks was an aging shoemaker, he was an amateur historian, as well.

Only after the ruin was secured, with keys in the hands of John Shanks, did the masons realize their fate. They would no longer be permitted to quarry the ruined cathedral. Tom Clachan was furious when he learned the news. At the town council meeting he spoke on behalf of his trade. "The stonemasons of Elgin have quarried the ruin for generations. Our work is needed now more than ever for

Elgin's new building projects. The council must reconsider!"

But the stonemason's appeal was firmly denied. "The time for change is afoot," Isaac Forsyth concluded, confirming the council's decision. "Now is the time to secure the cathedral ruin if we want to preserve our history." He looked directly at Clachan. With no compassion in his voice he said, "We must protect the remains of the ruin for posterity."

Tom Clachan refused to let Forsyth's words hang in the air unchallenged. "Aye. And the last time Elgin Cathedral was walled and locked four hundred years ago, it was to keep out the vilest man in the kingdom, a man of royal blood. I am not the Wolf of Badenoch, sir. Nor am I a descendant of the Privy Council who long ago ordered the removal of the cathedral's roof. We stonemasons are not the likes of Oliver Cromwell's men who ransacked the deserted cathedral's remains. I may be a lowly laborer, but I know our history as well as you, sir."

The council members grumbled their displeasure, but Clachan remained undeterred.

"The history of my family's craft spans more than five generations. Our ancestors were the builders and rebuilders of Elgin's first cathedral, the Lantern of the North. Our ancient Pictish roots in Scotland are widely known. We are not destroyers. We are builders. Our families have lived and worked in Elgin for hundreds of years. You talk of preserving what is left of the cathedral. We are doing just that, sir. Using the stones our ancestors laid down long ago to rebuild Elgin for the next generation."

For a thin slice of time, the council room was silent. Those present waited to see what might happen next. But Forsyth's unsympathetic voice interrupted all hope for a change of heart. "Thank you, Tom Clachan. Your words will be recorded in the minutes of this meeting." He gaveled the assemblage to a close.

Will had never seen his father so angry. The stonemasons and their families were shocked by the finality of the decision. The council's actions seemed irrational and unfair. In recent memory the masons had worked as partners with town leaders. Even helping shore up the old cathedral wall before it was locked. This shift felt like punishment for some phantom crime. The stonemasons had done nothing wrong. Nothing different from what they and their forefathers had done for hundreds of years. Now, quite suddenly, the masons were cast as destroyers, picking the carcass of a historic ruin.

The decision forever transformed Tom Clachan. The pleasant man who loved his work was now an angry man, threatening to single-handedly tear down the cathedral walls he helped repair. Pushing everyone away, Clachan silently wished the world would stop changing so fast.

Will Clachan yearned for the return of his father's good company.

He missed their long talks and Da's broad smile. The occasional pat on the back and playful tugging at Will's hair. Now his father was frequently away searching for work, leaving Will as man of the family. But when his father was home, Will tried to avoid Da's black moods.

One early spring day John Shanks arrived uninvited at Tom Clachan's croft. He asked to talk with the stonemason. Tom was irate to have Shanks at his door. But Charlotte Clachan encouraged her husband to step outside and see what the man wanted.

"What he wants!" Clachan seethed. "What about what I want?"

"Hush, man. Go hear what he has to say. And remember whose tenants we are, and to whom we pay our rents."

Clachan stepped outside but refused to shake John Shanks's hand.

"Walk with me," Shanks said. "I have a proposal for you." They moved down the track leading away from the croft.

As they passed a row of decaying houses near the River Lossie, Shanks finally spoke. "All these years and I am still unaccustomed to the quiet." He nodded toward the weather-darkened crofts. "When I was a boy, each home had a loom. On every street and lane, you could hear the clack and rattle. The sounds of womenfolk hard at work."

"Only a few remain," Clachan begrudgingly agreed.

"Do you remember those days? Before Johnston built the woolen mill?"

"I do," Clachan mumbled. "I am old enough to remember."

"Johnston brought machinery to comb the wool and spin it into yarn. With the mill's success came the end of every croft having a loom and a spinning wheel. Progress, I suppose," Shanks said. "Employment for townsfolk."

"And the end of women weaving woolen goods at home," Clachan pointed out. "Aye. I remember the old times well enough."

"A better quality of goods now," Shanks noted.

"At thrice the price."

Shanks shrugged. "There's always homespun goods at the Saturday markets."

"It's not the same," Clachan mumbled.

Shanks cleared his throat. "Change and progress—that is precisely what I have come to discuss."

"Only if you hear me out first," Clachan insisted.

Shanks stayed quiet as the stonemason revisited his grievances about rightful access to the ruin. "The cathedral was robbed out ages ago," Clachan argued. "You know the old stories as well as I do. How the rood screen was destroyed for firewood, and the bells carted off and melted down. How the cathedral's lead roof was dismantled and loaded onto a ship bound for Holland. And the ship's bad luck, sinking just out of Aberdeen Harbor. Aside from the stray coin or spoon or button, there has been nothing of value found on the site in years," Clachan insisted. He kicked at a rock embedded in the dirt. "And yet you felt the need to lock the ruin."

Shanks wasted no time restating his position. "As the ruin's appointed keeper and watchman, all decisions about access are now mine to make. And future access is entirely unsettled until we determine what is of value and what might be removed."

Picking up the loosened stone from the ground, Clachan harrumphed.

"And who is to judge what is of value?" Shanks asked. "You and your men value the stone, but this is a new age we are entering, Clachan. There is talk of a museum to be built in Elgin to house local discoveries. Who can say what lies beneath the ruin's rubble? The ancient Pictish Cross dug up last year near old St. Giles churchyard is a fine example. No telling what other antiquities we may find in Elgin."

Clachan walked on, so Shanks continued, "And who is to put a price on Pictish stones? Might they belong in a museum? Isaac Forsyth has received letters from a university historian regarding a visit to Elgin to see what is here. Are you suggesting you know more than a scholar about what we should value?"

Clachan stopped to study the rock in his hand. Spat on it and rubbed it with his rough thumb. "It is easy to invest in preserving a ruin when you are a wealthy man like Forsyth," Clachan pointed out. "But not so easy for men who need work to feed their families."

Shanks brushed a bit of dust from the sleeve of his worn coat and sighed.

Clachan smiled wryly. "You and I are more the same than different, Shanks. Though you might prefer to think otherwise, seeing as my croft is on land owned by the Shoemakers Guild of Elgin. Until your recent elevation by the town council, you were no more than a simple cobbler. You are a tradesman, and I am a craftsman, but you are a workingman just like me."

Shanks began to interrupt but Clachan held up a hand. "Let me finish. Imagine if this were happening to you. What if you were banned from getting the hides and silks and nails you need to be a shoemaker. And you were forced to travel abroad to gather the materials of your trade, even though they existed right here in the center of Elgin."

A shimmering dragonfly darted past and returned to circle above the men's heads. Clachan and Shanks gazed up at the beautiful creature as it flew away to the River Lossie.

Shanks cleared his throat, anxious to come to the point. "In some ways you are correct, Tom. Both of us are workingmen. Yet I am the newly appointed keeper and watchman of Elgin's ruin. And I will determine what should be carted away. Although I plan to spend most of my days in the ruin, I have a comfortable house and a warm bed in town. And I have shoes to make for my customers."

"Why are you telling me this?" Clachan asked.

"Because I need a helper in the ruin. I want someone sleeping nights in the keeper's hut to discourage looters and foragers."

"Are you calling me a looter?" Clachan bristled.

Shanks ignored the question. "I am no longer as spry as I once was, but I have the stamina of men half my age. Still, I will need assistance with the day-to-day heavy work. A young man with a strong back to help cart rubble."

Suddenly it became clear to Tom exactly what John Shanks had in mind. He wanted one of his sons. He wanted Will. At first the stonemason said no. "The boy needs to work at his trade. Stone-work is what he is trained for, not a guardsman."

"That is exactly why I want the boy as my helper. I can still fill a barrow and roll it to the rockery as long as there is light in the sky. But I recognize my limitations. I will need help moving larg-er stones," Shanks admitted, eyeing the stonemason's worn boots. "And I am willing to provide compensation."

Before Clachan realized it, he was listening to Shanks's pro-posal and negotiating terms of an agreement.

2

MOONRISE, SUNRISE, SECRETS

It was the beginning of something he never expected.

Will Clachan looked up at the sky through a gaping hole in the roof of the keeper's hut. The roof was more hole than shelter and it would need to be repaired. Still, tonight was special. His muscles twitched and his skin prickled as he watched the waxing moon begin to rise. If the sky remained clear he was certain to see something wonderful. The moon was about to illuminate the aperture in the ruin's stonework that once held an enormous rose window. Will shifted restlessly on the straw-filled pallet. Fleetingly, he imagined keeping an opening in the roof. A boyish romantic notion, easily entertained in a month when longer days were coming on. But he knew too well the full force of winter weather blown in from the North Sea. He quickly dismissed the idea.

Will tried to rest, but he was unaccustomed to the nocturnal quiet of the hut. He had spent almost every night of his life in his family's croft. Save for the times he traveled with his father or ventured far from town to hunt and fish with friends. Camping out and sleeping rough. To be entirely alone in the wee hours was a new experience for Will. At that very moment, he knew exactly what he was missing at home. The sounds of his father snoring, his mother tossing about in their bed, and the rhythmic breathing of three younger brothers sleeping on pallets near the stove. Will especially missed Jock the family dog chasing rabbits in his sleep by the door.

Few sounds broke the silence in the shadow of the great cathedral ruin. Only the wind sighing through new leaves on the wych elm trees and the stuttering call of a tawny owl preparing to hunt. Will closed one eye to track the fat moon's trajectory. He fingered the small carved stone he carried for good luck, imagining its mystical powers. Suddenly, the light of the full moon burst through the empty oculus like a great lantern. Long ago, Elgin Cathedral was called the Lantern of the North. Will wondered how high the towers must have reached to earn such a name.

Will yawned and burrowed deeper into his bedding. He was thankful for the woolen blanket his mother provided, along with bread and cheese for the morning. But after that his meals would no longer be his mother's responsibility. Will would be looking to John Shanks for food and shelter.

Will awoke to birdsong.

It was early, but he wanted to eat and dress before Shanks arrived. Will pulled on his new boots. Shanks had made them as part of the bargain with Da. There were boots for Will and for his father, and a pair of shoes for his mother. In keeping with the agreement, Will would be fed and housed in this hut near the ruin. Shanks would pay a modest stipend to Will's father and allow a small reduction to the family's rent.

At first, Will could not believe his father had struck a deal with a man he seemed to hate. But without resources the Clachan family needed income. And it meant one less mouth to feed. A mouth belonging to a boy fast becoming a man with fuzz on his chin and his voice adjusting to a lower octave. As part of the bargain, his father insisted that Will would visit his mother regularly. The agreement specified that payments for Will's work would go into his father's hand. Half paid at Whitsunday and half at Martinmas as was customary.

Tom Clachan had other reasons to strike a deal with John Shanks. "Sometimes it is wise to keep your adversaries close," Will's father explained. "You'll have the man's ear, and you will know what is happening. I expect you to tell me all that you learn." With a tight grip on Will's shoulder, his father had stared hard into his son's eyes. "If you earn the old shoemaker's trust, you might find a way for us to return to the ruin."

Will's stomach had churned when he learned his father's true aim. Long before the stonemasons were expelled from the ruin, his father had taught him the value of honesty. The importance of being forthright and respecting people you worked for. Will hoped the day would never come when he might be forced to choose between obeying Shanks or his father.

"Are you there, boy?" Shanks called toward the hut.

The old man had not seen Will standing ready and waiting at the ruin's entrance. "Here, sir!" he answered.

Shanks joined the boy and unlocked the heavy door in the wall with a large key. "A peaceful night, I presume?"

"Aye, sir. It was."

Will stood a head taller than the old shoemaker. Shanks noticed Will's trousers were too short. Likely from a recent surge in height. There were layers of patches sewn onto the knees, and his shirt was well-worn but clean. No doubt his mother's doing.

Once inside the cathedral grounds, Shanks bolted the door behind them. He smiled down at Will's feet. "How are the boots?"

"They need breaking in."

"Let's get to it!" Shanks pointed to a wheelbarrow filled with shovels and pickaxes. "Bring that." The old shoemaker set off through the piles of rock and debris.

Will followed with the barrow. He was familiar with the ruin's terrain and unconcerned about disrupting anything—weather and time had already taken care of that. The rubble littering the grounds was frequently rearranged, helped in recent years by destructive flooding in the Moray region. Will and his shovel were just one more force of nature having a go at the remains.

The ruin had been Will's playground and workplace. It was here he learned the stonemason's trade alongside his friends, brothers, and cousins. Even the youngest boys scavenged the extensive site. Chasing down odd bits of wood and metal scrap, or a particular piece of stone.

Will could walk through the town of Elgin and identify stones cut from the cathedral ruin. Many were used to build foundations. His father had shown him how to look for the color of the sandstone and identify the remains of ancient Pictish carvings. Sometimes the carvings were squiggles or curls or serpentine marks. Rarer were the bits of a face, an eye, or a wing. The carvings were difficult to spot in the old, weathered rock. But Will could identify stones cut by his father and his grandfathers. Not so long ago the stonemasons of Elgin had helped build Dr. Gray's Hospital and the new Assembly Rooms. Those important buildings had cathedral stones in their foundations.

"Time to work!" Shanks began shoveling rubble into the wheelbarrow.

Will wondered how much Shanks knew about him. Did he know that his first job as a small boy was fetching water for the stonemasons? Did Shanks have any idea how familiar he was with the ruin? Was it possible Shanks knew all the places Will had explored while playing and working here?

Will was certain he could learn a lot from John Shanks. But he was just as certain that he knew some things about the ruin that Shanks did not. Will still carried his secret good luck piece in his pocket. He had never revealed the tiny carved creature to anyone. Not even Mam. And now he intended to keep his secret from Shanks. He quickly touched the carved wings and resumed shoveling.

Will thought Shanks was an odd little man. Dressed in his warm coat, sturdy shoes, and stocking cap, he proceeded to talk nonstop as they worked. Recounting the history of the cathedral back to its beginnings.

"Imagine, Will. The oldest parts of this cathedral were constructed in medieval times—the age of knights in armor and the Holy Crusades. It was built to be the principal church of the bishops of Moray. The bishops were educated and powerful men." Shanks gestured toward the ruin's crumbling walls. "Do you know which part of this cathedral is the oldest? The part that was built first?"

"I do not," Will admitted. "Does it still exist?"

"Ah. An intelligent question, boy. Shows you are thinking." Pointing to the western edge of the ruin, Shanks said, "We believe the west front was built in the thirteenth century. It was a beautiful architectural achievement in its time. See the remains of those two towers sticking out of that mountain of rubble? Between them was once a processional entryway. Imagine the bishops, dressed in splendid robes trimmed in gold and red and blue, processing into the cathedral."

Shanks closed his eyes as Will watched the old man's face.

"And that oval recess in the center above?" Shanks's eyes were open again.

Will looked hard at the piece of wall rising above the rubble, attempting to see what Shanks saw.

"That cavity was once filled with a magnificent carved image. Possibly the Savior. Or the holy family flanked by angels. There is so much we do not know about what is buried under that wreckage. Waiting to be discovered." Shanks clapped his hands together. "Back to work!" he bellowed, and their digging resumed. Apparently, the ruin keeper needed an audience as well as a strong young back.

Will had to admit Shanks was a fine storyteller. Will's father and uncles told tales about the ruin, too. But it seemed Shanks knew a few that Will had not heard before. He had not given much thought to what the cathedral might have looked like in its prime. Nor cared about the people who once lived and worshiped here.

Catching the look on Will's face, Shanks said, "Imagination, boy. That's a gift not everyone possesses."

With Shanks's monologue and the nonstop work, the morning hours sped by. As Will's stomach began to rumble, a voice called from outside the door.

3

ΛLΛNNΛ

"Grand-Dey! I'm here with your dinner."

"Time to eat!" Shanks announced happily.

Will followed Shanks out of the ruin, wiping his grimy hands on his breeks.

"Will, this is my granddaughter, Alanna. She has brought our midday meal." Shanks turned to her and said, "Meet my new helper. My assistant keeper."

Will had been thinking only of food. But when he saw Alanna Shanks, his stomach quieted. His chest tightened. He prayed his voice would not crack. "It's a pleasure, miss." Unexpectedly smitten, Will could not pull his eyes away from the girl. He watched as she spread a cloth on the ground and set out their meal of cold pork pie and cider. Her hands were tiny, as were the delicate shoes on her feet. Will thought the girl might fly away if she had wings.

Shanks removed his coat and hat before settling onto the cloth. "Thank you, my dear. I'll bring the basket when I come home."

"Yes, Grand-Dey." Alanna lightly kissed the top of her grand-father's head. Then she walked off toward town without ever looking directly at Will, who could not stop staring at her.

"Sit down, boy." Shanks was already digging into a meat pie and had pulled the bung from a crock of cider. Apparently, the only time Shanks didn't talk was when there was food to hand. Will took a long drink of cider, trying not to be obvious about watching Alanna walk away. She appeared to be slightly older than he was, but that did not stop his heart from racing.

Busy finishing the last crumbs of his meal, Shanks was oblivious to Will's distraction. The old man looked ready for a quick lie-down.

Will needed to say something to relieve his excitement. "Do you have other grandchildren, Master Shanks?"

"Just Alanna." His eyes were closed as he lay on his back picking his teeth with a piece of straw-grass. "She is a very busy girl. She sketches and paints. She reads and writes poetry. And she helps see to the house. She's a good girl."

Shanks's words felt like a knife to Will's heart. Reminding him that the girl he just met—if you could call it a meeting—was the literate granddaughter of a burgh elder, and entirely out of his realm. By the time Will finished his dinner, Shanks was up from his nap and repacking the basket.

Once back inside the ruin Will daydreamed about Alanna. Thoughts of the girl filled his head while he shoveled. He wondered if he might see her every day. He wanted to know if she always wore blue to match her eyes, and if she had any suitors. He tried and failed to conceive of a situation where he and Alanna might have a conversation.

"Over there." Shanks pointed to what remained of the choir walls, interrupting Will's woolgathering. "Those are the walls that must be stabilized as soon as possible. I am meeting with the Office of Works Committee next month in Edinburgh to review plans for the project." Shanks watched Will to make sure the boy was listening. "There will be times when I will be away from Elgin. There are meetings I must attend and reports to write. I have important correspondence to see to. You seem like a responsible boy. I'm trusting you will work just as hard, if not harder, when I am away as when I am here."

"Of course, sir." But Shanks's words set Will to worry over a larger dilemma—the clash of expectations between his employer and his father.

Shanks began telling another story. For a while Will let the crunch and tumble of broken rock drown out the old man's voice. He knew the stories of the cathedral's ancient past: The rejection of Catholicism. The friction between the Church and the landed gentry—the earls and lairds and brodies of Moray. He tried to imagine the depth of hatred required to destroy a thing of beauty, no matter your religion. That bit of history brought to mind his father's anger at Elgin's town elders. It was a different kind of battle, but Will recognized the similarities.

By afternoon, Will felt the effects of weariness. His focus narrowed and the great ruin around him seemed to fall away. All that remained was the sound of his shovel scraping against the piles of rubble. Rubble that was once part of something massive and breathtaking to behold. *Ruin* was not a temporary condition. Every wheelbarrow full of bits and pieces reminded Will of that fact. There was no hope of anyone ever putting this cathedral back together again. By day's end, the novelty of Will's new life was already dwindling. He was left with the memory of his father explaining what was expected of him. *Keep your adversaries close,* Da had warned. Looking at Shanks now, Will found it difficult to think of the shoemaker as his enemy. What Will saw was a jolly old man with a shovel in hand and a nonstop story on his lips.

When at last they stopped work for the day, Shanks locked the ruin. He reached into the dinner basket and removed another crock of cider, and something wrapped in a folded brown cloth. "Your tea," Shanks said, passing the food to Will. "See you in the morning." With his shovel in hand as a walking stick, Shanks turned to leave.

"Sir? You introduced me to your granddaughter as your assistant keeper. Is that what I am?"

"I suppose so, now that I've seen you work. I am the official cathedral keeper and watchman. It is my ruin, and you are my helper. Now remember, you are staying in the hut to ward off any intruders. You must learn to sleep with an ear out. Keep your spade inside the hut for protection. I will have supplies delivered tomorrow to fix that roof, along with peat for your fire and some provisions."

"Thank you, sir." Hungry and weary, Will was anxious for Shanks to be gone. Long before the moon was up Will fell into a deep sleep. His newest fears and desires filled his dreams.

Will woke to sounds of a wagon approaching.

With nothing to eat, he hurried into his boots and stepped outside.

The driver offered Shanks a hand down from the wagon, but Shanks waved the man off. "Don't be silly, Morrison. I'm as strong as you are."

"Good morning, sirs!" Will was quick to help the driver unload the wagon. It was mostly roofing materials. Lengths of rope and twine, bundles of thatch, wadding, and wooden broaches, some thatching tools, and a sturdy ladder.

Morrison frowned at Will. "I expect to have my tools back in the same condition as they are now."

"I understand." Will nodded, doing his best to mirror the man's serious expression. But Will could not hide his smile once he saw the remaining items in the wagon were for him. There was a small table and a wobbly chair, a sturdy wooden bucket, and some mismatched cutlery. A tattered blanket cradling an oil lamp and an earthenware chamber pot. All of it was quickly unloaded.

"Hungry, Will?" Shanks took a small box from under the wagon seat and handed it to Will. "Cold storage for your breakfasts. Alanna stocked it this morning with crowdie cheese and bannocks. Enough to last a few days, I think. Go eat so we can start work."

"Are we roofing today?"

Shanks laughed. "That's your job, boy! You can thatch on your own time. This week you work with me in the ruin."

Will stepped inside the hut and quickly tore into a bannock. He swallowed without chewing and thought about Alanna's small hands preparing his food. Hands that touched the bread he had just eaten. But this was no time for daydreaming. Will was determined to impress Shanks. He wanted the old man to see that he was more than a boy with a strong back. He was a good listener, a fast learner, and he was worth something. Will heard the wagon departing. The bread would have to satisfy his stomach for now. He placed the foodstuffs under the eaves, hoping to discourage bugs and mice.

Once inside the ruin, Shanks and Will resumed their endless work. Will matched Shanks shovel for shovel as they filled the wheelbarrows with broken rock and rubbish. Without preamble, Shanks launched into a recitation of the cathedral's history. "More than three hundred years have passed since this cathedral was abandoned for Elgin's parish church. And when that happened, it was the beginning of the end for this place." Shanks gestured skyward. "The roof was dismantled for its valuable lead. The bells were carted away, the choir screen chopped up for firewood. The stones plundered. No doubt you have heard these tales."

Will nodded but did not reply. *Plunder* was not a word his family would choose to describe reusing a ruin's stones. But Will knew better than to contradict Shanks. "What I cannot understand, sir, is how anyone could destroy a thing of beauty. I have been very cold many nights in my life, Master Shanks. Yet I cannot imagine burning something as magnificent as a choir screen."

"Maybe not, Will. But surely you have imagined your ancestors carting away the stones long before the cathedral was a total ruin."

Will kept his eyes on his work without a reply.

Leaning on his shovel, Shanks continued, "A century ago, the central tower collapsed and destroyed the nave." He pulled a handkerchief from his back pocket and methodically cleared his nostrils. "By then this place had withstood nearly four hundred years of abuse and neglect by time, weather, and man."

Will was in no position to challenge his new employer. But he silently objected to the assertion that the stonemasons contributed to the abuse of the site. He shoveled faster and finished filling both barrows. "Where should I dump these, sir?"

"Over there. Close by the door."

Will hesitated. Shanks was telling him to dump the rubble where they had cleared the day before. Was the old man raving mad? Will was not afraid of hard work, but what was the sense of rearranging piles of rock. "Over there?" Will pointed to be certain.

Shanks was on his knees examining something on the ground. "Aye," he replied without looking up. And Will suddenly saw himself as an old man just like Shanks. Years from now still working in the ruin, moving piles of rubble back and forth. He grabbed the handles of his wheelbarrow and turned away to hide his frustration.

"Come look here." Shanks handed Will two heavy flagstones. "For your roof. To anchor the newly thatched corners."

Will hefted the stones.

"And Will. Don't dump the barrows where we cleared yesterday, and don't block the door. Soon enough we will start moving rubble out of the ruin."

Will was relieved to learn Shanks had some sort of plan and was not an imbecile, after all. Shanks resumed his recitation of Elgin's history, and together they made progress clearing a circular space not far from the cathedral's chapter house. The sun was high in the cloudless sky when Shanks heard Will's stomach grumble. "Sounds like time to eat."

"Is your granddaughter bringing our meal?"

"Not today. I brought a basket. We'll eat in the chapter house where it's cooler."

Will steadied his face to hide his disappointment. He had imagined seeing Alanna every day, and now he felt a bit stupid. After all, Shanks had said Alanna was a busy girl.

4

DREAMLAND

It was cool inside the chapter house.

Will's eyes adjusted slowly from the bright light outside. The chapter house was the only structure in the ruin still mostly intact. Once it had been a glorious place—a masterpiece in masonry, carpentry, stained glass, and wood. Built as the meeting place for the powerful canons of the church. More recently Elgin's tradesmen met here. Will loved this place. He did not realize how much he had missed it until he walked inside. He wondered if his brothers and cousins missed it, too. It had served as their refuge on hot summer days. And when the weather turned cold, the stonemasons and their sons had huddled here for warmth.

The octagon-shaped chapter house fascinated everyone who saw it. At the center of the room, a single column stretched up to a tall ceiling where it bloomed into a beautiful, vaulted web. Enormous windows towered on seven walls. Pieces of decorative trim still hung from the window frames, but not an inch of glass remained. The distance from the floor to the windowsills was the height of a man. Stone benches were built into the walls below the windows.

"Sit," Shanks instructed Will. He shooed away a few persistent flies and lifted a cloth from the food basket. The old man removed two large drumsticks, golden brown and gleaming with fat. Handing one to Will he explained, "Left from my meal last evening. Men's food!"

Will tore into the turkey leg while Shanks portioned out bannocks. They ate without talking.

Shanks belched and the sound echoed off the walls, making them both laugh. Long ago, the acoustics had enhanced the voices of chanting monks, respected canons, and praying bishops. But the reverberation of sound did not discriminate soulful from silly.

Shanks looked at the ceiling. "It is not always easy to determine when an old building was first constructed, and when it was repaired." He wiped the turkey grease from his mouth with the back of his hand. "Isaac Forsyth and I believe the most beautiful parts of this chapter house are at least three hundred years old. But the foundation and corbelled-out walls may date back to the origins of the cathedral in the twelve hundreds." Shanks glanced at Will to see if the boy was paying attention.

Will nodded. There was plenty he could say about the chapter house, and dozens of questions he might ask. But first he would listen and learn. He needed to be sure of his place with this man. Speak only when spoken to and try not to ask too many questions.

When the food was gone Shanks stretched out for a catnap. Will did the same. His memories were strong in this place. He let his eyes follow the rows of stonework along the ceiling. It put him in mind of a time when he was growing so fast that he frequently tripped over his own feet. His legs would twitch, making it difficult to rest. Will's father had suggested he try counting the ribs of stone on the chapter house ceiling. The counting never failed to put him right to sleep.

The stonemasons' sons called this place Dreamland. The walls were worn down and the stone floor weathered. Yet once your eyes adjusted there was always something new to discover. The remnants of artwork and carvings scattered over the walls seemed endless. Skulls and crossbones, five-point stars, bells, and a chalice were easy to identify. There was a spade and a shovel, a lizard, and what some said was a lion. A skeleton etching gave the younger boys bad dreams when the older ones spun stories of haints and ghouls. Will's favorite etched image was a small heart, but he kept that to himself.

They had frequently debated the more faded images. Was the face below the east window a bearded goat? Whose initials appeared in the coat of arms? Was that a C or a G on the shield? Most of the older boys knew their letters and numbers. A few could read a little. They made up names and rhymes and stories about the worn-away symbols and shapes. Although the walls were scoured by time, Will enjoyed closing his eyes and running his fingers over the shapes. He especially liked an intricate feather etching that invited human touch.

High above on the chapter house ceiling the spider web of roof supports formed a giant star. Fragments of ancient gilding still clung to the stonework overhead, and specks of bright-colored paint remained. The boys believed they saw angel faces and holy saints. But it was difficult to tell much, even on the sunniest days.

Once, when he was very young, Will sat on the lap of an elderly uncle who whispered stories in his ear. Sharing his memories of the chapter house from years before when the uncle was just a boy. Based on those stories Will could now look up and dream of red-and-blue flowing robes, clouds and wings, halos, and even the face of God. How many times had he stared up at this ceiling and fallen asleep on the cold stone floor?

When they returned to work, Shanks and Will spent the afternoon making a circular clearing close by the chapter house door. The old ruin keeper gave no explanation. Eventually Will could no longer contain his curiosity. "Sir, what is the purpose of this space we are making?"

Shanks removed his cap and scratched his head. "Have I not told you? I suppose not." He smoothed the sparse garden of hair on his head and replaced the stocking cap. Leaning on his shovel Shanks asked, "What do you know of the Pictish pillar? The great stone cross exhumed near St. Giles last year."

Will stopped shoveling. "The one they found while digging the new road?"

"Yes. Some called it a cross, but a Pictish stone for certain. It's been stowed for safekeeping. But now that the ruin is secured, Forsyth and the town elders have agreed to move it here. No easy task. The thing likely weighs a tonne. You and I are clearing a place for it. And we need a pathway for the workmen to maneuver the pillar into place."

Will eyed the distance between the entrance and the clearing. He tried to estimate how long it might take to finish. It depended on how wide the pathway needed to be, and how much larger they would make the clearing. Two weeks? Maybe longer.

Will flexed his hands. He felt the threat of new blisters forming atop yesterday's layer. "One last question, Master Shanks," Will spoke timidly. "Why did you choose a site for the pillar so far from the door?"

Shanks gave a great laugh. He looked at the ground and shook his head. The smile did not fade from the old man's face. "Ah, Will. Because right here is the perfect spot!" Shanks continued digging, his pace faster than before. As though the conversation had inspired a new urgency.

Will missed his family.

His body ached for a rest and his hands were stiff from shoveling. He was expected at home on Sunday. But he could not ignore the roofing supplies stacked beside the keeper's hut. He would need to repair the roof before Morrison reclaimed his tools. And he needed to show Shanks he was a responsible worker.

When Will did not come home as planned, his parents sent his brother Luke to see what was amiss. Luke was not dispatched empty-handed. Like all good mothers, Charlotte Clachan was concerned about her eldest son getting enough to eat. Will's father grumbled that they had plenty of mouths to feed under their own roof. But he did not stop his wife from sending a basket of oatcakes with Luke.

From a distance, Luke spotted Will up on the keeper's hut roof. He waved his arm and called, "Brother! I've come with bread from Mam. And Da wants news of you. Come down so we can talk."

Will smiled at Luke. Barely a year separated their ages. "Better you climb up here and give me a hand. We can share news while we thatch. And bring something from the basket. My stomach is howling."

Luke took two oatcakes from under the cloth in the basket and climbed up on the roof. "Good to see you," Will said before stuffing an oatcake into his mouth.

"More likely you are glad to see a bit of Mam's baking."

"Both, truly. I could use some help with this roof. Can you stay awhile?"

"As long as we talk while we work. If I return home without

news of you, we will both be in trouble."

Will repositioned himself so that he and Luke could work the thatch together. They swapped stories while pinning the wads. Will told Luke about working alongside Shanks. "And here is evidence of it." Will turned his palms up so Luke could see the damage. The skin on his hands was raw with cuts and blisters from shoveling and thatching.

"Next time I come I will bring some of Mam's salve," Luke promised.

"Aye. But the next time I see you, I hope it is under your roof instead of on top of mine."

Luke laughed.

"Explain to Mam why I couldn't come home. These tools must be returned, and I have precious little time to finish the work. I appreciate your help, Luke. And the food, too. Tell Mam that Shanks is seeing to my supper and tea. But the truth is I am mostly hungry unless I have just eaten."

"My stomach is like that even with Mam's good meals," Luke confessed.

"Aye. Well, count your blessings, brother."

Luke leaned back on his heels to assess their work. "Are you leaving a smoke hole in this roof?"

"I would, but I have no oilcloth or hide to make a cover."

Luke clambered down the ladder and hefted one of the flagstones from the ground. "This would do nicely over a smoke hole. And the other flagstone will anchor the newly thatched corner."

"But the ladder is not mine. It goes back to its owner when the roof is done."

Luke eyed the drop to the ground from the lowest edge of the roof. "You only need a short ladder." Remembering Will's mangled hands he offered, "I'll make you one."

Will felt a sudden gratitude for his younger brother's kindness. Although he had the skills to make his own ladder, it was time that he lacked now that he was employed by Shanks. The brothers worked steadily to finish the repairs before the afternoon light was gone. As they attached the straw bundles, they shared more news.

"Tell me, Luke, has Da found work?"

"Not yet. And he's been home more than Mam would like. *Too many men in this croft!* is still her favorite chant. At midweek she kicked us all out for the day, and Da took us fishing." Luke grinned. "And you know what that's like with the young ones. Forever getting their lines tangled. Falling in the water and scaring the fish. They giggle too much for Da's liking. When Andrew peed into the water upstream from Da's lines, that was the end of it. We packed it in and went home."

"Catch anything?"

"Five small trout. Ross got to carry the fish. His chest puffed out proud when he handed them to Mam. The fish made Mam happy to see us again. It was a good adventure. The boys needed a day with Da." Luke gestured toward the ruin with his chin, his hands full of thatch. "They will not get to run as wild as we did over there." The brothers exchanged a meaningful look.

"You're right. It's odd really—just Shanks and me in the ruin. The sounds are not the same as when the stonemasons were working. All of us boys running errands and playing 'til we dropped. Now it's just birdsong mixed with the scrape and rattle of a couple of shovels." Will frowned and shook his head.

"And Shanks?" Luke asked. "What is he like?"

"Much stronger than I expected. He's pleasant enough and a hard worker." Will paused. "And he is a talker." Will caught Luke's eye. "The opposite of Da."

Luke finished fastening another bundle of thatch. He stood and stretched the muscles in his legs and back. "Sounds more like Andrew. He talks from the moment he opens his eyes in the morning until he drops off to sleep at night. Mam must 'shush' him twenty times a day. He asks so many questions it makes her head ache."

"Good to know nothing has changed." Will grinned.

"Aye, it's only been a week, but it feels much longer without you at home." Luke descended the ladder for more wooden broaches to pin the thatch. Two rungs down he was face-to-face with Will kneeling on the roof. "He misses you, Will. We all do."

Will felt a squeeze on his heart, but he held his emotions in check. "More likely you miss my help with the chores." Will smiled.

"Please find your way home next Sunday, or Mam will be hanging us all out on the laundry line."

"Tell Mam next Sunday there will be no excuses."

After Luke delivered the broaches to the rooftop, he descended the ladder again. "Da and the men are hoping to gain access to Spynie quarry. And there is talk of permission from the Earl of Fife to remove collapsed stones from Pluscarden Abbey."

"Tell Da I wish him luck."

Luke reached into the basket and removed a fat bannock hidden beneath the oatcakes. Up on the roof, he ripped the bread in two and handed half to Will. Like a magic trick both halves disappeared.

"You remember that great piece of stone they pulled from the ground by St. Giles last summer?" Will asked.

"That Pictish pillar? I surely do. It was a massive slab. There must have been a dozen men hoisting it onto the wagon bed that day."

"Shanks says they plan to move the pillar to the cathedral grounds from a storehouse behind Commerce Street. Tell Da they may be moving it sometime soon. Maybe Da should see if they need more men for the job."

"I'll tell him, Will. But I cannot say if that news will make Da glad or angry."

"I know. But I promised him I would share any news."

The sun was headed for the horizon when Luke and Will climbed down from the roof. As Luke brushed at the bits of straw clinging to his clothes, he discovered a new hole in the knee of his trousers. "Mam's not going to like that," Luke muttered.

"When you tell Mam you were helping me put a roof over my head, she will forgive you." Will winced from his blisters as the brothers shook hands. It was something they had never done before, yet it felt right after the work they had accomplished together. A small acknowledgment that both stood on the doorstep of becoming men, and now lived under separate roofs.

"Goodbye, brother!" Luke snagged the handle of the empty basket and tossed the cloth square to Will. "Make yourself some bandages for those hands."

"Tell Mam I will be home next Sunday."

Luke waved over his shoulder. His walk broke into a trot, anxious to be home in time for supper.

5

THE WITCHES POOL

Shanks and Will spent several days clearing a site for the Pictish pillar.

Shanks made no mention of when the pillar might be moved. But Will knew it would take weeks to make a path wide enough to haul the ancient slab into place.

They had recently begun dumping rubble outside the ruin, heaping it along the wall. Will was becoming a skilled estimator of time and effort. He wondered why Shanks did not employ more men to make the work go faster. With so many idle stonemasons in Elgin, it seemed like lunacy having two men clearing the cathedral yard.

When Shanks announced he would be away in Edinburgh for several days, Will was relieved. "I have important meetings to attend with the Scottish Office of Works Committee," Shanks explained. "While I am gone, I want you to remove the rubble we've piled outside."

The expression on Will's face gave him away.

"Aye. Not an easy task but one we must begin. We cannot keep piling the rubble outside the walls. Never mind that the townsfolk dumped their rubbish here for years. We must cart away what we know to be worthless so we can see what lies beneath."

"Beneath what?" Will asked without thinking. He realized his witlessness as soon as he spoke and slipped a hand into his pocket. Just long enough to touch the wings of the stone talisman he secretly carried. His very own evidence of the wonders that might be buried within this shattered cathedral.

"You have seen me examining pieces as we dig. I am certain we will eventually begin to find…" Shanks hesitated, and Will wondered if it was a loss for words or a lack of trust. "It is difficult to imagine all that we might uncover," Shanks continued. "But I am convinced that one day people will come to Elgin from far and wide to see the fascinating relics we will discover here. But I am getting ahead of myself," Shanks mumbled. He cleared his throat. "We need to discuss the carting of rubble to the Order Pot."

"The Order Pot?" Will flinched. "You mean the Witches Pool?"

"Yes. The Witches Pool, as you choose to call it. And you have raised an interesting point. The 'Order Pot' was a name corrupted from 'ordeal pot.' It was the place where women thought to be witches underwent the ordeal by water." Shanks knew he was making the boy uncomfortable, but discussions about witches made most people squirm. "And criminals sentenced to death by drowning were also executed there. But that was a long time ago, boy. Nearly three hundred years have passed since the last witch was drowned there."

The history lesson did not ease the sickening feeling in Will's innards. He knew better than to speak his thoughts: Why the Witches Pool? Couldn't they just dump the rubble somewhere else? Leave it outside the wall or cart it into the nearby woods.

Shanks continued as though reading Will's mind. "I have given the matter much thought. The Witches Pool is the perfect place to take all this collapsed masonry. Whether old Tom-the-Rhymer's verse is true or nae, a bottomless watery pit seems just the place to dump this churchyard rubble."

Will stayed quiet. He tried not to think too far ahead. He did not want to dwell on all that rock they had recently shoveled and carted. Now he would have to refill the barrows and roll them down to the Witches Pool. By whatever name, it was well known as a haunted place in Elgin.

But there was a certain logic to Shanks's plan. Parish residents still dumped all manner of discarded items into that dark and deep watery hole. Just as it long ago swallowed up the bodies of drowned witches and criminals. Now it would receive the remains of one of the largest cathedrals in all the land.

A chill ran down Will's spine. He recalled each word of the old rhyme Shanks had mentioned. Some folks believed the rhyme was an ancient prophecy about this very cathedral as over the centuries it passed from splendor and glory into decay and ruin.

"The Order Pot and Lossie grey shall sweep the Chan'ry Kirk away."

Shanks carried a precious package.

He had one last stop to make at the ruin before heading to Edinburgh. At the keeper's hut Shanks handed Will the package and set a basket on the table. The basket emitted tantalizing smells of baked meat pies. The package was compact in Will's hands. Brown shop paper had been carefully folded around the contents. It was tied up with a length of waxed string long enough to make a bow on top.

"For your mother," Shanks explained simply, in answer to Will's quizzical look. "Please give her my regards. Tell her I hope she likes them."

Will gently fingered the string, imagining the things his mother might use it for once the package was unwrapped.

"Her shoes," Shanks explained. The old man's expression shifted slightly, revealing an impish grin. Will noticed a twinkle in Shanks's eyes that he had not seen before. As though Shanks the shoemaker might be somewhat jollier than Shanks the keeper of the ruin.

"I will take them to her in the morning."

"Good, good," Shanks murmured. It was clear he had more on his mind than delivering shoes and pies. "While I am away, I expect you to begin moving rubble to the Order Pot."

"Yes, sir." Will was growing impatient. They had already discussed carting the rubble. It was backbreaking work but uncomplicated. Will was hungry and the smell of food made him anxious for Shanks to be gone.

"I expect you to make good progress in my absence." Shanks fumbled something from his coat pocket. His short thick fingers were stiff and rough. "This is for you." Shanks handed Will a worn leather notebook. It was small enough to slip into a breast pocket. Small enough to fit a woman's hand. "I want you to make a mark for each barrow of rubble you tip into the pool. We are going to keep a count."

Will opened the notebook and Shanks handed him a stubby charcoal pencil. Several thin pages had been neatly torn away. Inside the cover Will noticed some words rubbed out. Shanks stepped closer and gently took back the pencil and notebook, holding it open for Will to see. "For each barrow you dump, I want you to make one slash mark, like so." Shanks put a small vertical line in the upper left-hand corner of the first page. "One…two…three…four…"

"Yes, sir. I know how to count."

"And after every fifth barrow, you make a diagonal slash mark across the four lines, keeping count in groups of five."

"I can do that," Will answered. His stomach had commenced a low rumble. "I know my numbers." He did not want Shanks to think he was dim. "And I've counted with slashes before." Although it had been in the dirt with a long stick, not in a leather notebook.

"I wrote the dates I expect to be away at the top of this page. You can make your slash marks beneath." Shanks put a large X through his sample and handed the notebook and pencil back to Will. "Carry this with you and make a slash after you tip each full barrow. Don't count in your head and make the marks later. You can lose track that way."

"I understand, sir."

"In my absence Alanna will bring your meals, and the ruin will remain locked."

Will had not considered being locked out of the ruin while Shanks was away. Clearly, he would not be trusted with a key anytime soon.

"And, Will?" Shanks stood in the doorway of the hut looking up. "I must say, that's a fine-looking roof."

When night came, Will was unable to sleep. Something about the shoes made him restless. Both Will and his father were already wearing their new boots. But he had forgotten about these shoes for Mam. And there lay the heart of his uneasiness. He was ashamed for not remembering the promise of shoes for his good mother. Part of the bargain with John Shanks. He closed his eyes and pictured the shoes his mother had owned for as long as he could remember.

A pair of brown boots with laces up the ankles, worn rough on the toes and thin on the heels. Mam wore them every day from the moment she woke until she placed them beside her bed at night.

Will sat up and carefully took the package from the table. It was compact and light in his hands. It could not possibly contain footwear to replace those brown boots. He considered taking a small peek at the contents. He was certain the shoes would make his mother happy. Holding the package made him realize how small his mother's feet must be. Lifting the bundle to his nose, he smelled the newly worked leather. It was exciting to be the bearer of this gift for Mam.

"Maybe just a peek," Will whispered. Curiosity tempted him to unwrap the shoes. But the precise folds of the paper and tightly knotted strings seemed to discourage even the tiniest look. And if he opened the parcel entirely, could he put it back together again? Will yawned. He did not want to be tired for his visit home. He returned the package to the table and reached to extinguish the lamp. But in that moment, he realized he could not sleep without first seeing the shoes.

Will was awakened by sunlight slicing through a crack near the door. He yawned and rolled over, hoping for another few winks. He had slept fitfully, pondering Mam's reaction when she opened the shoes.

The shoes! Before Will could close his eyes again, he saw the package perched awkwardly on the table. Seeing the shoes had seemed like the only solution to a good night's sleep. So, of course, he had peeked at them.

At first, he had barely slid the string to open a small fold in the paper. He had touched the soft leather with his finger and held the opening close to the dim lamplight hoping to see the color of the shoes. In the process, he managed a tiny tear in the wrappings. He decided the best course of action would be to unwrap the package entirely and put it all back together again. To his dismay, he had problems rewrapping the shoes. His fingers felt too stiff for the job. After several failed attempts he finally managed to cover the beautiful shoes with the brown paper again, hiding the rip and tying the string on top. But somehow the bundle was lopsided and no longer perfect. It bothered Will that Mam would not see the package as beautiful as it was when Shanks delivered it. But he knew it was not the wrapping that mattered. It was the shoes.

6

A VISIT HOME

Will was glad to be home.

From the front gate he saw Andrew sitting on a stool, his index finger poked into a small bowl. The bowl contained a thick concoction of baking powder and vinegar. Red splotches dotted the boy's arms, legs, and face. His eyes were swollen from crying. Mam was busy plucking stingers out of Andrew's hide.

"What's all this?" Will asked.

"Andrew discovered a nest of ground hornets," Mam calmly replied.

"I was only watching them," Andrew explained. "Climbing in and out of their holes in the dirt. I wanted to know what happens to them when it rains. So, I used a rhododendron leaf to trickle some water into their holes." The hornets had shot out from their nest and attacked Andrew as he ran shrieking for home.

"I have something for you, Mam." Will wanted to give his mother the shoes straightaway. But she crinkled her freckled nose and pulled back from her welcoming embrace.

"You smell like a young man who has not seen a cake of soap

for weeks," Mam informed him. She insisted he clean up before entering the house. At the edge of the garden Will stripped to the waist and washed from a wooden bucket. Mam wiped tears from her cheeks.

"Now, Mam, it's not been that long."

"My eyes tell me different." She could not help but admire her eldest man-child. Seeing her son's bare shoulders she declared, "You have grown new muscles since you left. And you look taller than your father. Nearly as tall as me."

"That's the new boots." Will blushed.

She handed him a clean rag to dry himself, and then one of his father's shirts. As Will attempted to fasten the buttons Mam noticed his scabbed hands. "Goodness, Will. Luke told me you needed salve, but I had no idea…" She stepped quickly into the house, returning with her rag basket and a brown crock covered with a clean linen square.

Seated together on the wooden bench at the edge of the garden, Mam gently massaged ointment into Will's raw and blistered palms. He winced and she grasped his hand more firmly. "If you are tough enough to create these scars you are strong enough to withstand my treatment."

Held captive, Will surveyed the yard. The family's small garden contained much more than the average North Coast kaleyard. His mam grew cabbages, onions, leeks, turnips, carrots, and potatoes—as well as kale. She had her own gooseberry bush, even though a wild patch thrived just up the road. Will recognized the sage and rosemary plants. But he could not recall the names of all the herbs Mam cultivated. The new crops looked healthy, warmed by the heat absorbed and released from the garden wall.

Will and Luke had helped their father build that wall some years before. When the work was done, Da let the boys carve their initials into a modest cornerstone. Will looked for and found the rough-cut *WC* and *LC* peeking through a tuffet of field grass. The wall protected his mother's vegetables and medicinal plants from cold north winds and late spring frosts. It also blocked from view the family's rabbit hutch and chicken coop. When Mam looked out her kitchen window, she preferred not to see the small beasties that eventually became the family's meals.

Mam took her time nursing Will's hands. She wrapped his palms in clean strips of linen rags. Carefully she tied small knots so they would not impede the use of his hands. Her binding skills reflected years as a matron in a family of stonecutters. As she worked, she talked about small things Will had missed at home. And she asked about Master Shanks. More specifically she wished to know, "What is he feeding you?"

Will flexed his fingers, admiring his mother's work. "Not to worry, Mam. He sees to my meals regularly." Will ran one bound hand through his wet hair, smoothing it into place. Mam gave her son a quick kiss on the cheek as she slid a stray strand behind his ear. "About Master Shanks, Mam—I have a parcel for you in my bag."

The shoes caught Charlotte Clachan by surprise. Wrapped in brown paper and tied up with string, the package was smaller than she anticipated. Certainly, this bundle could not contain the shoes John Shanks promised to make for her. The shoemaker had come to the croft on two occasions to measure and remeasure her feet. She was anticipating some sort of laced-up black leather half boot. Something sturdy and practical. Her old boots were a secondhand pair with holes in the soles, and heels worn akilter. With proper waxing and wadding they kept her feet mostly dry and warm.

Oh, but what shoes John Shanks had made for her! Fashioned from moss green leather, silk, and calfskin with dove gray straps.

She blushed holding them in her hands. Held them up to her nose and then to her cheek. When she slid them on her feet the fit was perfect. Charlotte loved the new shoes. They smelled so nice and were very dear. She did not care that they lacked any manner of practicality. They were like the shoes one might wear in heaven.

Will had known the shoes were special the moment he folded back the wrappings. In his dimly lit hut, he could not imagine these beautiful shoes on his mother's feet. And yet that was exactly where they ended up. The green shoes made Charlotte Clachan exceedingly happy, and she danced around the cottage.

But the shoes did nothing to improve her husband's mood. "Dancing shoes. Bah!" Tom Clachan snarled when he laid eyes on them. "What does Shanks think you do all day? Life is more than a pair of fancy shoes, Charlotte," he lectured.

"Maybe for you!" she snapped back. "And easy for you to say. But I am on my feet every waking hour, and it is my feet that drive my happiness." In recent days, it most certainly had not been Charlotte's husband making her happy. She refused to let Tom's grouchiness ruin her joy.

As she finished preparing Will's homecoming meal Mam hummed a tune unfamiliar to her sons. Her joy was contagious. Jock the dog followed her to-and-fro, wagging his tail. She would not be denied this bit of bliss. Her movements were light and nimble, as though the shoes had magically changed her into a younger woman. But those shoes sent her husband stomping out the door, mumbling under his breath.

In a way, Will understood his father's point of view. Surely his mother would have found more use in a practical pair of working boots. Shoes to wear for housework and yard work and walking to market. Instead, Shanks had made a most lovely pair of dancing shoes. The kind one might wear to climb into a horse-drawn chaise and visit friends. Or wear to a dance or a party. But except for the annual Saint Andrew's Day celebrations, his mother did none of those things. It was unthinkable to own shoes worn for only one occasion. Yet once the shoes were on Mam's feet, it was clear that she might dream of such things. And impractical dreams made Will's father irritable.

Will followed Da into the yard. He stood eye to eye with his father, whose Pictish heritage was unquestionable. Short in stature, Tom Clachan was broad-shouldered and muscular with a dark complexion, shiny black hair, and feet that seemed almost square. A fact Will's mother believed made her husband a poor dancer.

Will kept quiet while Da lit his pipe—the one with a feather carved on its bowl. A gift from Mam on his father's last birthday. Da's pipe-lighting required him to pause his muttering. Will used the opportunity to change the subject.

"Did Luke tell you about the plans to move the Pictish pillar to the ruin?"

"He did. But nothing has come of my inquiries. What other news do you have for me, son? I am anxious to hear how it goes with John Shanks."

Jock had shadowed the men into the yard. The small dog was eager for Will's attention. Will plucked an old rag ball from a patch of tall grass. He threw it into the field abutting the yard. The dog shot off to retrieve it.

"We have cleared a place for the pillar and begun a track across the grounds. We are hauling out barrows of broken stone and rubbish. Shanks has decided to dump the rubble into the Witches Pool."

"The Witches Pool!" his father guffawed, coughing, and blowing smoke from his nostrils. "The man's gone daft."

"Aye. But that's what I'll be doing while Shanks is in Edinburgh."

His father's face brightened. "Did he leave you a key to the ruin while he's away?"

"No, Da. I will be carting rubble from outside the walls."

"Then you have yet to earn the man's trust."

"I believe he is trusting me more each day as he comes to know me better. I am working hard." Will held out his wrapped hands as evidence of his claim. "And I am doing all he asks of me, even repairing the roof on the keeper's hut. I am doing my best to convince Shanks that I am a worthy assistant keeper."

"Assistant keeper! Is that what he's calling you? I need resources and you bring home a title and a pair of useless shoes. Bah!" His father spit on the ground.

"I am trying my best, Da." Will's voice shook with anger and heartache. "What else do you expect from me?"

His father's voice was intense. "I expect you to convince Shanks to give you a key."

Will paused before whispering, "And then what?" The question surprised them both. He had challenged his father without thinking. A moment of silence hung in the air. "When that day comes, Da, what will happen when I hand you the key to the ruin?"

Tom Clachan narrowed his eyes and blew smoke. "Hold your tongue. I deserve your respect." Will's question remained unanswered, but he could imagine what might happen if Shanks ever trusted him with the key. It would not end well.

Jock reappeared. He dropped the ball in the space between the two pairs of new boots. The dog looked up expectantly.

Luke poked his head out the door. "Supper is on the table!" Jock slipped into the house on Luke's heels.

It had only been weeks since Will left home. But his stomach misjudged it to be much longer, influenced by the aroma of his mother's cooking. The Clachan family took their seats at the table, excited to have Will home. Mam placed a basket of warm oatcakes between Ross and Andrew.

"Come now, Charlotte. Take a seat," Tom instructed, looking into his wife's eyes.

Will attempted to read his father's expression. He wondered if the homecoming excitement displeased him. Luke leaned into Will's shoulder and whispered in his ear, "Mam has been cooking for two days straight!"

Andrew and Ross simultaneously reached for the bread basket but recoiled at their father's stern instruction. "Grace first!" he commanded, sending his best evil eye in the direction of the youngsters.

"Hands," Mam's voice was gentle. She closed her eyes and extended her hands to Ross and Will. With all hands joined around the table, the family recited together:

"Some hae meat and canna eat.

And some wad eat that want it.

But we hae meat, and we can eat.

And sae the Lord be thankit."

"Amen!" Andrew and Ross sang out in unison and helped themselves to oatcakes.

With a flourish, Mam removed the lid from a large covered dish in the center of the table.

"Inky Pinky!" all four boys exclaimed at once. "And it's not even washday!" Andrew pointed out. Everyone laughed, including Da.

"Will's favorite." Ross smiled sheepishly. A fop of thick black hair fell across the boy's eyes. He quickly reached to put it back in place, but not before Da could say, "That boy needs a haircut." It was what Da always said about Ross's unruly hair. Ross was a quiet child, the baby of the family. Mam liked to point out that no one knew for certain whether Ross was truly quiet, or simply silenced by Andrew's constant chatter. Ross was his father's son in all ways. He resembled his Pict ancestors and the Clachan stonemasons. He was compact with a dark complexion. But his eyes were as green as grass in springtime. Some said they were disturbingly green, shining out from under the black fringe forever hanging in his face. When anyone told Tom that Ross was his spitting image, he was quick to answer, "Except for the eyes. Those eyes are from his mother's Celtic relatives on Charlotte's side of the family."

Luke winked at the younger boys. "Imagine! Serving Inky Pinky on a Sunday."

Andrew could barely sit still. His constant chatter was only temporarily slowed by his consumption of food. "Mam must love you a lot, Will, to make Inky Pinky on a Sunday." Talking with his mouth full, Andrew earned a stern look from Mam.

"And extra gravy." Will beamed in appreciation. He leaned over the table and inhaled the aroma of the beef slices. After stuffing a gravy-soaked oatcake into his mouth, Will left his seat to hug Mam. She smiled lovingly at her men.

"Tell me again who gave you this recipe, Charlotte," Da asked, helping himself to a second slice of meat. "Who gave this meal its name?"

"An old friend," Mam answered. "Meg Dods. She was an exceptional cook."

"But not as good as you, Mam." The expression on Andrew's face was the kind of loving look only a nine-year-old boy could unabashedly give his mother.

"The name Inky Pinky is so old, no one is certain where it came from," Mam explained. "But it has always been served on washday because it is easy to make with leftovers from Sunday roast."

"More tatties, please?" Ross asked. In the presence of three older brothers, he was unsure if he could claim any of the remaining potatoes. Luke judiciously shared out the remaining veg.

Will glanced across at Andrew. Bits of dried paste dotted his young brother's face and hands. The boy was still puffed up in places. But he no longer wore an anguished look. Even after a hornet attack, Andrew could not be subdued for long.

Surrounded by her men, Charlotte Clachan was never happier than when the faces she loved most began to look sated. This was her favorite moment of a family meal. With a quick wink at Ross she asked, "Who wants pudding?"

"I do!" the boys answered in unison. Da rolled his eyes.

As Charlotte rose from her chair she refastened a strand of mahogany hair worried loose from the bun at the nape of her neck. She wiped her hands on her apron and uncovered a pan of baked apples stuffed with currants. The apples had been cooling for some time, and the aroma was impossible to disguise. It filled the croft with a lovely scent. Even Jock was drooling.

Luke whispered in Will's ear, "Mam wanted to make a Dundee cake. Da said certainly not."

Will eyed their younger brothers. "Some of us will enjoy the apples more."

Mam topped each apple with a dollop of gooseberry jam and brought them to the table. Save for the sounds of spoons scraping bowls, all was quiet while they savored the warm fruit. Jock panted, anxiously waiting for someone to drop a gooseberry.

Will looked down the table just in time to see his father's expression change. Da's brow creased and his eyes narrowed. His brief good mood slipped away.

Pushing his half-eaten apple aside, Da leaned forward in his chair to focus his attention on Will. "Aye, Will. It is good to have you home. And while you have been working for Shanks, I have been busy as well, estimating how much usable stone remains in the ruin. Thinking of projects where it might be put to good use."

Everyone grew quiet. Even Andrew, who was busy scraping bits of baked apple from his bowl, put down his spoon.

"I have spoken with several town elders about my plans."

Will held his breath, dreading what Da might say next.

"I know there are those in town who agree with me, even if the town council does not. There are wonderful great houses yet to be built in Elgin. Built with stones from the cathedral ruin."

"Oh, Tom," Mam sighed.

"Charlotte, this is important for Will to hear. For all of you to hear. I have been talking with local contractors. I might have potential customers. Families who want fine houses built outside of town."

Everyone kept silent. Only Andrew seemed briefly distracted, eyeing the remains of Da's pudding.

"This is where I need your help, Will. Do we understand one another?"

Will kept his head lowered. "Yes, Da," he replied quietly.

"Because I cannot do this work without your cooperation."

"I will try harder." It was the best Will could offer.

"Good. I want it to be clear what is expected of you."

Will nodded wordlessly. His father's talk was likely a pipe dream born of desperation. There was no doubt Da was trying to secure new work, but his recent bad temper had estranged him from town officials. His easygoing reputation was eroding with every angry confrontation. There were some who now saw him as too difficult to employ.

Luke and Mam cleared the table. The rest of the family followed the dog into the yard. They took turns throwing the rag ball for Jock. Will felt the start of a small ache in his chest. He had missed Ross and Andrew. Even more it seemed he missed the family dog. Only his father's clean shirt on his back kept Will from joining his young brothers wrestling with Jock on the ground. But he gave the dog plenty of rubs and pats.

While the boys played with the dog and her husband smoked his pipe, Mam quietly tucked a few things into Will's empty bag. Another clean shirt, a cake of soap, a tin of salve, a small crock of potted meat and day-old rolls.

The day faded away too quickly and soon it was time for Will to leave. It was a strange and awkward moment. Regardless of Da's temperament, Will found himself wishing he could stay the night. By comparison, the keeper's hut seemed a lonely destination. It was Mam who knew best how to dispel uncomfortable moments, even as she regretted Will's departure. Will hugged Mam and kissed her on the cheek. She lifted her skirts and danced a little jig to show off her new shoes. "Take care of those hands," she told him. "I've put some salve in your bag."

Da gave his oldest son a firm pounding on the back. "Aye, boy. Now don't be expecting such a homecoming next time you show your face. At least not without considering your own contribution to the food on the table."

Will understood the veiled comment. It was more about securing the key to the ruin than bringing home a rabbit or a string of fish.

"Work hard and remember what I have told you." Then Tom Clachan looked to his wife. "And woman—you cannot fool me. I know you're sneaking the boy those rolls."

Will resettled the bag on his shoulder and tousled Ross's hair.

When Luke appeared from the far side of the house, he was carrying a roughly built ladder. "It's not handsome"—Luke grinned—"but it is sturdy."

Will tested the gift by balancing on the bottom rung. "Thank you, Luke," Will said, blinking back tears of gratitude. Instead of a handshake the brothers embraced.

Will scratched Jock's ear once more. The dog barked and spun in circles. With his loving family at his back, Will headed in the direction of the ruin. He was filled with mixed emotions about his future and his past. He waved a hand above his head but did not turn around for fear the tears on his cheeks would show. He was not far down the road when he heard panting. Jock was tagging along behind him, smiling foolishly. Twice Will tried unsuccessfully to send the dog back home, but Jock was too busy barking and running in circles. The dog tried to tug the ladder from his hand, as though it were a stick to play with. Will stopped walking. Through his tears he pointed down the road and sternly ordered the dog, "Go home!" Whether tempted by the smell of the food in Will's bag, or the fun they might have playing with the ladder, or simply the dog's unchallengeable love for Will, Jock refused to obey.

At last, Luke came running to where Will and the dog faced off. Will quickly wiped a sleeve across his eyes. He did not want his brother to see him crying. Luke was grinning when he caught up to Will. "I told you I built a fine ladder. Even the dog wants it." He winked at Will and scooped up the dog. With a firm hold on Jock, Luke squeezed Will's shoulder. "Do not worry yourself about Da. He will come around soon enough."

"I hope so, Luke. I hope so."

7

BARROWS TO THE POOL

The keeper's hut was too quiet.

Will wished Jock had followed him to the ruin. The wee dog would have been a comfort. The salve, soap, and food Mam tucked into his bag made his heart ache. Dinner with his family had reminded Will that the joy of food came from eating it in good company.

Will turned his attention to everything he needed to accomplish while Shanks was away. Time on his own might help with his daily routine. He would rise early and fetch the day's drinking water. He needed a small cistern to collect rainwater. The wooden bucket could only hold so much.

Will wanted time to forage. Before long there would be windblown fruit to scavenge. In the woodlands he could trap rabbits and gather birds' eggs. He could fish the streams that fed the Lossie. Yet all these plans required time. And he had precious little time for anything beyond work and sleep.

Mam's bar of soap reminded Will of other tasks. He might have overlooked washing his clothes and bathing, except for the memory of his mother's face repelled by his unwashed state. Women cared about such things. If he cared about women, he would need to clean himself up now and then.

Will yawned. He put out the light and closed his eyes. Undoubtedly, he would need a good night's sleep.

Down was a good direction to go when pushing a full wheelbarrow. That was Will's first thought as he pulled on his boots. The terrain from the cathedral to the Witches Pool was mostly level. And where it wasn't level, it was downhill. Pushing a wheelbarrow full of rubble weighing the sum of two men would be difficult even on flat ground. Thankfully it would be empty on the return trips uphill.

Will crammed one of Mam's rolls into his mouth, sliding another into his pocket. He considered his route between the ruin and the Witches Pool. If he kept to the pathways, it would take three times as long as the shortcut through the meadow. Crossing the meadow at a fast pace he could reach the Witches Pool in less than a quarter hour—but longer with a full wheelbarrow. Yet there were good reasons to keep to the well-worn track crossing the old Aberdeen Road and not risk getting stuck in the meadow. All those plans were well and good until Will stepped outside.

In this northeast corner of Scotland, a stranger might suspect a cold and desolate region. Many newcomers were surprised by the lay of the land, the quality of goods, the flora, the fauna, but particularly the weather. From Easter until autumn the skies frequently offered near-perfect days. A mix of weak sun and scattered clouds. A cool breeze off the Moray Firth. Hints of warming that may or may not materialize. Tolerable days when fruit trees sprouted crowns of pastel fuzz. One might begin to feel warm enough after the trials of a Highland winter.

Caught up in estimating how many barrows he might mark down in Shanks's notebook, Will had misjudged the weather. Yesterday had been springlike. But as he stepped outside a dense mist consumed him. For all his calculations a *smirr* of bad weather was the last thing Will anticipated. The bleak day was devoid of even the weakest sunlight and a fine drizzle dampened everything. Will lifted his coat collar and imagined he was the only person in Elgin not huddled near a warm fire.

Through the mist the rubble piles along the wall resembled stout guardsmen. How long would it take to move it all? How many trips to the pool? How much rock could he move in a day, in a week, in a lifetime? How many loads before he might prefer to throw himself into that bottomless pool?

On Will's first trip with the wheelbarrow the ground mist was thick. He took care where he placed his feet. He could barely see past the barrow's front wheel. Reaching the pool, he left the barrow and walked to the water's edge. As a young child he had been warned away from this place. "Stay away from the Witches Pool!" mothers frequently reminded their children. But plenty of boyhood dares in Elgin involved the Witches Pool.

Even in the mist, Will knew the pool's shape and size—circular and about seventy feet in diameter. Keeping away from the swampy reedbeds, he carefully paced the rim until he found firm ground. A solid spot so that he and the wheelbarrow would not end up in the pool along with the rubble.

As Will watched the rocks slide into the Order Pot, he tried not to think about witches. The noise of the rubble hitting the water would scare away anything living in the pool but attract the attention of anyone nearby. Once the splashing settled nothing made a sound. It would be impossible to dump all the loads in one location. Bottomless or not, eventually he would need to adjust his launch point. But for now, this place would do.

Will did not linger. He needed to listen for the chimes from St. Giles to know when to expect Alanna with his meal.

Will felt embraced by the fog.

He was about to refill the wheelbarrow when he remembered Shanks's notebook. He set aside the shovel and reached into his damp coat. To his relief the notebook was still dry, but he fumbled the pencil to the ground and cursed. As he bent to retrieve it, a deep voice startled him.

"Pray tell, Will Clachan. Are you working or writing?"

Will yelped and dropped the pencil a second time. The hairs on the back of his neck tingled. "Who goes there?" he demanded. He tried to keep his voice steady, but it cracked fearfully.

"Morrison," came the answer as the man emerged from the mist. He held a large basket draped with heavy burlap. "Sorry to startle you, young Clachan. It was not my intent." Morrison's stoic expression struggled to hide a smile.

"I was expecting Mistress Alanna," Will explained. "Master Shanks said she would deliver my meals. But you have come instead on this miserable day, and I am grateful."

"This is not the best weather for carting stone, but I see you are showing your worth."

"It is what Master Shanks instructed me to do. I was startled because I was not expecting you. And the Witches Pool on a day like this..." Will paused to choose his next words carefully, not wanting to appear weak. "It can be eerie, especially working alone."

"Aye, it can," Morrison agreed, leaning against the cathedral wall. He pulled the brim of his hat lower on his brow. "When it comes to witches it is best to know the facts. Instead of letting your imagination run wild."

"I suppose," Will offered cautiously. "But the facts about the Witches Pool—or the Order Pot as Master Shanks calls it—are plain enough to me. It was where they drowned lots of witches a very long time ago when there were still witches in Elgin."

"There is one witch's story worth retelling," Morrison offered. "It is a true one, and it happened right here in Elgin. On these once hallowed grounds near the cathedral's Pans Port. We know the story is true because a witness wrote it down. And that very old document still exists."

The wind was pushing a thick bank of fog up from the River Lossie. Will moved closer to see Morrison's face. "Have you seen that document?" Will asked.

"I have. In an ancient book about Moray's history. I do not read much, and it was written in the way people wrote long ago. But I was in the room when it was read aloud to a group of educated men. And I have a very good memory."

Will held his breath for a moment. He wondered if Morrison would share the story.

"There was a scholar present at the reading," Morrison continued. "He believed the events the witness wrote about happened three hundred years ago."

Will leaned into the wall. He was hungry and wet and weak in the knees. If Morrison was going to tell his story, Will was anxious for the man to get on with it.

Morrison cleared his throat, closed his eyes, and slowly began reciting from memory. "Great multitudes rushed through the Pans Port of Elgin Cathedral and across the meadowland. They surrounded the Order Pot. And here they dragged through the tumult an old woman named Marjory Bysseth."

"This very same meadow I have been crossing with my wheelbarrow?"

Morrison opened his eyes. "The very same."

Will felt a seed of sickness in the pit of his stomach.

"May I continue?"

Will nodded.

"Marjory Bysseth was in sore plight with her gray hairs hanging loose and crying 'Have pity on me, have pity!' Now Master Wyseman, the same clerk who stood up at her trial, stepped forward and said, 'I know this woman to have been peaceable and unoffending, living in the privacy of her widowhood and harming no one, and speaking against no one. What have you further to say against her?' There was a great murmuring of displeasure among the people. But Master Wyseman, hearing no accusations, once again asked the question, 'What have you further to say against her?' Then did the friars repeat how they had witnessed this slattern and unkempt woman muttering her Ave Marias backward. And others claimed to have seen her barefooted prints in the dirt leading back to her dwelling from a field where many cattle had died by her wrongdoing. But she, hearing this, cried the more. 'Pity! Pity! I am guiltless of these false crimes, never so much as thought of by me.' Suddenly, there was a motion in the crowd and the people made way. A leper came forward…"

"Pray tell, Morrison, what is a leper?"

Morrison sighed. "I was about to do so. Please, try not to interrupt the story. It makes the telling more difficult."

Will apologized. He silently vowed not to speak again until Morrison finished.

"A leper came forward," Morrison continued, "and in the faces of the people he bared his arm, which was withered and covered over with scales, most piteous to behold. The leper said, 'At the day of Pentecost last past, this woman did give unto me a shell of ointment with which I anointed my arm to cure an abscess that had come over it. And behold, from that day until this, my arm has shrunk and withered as you see it now.'

The crowd became clamorous and closed round the accused woman. Marjory Bysseth cried piteously that God had forsaken her. That she only meant good and not evil, and that the ointment was a gift of her husband who had been beyond the seas, and it was a gift to him from a holy man. She had given it free of reward or purchase, wishing only that it might be of good use. But that good gift had been paid back with evil and sorrow. Whereupon the people again pressed round the woman and dragged her to the pool, amid many tears and cries. 'Witch! Witch! Witch! To trial! To trial! To the Order Pot!' And they plunged her into the water. There was a great shout as she rose again and raised up her arms, as if she would have come up. Silence overtook the crowd. When again she went down with a bubbling noise, the crowd shouted, 'To Satan's kingdom she has gone!' Forthwith the crowd dispersed and went their ways."

Morrison opened his eyes. Will had slid down the wall, his hand covered his mouth. Morrison thought he looked more like a child than a man. "Not a pleasant story," Morrison sighed. "Many witches were drowned in the Order Pot, but no one knows how many."

Will could not bring himself to thank Morrison for giving him so many unpleasant images to dwell upon. He got to his feet and reached for the food basket. He was anxious to stop thinking about witches and eat something. He invited Morrison to join him, but the man declined. "I have other work yet to do." Then Morrison handed Will a pair of worn work gloves. "These might help protect your hands."

Will nodded appreciatively. "I will return them to you when my hands heal."

"No need, boy. They are yours to keep." Morrison glanced at Will's bandaged hands. "You've earned them."

Inside the keeper's hut Will lit a turf fire. He moved his chair close and propped his cold feet at the edge of the grate. It was impossible to dry out before returning to work, but warm and wet was better than cold and wet. Even a small fire was sure to make the hut smoky, but Will was too tired and hungry to climb Luke's ladder and uncover the smoke hole. Although it might release the smolder, it would certainly admit the rain.

The basket contained a generous assortment of foodstuffs, but Will would have given anything for a hot bowl of soup or thick brose. He felt ashamed for wanting what he did not have. The basket held enough food for at least two days. Everything was carefully wrapped and arranged, suggesting Alanna had prepared it. It was unlikely a man would have taken such care. Yet Will would have found it impossible to imagine Morrison doing any of the things he had just witnessed.

And then there were the gloves. Will lifted the weathered work gloves from the table. He recognized the mark on the inside cuff, made by the one remaining glovers in town. Will had assumed Morrison to be a difficult man. But here was evidence to the contrary. His unexpected thoughtfulness seemed out of character for a man so stern.

Once his hunger was satisfied, Will made two marks in Shanks's notebook. One for each barrow of stone tipped into the Witches Pool that morning. He was acutely aware he had not followed Shanks's directions to mark down one barrow load at a time. "How dim he must think I am," Will muttered. Still, he would attempt to do what Shanks ordered.

The rain had yielded, but not the fog, when Will returned to work. Making his way to the wall he could barely see the piles of stone until he was upon them. He pulled on the work gloves and wondered again about Morrison's motivations. The man had said plainly Will did not need to return them. And yet Will wondered what he might be expected to do in exchange.

Will struck his shovel into the nearest pile and pivoted to deliver the rocks into the wheelbarrow. To his surprise, the barrow was already filled. Will squinted into the low clouds clinging to the ground. He looked around, hoping to discover the person responsible for filling the wheelbarrow. His senses told him he was alone. Morrison had done him another kindness.

After hearing Morrison's story, Will's thoughts were no longer his own. He found it impossible to tip rubble into the Witches Pool without imagining the bones of the souls drowned there. Bones he was now burying firmly beneath the cathedral's wreckage.

As Will carted his next load over the soggy ground, the wheelbarrow developed a new noise. The distinctive sound was coming from the wheel. A scraping swish that hurt the ears. With every round the wheel seemed to whisper the one word foremost on Will's mind: Wit-ches. Wit-ches. Wit-ches.

8

FUNERAL FOR A CAT

The bells of St. Giles began to toll.

Will counted five chimes ringing from the new church tower. It was good to hear the ancient bells again after months in storage. During the reconstruction of St. Giles, Elgin had been a town without bells. A young boy was employed to cry the hour. His name was Reginald Smith, but he quickly became known as Reggie the Screecher. Reggie was diligent and dependable, never missing an hour between dawn and dusk. His painfully shrill voice traveled far on the wind. Regrettably, it was not easy on the ears. A wealthy parishioner despised the crier so much that he paid for the quick completion of the new bell tower long before the rest of the church was finished.

Will decided to cart a last load of rubble to the pool before dusk. Wrestling the full wheelbarrow down the mucky hill seized all his remaining strength. He had expected faster progress, but this was backbreaking work. Although the rain had stopped, the route was now a muddy ditch. His vision of racing to the Witches Pool and back had been pure fantasy. Exhausted, Will closed his eyes every few steps preferring not to see his own slow progress. It felt a bit like sleepwalking.

Will could not chase Morrison's story from his head. Although it was long ago, Marjory Bysseth's trial was not held in a place far, far away. It happened here at this pool. And those townsfolk who called for the drowning of the witch? Likely many of their descendants still lived in Elgin. Will wanted to believe his ancestors were not among the rabble the day they drowned Marjory Bysseth. Yet he was forced to admit that such a thing was possible. Killing accused witches was part of what happened in places like Elgin back then.

At the edge of the Witches Pool Will tossed a few rocks from his barrow into the water. He imagined the layers of ruined cathedral piling atop the bones of the dead at the bottom of the pool. He was ready for this day to be done, and he longed for his supper and his bed.

A thick mist swirled up from the River Lossie and clung to the Witches Pool like a shroud. Will found a firm bit of shore and slowly tipped his barrow.

A slender motion at the edge of the pool caught Will's eye, but the reeds and mist obscured his vision. He righted the wheelbarrow before it was empty. Sensing the presence of another, he discreetly lifted a fist-size rock from the barrow. Will heard the voice before he could locate its source.

"What are you doing?" The words were broken and craggy.

Will could not tell if it was a man or a woman. He tried for a better view but cautiously kept his distance. The child-size figure seemed to float on the mist. Will remained quiet, hoping to be invisible.

"What are you doing?" The brittle voice was insistent.

A light breeze stirred the reeds and the curtain of mist all at once sank to the waterline. Will now saw a very small person clothed in a tattered brown cloak. She clutched the rag close around her. Bits of gold-and-red threads hung broken from the garment's tattered edges. Other than her question she made no sound.

Still spooked by Morrison's story, Will gripped the rock in his hand more firmly and held it out of sight. He wondered if the figure was a passing spirit that might vanish as quickly as it appeared. But flesh and bones or not, she was staring in Will's direction. With the mist gone, he now had a clearer view of the robed stranger. She was an ancient sprite of a woman, her face wrinkled and folded in upon itself. Will startled when the woman spoke again.

"I-am-the-breath-and-voice-of-sea-and-land. Let-no-one-desecrate-this-place-I-stand. What are you doing here, boy?"

Will was in no mood for explaining his endless chore to a stranger. He thought—but did not say aloud—that he was doing the work of a madman, dumping rubble at the feet of an old madwoman here at the Witches Pool. Instead, he settled for a simpler response. "What am I doing? Good woman, can you not see that I have been tidying up the churchyard?"

Will should have stopped there and pushed his barrow back up the hill. But before he realized what he was saying, Will asked, "And what brings you to this sad place on a cold and haar-filled day?"

In answer, the old woman pulled something from under her cloak. She held it out to Will as though it were an offering. It was just large enough to require the use of both her gnarled hands. It was the size of a loaf of bread and wrapped tightly in strips of dirty rags. "It is my cat." She paused to amend her statement. "It was my cat. Now it is dead." The frailty of her voice made Will take a step closer. The dead cat had snagged his interest.

"I have brought her here for a watery burial."

"Why here?" The question escaped Will's lips at the same moment his brain asked why he remained rooted in place, conversing with this hag.

"I am the last from a family of wayward sisters. A very old family," she answered, gazing across the surface of the pool. "An ancient family that lived in Moray for hundreds of years, roaming heather and hillock. My ancestors were advisors to royalty. Kings and thanes." She briefly lifted her chin and straightened her bent frame. Then she sighed and relinquished the effort. "That was long ago, and no one recalls their names. But their stories were passed down, grandmothers to daughters and granddaughters, sisters and aunts and cousins."

"Have you come far?" Will asked.

"Away off to the east near Brodie Castle," she replied. "But memories of my ancestors are strong here in Elgin. Some are even…" She hesitated as though searching for words. "Some are even buried here," she sighed, looking down into the pool.

Will's heart raced. Yet the hag's honesty prompted his courteous response, "Yes, of course. Many have family long buried in the cathedral grounds and nearby churchyard."

The old woman made a noise. It might have been a stifled laugh or a sob. Will decided to say no more about graveyards and tombs. And yet there was still the matter of the cocooned dead cat. And whatever ceremony the old woman had come to the pool to perform.

"For many years this old gray cat followed me wherever I traveled. It came and departed from my home as though it lived there, too. Yet I never invited it in. It expected me to feed it and share my milk, never hesitating to drink from my cup. It would disappear for days and weeks. Sometimes longer. It was an intelligent animal. Have you ever owned an animal that seemed to know you better than yourself? Knew your every thought and mood?"

Will nodded solemnly, thinking of Jock.

"I hated this cat. But when it left, I missed it. It was a sentient being in my otherwise empty life. I would tell myself, 'Tis just a cat!' But its eyes…they seemed to comprehend every word I uttered. It watched me like a hawk watches a mouse. It was as though the cat knew my mind and my soul. I grew suspicious. And eventually I realized, the cat was waiting me out."

Will wondered if that was the end of her story. Tired of standing he leaned against the wheelbarrow. "Waiting for what?" Will asked.

"The old gray cat was waiting for my demise. For surely this cat was a witch, as I had suspected for years." She paused. "Or maybe not." The hag shifted the bundle into her other arm. "In any case, witch or cat, she belongs at the bottom of this pool—" The old woman hesitated and looked directly at Will before finishing her thought "—with all the rest."

Will swallowed hard.

"Now, boy, if you would be kind enough to give me that rock in your hand, I will tuck it into this beast's shroud and assure it finds its way to the bottom of the pool." She extended a hand of thin crooked fingers to take the rock Will clutched. He did not remember walking toward her. Only arriving and placing the stone in her open hand. A stone large enough to do the job.

"Did the cat have a name?" Will asked.

"Ashes," the old woman answered without hesitation. She stuffed the stone into the bundle. Holding the compact sarcophagus over the water's edge, she mumbled what sounded to Will more like a chant than a prayer. He could not make out the words she spoke. It was all unfamiliar gibberish, as though her thin-lipped mouth were full of pebbles. Or maybe it was just her lack of teeth that made her recitation unfathomable.

Will returned to his barrow to finish his work. Cat or no cat, he would not wait any longer for the conclusion of this funeral. As Will tipped the rest of the stones into the pool, the old woman retracted the bundle. Now she held it more like a baby than a dead cat. Tottering closer, she squinted up into Will's face. Before he could retreat, she chanted, "Someday you'll meet a ruler of the land. Show her when you bend to kiss her hand."

Hearing the hag's rhyme, Will resisted an inexplicable urge to show her the winged talisman in his pocket. Before he could think what to say next, the hag startled him once more by asking, "Do you know how to tell if a woman is a witch?"

Will groaned. "Enough witch stories," he muttered.

"Let me tell you, boy," the hag continued, "if you are dumping that ruin of a cathedral into this Order Pot, you likely need to know a thing or two about witches."

"I must get back to my work," Will protested.

"Nonsense and twaddle! Anyone can see plain that you are done."

Will blushed, caught in a lie. Twice he opened and closed his mouth searching for words that would hasten his escape but none emerged. He felt some morbid curiosity about what the old woman might say and do next. "This is what happens," Will thought aloud, "when a person lingers too long at the edge of the Witches Pool." Exhausted, he sat down beside the wheelbarrow.

The old woman continued, "I shall ask you again. Do you know how to tell if a woman is a witch?"

Will muttered an unintelligible reply.

"In days of old, there were many ways to test a woman to determine if she was a witch. Or so they say. The last witch was suffered to drown in this Order Pot more than one hundred years ago.

No one remains alive that was alive then. Or at least it is unlikely. Unless there is some other old witch who we do not know about, living in the woods somewhere." The old woman cackled, amused by her own speculation.

Will did not smile. Cornered into listening to another witch story, he was confronted with the possibility that this ugly old woman might be talking about herself.

"But if there were such a person, such a witch, and someone were to find her, likely she could tell us about the true test for witches. Not just the tests people made up, invented solely to dispose of an irritating neighbor, or an unwanted woman with child." She grunted and tucked the dead cat bundle under her arm before she continued, "And what were these tests to determine a witch from an innocent? Some said witches were incapable of shedding tears. And some said they danced naked by the light of a full moon. But that is not an image a boy like you should dwell on. Others claimed witches possessed the power to converse with wild animals. And most everyone agreed it was rare for a person to be born a witch. A woman became a witch by bargaining with the Devil himself."

Will moaned. For certain he was doomed to a night of turbulent dreams.

"Since there was much confusion and uncertainty about how to tell for certain if a woman was a witch," the hag continued, "the authorities eventually agreed upon one true test. And it involved water. Witches, you know, do not tolerate water. And that is how this pond became the Order Pot. It was the place where witches were dispensed with—once they were judged to be witches."

With a motion faster than Will could comprehend, the old woman unceremoniously flung the white bundle of dead cat out into the pool. It traveled much farther than Will imagined possible. He watched the bundle sink swiftly and disappear. The rings from the impact rippled toward him. The skin on his scalp prickled. As the pool filled with concentric waves, Will thought to ask the old woman her name. But when he looked in her direction she was gone.

Will did not linger. He trudged up the slope pushing the empty barrow. Dark clouds sent sharp pellets of rain, stinging his face. He resisted the urge to glance back at the Order Pot until he reached the top of the track. Will looked over his shoulder. At the edge of the pool stood the ancient crone—arms outstretched, palms up, fingers bent like claws, her lips rapidly moving. But Will was too far away to hear her voice. The wind came up strong and the clouds burst open, flooding the skies over Elgin with angry rain. Will wiped a sleeve across his face. When he looked again the hag was gone.

9

ALANNA'S BOOK

The skies cleared in Elgin and Will returned to his work.

Bright sunlight helped ease the ominous feeling in his chest. But he still glanced cautiously over his shoulder whenever he turned his back on the Witches Pool. Will carted rubble and marked each load in the notebook. The memory of the crone and her dead cat became more dreamlike than real. Will wanted to stop thinking about the old woman. He wanted to shake her words from his head. He began looking forward to Shanks's return and the old man's stories.

Will took advantage of the good weather to clean his clothes and bathe in the river. He picked a small handful of wild strawberries and ate them as he walked back to the ruin. He had removed his mother's bandages and his hands were slowly healing. Morrison's gloves were fine protection.

The nice weather improved Will's mood. He wondered if Shanks would be more impressed with the diminished rubble piles, or the number of marks in the notebook. Will hoped Shanks would be pleased, but he was uncertain about the old ruin keeper's expectations. His own ambitions were his biggest frustration. Will had eagerly overestimated the amount of rubble he could cart in a day, even in the best circumstances. Yet he remained optimistic about his progress.

Working through the morning hours Will's thoughts returned to food. The basket Morrison had delivered was almost empty. The cheese and potted meat were just a memory. His stomach rumbled. He reached into his coat pocket for the last crowdie roll. He broke off a piece and popped it into his mouth. The stale bread held good flavor. The hardness was a benefit, lasting longer before swallowing. He wished Alanna would bring him a meal as Shanks said she would. Otherwise, he would need to set a rabbit trap or sink a trout line.

After making his thirteenth mark in the notebook Will returned to the hut. He drank some rainwater from the bucket and checked his food box for crumbs. As the church bells struck eleven, Will heard a cart approaching. Alanna had driven her pony cart to deliver his meal. Will offered his clean, unbandaged hand to assist her from the cart. He was glad for the timing of his bath.

Alanna picked her way carefully through boggy patches left from the heavy rains. She wore fine calfskin gloves and an embroidered drawstring pocky hung from her wrist. "I have brought you a nice food basket," she said. "Would you kindly carry it from the cart?" Alanna lifted the large cloth folded over the food. To Will's surprise she pointed to a patch of dry grass at the base of the cathedral wall. A spot where the sun's reflection had dried the ground. "Over there," she said. Together they spread the cloth and Will placed the basket in the center of it. "I hope you like the food," she said with a smile.

Will hesitated, suddenly uncomfortable in Alanna's presence without Shanks there to chatter and unpack the meal. But the smell of fresh bread elicited growls from his stomach. He knelt carefully on the edge of the blanket and risked a glance in the girl's direction. She was not looking his way. The breeze danced the ribbons on her bonnet and bobbed the Scots bluebells tucked into her hatband. He could see her dainty blue shoes but not the eyes that matched them. With an air of formality Alanna remained standing, unsure whether to stay or go.

"Would you like to sit, miss?" Will asked. "I could fetch a chair from the hut."

"That's not necessary. I am enjoying the sunshine. I often sit upon the ground when I read under a tree, or when I sketch and paint in the meadow." Alanna remained on the far edge of the blanket, her eyes closed, and chin tilted skyward. She was thinking about the characters in a book she favored. Imagining how her plaid shawl and the puffed sleeves on her dress resembled the costumes worn by heroines in Walter Scott romances.

Will noticed a soft citrus scent. It tickled his nose each time Alanna swished the flounce of her skirts. The odor was familiar. Something his mother grew in her garden. Bog myrtle came to mind. Or was it sweet gale? What he remembered was the plant's practical value. The crushed leaves gave off a citrusy scent to repel midges.

As hungry as he was, Will could not decide if he was more tempted by the smell of the girl or the aroma of the chicken. "Would you mind if I eat now, miss? Or should I wait until you leave."

"Oh goodness, please eat. There's a nice bit of roasted fowl and plenty of bread. Morrison told me young men never tire of eating good bread. There's also cider and other provisions. Enough for two days…" As Will quickly finished a chicken leg and made a roll disappear, Alanna wondered if her words could possibly be true.

She had not planned to stay. But neither had she given it much thought beyond delivering the basket. She spread the blanket only because that was how her grandfather instructed her to do it the first time. It occurred to Alanna that the boy could have eaten in his hut if she had delivered the food and left. On the other hand, she wondered if this broad-shouldered scarecrow of a boy might enjoy some company.

A butterfly fluttered past and paused on a lone thistle rooted near the base of the wall. "Oh! It must truly be spring!" Alanna clasped her hands together in delight. "Do you know what that is?"

"A butterfly, miss, and a very fine spotted one at that."

"It's not just any butterfly. It is a green fritillary. A nice specimen, I'd say."

Something in Alanna's voice suddenly reminded Will of her grandfather. "Green?" Will frowned. "Why do you say it's green when it has golden wings with brown-and-black markings?"

"Look again. When it lands on the moss-covered bark of a Scots pine tree it will fold tight its wings. The dark green fur on its body helps it disappear into the thick moss."

Before Will could ask how she knew so much about butterflies, she told him.

"Isaac Forsyth has an extensive butterfly collection in his library. Sometimes when my grandfather visits him, he takes me along and I am allowed to borrow a book. When I get tired of reading, I study the butterflies. They are pinned in cases and labeled with their names. The collection contains at least two hundred specimens. Most are from Scotland, but several of the cases came from faraway places once visited by Dr. Alexander Gray. He was a famous surgeon for the East India Company. Many of the butterflies are from his collection. He sailed all over the world before returning home to Elgin. When he died, he left a good portion of his fortune to build Elgin's hospital. And he left many of his books and collections to Isaac for his library. Isaac Forsyth is one of the best-known booksellers in this part of Scotland, you know." The gush of words seemed to exhaust her. "Perhaps I will sit for a while," she said. Alanna settled carefully on a corner of the cloth, the food basket serving as a small barrier between them. She removed her gloves and reset the shawl on her shoulders. Sliding a book from her bag she asked, "Do you read?"

Will froze midchew. He was unsure how to answer. She had not asked if he could read, but if he did read. And never before had he been asked the latter.

Sensing Will's hesitation, Alanna did not wait for his response. "Of course, I suppose you would have little time for reading." Running her hand over the small book in her lap, Alanna kept talking, "But might you have a favorite book?"

"I have not given that question much thought, miss," Will replied, careful not to look directly at Alanna for fear she would see his awkwardness. Instead, he unstoppered the cider and drank.

"My favorite book is the one I am presently reading." Alanna patted the book in her lap. "*Ivanhoe* by Walter Scott. He is my favorite author. And Amy Robsart in *Kenilworth* is my favorite heroine. I have imagined what it must have been like to be her." Alanna paused, rearranging her thoughts and her skirts at the same time. "Not the falling-down-steps-to-her-death part, of course." She paused again.

It was clear to Will that the girl was working through a particular thought. But he lacked skills for reading the minds of the fairer sex.

Alanna blushed a bright red as she realized all that remained to be imagined about Amy Robsart—apart from her dramatic death—were her love affairs. She turned her face away and touched her temples with a lacy handkerchief. Wordlessly, Will offered the cider crock. She shook her head and busied herself with replacing the handkerchief in her bag.

"I do read some," Will whispered. And, of course, he knew of Walter Scott. The man was a national figure. Even if he had little to add to the conversation it was nice to have a friendly voice nearby.

Alanna was no longer reflecting on Will's reading abilities. She had moved on to thoughts of Ivanhoe and the beautiful Rowena, romantic characters in the book she held in her lap. "Would you mind if I read aloud while you eat?"

"I would like that. If you do not mind me eating while you read."

She nodded her agreement. "The rain has kept me indoors and reading helps pass the time with my grandfather away. *Ivanhoe* is the name of this book and also the main character," she explained. "Actually, his name is Wilfred of Ivanhoe. He is the son of a knight who was devoted to King Richard during the Crusades. And there are many more characters: ladies and knights, outlaws, servants, and monks. A jousting tournament is underway and…" She paused. "Maybe it would be best if I just read." Once she found her place in the book, Alanna adjusted her bonnet to shade her face. She daintily cleared her throat.

From the sound of her voice, Will sensed Alanna's devotion to the story. Her reading voice was easy and steady without pretension. Will was glad of it. Other than the Holy Bible, he could not recall anyone reading a book aloud to him. There was plenty of storytelling in his family, but that was different than reading from a storybook. He concentrated on the words and was quickly transported.

"'The trumpets had no sooner given the signal, than the champions vanished from the posts with the speed of lightning and closed in the center of the lists with the shock of a thunderbolt. The lances burst into shivers up to the very grasp, and it seemed at the moment that both knights had fallen, for the shock had made each horse recoil backward upon its haunches. The riders recovered their steeds by use of the bridle and spurs; and glared on each other with eyes that seemed to flash fire through the bars of their visors. And between every pause was heard the voices of the heralds exclaiming, 'Fight on brave knights! Man dies but glory lives!'"

Will closed his eyes and settled into the story. She read and flipped pages and read some more.

"'One by one the archers stepped forward and delivered their shafts bravely. Of twenty-four arrows shot in succession, ten were fixed in the target, and the others ranged so near it that it was considered good archery. Hubert shot so successfully that his arrow alighted in the very center of the target. 'Thou canst not mend that shot, Locksley,' said Prince John with an insulting smile. 'I will notch his shaft for him, however,' replied Locksley. And letting fly his arrow, it lighted right upon that of his competitor, which it split to shivers.'"

Will pictured the tournament's pomp and pageantry. The pennants and tents. The archers, and the woodsman named Locksley. What it might have been like to be among the crowd on the hill that day. He opened his eyes to watch the girl reading to him. Fell in love with her ability to transport him with her voice. With a book. With a story.

Alanna paused. She, too, had been engrossed in the tale. And no wonder, Will thought. What young woman could resist men like Locksley and the Disinherited Knight? A new inadequacy crept into Will's thoughts. How could he—a rubble-carter—compete with valiant knights and a heroic archer like Locksley? Did it even matter that he was a real person, and Locksley just a scatter of words on a page in a book?

As if Alanna could read his mind, she flipped back to the beginning pages and read aloud, "'The knights are dust, and their good swords are rust, their souls are with the saints we trust. Their castles are but green mounds, and shattered ruins the places that once knew them, know them no more. Nay, many a race since theirs has died out and been forgotten...'"

The wind changed direction. The reader and the listener both looked skyward. Dark clouds were gathering, and a new storm was forming. Another gust pulled at Alanna's hat.

"I should go," Alanna said. And with more speed than she had previously demonstrated, the girl retrieved her things and made her way swiftly to the pony cart.

Will trailed after her, unsure about leaving the cloth and the basket.

Alanna interpreted his backward glance as a longing look at the uneaten food. "Hurry!" she encouraged, checking the sky. "Don't fret. I'll collect the basket next time. A hand, please?"

Alanna settled herself on the bench of the cart and Will helped point the pony in the right direction. "Does he spook, miss?" Will asked.

"Daisy is a calm and matronly beast. *She* will see me home safely." Alanna clucked her tongue to the pony and shook the reins. As they trotted off, she called over her shoulder, "Nearly forgot! Grandfather sent word. He is delayed in Edinburgh."

Will shoved his hands into his pockets and watched her go. He felt a sudden sadness. In the stiff breeze the clouds were moving fast. As he retrieved the basket and the cloth, it crossed his mind that he should have seen the girl home. It was a missed opportunity to be chivalrous. Will picked up a flower dislodged by the wind from Alanna's hat and dropped it into the basket. His thoughts returned to the knights in the story. He wondered what would happen next, and how he would ever find out. But foremost on his mind were two words Alanna had spoken: *next time*.

10

COUSINS

He should have known.

Will had sensed someone nearby as he dumped another load of rubble into the Witches Pool. He tried to ignore the rustling reeds, but the phosphorous odor of a Lucifer match tickled his nose. Will was in no mood for another encounter at the pool. But when he turned to leave, he heard Johnny's voice.

"So, this is what you're up to now. Carting rubbish and picnicking with girls." Johnny emerged from the reeds holding a clay pipe. Davie and Walt were close behind.

Walt snickered when Davie asked, "Aren't you afraid of disturbing the souls of dead witches?"

These boys were Will's cousins, his mates, and his friends. Boys whose company he regularly kept until the wall went up. It was strange how a wall could change people's lives. Keeping them in or out. Scattering them to other places. Will knew that Davie, Walt, and their father had found new work. And Johnny? Most likely he was drinking and causing trouble. Will turned his attention to Walt. "Are you still roofing the Episcopal Chapel?"

"Aye, we're almost done. And if work on St. Giles goes as planned, a lot of us hope to be taken on there."

"That's good news," Will said.

"It is," Walt agreed. "Looks like we won't need to leave town to find work. At least not for a while."

"Speak for yourself," Johnny muttered.

"What are your plans now, Johnny?" Will wanted to know.

Johnny kicked the dirt. "Not everyone is equally blessed," he snarled.

Will glanced at Davie and Walt before asking Johnny a familiar question—a question these boys had frequently discussed. Ever since they were old enough to meet after dark with stories to swap and a purloined inch of whiskey from some unfinished bottle. It was a game of sorts, and Will was certain where his question would lead. Ultimately, he hoped to defuse the anger lurking behind Johnny's eyes. "So, Johnny. Tell me. What might you wish for today?"

A smile teased Johnny's lips. His reply was always the same. "Can I wish for anything?"

"Anything at all," Will said.

Johnny shaded his eyes and squinted past Will's shoulder. As he touched a hand to his chest, the present faded away.

Up the rise toward the meadow, outside the Pans Port, something seemed to move. The sunlight was unusually bright. In Johnny's imagination he could see them all together up there. Davie and Walt and Will and a dozen more cousins. Back when they were eight and nine and ten. When they would escape the ruin and run into the open field. Choose up sides to play at war with weapons both pretend and imagined. Recreating their own version of the battle on Culloden Moor. A real place, not far away to the west of Elgin. A real battle that happened long ago between British soldiers and the Highland Clans.

The wind shifted. The clouds moved. The sunbeams holding the young boys' images on the hillside faded as quickly as they had appeared. Once again, Johnny let his hand stray to his chest, just long enough to graze the front of his shirt. Underneath, a small leather pouch hung close to his heart. The square of Murray plaid secured inside the pouch was lighter than a downy feather. The cloth was stained with the blood of Johnny's grandfather who died at the battle of Culloden. Some had seen the pouch, but Johnny never revealed its contents, fearful it might be taken from him. He alone possessed its power to conjure the bitter family memories passed down to him. That tiny bloodstained bit of cloth made it all real.

Returning from his reverie, Johnny repeated Will's question. "What might I wish for? I have a new wish."

"You do?" Will was surprised.

"I would still wish to have fought at Culloden. But—"

Davie and Walt groaned in unison. "There it is." Davie rolled his eyes. "Same as always."

"Quiet, Davie. Let him have his say." Will nodded and Johnny continued.

"Davie has a point. But usually when I talk about Culloden, I'm less sober than I am now. I always believed if I could have fought at Culloden, I would have fought with the clans like my great-grandfather did. And I would have gladly died on that battlefield to avoid being born a meager remnant of the great clans three generations later."

"That's not a kind thought, Johnny." Walt scowled.

"But recently," Johnny continued, "I've had a change of heart. If I could wish for anything, maybe I should wish to fight at Culloden," he hesitated to be sure he had their attention, "with the British."

"You cannot mean that," Davie whispered.

"Aye. I think I do. When the battle on Culloden Moor happened down the road, the people in this town were not all on the side of Bonnie Prince Charlie, just because they were Scottish. In truth, this town was split down the middle. Half supported the clans and half aligned with the British. When I look around Elgin now, those whose ancestors backed the British at Culloden came out better than those who supported the clans."

"What about the Andersons?" Walt insisted.

Johnny smirked and shook his head. "Aye, the old widow Anderson. Who sheltered the Bonnie Prince and nursed him back to health in the days before the battle. Who saved the sheets the Young Pretender slept in; and when she died had herself wrapped in them as her burial shroud. That's a fine story indeed. But the Andersons of Elgin were the wealthy exception." Johnny continued, "If my great-grandfather had chosen to side with the British, his odds of surviving Culloden would have been better. And my lot in life would have been better, too. That's a fact. So, there it is, boys. If I could wish for anything, it would be to fight with the British on Culloden Moor and live to reap the rewards."

It was a relief when Johnny stopped talking. But a sense of pending manhood caught each boy silently wondering what the winds of change might bring next.

"What will you do now?" Will asked Johnny.

"New contractors are moving into Elgin, taking work from the local tradesmen. Don't fool yourselves. There's nothing for us here anymore. My father says Elgin is changing so fast that soon we won't recognize it. And have you heard about the new school for orphans? Imagine that! Orphans getting a book-learning education instead of being sent to the poorhouse. Where does that leave the likes of us, sons of stonemasons?"

That thought had never entered Will's head. Work did that to a person—wiped away any time for sorting thoughts. Idleness, on the other hand, provided time to gather reasons to be disgruntled. The mention of book learning reminded Will of his discomfort when Alanna asked him about reading.

"That's all fine and good, Johnny, but what will you do instead?" Will was sincerely interested to learn what plans his black sheep cousin was considering.

"Aberdeen," Johnny said. "Signing on to a sailing ship as a deckhand for the East India Company if I have my way. To London and on to Bombay." Johnny was pleased with the surprised looks on his cousins' faces. "See the world. Do something other than cut and lay stones," he said enthusiastically.

"You would leave Scotland?" Walt was shocked at the thought.

"Why not? If my life has to change, at least I'll be doing the changing."

"That's a rough life, Johnny." Davie frowned.

Johnny laughed. "Can't be rougher than what I got now."

Considering his cousin's violent homelife, Will thought Johnny might be right.

"What makes you think they will take you on in Aberdeen?" Walt asked.

"I'm young and strong and…" Johnny hesitated. "And if they don't, I'll stow away. Worst of it they'll put me ashore in London."

The boys were awestruck imagining their cousin as a stowaway on an East India Company ship.

"Not sure exactly when I'll go—if I do," Johnny added.

Will stopped leaning on the wheelbarrow. "I need to get back to work."

Johnny squinted hard at Will; his face gone mean. "So, exactly what is it you're doing here?"

"I could ask you the same." Will returned Johnny's glare.

"Are you getting paid for this, or what?" Johnny took a pull on his pipe and spit on the ground. He picked a small bit of leaf from his tongue.

"Daft question," Will replied, looking to Davie and Walt for support.

"Ruin keeper is it, now?" Johnny moved closer.

Will stood his ground.

Johnny looked over Will's shoulder, up the hill once more. "You seem overanxious to be on your way, cousin. Is that girl waiting for you? Up in the hut? Does she come with the job? A bit of your pay?"

Will's face raced red. He called Johnny a name he'd never used before. He stepped around the barrow and took a swing, grazing Johnny's ear. Johnny was the more experienced fighter. His response was fast and powerful. The punch struck Will near his right eye. Will lowered his shoulder and ran at Johnny, shoving him hard. Knocked off-balance, Johnny fell backward toward the Witches Pool. He reached out and grabbed air in one hand and Will's arm in the other. Johnny struggled for footing, but Will's upper body strength was enough to knock his cousin off his feet and into the water. The clay pipe flipped out of Johnny's hand and plopped into the pool with a sizzle.

The surprised look on Johnny's face satisfied Will. He had never been the strongest, but it seemed the balance of physical power among the four boys had rearranged itself. Will's days of being bullied by Johnny Murray were over. Or so it seemed to Will.

Davie and Walt were laughing as Johnny struggled out of the pool.

"You'll be sorry for this, Clachan," Johnny seethed.

But Will was already far up the hill with his barrow.

11

BAPTISM, DAMNATION, AND PLACES BETWEEN

Throbbing pain woke Will before dawn.

He reached for his face and remembered. Gingerly touching his eye made him wince, but at least it was not swollen shut. "Why did you have to punch me in the face?" Will mumbled into the darkness.

His stomach growled, undaunted by the pain in his eye. But even more important than food, Will needed water. He would start his day with a walk to the Bishop's Well in the nearby woods. Long considered a sacred spring, it was known for its purity and freshness. Folklore claimed the water from the Bishop's Well possessed healing powers. The thought of cool water cupped to his sore eye was enough to lure Will to the spring.

Will made his way to the edge of the woods. The empty bucket he carried knocked against his leg as he walked along eating his morning roll. He was thankful Shanks was still away. Will hoped the delay might continue long enough for his eye to heal. He had no desire to discuss the incident with Shanks. It was hard enough for Will to understand why he was the target of Johnny Murray's anger.

People were always trying to explain the unexplainable. It was human nature to do so. Although, Will had to admit, he'd met several dogs and a horse that were smarter about cause and effect than some people he knew. His father once told him that religion was invented to explain good and evil. And there were wise men who believed that book learning was every bit as important as prayer for sorting out the human condition. But Will's thoughts about Johnny were still unresolved when he reached the Bishop's Well.

The spring was lively. It bubbled up among green ferns and soft moss. A little Eden in miniature. There were tiny white flowers no bigger than a pinhead, and clusters of small wild strawberries. The gently splashing water gave off a clean mineral smell. Will knelt and placed his hand under the steady font. He lifted the fresh water to his swollen eye and its coolness quickly eased the pain. He repeated the eye bath several times before cupping handfuls of water into his mouth. This spring tasted different than the rainwater he collected. It bore no resemblance to the water from the Lossie. When Will was younger, everyone in Elgin drank water from the river. But that was before the town piped its wastewater into the Lossie. Now people were more careful. They washed and bathed and fished upstream.

Will stretched out on his stomach and put his mouth to the source, drinking long and loud, quenching his thirst for the first time in days. When Will could drink no more, he settled himself on the ground. He let his eyes follow the narrow stream to where it left the far edge of the woods to empty into the river. He listened to birdsong and the wind stirring the treetops. He had work to do, but there would always be more work. For a heartbeat, Will let go of his worries and felt free.

"Aren't you the boy who's dumping the cathedral rocks into

the Witches Pool for old John Shanks?"

The voice startled Will onto his feet. A small man with an unfamiliar face stood on the opposite side of the stream. He was toting two large buckets. Will noticed the man's clean scrubbed hands and his worn but tidy garments. "My name is Will Clachan. I work for Master Shanks, the ruin keeper."

"Good morning, Will Clachan. I am James Thompson, a newcomer to Elgin. I arrived at the start of last school term to take a teaching position at the Free School."

"A pleasure, sir."

"I instruct young boys in mathematics and history." Thompson paused, assessing Will in some unfathomable way. He glanced around the woods as though concerned about who might be lurking or eavesdropping. "However," the teacher continued, lowering his voice, "my true interests lie in the study of natural history. Geology, astronomy, zoology, fossils, and botany. Employing the scientific method to learn more about the world around us through observation."

"You study trees and animals?"

"And stars and rocks."

Will could not guess the man's age. He seemed a mix of elfin youthfulness and wizardly wisdom.

"It appears we are both here for the same purpose." The teacher lifted his chin toward Will's bucket and placed his own pails on the ground. "Do you know the history of this well?"

"A bit, sir. Likely not as much as you, a teacher of history. But I know it is called the Bishop's Well. And it offers the finest fresh water."

Thompson squatted near the source for a drink. He splashed water on his face and head and ran his fingers through his hair. "Originally it was called Saint Anne's Well," the teacher said. "It was once a clootie well—a holy well—and people visited here hoping for a cure to whatever troubled their bodies and souls. Seeking relief from their infirmities, people came to the well to wish for cures. The water was an important part of the ritual, yet there was something more to it. A piece of cloth, a clootie, was soaked in the healing well water and rubbed on the affected body part. Prayers were said and the cloth was tied to a nearby clootie tree. Folklore claimed that once the cloth rotted, the person's sickness would disappear. The practice dates to pagan times. But like many beliefs, the wells were adapted and modified by the early Christian church." Thompson paused. He looked at Will and grinned lopsidedly. "Is that what brings you here?" Before Will could answer, Thompson pulled a clean handkerchief from his pocket. With a wink, he offered it to Will, gesturing to his swollen eye.

Embarrassed, Will hesitated. He was unsure if the man was seriously offering him his handkerchief as a clootie or attempting a bit of humor.

"Not exactly," Will replied, waving off the proffered linen square. "I was in need of drinking water." Will lifted his bucket and tucked it under the flow. "And yes, the cool water has proved useful for soothing my eye."

"Have you seen a clootie well before?" Thompson asked. "There is another one not far from here in Culloden Woods. Saint Mary's Well, it's called. And there are others scattered about the countryside in secluded and mysterious places."

"But there is no clootie tree here." Will looked up into the surrounding trees in this place he knew so precisely.

"Not anymore," Thompson said. "But six hundred years ago there existed a magnificent one."

"What happened to it?" Will asked.

"The cathedral was built. The nearby spring was an asset, but the bishops were not fond of superstitions and folk stories. Bishop Andreas renamed the spring the Bishop's Well. When the people continued in their old traditions, he had the ancient clootie tree cut down. At the time it was thought to be eight hundred years old. But it may have been twice that, for all we know."

"Eight hundred years." Will tried to imagine it as he looked up into the trees. "I would love to have seen it."

"In a way, you still can. See that clearing just beyond?" Thompson pointed deeper into the woods, not far off from where they sat.

"Where the moss grows on the stones in a large circle?" Will knew the spot well from childhood adventures.

"Those are not stones," Thompson beamed gleefully.

"Not stones?"

"You should examine them more closely sometime. That ring of stones is what remains of the outside circumference of this well's ancient clootie tree. Most likely a massive beech tree or an enormous oak. Brought here and planted during the Bronze Age. The area inside the circle was once occupied by the tree's trunk."

"No!" Will whispered in disbelief.

"Imagine its branches," Thompson continued. "Eight hundred years of branches covered in bits of rotting cloth. An assortment of faded colors and textures reaching up into the sky as high as the eyes could see."

Will tried to fathom what the teacher had described. At the corner of his vision, on the far side of the clearing, Will imagined a bearded man with an ax on his shoulder, looking skyward. The woodsman took a few steps and disappeared into the trees.

"It must have been an awe-filled sight," Thompson continued, "which was why the bishop had the clootie tree removed."

Will stood and walked closer to the clearing. He stared into the empty space that he had only known as a glade in the woods. Now it was something more.

"One can assume it took months for the woodsmen to cut it all down and haul it away. Some of its branches would have been larger than the trees that grew around it."

"Then what happened?"

Thompson shrugged. "People went to church." He bit his lower lip for a moment, gauging his audience. "I am told this well was used as a source of water for baptismal fonts in the great cathedral, and more recently in St. Giles Church." Thompson repressed an escaping smile. "I have also been told that, occasionally, the young acolytes were lazy."

"How so?" Will asked.

"Sometimes they dipped water from the River Lossie instead of coming here to the holy well. And in very bad weather, some of the acolytes would dip water from the Order Pot to fill the font, since it was nearer the cathedral. The boys rationalized that it would make no difference since the water was made holy by sacramental blessings. But here in Elgin, people likely wondered how it was that some of those baptized became good people, while others turned bad—as though the baptism did not 'take.' And although the Presbyterians might reason it away as predestination, others needed a plainer explanation. Eventually, word leaked out: the holy water was not always from the purest source." Thompson smiled to himself, considering the word *leak*—another potential source of fouled baptismal water. "Blessings by priests and bishops could only do so much for tainted water. Even the Lossie, when she overflows her banks, becomes mixed with the Order Pot. Just like the Holy Trinity, this Bishop's Well, and the River Lossie, and the Witches Pool are also three-in-one."

Will's brain raced to keep up with the flood of words.

"Like you, I happily drink from this clear spring. And I enjoy fish from the River Lossie. But I would prefer to die parched before I would drink from the Witches Pool," the teacher concluded.

Struck by such a storm of observations, Will felt the need to sit down again. His own throat was suddenly dry from all the talking Thompson had directed his way. Will dipped his hand into the stream for a drink. Hesitated. Laughed, and drank again. Although overwhelmed by the man's stories, Will was grateful for the wealth of ideas this teacher had given him.

"What tales you tell!" Will made it sound like a compliment. He finished filling his bucket. "You are better than a book, Master Thompson."

"Do you read?" the teacher asked.

There it was again. The same question Alanna had put to him.

"A little," Will answered.

James Thompson looked straight through Will. He knew from years of teaching exactly what that response meant.

"I'd like to learn to read better," Will added.

"What have you read recently?"

It was tempting to lie, but Will thought better of it. "Recently? I had some parts of *Ivanhoe* read to me. I heard enough of it that I would like to be able to read it on my own and find out how the story ends." Will shook his head. "But now I must be back to work. The cathedral ruins won't march into the Order Pot by themselves."

Thompson laughed. "See you again, Will. Nice to meet you."

"And you, sir." Will bobbed his head deferentially.

"No need for that, Will. You're not my pupil. At least not yet."

12

WILL'S FIND

Will began work before the first church bells rang.

His mind wandered to knights' tales and clootie wells. His thoughts only returned to the present when he made a slash mark in the notebook.

After three trips to the pool, he set the wheelbarrow firmly on the ground and settled himself beside it. Will was too tired to worry about lingering by the pool. Too tired to think about angry cousins, or old women who looked like witches. The setting was almost pleasant if you could forget what lay at the bottom of the pool. True, there was a fetid smell from the stewing bog, but despite the pool's connection with death, life still lingered at its edges. A passerby might spot the occasional gull or a long-tailed duck. There were warblers, siskins, and pipits in springtime. Toads and newts made their homes here, too. Will ignored any connection between those creatures and witches. He wondered what the pool was called before the first witch was drowned here. If not for its horrific history, the Witches Pool might have been a pleasant spot with a nicer name. Yet at the rate he was dumping rocks into it, Will could almost picture a day, far in the future, when the pool was entirely filled in. The thought made him laugh.

Back at the ruin, Will was scooping another shower of rocks into the wheelbarrow when something caught his eye. A smooth white flash that was quickly covered by more rocks. Will searched until he found the piece again, picked it out, and brushed it off. He removed his gloves to examine the piece carefully. The unbroken surfaces were carved and polished. It appeared to be a piece of a tiny carved hand with a dimpled knuckle.

Will stared at the broken hand in disbelief. He felt light-headed when he realized he might have dumped it into the pool. He wondered what Shanks would say when he saw it, and if it had any value. He gently set the piece aside, but all afternoon he cautiously watched every wheelbarrow of rubble tipped into the pool. Spying something at that point would be too late of course. Value and beauty lost all meaning once something precious disappeared into the Witches Pool. Will considered his own carved creature rescued from the ruin. It might be wise to inspecting the rubble more carefully.

Later, back in the hut, Will set the broken white hand on the table. He pulled the winged creature from his pocket and placed it next to the hand. His own small carved wonder was a bit of sculpture that bore little resemblance to the broken hand. Carefully turning the creature in his fingers, Will smiled at its peaceful face. He considered what other small finds might be lost forever, without more care for what they were dumping.

Will knew there was no way he could talk to Shanks about any of this without showing him his good luck piece. And he was not about to do that. Will was sure if he revealed his little creature to anyone, it would be taken away and lost to him forever. The wings, the tail, the claws, eyes, and scales of the tiny carving were like nothing Will had ever seen in his own world. He reasoned that since he had found the creature long before the ruin was locked up, it belonged to him alone. That was Will's point of view, but not one he wished to debate. He rubbed the creature's wings and returned it to his pocket.

Will knew there were consequences to his small secret. He alone would be keeping an eye out for what might be lost in the rubble destined for the Witches Pool. Shanks had made his own position plain. His objective was to clear the cathedral grounds as efficiently as possible. It made no difference whether Will agreed with the old shoemaker's methods. He could only hope the little white hand might change Shanks's mind.

Will did not own a mirror.

Other than by touch, he could not tell how fast his eye was healing. But his mother possessed a tiny looking glass. It was a wedding gift from Da. Not much larger than a playing card and set in a mahogany border that matched the color of Mam's hair. Da said the mirror likely came to the Isles on a trading ship. It had been a rare extravagance wrapped in a half sheet of fine writing paper bearing a fragment of poetry.

Once when Will was younger, he happened upon the folded paper. He recognized a few words, but not the important ones: *beauty* and *vanity* and *reflection*. Will left a thumbprint on the mirror before Mam discovered him. "Not for you!" she scolded him and snatched the paper from his hand. "Learn to stay out of my things." She sent him off with a halfhearted smack on his bum.

Will considered going home to use Mam's mirror. Then again, the look on Mam's face might be mirror enough. This visit would need to be short. Since Shanks had been gone longer than expected, Will had no idea when he might return.

Will had reduced the rubble piled outside the ruin and stopped worrying about Shanks's expectations. There was no rushing heavy labor, and he would be no use to anyone if he injured himself. His father had taught him that lesson.

As he walked home Will considered the questions Shanks might ask on his return from Edinburgh. The events he might share with the old ruin keeper, and those he would choose to leave out. He would show him the notebook with thirty-one marks on the page. It was the best way to talk about his accomplishments. But Will knew Shanks would be the one asking the questions. He only hoped the first topic would not be his swollen eye.

Will was proud of every mark in the notebook. Early on, he had considered what would happen if he added a few extra slash marks. How would anyone know? But of course, he would know. And Will quickly realized he was not the kind of person who could live with himself as a bald-faced liar. He would answer truthfully any questions Shanks asked. But aside from discussing the weather, Will did not intend to mention the visit from Morrison. Nor his fight with Johnny or his encounter with the hag.

A sudden thought slowed Will's pace. His shortsightedness arrived like a noose draped around his neck. Until now, he had not once considered what he might say to Shanks about his conversation with Alanna. Would the girl tell Shanks about reading to him? Will turned scarlet at the thought, instantly worried about how Shanks might misinterpret her good intentions. How he might perceive Will as loafing with his granddaughter, without an escort, and listening to stories when he should have been working. Looking back on it, he imagined all the ways their brief meeting might be misconstrued. Especially if his spying cousins spread false rumors about Will and the girl. But what was done, Will could not undo. And wishing it away seemed harsh when Alanna was only showing him a kindness. He would not trade those moments hearing her read *Ivanhoe* for anything.

Ivanhoe. Will closed his eyes and imagined the valor of the Disinherited Knight. If challenged about his encounter with Mistress Alanna, Will would be truthful. He had nothing to apologize for.

"It seems you only find your way home when you need doctoring," Mam muttered as she stood over her oldest son seated on the garden bench.

"Ouch!" Will flinched.

"Hold still!" she demanded, massaging ointment into the puffy flesh around her son's bruised eye. Mam was not happy with him. There was no motherly concern in her voice when she asked, "Who did this to you?"

His father also showed little sympathy, especially once he learned the fist that did the damage belonged to Johnny Murray. "You know better than to keep company with that boy. He's nothing but trouble these days."

"He was the one—"

Will's father held up a hand, shook his head, and stepped back inside the cottage. Will was finding it difficult to convince his family that he was the victor in the fight. But it was Mam's reaction that surprised Will the most. It required a lot to raise his mother's ire.

"Stupid boys," she muttered over the top of his head, her hands working some small miracle on his face. Will imagined her anger was widespread, containing a womanly point of view about men making messes of things. She sighed. "Was this another argument about Culloden?" she asked.

"No. Not really. But we were talking about the battle just before. Mostly it was Johnny talking."

"Why must men be so *doaty*!" Mam seethed. "Did I ever tell you…" She hesitated, calming her voice. "Did I ever tell you about how all you boys became cousins?" Mam did not give Will space to answer. "There are several ways to be related to another person who is not your blood brother or sister. Cousins are cousins because of the relationships of their mothers and fathers. Your father talks a lot about his Pictish side of the family. The Clachan side, with all its other surnames. But in truth, the boys who grew up together in the ruin these last generations were mostly related through their mothers."

"What about—"

"Hush I said. This is my time to talk."

"Do you have to keep massaging my eye? It smarts."

"If you want it to look well when Master Shanks returns, keep quiet, and let me work while I talk." Mam's fingers begin to move more tenderly.

"After Culloden, it was women who helped men find ways back into the community. Helped them return to work, and ushered life forward to some better condition. It was women who put their lives back together again after men tore them apart. It took a long time. But the Murray women were strong and driven by survival, especially for the sake of their children. They banded together and fiercely supported one another. They needed to believe in a better life. One that did not demand the sacrifice of their young men in battles like Culloden. There was no glory, Will. Only survival. It was the Murray women who chose to stand together by marrying stonemasons. Mind me—these women had relations and acquaintances that fell on both sides of the Culloden battlefield. Most fought with Prince Charles. But some saw the folly of supporting an outsider so they sided with the Crown. But after—" Mam fought to steady her voice. "When the battle was done there were few victors. You cannot look on the aftermath of a slaughter and celebrate, even if you were on the winning side."

Charlotte Clachan took a seat beside her oldest son. She looked at him with the assessing eyes of a healer, and the loving eyes of a mother. "Listen carefully, Will. Fighting should always be a last resort."

"But—"

She held up a hand to silence him. "Learn to talk your way out of confrontations. As for Johnny…" She slowly shook her head. "Be angry with him for hitting you, but be thankful that you do not have his life."

She took Will's fuzzy chin in her strong hand and looked him hard in the eyes. "Understand?"

"Aye, Mam. I truly do."

"Now, then. Let's see about something to eat. The boys took Jock and went fishing this morning. I don't expect to see them again until supper. But we shall have some lunch," she announced.

Hearing this, Will's father smirked. Lunch was a meal mostly reserved for the longest days of the year, when work began early and continued late. The rest of the year, when it was pitch-dark by four in the afternoon, dinner was served at dusk, making lunch an unnecessary meal. Looking at her son's gaunt face, Charlotte rationalized her decision. It was close enough to Beltane to fix her son a midday meal.

Lunch consisted of cheese, Mam's bilberry jam, and thick slabs of brown bread, served alongside bowls of nettle soup. The soup was a rich green broth full of spring spinach, nettles, potato, and wild garlic. It was already simmering, ready for the boys when they returned.

Will appreciated his mother's wisdom nearly as much as her skillful way with food. She could concoct flavorful dishes from the most meager provisions. "Oh goodness," he said with his first mouthful.

"And good for you," Mam told him—not for the first time.

Before coming to the table, Tom Clachan had been studying construction plans for a sizable house. To Will's surprise, his father did not ask questions about Shanks or the ruin. And he said very little about Will's black eye. But then Mam had been angry enough for them both.

"Do you have a new project, Da?" Will asked, nodding toward the drawings.

"I might. It depends. For now, we wait and see."

A look from Mam cautioned Will to leave the matter alone.

This was as calm as Will had seen his father in months. Instead of Da pressing him for information, his father had news of his own.

"I know of Shanks's whereabouts, and why he's been delayed." His father wore a prideful look. Tom Clachan knew something his son did not. And he seemed eager to share it—just as soon as he scooped a spoonful of soup into his mouth. "Word has come back to Elgin that Shanks has gained the attention of the Scottish Office of Works Committee. He has been in Edinburgh discussing a petition for financial assistance to maintain the cathedral ruin. Shanks is trying to convince committee members to come to Elgin and inspect the ruin."

Will kept eating without comment. He wondered who in Elgin was willing to share such details with his father.

"Some funds have already been allocated by the Crown. Robert Reid himself has endorsed a new roof for the chapter house. Yet

Shanks is pressing for additional commitments. He wants the committee to see firsthand the need for stabilizing the ruin's ancient walls."

Mam did not look up from her bowl, but Will stopped eating. It had been a long time since he heard his father speak so many sentences all at once.

"Who is Robert Reid?" Will asked.

"Robert Reid is one of the most important men in the country, son. I am surprised Shanks has not spoken of him. He is the Master of Work to the Crown of Scotland. A most famous architect. He designed the new facade for Parliament Square in Edinburgh, and he is responsible for all public works projects in Scotland. If I were you, I would not be dallying after your lunch. Shanks is likely to return anytime now." Da looked hard at Will before returning to the business of wiping clean his soup bowl with a crust of bread.

"Yes, Da. I will."

"The boys will be sorry they missed you." Mam patted Will's arm.

Will hesitated. "Da. May I ask—"

"Where I heard this news? You may not."

"I understand. But that was not my question."

"What, then?"

"Do you know where I might get a waterskin?"

His father's face shifted. Possessions and information were both things Tom Clachan did not part with easily. "Ask Shanks," he replied. After a stern look from his wife he added, "But if he cannot provide, I will watch for one at the market. Now best be off with you."

Will did not miss Mam's glare.

"Charlotte, I am only looking out for the boy."

"Da is right, Mam. I should get back."

"I think I will go check on the boys," Da said, gripping Will's shoulder lightly before heading out. "I will have them back by supper." He winked at his wife.

When it was just the two of them, Will sheepishly asked his mother, "Might I look into your wee mirror, Mam?"

"There is really no need, Will. Your eye will heal just fine." But the look on her son's face melted her heart. She went to her bureau and opened a drawer. "One quick look," she told him.

Mam raised her palm, holding the mirror up to Will's face. He dipped his chin and tipped his head to locate the reflection of his damaged eye. It was not as bad as he feared, nor as improved as he hoped. Before he could take a second look, the mirror was back in the drawer. Mam handed Will his bag and walked him to the door. "You need to be at the ruin when Shanks arrives. Black eye or not."

There was something about the way his mam waltzed him to the door that made Will look down at her feet. To his surprise, she wore a handsome new pair of brown leather boots. "Where did those come from?"

With an impish glare she lifted her skirts just enough for him to admire the lace-up boots. "You did not truly believe the shoemaker was only making me a pair of dancing shoes. A boy delivered these after your last visit home." With a gentle peck on his cheek, Mam pushed her son out the door. "Now be off with you. Work more, worry less."

At day's end, the Clachan men came home and ate their supper. Later still, as Luke settled the younger boys for the night, Tom whispered to Charlotte, "I heard what you said to the boy. While you were seeing to his eye."

"Someone needs to give him useful advice."

"I agree with you. What you said was true. But, Charlotte?"

She lifted her eyes from the mending in her lap.

"There is something else young men have been known to fight over."

She raised an eyebrow. "What would that be?"

"A girl."

13

THE SHOEMAKERS OF ELGIN

Shanks studied the remains of the rubble piles and smiled.

He unlocked the door in the wall and stepped inside the ancient ruin. With fresh eyes he assessed the grounds. Soon they would have visitors from Edinburgh, and Elgin would need to be ready to receive them.

"Sir?" Will poked his head around the open door.

"There you are, boy."

"I was dumping rubble at the pool, sir."

"Good lad. You have made fine progress I see."

"Would you like to look at the notebook?" Will removed his gloves and dutifully added a mark on a page filled with slashes. He placed the notebook in Shanks's hand as though it were a precious thing.

Shanks held the open book at arm's length and squinted. He moved his lips silently counting. "Nearly fifty. Well done, boy."

Will beamed at the compliment but winced when the smile tweaked his sore eye.

"What's that there?" Shanks moved closer to examine Will's

face. "Not an accident, I hope."

An accident would have been the perfect excuse, but Will stayed with the truth. His mother's voice in his head reminding him that the truth made life less messy. "Not exactly, sir. It's more like a blackened eye." Attempting to change the subject, Will produced the broken white stone from his coat and offered it to Shanks. "I saved this bit from the Witches Pool." Like a dog presenting a retrieved stick, Will anticipated praise. But Shanks remained silent as he turned the piece of marble over in his hands and held it up to the sunlight.

Will spoke softly, spellbound by his own discovery. "I wonder if we might find the rest of it. Angel or child or whatever it once was."

Shanks laughed, making Will feel silly. "Will Clachan, we are far past putting things back together again. Our only purpose now is to maintain what remains here." Shanks glanced at the broken piece of marble in his hand. He slid it into his jacket pocket and sighed.

The old ruin keeper's action baffled Will. If the piece was worthless, why keep it? Why not just toss it back into the piles?

St. Giles church bells began to chime, and Shanks perked up. "Let's eat. We have much to discuss."

In the chapter house with food in hand Will asked, "Did your meetings go well in Edinburgh, sir?"

"Aye. They did. But first, I would like to hear about your eye."

Will chose his words carefully. "I had a disagreement with a cousin, sir."

"What was the disagreement about?"

Will was unsure how to answer. There was no easy way to explain how he and Johnny Murray came to blows. Not without a long explanation that would leave no one in a good light. So, he kept his answer brief. "Culloden," Will said.

"The battle?"

"Yes, sir."

"What about Culloden?"

Will realized Shanks was going to insist on some sensible story to explain a foolish argument. An argument that involved much more than Culloden. But Will was determined never to utter Alanna's name during this conversation, nor mention defending her honor. Instead, Will said, "The disagreement grew from jealousy. Things here in Elgin are changing. Some folks are faring better than others. Some are working." Will shrugged. "Some are not."

"And how does Culloden fit into it?" Shanks took another bite of his meat pie while Will considered his answer.

"There were haves and have-nots after Culloden, too."

That explanation seemed to strike a chord with Shanks. His expression changed. "So, you and your cousins still talk about Culloden?"

"Sometimes. Not often. Not anymore. Except this last time…"

"Yes, I see. Just when you think some painful bit of history has faded from memory, something happens that brings it back to mind, like a blow to the face." Shanks fought a smile and lost. "In your case, quite literally."

Will was relieved to see Shanks looking less serious. But the man was born for storytelling. Their conversation had sparked a memory and Will was grateful for the distraction.

"Not long ago," Shanks began, "I was searching the Burgh of Elgin's old records for a particular bit of information about the cathedral. I was reading council minutes from decades ago. I paged through entries about land disputes, hiring new teachers, and allocating money for the poor."

Will nodded.

"Then I came across an interesting fact. Leading up to the battle at Culloden, there was no mention in those council minutes of the skirmishes and clashes in this region. Not one. Then I checked the dates of the Burgh Council meetings. This council had met monthly for more than one hundred years." Shanks took a sip of his cider. "And then there was a nine-month gap with no minutes at all. That gap began in March 1746, the month before the battle on Culloden Moor, and continued into the new year. When the council minutes resumed, there was no explanation for the long break."

Shanks checked to see that Will was following his story. "As it turned out, the town was so divided over the return of the Bonnie Prince, that even the Burgh Council members did not see eye to eye. So, they chose not to convene from March through December 1746. There are no minutes, no notes, no mention of their decision to stop meeting. And no comment on their decision to begin meeting again. If you look solely at the council's minutes, it is as though nothing happened on Culloden Moor in April 1746. The only clue is the council's nine months of silence. Understand me, Will. These record books detail the council's most insignificant decisions. Which makes the 1746 blank space in the records a breathtaking discovery." Shanks took a swallow of cider. "I could not help but wonder how the Burgh Council could have been so divided that they took a nine-month hiatus. Then months after the battle, they gathered in the council room and gaveled a meeting to order."

Will could hear the emotion building in Shanks's voice.

"The same men in the same place picking up where they left off without a single recorded word about Culloden. The minutes of that first meeting were sparse. The council approved a small payment to repair a retaining wall along the Lossie. They drafted a formal letter of congratulations to the Earl of Fife on the marriage of his daughter. But nowhere is there an account of the Rebellion. Not a single sentence about the two thousand souls who lost their lives on Culloden Moor, less than a day's march up the road from where the council met. I can only imagine all that went unsaid."

Will had never heard anyone say how many men had died in the battle. He was unable to imagine so many people dying in one day, all in one place.

Shanks handed Will another meat pie. "There is one more Culloden story I wish to tell you, Will. My own family's story."

Will nodded, relieved not to have the conversation return to his bruised eye.

Shanks resettled himself on the bench. "Likely you know the Pretender, Prince Charles, stayed in Elgin before the battle."

Thanks to Johnny, Will did know that fact, but he stayed quiet.

"The Bonnie Prince was a guest of Mrs. Anderson at Thunderton House. She was a known Jacobite sympathizer. Members of the prince's staff were quartered in townspeople's homes. My father was a young shoemaker in Elgin and a member of the shoemakers' guild. This was before I was born, of course. While Prince Charles rested in Elgin for eleven days recovering from a fever, my father was approached by one of the prince's generals. A man named William Boyd. Boyd asked about my father's sympathies, and his skills. The regiment he commanded needed shoes for the men, and he needed them quickly. A deal was struck. My father organized the swift production of seventy pairs of shoes through the shoemakers' guild so that the men under Boyd's command would not go barefoot into battle. Each shoemaker in the region furnished his portion. Before he marched his freshly shod regiment up the road, Boyd made arrangements to compensate the shoemakers."

Shanks barely paused before finishing the unhappy story. "After the battle, William Boyd, the fourth Earl of Kilmarnock, was captured and taken to London for execution. From prison, Boyd wrote to a friend concerning the shoemakers of Elgin. In his letter, Boyd told of a debt he wished to have settled on his behalf. A debt for which he said he was 'liable if not paid, owing to poor people who gave their work by my orders.' He wrote about the shoemakers of Elgin, and the seventy pairs of shoes so swiftly produced. Although they were to be paid three shillings and sixpence each, Boyd later learned Elgin's shoemakers had not been paid, after all. The funds diverted for other causes. Boyd asked his friend for assistance with righting the matter. He wrote that it would greatly ease his heart if payment could be arranged from his family's estate to compensate Elgin's poor shoemakers. He closed the letter by saying that had he lived, he would have attempted to right the matter himself. But with his execution imminent, any such action was now impossible."

For a long moment Will and Shanks sat in the silence of the chapter house.

"I have that letter," Shanks said at last. His voice barely a murmur. "The letter the earl wrote to his friend about the shoemakers of Elgin. I keep the letter in our family Bible. The paper it is written on is now fragile. I had Alanna copy the words so that its message is never lost—even if the ink fades away."

"How did you manage to come by the letter, sir?"

"Forsyth helped me acquire it from the earl's family estate several years ago." Shanks paused, listening to a strong wind buffeting the ruin's walls. "It was a heartbreaking and generous thing for a man to bother with on the eve of his execution, don't you think?"

"I cannot imagine." Will shook his head. "I have never thought much about all that came before and after the battle. The desperate need for soldiers' shoes, and the execution of an earl."

"Imagine is all we can do." Quietly, Shanks continued, "My father's lot in life was improved by the wish of a dying man."

Will tilted his head. He did not fully understand.

"The debt was well paid, although it took some time. It was money none of the shoemakers ever believed they would see in their hands after Culloden. The payment helped keep many of Elgin's shoemakers in business. Kept some of them from starving. When the money for the shoes finally arrived, my father was placed in charge of ensuring every shoemaker received his due. You see Will, when the prince and his men rested in Elgin, the earl was quartered with my father. My father lived in bachelor rooms above the shoemaker's shop. William Boyd knew he could entrust my father with the responsibility of distributing the payments. That was why the money was sent to him. In the end, my father was much admired by his peers."

"How was he able to have his own workshop and rooms when he was so young?" Will asked.

"He was apprenticed to his uncle for a time," Shanks explained. "Then his uncle disappeared, leaving my father temporarily in charge of the business. Only later did my father learn that his uncle had gone to support the Rebellion. He never returned. But the windfall that eventually came back from the estate of the earl helped make my father a successful shoemaker. He gained a certain status in the community, exceeding his vocation and his age."

Will listened quietly, trying his best to understand Shanks's meaning.

"My father became the most successful shoemaker in the region. I was born a decade later. But I like to think that if it were not for the determination of a good man on the eve of his own execution, I might not have been born at all."

"Did your father ever talk to you about Culloden?" Will asked.

"He did. Aside from telling the shoemaker's story and Boyd's restitution, he had only one comment when anyone brought up the battle. Two sentences that never changed: 'At Culloden, the High-landers were mowed down like grass. Prince, chieftain, and peasant were scattered like autumn leaves, never to meet again.'"

For a time, Will and Shanks kept still. The expression on the old shoemaker's face was weary and sad.

"You are a quiet boy."

"Aye, sir. I am."

14

CHE PICCISH SCONE

Shanks leaned back and looked up.

Will followed his gaze. With a gnarled finger, he pointed up at the vaulted ceiling. "The Scottish Office of Works Committee has recommended a new roof for this chapter house, with plans supervised by Robert Reid. Now the Crown must agree to fund the project."

"Does that mean the committee was pleased with your report?"

"So it seems. But it was the lord provost of Elgin who first requested funds for a new chapter house roof. My report concerned the historic importance of the cathedral ruin in its entirety, including work to stabilize what remains." Shanks stirred. "I cannot sit any longer. Let's go outside."

Shanks led the way to the circular clearing. "I invited members of the Works Committee to Elgin to tour the ruin and see the need for additional funds. A date has not been set, but we must prepare for their visit. We have our work cut out for us, Will."

"Might Robert Reid come to Elgin?" Will asked.

"That is my hope but not my expectation. He is kept very busy in Edinburgh."

"Does he approve the funds or is it the Works Committee?" Will dug for details.

"So, you have been paying attention, boy. Do you know who Robert Reid is?"

"A very important man."

Shanks laughed. "Aye. You've got that right. He is the head of the Scottish Office of Works. He is a great architect. His newest title is Master of Work to the Crown of Scotland. Before that, his title was the King's Remembrancer."

"The King's Remembrancer?" Will asked, puzzled.

"It was a most unusual title. He served as the administrator of the Crown's treasure trove, including estates and properties that fell to the Crown. Many of those properties were once held by the church," Shanks explained.

"Like our cathedral ruin?"

"Yes. Including Elgin's cathedral ruin."

"Are there jewels and gold and silver in the Crown's treasure trove, sir?"

"All of that and more. There are many antiquities and artifacts kept safely locked away." Shanks thought for a moment. "A shame really. There are countless items that would be very interesting to inspect."

"When will work begin on the new chapter house roof?" Will wondered.

"It's difficult to say. There are details still to be worked out."

"What sort of details?" Will asked.

"Primarily the choice of material for the new roof," Shanks explained.

"Wouldn't it be flagstone, like the roofs on most church buildings?" Will was unable to staunch his flow of questions.

"That was likely the assumption when the lord provost requested the funds," Shanks said. "However, Robert Reid has posed a set of questions about the building's structure. Concerns he wishes to have addressed before work begins."

Will recognized a disquieted look on Shanks's face and waited for further explanation.

"In the interest of what Robert Reid refers to as historical conservation, he insists the roof repairs must not further damage Elgin's chapter house. It is the only octagonal chapter house in Scotland. Although the ancient design was also fashionable in England." Shanks shrugged. "The York Minster has one. And Westminster Abbey."

Will attempted to keep up with the details.

"It was assumed Elgin's original chapter house roof was made of lead, like the cathedral buildings around it. But Reid does not agree. He believes the reason this chapter house has survived so well is due to the composition of its original roof. If the roof had been covered in lead, it would have been removed when the rest of the lead roofing was stripped away. And the chapter house would have suffered similar decay and damage as the other buildings. Instead, Reid has proposed that the roof was once made of either stone, or wooden shingles from ancient hardwood trees. The interior supporting column, and the vaulting in the ceiling suggest stone was likely the original roofing. Before he decides, Reid wishes to see sketches and measurements of our chapter house. He wants the roof repair to be historically correct without collapsing the ancient building."

Will silently wondered who might be hired for this work.

"In the meantime, the Pictish stone must be moved here to the ruin. While those arrangements are sorted out, you and I will remove rubble from around the most fragile sections of the choir and transept walls. Now we must get back to work."

A year had passed since the discovery of the Pictish pillar.

With the reconstruction of St. Giles Church underway in the center of Elgin, the town council took the opportunity to reconfigure the surrounding roadworks. A "big dig" to improve Elgin's roads and drainage systems. Not long into the project, workmen made an unexpected discovery. Beneath the streets the ground was filled with bones. They were unearthing an ancient section of St. Giles's cemetery buried deep by centuries of change. The road crew was uncovering a massive boneyard with graves dating from the twelfth century. A surprising discovery since the oldest markers in the current churchyard dated from the 1600s.

But it was not a good surprise. This was a construction project, not an archeological dig. The crew had signed on to build a road, not exhume the resting place of old souls. The men holding the shovels were unsettled.

Urged on by the project foreman, the workmen continued to dig—until one old worker dropped dead. Rumors spread and the men spooked. This was not good work for those who valued peaceful sleep. No one wished to be cursed and haunted by an army of long-dead souls. The workers walked away. The wage was not worth the risk.

With the town unsettled by the great boneyard laid bare in the heart of Elgin, the town council begrudgingly agreed to extra wages. Hoping to finish the work quickly they added a night crew. But local men stayed home. Even an extra crown—payable to anyone who worked until the project was done—did little to attract enough able-bodied souls to do what needed to be done. The foreman was forced to look beyond Elgin for replacement labor.

Eventually enough poor farmers were lured by the wages to finish the project. Many who signed on hoped to discover something of value to secretly pocket.

As the magnitude of the ancient internment grounds was revealed, piles of human skeletal remains were carted off to a newly dug pit outside of town. The mass grave was discreetly consecrated and blessed by St. Giles clergy.

It was among the ancient wreckage of death in the heart of Elgin that workers found a great stone with curious markings. Its size and weight required special equipment to lift it from the ground. After inspection by town elders, the Pictish pillar was moved to safe storage in a private location.

15

Chicken and Egg

Will felt like he had moved a mountain.

Once the piles of rubble were at the bottom of the Witches Pool, he resumed making pathways through the ruin. Keeping a tally in the notebook had become his responsibility. Shanks still unlocked the ruin and brought food for Will, but they seldom ate together. The old man spent his time pacing off distances and scrawling notes that he crumpled into his pockets.

Will knew something was amiss when Shanks stopped mentioning the Pictish pillar. Although he dreaded asking, Will could not go home without some news for his father. "Sir? I thought by now the Pictish pillar would be—"

"There has been a delay," Shanks interrupted, waving his hand at Will as though shooing flies.

"A delay, sir?" Will's voice threatened to crack.

The old man sighed. "A concern has been raised. Some differences of opinion. Our lord provost, Peter Nicholson, has questioned the order of the work. Whether repairing the chapter house roof should be done before bracing the ruin's oldest walls or moving the Pictish pillar. He is worried about unstable walls falling on the Pictish stone," Shanks huffed. "It has become a chicken and egg conversation with the lord provost."

Will's mind raced with questions that he dared not ask.

"I have written to the Office of Works Committee, requesting their prompt commitment to the ruin's conservation in its entirety. I asked them to speed their visit. We are trying to convince the lord provost to let us move the Pictish pillar to the ruin without further delay."

"My father once said that massive pillar weighs more than a tonne. It will take many strong men to move it. Do you need more men, sir?"

"We already hired an experienced team," Shanks replied curtly. "What we need now is the necessary approvals."

The lord provost's blessing required a special visit to the ruin. He wanted to see for himself the planned location for the Pictish stone. Shanks began referring to Nicholson as Doubting Thomas. "He needs to lean against the walls himself to be convinced they won't topple over," Shanks grumbled.

When Nicholson finally visited the ruin, he did not come alone. To everyone's surprise he brought along Tom Clachan. Nicholson knew Clachan to be a skilled stonemason familiar with the ruin. And the lord provost had recently employed Clachan to build his new family home. Nicholson had made it known that he wanted the house to have a cornerstone cut from the ruin. A symbol of status and wealth.

Shanks was surprised to see Tom Clachan accompany the lord provost. While Tom went about his business, taking measurements and dropping plumb lines, Shanks kept his distance. Then the lord provost waved Shanks over to join his conversation with Tom. It was the first time in many months that Clachan and Shanks stood within handshake distance.

"There's been little change in the lean of these walls since last year," Tom began.

"We know that," Shanks replied curtly. Seeing Nicholson's disapproving expression, Shanks softened his tone. "It is the long-term degrading of the pitch of the walls we are worried with. That is why we requested funds. Not for short-term solutions."

"Most sensible," Clachan agreed. "We can all assume that these walls will eventually fall if nothing is done to them. And we know the lean of the walls will accelerate with time, until they collapse."

"Yes, of course," Shanks said. He was flustered that Tom Clachan could sound so professional while stating the obvious.

Clachan continued, "If you are putting all this into a report to the Works Committee, it is worth noting that the speed at which these walls might fall will be affected by the weather. Last year's heavy rains and flooding took their toll."

"The report to the Works Committee is not your concern, Tom," Shanks replied.

"Not so quick," Nicholson said. "You may not be interested in learning what Clachan has to say, but I am. And I believe he knows as much about the status of this ruin as anyone in Elgin."

The ruin keeper's face turned red. He swallowed his unkind thoughts. If Tom Clachan could convince the lord provost that it was safe to move the Pictish pillar to the ruin, so be it.

A noise behind them, a crunch of stone, made the three men turn. Will stood just inside the ruin. There was no telling how long he had been there. Off carting rubble, he knew nothing of his father's arrival. The expression on the boy's face was a mix of surprise and alarm. No one acknowledged Will's presence, but the look from his father was a familiar one. His eyes told Will to keep still and not interfere.

Nicholson asked Tom to walk with him around the ruin. "A bit of a tour, shall we?" The two men moved toward the old Pans Port without asking Shanks to join them.

This was Tom's first time back inside the locked ruin. As the lord provost chattered on about plans for his new house, Tom noted the changes in this place he knew so well. He was impressed to see the newly cleared pathways. A feeling of pride in Will's work crept into Tom's thoughts, and he allowed himself the slightest smile. Tom was unconcerned about whatever Peter Nicholson was saying just then. After all, Nicholson was lord provost of Elgin. If the man wanted a stone from the cathedral ruin, he was likely to get it. Tom stared at the ground so his thoughts would remain his own. One could never know for certain where life might lead.

On their way out, Nicholson and Clachan bid Shanks a good day. Passing by Will, Tom nodded to his sweaty son and was amused by the boy's confused expression. "We look forward to seeing you at home on Sunday." He patted Will firmly on the shoulder but did not look back at the old shoemaker.

In the end, the lord provost could see no reason to delay moving the Pictish pillar into the ruin. Nicholson was certain his decision would speed funds from the Works Committee. Everyone involved hoped the lord provost was right.

Tom Clachan was anxious for news.

One sunny afternoon Shanks and Clachan unexpectedly came face-to-face in town. "How timely to see you today," Clachan began. "Now that the way is clear to move the Pictish pillar, I wish to offer my services." His voice was more congenial than he felt, but Clachan's motivation was sincere. He hoped the project might help restore his reputation, and he knew men who needed work. "I can offer skilled and reliable workers, and the tools to do the job right."

Shanks was caught off guard by Clachan's forthright offer on a public street. He hesitated just long enough to consider and dismiss Clachan's new relationship with the lord provost. "We already have all the men we need, Tom. The town council has secured workers with the proper skills. Now, I am late for an appointment, so I bid you good day."

As Shanks moved swiftly down the street the expression on Clachan's face was as good as calling the old shoemaker a liar. But Shanks had been truthful. A small team of experienced men had already been hired. Most of them were not from Elgin, a deliberate decision by the town council. When it came time to move the pillar, the council was determined not to repeat the labor problems encountered during the big dig.

Shanks still worried about resurrecting the fears that originally surrounded the massive stone. He was anxious for people to find the Pictish relic fascinating instead of fearing it. That was the reason for hiring workmen not from Elgin. When the time came to move the pillar, Shanks wanted it to go well.

Tom Clachan was incensed when he learned of these plans. Although he held his tongue in public, he had plenty to say to his son when Will came home. "The man purposely infuriates me!" he seethed.

"I understand, Da. It seems wrong not to hire Elgin's own workers to move the pillar. No doubt Shanks has his reasons, but he has not shared them with me."

"No doubt he does, son. But I sincerely question the man's

logic."

Will wanted to ask his father about his visit to the ruin with the lord provost, but he thought better of it. He wondered whether Nicholson had the power to give his father access to the ruin. But his father made no mention of it. Nor did he talk about the key to the ruin or ask how Will was getting on with Shanks. When it came time for Will to leave, his father handed him a folded note. It was sealed with wax and addressed to John Shanks. "Deliver this for me," his father instructed.

Will hesitated but did not protest. He accepted the note with a solemn nod.

"This is between me and Shanks. Not for your eyes, Will. And not for you to worry over. I am offering my experience, should he need it. Nothing more."

Although his father had insinuated the note's purpose, Will speculated about its true contents. He did not look forward to giving the message to Shanks. Will felt uncomfortably caught in the middle.

When he presented the message to Shanks, Will did his best to steady his voice and his hand. "From my father," Will explained.

The old shoemaker made no comment as he slid the sealed paper into his pocket.

Once a date was set to move the Pictish pillar, discussions became preparations. Shanks kept Will busy dispatching messages, running errands, and accompanying Morrison to fetch supplies. Will still shoveled in the ruin, but other tasks now took him around town. Will realized how much he missed working with others. Especially with Shanks frequently out of the ruin. And no matter how much the man talked, John Shanks alone could never replace the family and friends that had been part of Will's everyday life.

One afternoon, while riding in the wagon with Morrison, Will saw Alanna. The wagon turned a corner and there she was, pulling on her gloves as she came out of a shop. Will turned around craning his neck to prolong his view of the girl.

Morrison clucked, and it was not meant for the horse.

"I have not seen Miss Alanna for quite some time," Will explained.

"She recently returned from Edinburgh," Morrison offered, "Visiting distant cousins, I believe."

Will gave the briefest nod before changing the subject. "Do you believe the Pictish pillar is cursed?"

Morrison shot Will a sidelong look and shook the reins before answering. "No. Of course not. Who says so?"

"When it was first discovered, people talked a lot about a curse. Cursed to the touch, cursed to move it, cursed if you looked upon it. The stone made people talk about bad things happening."

"Pure nonsense. Stirred-up fear can be contagious, Will," Morrison cautioned. "But tell me, where did you get such ideas?"

"Just rumors, mostly. From a cousin whose father worked the big dig. He told me how the stone was discovered. The workmen believed it to be cursed and wanted to cover it back up. But some imagined a Viking hoard of coins beneath it. The workman whose shovel first struck the stone fell ill and died. His family believed he had been cursed." Will turned to check Morrison's reaction, but his face was like stone. "After that, no one wanted to touch it."

"Anything else?" Morrison raised a bushy eyebrow.

"My father told me the town hired Archie Duncan to build a massive block and tackle strong enough to lift the stone. That it was moved away in the night, but no one knows where. Eventually people stopped talking about it once the roadwork was done. But that does not mean people have forgotten or changed their minds about the curse. That's why I wonder about Master Shanks's decision to move it into the ruin." Will shrugged. "That's what I know."

"Archie Duncan is a retired shipwright from Aberdeen. He possessed the skills to build a block and tackle big and strong enough to lift the stone. That much of your story is true. The rest?" Morrison pulled a face and shook his head. "I do not put stock in rumors about curses."

Will shifted on the wagon seat to look directly at Morrison. "You do not put stock in stories about curses. Yet you went out of your way to tell me the story of the witch. How can you dismiss one story and embrace another that is so similar?"

"You do not see the difference?" Morrison seemed surprised.

"No, sir. But I would be glad to hear your explanation."

"It is quite simple, really. The tale of the cursed Pictish pillar is just that. A wild tale constructed by fearful people. The story of Marjory Bysseth is from an eyewitness's written account of what happened the day she was drowned as a witch. Although the account contained accusations of curses, they were not factually proven."

"What about the workman who died? The one whose shovel first touched the stone. That happened," Will insisted.

"We know the man died. But there was no proof the stone caused his death. No physician in Elgin would state such a thing to be true."

"Are you saying it cannot be true?"

"I would have to believe in curses, which I do not. Cause and effect is a fragile thing, Will. It requires more than hearsay and assumptions."

"I will have to think on that," Will replied. And he would

when he was alone and could give the matter his full attention. But now they were approaching the ropemaker's shop, and Will's mind jumped to a new set of questions.

"What type of rope will we need?"

"Seamen's rope," Morrison told him. "The sort used on ships to haul anchors. Masters Forsyth and Shanks do not wish to risk using anything less. It would be disastrous if a rope broke during the move and the stone dropped and cracked."

It had not crossed Will's mind that such a thing could go so wrong. But now he could not shake the image of the Pictish pillar lying broken on the ground.

16

SUMMONING THE PICTOLOGIST

Finding a Pictograph expert was not an easy task.

Nearly a year had passed since the Pictish pillar was locked in a carriage house owned by Isaac Forsyth. It remained caked with all manner of clay and mud, except for where a workman had scraped off enough muck to reveal a series of runes. It was those exposed surfaces that drove Forsyth to rescue the stone. And then he set about finding an expert to inspect their discovery.

Forsyth wrote to his friend Robert Reid who had found buried relics on his workplaces in Edinburgh. Reid directed Forsyth to a historian who had worked for the British Museum, helping unpack the Elgin Marbles. Forsyth followed the fate of the Elgin Marbles with interest. For better or worse, the marbles' moniker linked their small burgh to the famous Greek treasures. Named for the man who removed them from Greece and shipped them to Britain. Thomas Bruce, seventh Earl of Elgin and Ambassador Extraordinary, was equally admired and vilified for his efforts. Forsyth considered writing the British Museum about the Pictish pillar. But he knew it could be years before they might examine a gravestone in

Elgin, Scotland.

Instead, the historian in Edinburgh referred Forsyth to a Pictish stone expert residing in the far north of Scotland near Tain. His name was Allan Ross. In an exchange of letters Forsyth sought guidance from Ross, who referred to himself as a Pictologist. He advised Forsyth to keep the stone covered in a dry place. Because Ross discouraged cleaning the stone, Forsyth resisted any temptation to take a bucket of water and a curry brush to the dirt-caked slab.

When the decision was made to place the stone in the cathedral ruin, Forsyth wrote once more to Ross asking him to come to Elgin. The Pictologist did not delay. He was curious to see the stone Forsyth had so effectively described in his correspondence. Ross assembled every necessary tool of his trade into a large travel case. Brushes and rags and special cleaning solutions. Potions he had personally developed. Everything he needed to clean ancient sculptures after centuries in the ground.

Isaac Forsyth lived alone in a house with many empty bedrooms but preferred to lodge his visitors in nearby rooms. At least until he made their acquaintance and assessed their character. When Allan Ross knocked on his door, Forsyth only needed to see his face to feel sorry for the man. To reach Elgin from Tain Ross had been on the road for days. He looked to be in desperate need of a comfortable place to sit down. Somewhere that was not in motion. Forsyth quickly ushered him into the parlor.

Forsyth's houseman tried to take the traveler's bag, but Ross shook his head. "I prefer to keep it, thank you." The Pictologist was an odd little man with an odd little voice. His accent was unfamiliar to Forsyth, who considered himself well-traveled. But Tain was not a place he had seen.

"Janet!" Forsyth called to his girl. "Some water for my guest at once, please."

Allan Ross rucked up his face in an absurd fashion.

"Or perhaps some tea?" Forsyth asked.

To which the man shuddered vehemently.

"Buttermilk, then?" Forsyth tried once more, unsuccessfully.

"Err…perhaps something a wee bit stronger if ye dinnae mind, sir. To be honest, I was uncertain I would make it here alive. If ye might find me a wee dram of aqua vitae it would be appreciated."

"Janet, kindly fetch a glass of sherry for Mr. Ross. We have no stronger drink in the house, sir," Forsyth unapologetically informed his guest. "I find it clouds the mind."

Once the men were settled in the parlor Janet arrived with the sherry and a glass of water for her employer.

"I am glad you are here, and I am sorry you had a difficult journey. I have never been as far north as Tain," Forsyth admitted.

The Pictologist sniffed his glass before sipping. "I fear I lost count of the number of times I changed mail coaches. Please forgive me when I tell you that I do not look forward to my journey home, but I will likely be most happy to get there." Ross bolted his sherry and sadly examined the empty glass. He slumped deep into his chair near the fire.

Forsyth cleared his throat, drank his water, and stood up. He was known in Elgin for many things, including his directness. "You will need time to recover from your journey. After you have rested, we will meet again. For dinner, perhaps? Or a later supper if you prefer." He did not give Ross time to object. "Janet, please walk our guest across the street to the rooms we have arranged for him."

Janet was already making her way to the door with the man's bag. Unsure whether he was coming or going, the Pictologist removed and replaced his hat. He nodded to Forsyth before reclaiming his bag and followed the girl out the door. Forsyth hoped with all his heart that he had not made a grave mistake.

By four o'clock the sun was dipping toward the horizon. This was the hour most families in Elgin sat down to their last meal of the day. Forsyth's cook had prepared a light supper, and Janet was sent to rouse Allan Ross and bring him to the table.

Feeling a bit guilty for his initial intolerance of the stranger, Forsyth greeted Ross at the door and delivered a generous glass of sherry into his hand. "Let us go straight into supper." Forsyth guided his new acquaintance to the dining room.

"Please sit here, Mr. Ross." An oversize dining table filled the room and the two men sat at the far end. Seated in the great chair at the head of the table, the man from Tain seemed the size of a young lad. Forsyth offered up this place of honor to make amends for his own behavior earlier in the day.

Water was poured, along with a glass of fruit juice, a personal preference of the host. Ross's sherry glass was whisked away as soon as it was emptied.

"I am grateful that you have made the trip to examine our Pictish artifact," Forsyth began. "I trust you will recover after a good night's sleep."

Before the guest could answer, steaming bowls of mussel broth were set before the men. The dining room was quickly filled with aromas of shellfish, buttery onion, bay leaves, and thyme. Janet placed a plate of warm soda bread scones between the two men.

"I am glad for your presence at my table, Mr. Ross."

Ross sat up straighter and moved his spoon more gracefully through the broth than Forsyth expected.

"I thank you for inviting me." Ross slipped a mussel into his mouth and closed his eyes, smiling.

"I hope your rooms are acceptable."

The little man paused, his spoon halfway between bowl and

mouth. He looked around at the grand dining room with its ancestral portraits, sparking chandelier, and highly polished furniture. "Yes," Ross sighed. "Adequate, thank you."

"I appreciate you coming all the way from Tain. "

"North of Tain, actually," Ross corrected his host. "And yes. Tomorrow we shall see what you have dug up."

"Do you doubt me? After all our correspondence?" Forsyth frowned.

"Your descriptions and illustrations were very fine," Ross replied. "Still, not everything with carving on it is Pictish."

Forsyth bristled, but Ross continued, "Do not fret, Mr. Forsyth. Your correspondence gave me sufficient confidence to make this journey. That is no small thing. I do not say yes to everyone."

"I see," Forsyth replied flatly.

"You mentioned in your letters that the stone is in a carriage house. Is it nearby?" Ross asked.

"Very close by."

Ross dabbed up the last of his broth with a scone.

"I am a most curious man, sir. How is it you came to be a Pictologist?" Forsyth had been unable to find any reference to such a word in his vast library. Though it made sense that if those who studied ancient Egyptian artifacts were now referred to as Egyptologists, someone who studied relics of a place once called Pictland might call himself a Pictologist.

"Ah. Hmm. I suppose one becomes an expert at something after doing it for a long time. In my case, I have spent years examining pieces of stone dug up from fields, meadows, and streambeds in the northernmost regions of Scotland. I have recorded and sketched the images found on these stones. I have cataloged many runes and other markings, along with where the stones were found."

Janet came into the room with small plates of poached salmon.

She set them in front of each man and left again.

"It began with my father and older brothers. They were attempting to farm in a place inhospitable for growing much of anything. The northern coast has never offered a reasonable growing season and yet my family tried. Every time they set their plow to work the fields, they would break a plowshare. And then they would spend days digging up another tablet or pillar or piece of broken stone decorated with unusual carvings." Ross took a sip of his juice and made an unpleasant face.

Forsyth was busy checking his fish for small bones. The poaching sauce was lovely, but his cook was growing old. Her eyesight was not what it once was. Detecting and removing small bones from a poached fillet was no longer her specialty. Forsyth considered warning his guest, but he did not want to interrupt the man's story. The Pictologist seemed to be growing taller the more he talked. Or possibly it was the food reviving him.

"Eventually, I sent some of my drawings and notations to the British Museum, after exhuming a remarkable cross-slab. There is interest in classifying the discoveries," Ross explained.

Forsyth began to feel more impressed with his guest, even if his voice and mannerisms were a bit odd. After all, it was a known fact that brilliant men rarely seemed normal. He sincerely regretted his initial lack of compassion for the man's rough journey. "Is this the farthest you have traveled to examine a specimen?"

"It might be the farthest, but I've suffered more difficult journeys."

"Where was that?"

"Twice I have traveled up to the Orkneys. The Pictish stones there are like no others. But I am not a good sailor, sir, and the seas are rougher than you might imagine. I believe I would rather die than go back a third time." There was no drama in the little man's voice, only weariness.

When a final course of fruit and cheese was brought to the table, Forsyth noted the disappointment on his guest's face. Ross seemed sad the meal ended without further courses. He kept looking to the door through which the food had been delivered. No doubt he was hoping for something sweet, however Forsyth believed cakes and puddings were best left for special occasions. The Pictologist shared Forsyth's perspective, but he believed his own presence was reason enough to put a tart on the table.

Shanks arrived at Forsyth's home the next morning. After introductions, the Pictologist picked up his large bag. "Shall we proceed?" Ross suggested.

At the carriage house, Forsyth unlocked the barn-style doors, propping them open to admit daylight. The stone was inside, laid on a wagon bed. Forsyth walked the perimeter of the nearly empty space, lighting lamps. He wanted as much illumination as possible for examining the Pictish pillar.

The Pictologist set down his bag as Forsyth folded back the canvas tarp covering the great stone. "Wait," Ross said. He retrieved an empty wooden crate from a corner of the carriage house, placed it strategically beside the wagon, and stepped upon it. "Please proceed." Ross nodded. With the tarp folded back, Ross leaned over the stone as though it were a patient on a sickbed. "Please bring a lamp closer."

"Of course," Forsyth replied, anxious to be of assistance.

The little man fished about in his bag for a long, thin metal probe at the end of a polished wooden handle. "Let us begin at this end." Very slowly he let his fingertips explore the caked mud and dirt on the surface of the stone. "Now, if you could hang that lamp right above me," Ross instructed.

Shanks noted the expert's concentration but was unsure what Ross was focused on. He watched the man's fingers, as small as a woman's.

The Pictologist dipped his head and sniffed. He licked a finger and ran it along a few inches of filth where the caked dirt was knocked away. He scraped a bit with his probe and licked his finger. Again, he smacked his lips and made a face one might expect after eating dirt.

Shanks's head filled with pressing questions. "Sir, if I may—"

"You may not," Ross interrupted. "I will answer questions soon enough." More probes came out of the bag, followed by several covered tins and clay pots. Finally, Ross brought out a few soft brushes that looked more suitable for painting portraits than cleaning a massive piece of rock.

"Do you need water? Or other solutions?" Forsyth offered.

The Pictologist looked up, mildly surprised to see the two men still nervously lingering nearby. "Water? Most certainly not. At least not at this stage. First, I must judge the state of this massive stone you have unearthed. Kindly allow me some time with it. I will gladly give you my recommendations in an hour or two. In the meantime, may I suggest you step away for a while and let me do my work?"

Forsyth was not yet sure he trusted this man enough to leave him alone with Elgin's prized relic.

Ross could read Forsyth's face as he lingered, searching for an excuse to stay.

"Good God, man!" Ross squeaked, "It's a one-tonne rock. I'll nae be running off with it!"

Shanks removed his pocket watch. "We will be back at eleven

to see how you are coming along." Shanks took Forsyth by the arm. "Shall we return to your study?"

Forsyth was not comfortable being shooed away from his own property.

"A strange little fellow," Shanks mumbled, once they had walked a bit. "Let us hope he is skilled at his trade."

"You know as well as I, he came highly recommended." Forsyth frowned.

"Archie Duncan and his men should be here at noon," Shanks said.

"And the team of horses?" Forsyth asked.

"All arranged for, as well."

Later, when Shanks and Forsyth returned to the carriage house, Allan Ross was up to his elbows in dirt. A smudge of red mud streaked one cheek, and it was plain to see where a messy hand had scratched his nose. But the look on the Pictologist's face revealed his findings. "Fascinating! Absolutely fascinating," Ross declared before either man could ask a single question. Two small areas on the stone had been carefully cleaned, revealing a pair of hands and what appeared to be a border of serpents. The worn carvings were remarkably detailed.

"Is it Pictish, do you think?" Forsyth asked anxiously.

"It seems so. Although I still cannot say for certain. But I can tell you this—what you have here may prove to be unique."

"How do you mean?"

"I prefer not to say until I have cleaned and examined more areas."

To Forsyth's great relief, the man appeared to be firmly in his element, his skills on full display. It seemed Allan Ross could be both quirky and brilliant.

17

WHAT'S IN A NAME

Brute strength and fearlessness do not always go hand in hand. Forsyth's carriage house could barely hold the burly workmen as they coiled ropes and inspected the wagon. But all were careful not to touch the Pictish stone.

When Morrison and Will arrived at the carriage house, their presence went unnoticed. Everyone's attention was on an odd little man perched on a crate and flanked by Shanks and Forsyth. He was addressing the group gathered around the wagon where the pillar lay exposed. Some of the dried mud and caked clay encasing the stone was cleaned away.

The man on the crate spoke in a nasal brogue. "I will need a day or two for cleaning this exposed side but the downfacing side will wait. We want to move this stone as few times as possible. After it is placed in the ruin, I will clean the reverse surface." He bent his knees and squinted at the intersection of stone and wagon. "Based on my experience, it is likely blank."

The workmen did not share the stranger's curiosity about the pillar's downfacing surface. Their job was to determine the best way to move it undamaged to the ruin. The men quietly worried over the strength of the wagon bed, the age of the wagon wheels, and the condition of the road between the carriage house and the ruin.

"If the weather holds, we plan to move the stone in three days' time," Forsyth announced. He looked around the carriage house for the foreman Archie Duncan but could not spot him. "That will give our historian sufficient time to prepare the stone."

Ross rolled his shoulders as though shrugging off belonging to anyone.

Questions were asked and answered. None of the men spoke loudly, concerned about awakening the relic's curse. Forsyth still had not spotted Duncan.

"Any last questions?" Forsyth asked.

Will stepped from behind a workman to ask, "What type of rock is it, sir?"

Morrison's lip twitched.

The men looked in Will's direction, surprised by the boy and his question. Then everyone looked at the stone as though seeing it for the first time. Isaac Forsyth stared at Will, newly aware of his presence.

The historian piped up, "The stone is red-gray granite. Some may say pink, but no. It is distinctively similar to granite found in Aberdeenshire. It is a foot thick, six feet in length, weighing approximately in excess of one tonne, and—"

"Your name, boy?" Forsyth pointed at Will, interrupting the Pictologist. Shanks began to answer but Forsyth hushed him, waiting for Will's response.

"Will Clachan, sir." It was irregular for a worker to provide both his names to a gentleman, but Will wanted Forsyth to know he was Tom Clachan's son.

"Clachan, is it?"

Will nodded, grateful his voice had not cracked.

Every man has the power to believe what is true.

Morrison and Will were unloading their wagon in a nearby storehouse when Shanks appeared with urgent news. "Archie Duncan has taken ill," Shanks informed Morrison. "We will need another foreman."

Morrison cursed under his breath. "Any chance of a quick recovery?"

"Apparently not." Shanks was clearly upset.

"He will be difficult to replace." Morrison furrowed his brow.

"Let's hope his men will still work for us," Shanks grumbled.

"Aye." Morrison hesitated. "Then there is the matter of the horses, and the block and tackle. Duncan may not let us use his men and equipment without him."

Shanks muttered some bit of Gaelic. The men began to consider replacements for the ailing foreman. "It must be someone well-qualified for the work," Shanks insisted.

Will's thoughts spilled out. "My father can take Archie Duncan's place. He has the experience, the equipment, and the men."

Shanks scowled without looking in Will's direction. "I assume you were attempting to be helpful, Will. Nevertheless, no one asked for your opinion. Isaac Forsyth and I carefully selected these men to move the Pictish stone. We have our reasons for who we chose and why."

Something in Will's demeanor made Shanks reconsider ending the conversation. "We will not have superstitious men involved in this effort. Not a single man who still believes in fairies, witches, and ghosts."

For a moment the only sound in the storehouse was from a pair of swallows fluttering in the rafters. Morrison looked down at his boots, praying Will to keep silent.

But the boy's voice was quiet and firm. "My father is just such a man, sir. A man of good judgment who has never shown the smallest interest in fairy stories or demons."

"True enough, I'm sure. Yet these matters are my business, Will. Not yours."

Will hung his head. Any hope of carrying good news home to his father was gone.

Shanks pointed a finger at Will. "Have you heard of William Hay, the poet?"

Will began to answer, but Shanks did not give him a chance.

"Hay wrote of Elgin:

'Tis the land of the famed Knock of Alves

Where fairies and spirits repair

To revel and dance in the moonbeams

Or trip o'er meadows fair.'"

Shanks spat out the lines of poetry as though they were foul. "Hay's poem is like a curse on this town. We cannot seem to escape what the man committed to paper. Do not believe all that you hear and choose carefully what you believe to be true." Shanks left the storehouse and Morrison followed.

"What was I thinking?" Will muttered. He would quickly need to make amends.

As Shanks left the storehouse an uncomfortable thought made him hesitate. What if Archie Duncan's illness revived fears of a curse and spooked his men? Shanks removed the message from Tom Clachan from his pocket, still unsealed and unread.

When the Pictologist finished cleaning the exposed side of the Pictish stone all who saw it were amazed.

Unfortunately, Archie Duncan remained abed burning up with fever. Unsettled by their foreman's sudden illness, his men decided only half the job was safe. They were willing to haul the stone to the ruin, but they would not agree to unload it. With that obstacle made clear, it left Shanks and Forsyth in need of a second team to set the pillar in the ruin.

The obvious solution left Shanks and Forsyth out of sorts. At the ruin Tom Clachan and a team of stonemasons would finish the job. Using levers and a block and pulley, a team of seven strong men with years of experience would raise the Pictish pillar from the wagon and place it in the cathedral ruin.

On the day of the move Duncan's men arrived at the carriage house with a fine-looking team of workhorses. A set of Garrons sired by Clydesdales, low-slung, wide-chested, and built for work. As the men were hitching the team to the wagon one of the horses spooked. Wild-eyed, it whinnied and reared. Two men lassoed the horse and walked it down the road and back. They ran their hands along the beast's strong neck. Crooning lovingly in Gaelic, they hoped to settle it down.

The other workmen stopped to watch. The skittish horse became a distraction. The men muttered and shook their heads, kicked at the roadbed, looked at the sky. Searching for any excuse to walk away.

Archie Duncan's headman turned to Shanks. He removed his hat and twisted it in his hands. "Aye, sir. Maybe today's not such a good day to move that stone, after all."

Shanks flew into a rage. "We have an agreement! Today is the day. You agreed to hitch and pull this stone on this wagon from here to the ruin. That's your part in the bargain—with no need for any of you to touch the stone!"

Before Shanks could say more, Forsyth intervened. "Let us all take a moment to settle down," he suggested calmly.

But again, the horse whinnied wildly. The workmen looked away and shook their heads. They were now nearly as skittish as the horse.

"Maybe another day, sir," the headman offered.

Watching from the carriage house Will mumbled, "So much for choosing men who do not believe in evil spirits."

"I am certain all will be well," Forsyth coaxed.

A high nasal voice pierced the air and Allan Ross stepped out among the men. "Most of you saw me the other day. I am Allan Ross. Come from Tain to inspect this stone and clean it for display in the cathedral grounds. Some say I am an expert on Pictish stones and the carvings upon them. I have been examining and cleaning and keeping records of such things for a very long time."

Forsyth cringed, fearful the man's voice might further spook the horses.

"Can anyone guess how many Pictish stones I have dug up and cleaned?"

The workmen glanced around as they realized the little man was speaking to them.

"Anyone?"

"Five!" one workman shouted.

"Ten!" said another.

"Just the one," someone offered.

"What makes you say 'one?'"

"Since yer still alive, you must really only have handled the one. And likely you won't be livin' to clean another."

The workmen laughed nervously.

"Incorrect!" Ross squeaked. "I have examined twenty-nine Pictish stones in my lifetime before coming to Elgin. And I have never been ill a day in my life!"

The men began mumbling again, but Ross had their attention.

"I perceive," Ross continued, choosing each word carefully, "that some among you might be concerned about ill effects from such artifacts as this one." He waved his hand toward the reclining stone strapped to the wagon, but he did not look away from the men. "My brothers are farmers up north of Tain. They have dug up many stones like this one, out in their fields near the coast. They remain hale and hearty men. If moving Pictish stones is a death sentence—if it somehow could magically kill a man—my brothers and I would all be dead ten times over!"

The men allowed themselves some small nervous laughter.

"But yer so puny," one man replied.

"Aye. I've been puny since the day I was born, sir, but never sick a day in my life. Discounting seasickness, which is not a sickness at all. Just an aversion to a rocking boat on wild seas." Ross gyrated his small body to demonstrate, then feigned a face of anticipated vomit. The men laughed. He smiled and nodded. "So, you see there is nothing to worry about here. I have been touching this stone for days now and I feel fine. The only way this stone could kill a man," Ross paused for effect, "is if it falls on you. But then, anything weighing a tonne that falls on a man would likely crush 'em. Aye? So, mind you—get on with your work and do the job well!"

Apprehension faded into laughter, and Duncan's men kept their part of the bargain.

18

THE ELGIN CROSS

The Pictologist slowly ran his fingers over the glyphs.

The stonemasons had performed their work at the ruin without hesitation. After carefully lowering the Pictish pillar into place they packed up their equipment and left.

Allan Ross was awestruck when he cleaned the reverse side of the slab. "I have never seen anything like it," he told Forsyth.

"Nor have I," Forsyth agreed. "It is a most amazing relic."

"That it truly is, sir," Ross assured Forsyth. "I'll return in the morning to make my sketches. Then I hope to be on the afternoon mail coach."

When Will asked permission to touch the magnificent pillar Shanks laughed. "Of course, you may," the ruin keeper replied. "Lord knows it's seen worse."

Crouching close to the stone, Will could just make out the faded outlines that the Pictologist's work had revealed. Symbols of gospel saints: an angel for Saint Matthew and an eagle for Saint John. Looping edge decorations like intertwined serpents. *Runic convolutions,* the Pictologist had called them.

Will moved to the opposite side of the slab where the newly revealed images had surprised them all. The carvings on this side were very different from the saints and serpents on the reverse. Here were images of pagan symbols. A crescent and two circular markings united by a zigzagging band. "Runes," he heard Ross name them, "and a mystic knot." Will let his hand explore the eroded carving of a man on horseback carrying a bird of prey. Three dogs—one with a doe in its teeth—completed the hunting scene. Will's fingers lingered on the bird's wings, reminding him of the wings on his little stone creature. He was familiar with odd bits of Pictish carvings. Worn-away marks and small symbols. But he had never seen images like this.

Will was up early the next morning when Shanks arrived with Ross. Alanna had come along to see the stone and watch Ross make his drawings. The Pictologist wasted no time settling himself on a milking stool Shanks had brought along. The light was fine and clear. Ross removed a leatherbound book from his bag and turned page after page of sketches until he found a blank sheet. He took up his charcoal pencil and began to draw. A moment later he stopped. Alanna, Shanks, and Will stood peering over his shoulder. Ross cleared his throat. "Some room, please. I'll gladly show you the drawings when they are finished."

It was difficult to say which held Will's attention more: the deliberate strokes of Ross's pencil, or Alanna's face as she eyed the man at work.

Ross kept his word. Although anxious not to miss the mail coach, he obliged Alanna by turning every page in his sketchbook for her to see. She cooed admiringly, making Ross blush. Will damped down his feelings of jealousy, reminding himself Ross lived in the far north of Scotland.

News of the Pictish pillar spread quickly.

Soon there were inquiries addressed to Shanks from the Office of Works Committee. Hailing from Aberdeenshire, committee members David Grant and Thomas Fraser planned to visit Elgin. "We hope to meet with you and the lord provost," their correspondence read. "We wish to inspect the ruin and discuss proposed repairs."

The news set John Shanks in motion. Together with Forsyth and the lord provost they made plans for a modest event at the ruin. Invitations were sent to a select list of Elgin's citizens. Shanks planned to lead a private tour for the committee members, followed by a small reception. But the list of invitees quickly grew to accommodate everyone who no one wished to offend. These included the Earl of Fife and his family, magistrates, council members, and most of the respectable inhabitants of Elgin.

In his excitement, Shanks announced he would make the key speech of the day, ceding lesser remarks to town leaders. Setting aside etiquette, the lord provost allowed the old shoemaker to have his way.

While her grandfather worked on his speech, Alanna worried over the refreshments and what she would wear. She also gave Will a set of clothes to don for the reception. "This is an important event," she said, handing him the neatly folded bundle. "We must all make a good impression on the Works Committee members."

After Alanna left, Will tried on the clothes. He looked down at himself dressed in the ensemble of trousers, shirt, jacket, and tie.

They were certainly in better condition than anything he owned. Unfortunately, the jacket and shirt were much too large and did not fit him at all. Will could think of only one possible solution. He bundled the jacket and shirt into his pack and headed home.

"Tell me again where you got these clothes." Charlotte Clachan frowned as she held up the suit coat.

"John Shanks's granddaughter, Mam. Alanna is her name. She said everyone attending the ceremony for the Pictish pillar must make a good impression. But these clothes are much too big."

"I can see that." Mam smiled.

"There are trousers, too, but they fit me fine. I thought you might have some idea what I should do."

The distraught expression on Will's face touched his mother's heart. "You could not attend," she offered, examining the voluminous sleeves and shaking her head.

"Oh no, Mam. I dare not do that. I am…" he hesitated, searching for the right words. "I am expected, you see. Expected to attend."

"You could bring along a friend. This jacket is large enough for two of you." She laughed a little, hoping to make Will smile, but she could see the concern in his eyes.

"Is there anything you can do, Mam?" Will pleaded.

"I might…" she hesitated. "But first—did the girl say she was giving you these clothes? Or is she expecting you to return them."

"I do not know, Mam. I did not ask."

"We don't have much time, Will. I could alter these clothes to fit you better. But it will take some work and require cutting and sewing the fabric in ways I cannot put back."

"What should we do, Mam?"

"It is up to you, son. I suggest you find this girl and ask if she expects to have the clothes back as they are. But if you cannot find her quickly, I will not have time to alter them." She waited for Will's reply, but he was as frozen as a scared rabbit.

"Mam, do you think these clothes belonged to her grandfather?"

"Possibly. But whether they are his or no, these clothes have not been worn for a very long time."

"How do you know?"

"The creases tell me they have been folded away in storage. And the smell." She offered the coat jacket for Will to sniff.

He crinkled his nose. "It smells like your herb garden."

"Aye. A bit of lavender and rosemary to ward off vermin from chewing the fabric."

"I will find Alanna and ask about the clothes. But Mam—"

"Yes?"

"How shall I ask the question without sounding like…well… like an eejit."

"Honesty is always best, son. Tell her the truth. The clothes are very nice, but they do not fit you. Your Mam has offered to alter them but will not do so if the clothes must be returned in their present size."

"I'll run all the way and be back as fast as I can."

"First let me pin everything up. While you are gone, I can start basting. But I will not cut a thing until you return."

Will hugged Mam and kissed her cheek.

"Hurry now," she ordered, reaching for her sewing basket.

On the road into town, Will encountered Shanks heading for home. As Will explained about the suit an odd expression crossed the old man's face. He seemed wistfully amused. "Oh aye, Will. No one has worn those clothes for a very long time. Altering them will not cause anyone heartache."

"Thank you, sir. I will come back before the light is gone."

"Take your time, boy. I already locked the ruin. See you in the morning."

As Will sprinted away Shanks called, "Give your mother my regards."

When Will was nearly home, he saw his father farther up the road headed in the same direction. He called out, but Da seemed preoccupied. "If only I could whistle," Will mumbled. Whistling was a skill he had never mastered but not for lack of trying. Then Will noticed Jock coming to greet them. Da extended his arms and called for the dog but the wee beast passed him by and leaped into Will's arms instead. Jock licked Will's face and pawed his chest.

"Well, at least the dog misses you," Da laughed.

After Will told Mam what Shanks had said about the clothes, his father took him by the shoulders and examined his face. "I believe it's time you learned to shave," Da announced. "You, too." Da pointed at Luke.

The Clachan men, and the younger boys, too, went outside. Da handed Will a wooden bowl of water, a clean rag, and a cake of soap, but he held on to his straight-edge razor. The boys sat on the garden bench, oldest to youngest. "First, watch and learn." Da lathered his own face, opened the razor, and began shaving without the benefit of a mirror. The boys had seen Da shave many times but this was different. This time Will knew he would be expected to do the same to his own face. With each swipe of the blade over their father's jaw the boys grew more uncomfortable.

"Watch now. This is important. Before you give it a try, you must know how to sharpen the blade."

"Do you sharpen it every time you use it?" Will asked.

"Aye, I do. You are more likely to cut yourself with a dull blade." He carefully wiped the razor with the towel and looked directly at Ross. "Youngest first!" Da grinned. The little boy squealed and ran off with Andrew close behind.

Luke stood up. "Alright, then. Me first." Da guided Luke through the process, with only a small nick on his chin.

When it was Will's turn his hand shook on the first slow swipe. Da reached to steady the blade. "It can be tricky at first, but I never knew a man who cut his own throat while shaving," Da laughed. "Take heart, son. It's part of becoming a man."

Will liked the feel of his face without whiskers. "How often do we shave, Da?"

"Weekly maybe. And for special occasions like the ceremony you'll be attending. Also, women seem to like clean-shaven men. If you do not believe me, ask your mother. Before long you'll be caring about such things." Will blushed and Luke laughed, revealing which of his sons was noticing girls.

With a flourish, Da produced Mam's shears from his jacket pocket. "Time for haircuts! Where's Ross?"

There were plates of cold meat and rolls for supper. The boys saw to the meal while Mam sewed. Twice she insisted Will try on the clothes and the younger boys snickered.

Mam finished the alterations by lamplight long after Da and the boys were asleep. Will's eyes were drooping, but Mam would not let him rest until she was done. "I am surprised the trousers truly fit you, Will."

"Aye, Mam they fit fine with the belt."

"Whoever owned these clothes must have been a sailor to have a chest and arms so large and legs so trim."

Will tried on the refashioned shirt and coat and Mam made him practice tying the neck scarf. When he hugged his mother and kissed her cheek Will saw past the weariness in her eyes and realized she was trying not to cry.

"My beautiful boy is becoming a man. You look like a young gentleman, Will."

In the morning, only Da was up when Will gathered his things to leave. With a prideful look his father clapped him on the back and slid his horn-handled razor into Will's hand. "You will need this to practice shaving."

"Thank you, Da."

"It's your mam deserves the thanking, and you'd best remember it."

"I will be sure to let her know."

"One more thing, Will." His father pointed at Will's feet. "Remember to shine your boots."

19

UNVEILING CEREMONY

Will was waiting outside the ruin when he heard Morrison's wagon in the lane. He was delivering Shanks and Alanna, along with the refreshments for the guests. It was quiet now, but on the previous day the ruin had buzzed with preparations for the unveiling ceremony. A temporary platform and podium were now in place along with chairs for the speakers and special guests.

The tour for the Works Committee members was scheduled for immediately prior to the afternoon ceremony. Shanks, Forsyth, and the lord provost planned to escort their guests through the grounds. Only Shanks had previously met Grant and Fraser, but he did not know them well. The tour would include the chapter house and the derelict choir walls that needed buttressing. Then, at the appointed hour, the invited guests would be admitted to the ruin. The speeches and the unveiling of the Pictish pillar would follow.

After helping Morrison with last-minute chores Will returned to his hut to change into his new clothes. When he reemerged, he saw a long line of wagons approaching from town. And although the day was warm and muggy a line of local guests was forming outside the ruin.

Will found Shanks and alerted him to the early arrivals. "Guests are beginning to gather outside, sir. I thought you should know."

John Shanks gave Will a quizzical stare. Then a broad smile took its place. "You certainly clean up nicely, Will. I am giving you a new job today. I need you to look after the crowd outside while we tour the committee members through the ruin. When I give you the nod, you may admit only those who present invitations. Do you think you can manage?"

"Yes, sir, I will do my best."

Alanna stood staring at Will. She had not immediately recognized him. The tailored clothes made him look like someone other than the boy who had helped unload the wagon.

"Alanna," Shanks called. The girl's flowing dress was not what her grandfather might have chosen for this event. "May I suggest you water down the punch, my dear? A milder punch is advisable to keep our guests upright in this heat."

"Yes, Grand-Dey." Alanna smiled.

Forsyth did his best with the Works Committee members while escorting them to the ruin. David Grant was ancient. His deafness required Thomas Fraser to repeat what was being said by shouting it directly into the man's ear. It made normal conversation impossible. Will quickly ushered the men into the ruin where Shanks and the lord provost were waiting.

With guests already gathering, and the challenge of Grant's poor hearing, Shanks proceeded apace with his tour. He had hoped to tell a few stories about the history of the ruin, but the loud repetition of everything he said made good storytelling impossible.

As Shanks called attention to the ruin's leaning walls, the gentlemen seemed inattentive. The day was growing warmer, and Grant pulled at his cravat. Shanks exchanged looks with Forsyth and they quickly moved their guests to the chapter house. After Shanks pointed out the severely damaged roof, they stepped inside where it was cooler. Here the history could speak for itself. "In the midst of so much ruination, this ancient piece of Elgin cathedral miraculously remains standing," Shanks needlessly proclaimed. Anyone could see the wrecked roof needed replacing to save what was left of the interior. Craning their necks to take it all in, the visitors nodded appreciatively. Grant looked up at the beautiful pillar blooming toward the ceiling and shook his head, concerned. No shouted words were necessary to explain what was at risk here.

Forsyth nervously removed his watch to check the time. Everything was taking longer than expected. "Let us reconvene after the ceremony, gentlemen. We will answer any questions over a cup of punch."

Settled on a cool stone bench, Grant was relaxed in a way that suggested a nap.

"There are chairs for you both on the dais in the shade," Shanks announced in a loud voice. "The lord provost will show you to your seats and I will join you shortly." John Shanks hustled off to find Will. It was time to admit the local guests.

Alanna stood next to the punch bowl ready to serve. With her handkerchief she shooed away the occasional flying insect. Shanks took two cups of punch from Alanna. He met Grant and Fraser on the dais as the lord provost helped them to their seats. Settling in for the duration, the men seemed to appreciate the beverages.

At the entrance, Will checked invitations while Forsyth ushered guests into the ruin. Of course, the Earl of Fife and his family did not wait in line. They moved smoothly past Will without looking in his direction. "It's fine, Will," Forsyth whispered before greeting their most distinguished guests.

As word of punch filtered back through the crowd, the line picked up speed. When all the invited guests were inside the ruin a few townsfolk still lingered by the door. Dressed in their best clothes but without invitations, they hoped for a look at the Pictish pillar after the invited guests departed.

Within the ruin, all were intrigued by the blue velvet cloth draped over the Pictish pillar. Once everyone was in place Forsyth stepped to the podium. "Welcome, friends and honored guests."

A slight commotion behind him made Forsyth pause. "When do I get to see the damn stone?"

"Very soon!" came a loud reply. A ripple of laughter moved through the crowd.

The ceremony proceeded with a string of speakers. Threatening skies kept most remarks short, but not those of John Shanks. His closing speech would be the one guests remembered.

"In a few moments," the old shoemaker began, "I will unveil an amazing discovery. That is why you are here today. But first, let me tell you what we know about this ancient stone. It was likely carved here in Scotland at the start of the Christian era, as it incorporates the image of the cross. It was erected by the natives of this very soil to commemorate an event in their history. It probably dates from an era after the Druids, who only used rude and shapeless stones for their circles. This stone was carved sometime before the introduction of written characters, when this land of ours was called Pictland. We may never know if the Picts' runelike characters were an attempt at written language, imitating the Romans or the Scandinavian invaders."

Most of what Shanks was saying had been gleaned from the Pictologist, and Will worried Shanks might launch into a lengthy history lesson.

"Evidence of the Picts has been found throughout Scotland. These stonecutters left their mark with their intricate designs. And their descendants worked side by side with French and Italian craftsmen who built our cathedrals."

Realizing Shanks was referencing his ancestors, Will stood a little straighter.

"This great slab uncovered last year near St. Giles has been referred to by many names. Now that it is here in Elgin's cathedral ruin it will henceforth be known by one name alone: the Elgin Cross."

Enthusiastic applause erupted as Shanks left the podium and moved through the crowd. With a flourish he lifted the blue velvet cover from the Elgin Cross and the crowd pressed closer.

Will retreated to the refreshments table for a glass of punch. Done with his assigned responsibilities, he was free to watch Alanna charm the guests. Having been among the first to see the cross up close, Will felt special. He had enjoyed talking to people about the Pictish stone as they waited in line. And no one seemed to think him out of place checking invitations. Even the people who knew him. But of course, it was the clothes and the haircut and his smooth chin. As Mam had said, he was dressed the part of a young gentleman. Although he had neither the breeding nor the education, at least now he had an inkling what it felt like.

Will noticed Alanna staring at him. Blushing, she quickly turned away to fill another glass.

Shanks placed the key to the ruin into Alanna's hand and whispered in her ear. The girl nodded solemnly. She glanced in Morrison's direction, where he was busy stacking chairs.

The lord provost and the Works Committee members had adjourned to Forsyth's parlor and Shanks was anxious to join them. He turned to Will. "Before Alanna locks the ruin, I want you and Morrison to inspect the grounds. Make a thorough job of it. Let's be certain no stray visitors took a lie-down after too much punch." Then Shanks left for town.

As Will went to find Morrison, he noticed a few last guests leaving the ruin. Then a single figure slid by going in the opposite direction. Likely it was someone retrieving a dropped shawl or a stray glove. But then Will saw the person's face and his heart sank. It was his cousin Johnny.

Will's first thought was to follow his mischievous cousin. But glancing down at his clothes made him pause. Will hated to think what might happen to the suit his mother worked so hard to make perfect. And he did not have the heart, nor the bad judgment to go after Johnny alone. Instead, Will ran to get Morrison.

"Some nerve that boy has," Morrison seethed. "Just wait until I find him!"

"Shall I come with you?" Will asked.

"No. You stay with Mistress Alanna. Do not let her out of your sight."

Will found Alanna and explained what was happening. He described Johnny, but he did not mention the boy was his cousin. A distant cousin but related all the same.

"I know that boy," she told Will. "I saw him in town not long ago. He refused to step aside when my friend and I tried to enter a shop. He snarled nasty words in my face. Then the shopkeeper came to our rescue and beat him down the street with a broom." She shivered at the memory. Will carefully draped his jacket around her shoulders and Alanna smiled.

When Morrison returned, he did not have good news. "I canna find the young tramp anywhere. If we lock him inside the ruin, I fear he might damage the Elgin Cross."

Will could imagine that, too. "I'll stay," Will said without hesitation. "Lock me inside and I'll keep watch until you return. Just let me fetch some things from the hut."

"It may take me a while." Morrison sounded concerned. "I'll need to see Alanna safely home and then find Master Shanks or Forsyth."

Will was already halfway to the hut. "Just let me get my warm coat."

"Aye. And you might want some fuel for a small fire." Morrison followed Will into the keeper's hut. He hefted the cold grate and the peat. Will gathered his coat, pocketed matches, and pulled the woolen blanket from his bed. "Hurry," Morrison urged.

Back in the ruin Will settled his supplies near the Elgin Cross. He kept his shovel nearby as a weapon.

"Are you certain about this, Will?" Morrison asked.

"Aye. I'll keep watch, even if it takes all night."

With the key in her hand, Alanna gave Will one last worried look. Then she locked the door from the outside. Will heard the wagon move off at a clip with Morrison urging the horse.

Will sat down by the Elgin Cross, but he did not light the peat. The fire could wait. He pulled his coat close and settled in to keep watch.

Back in town, Shanks, Nicholson, and Forsyth were meeting with their Works Committee guests. They had settled into Forsyth's upstairs reading room, and while four of the men conversed, the fifth softly snored. It was no longer necessary to shout. Discussing the recommendations in Shanks's report to the Works Committee, it was evident that funding was the sticking point. A sizable cost variable depended upon who might complete the repairs.

Shanks held strong opinions on the matter. "I believe hiring Robert Reid's Edinburgh laborers is preferable to using Elgin's local workers."

The lord provost glared at Shanks. "Our workmen have been laying the roof on the new St. Giles church these past months. What more experience do you need?"

Shanks was adamant in his opposition. "To assure the repairs are done once and for always we need the best workers." He paused. "And then there is the matter of trust."

"Trust?" Fraser asked.

The lord provost shook his head. "The stonemasons proved they can be trusted to do good work when they moved the Pictish pillar."

"The Elgin Cross," Shanks corrected Nicholson as Forsyth rolled his eyes.

"It's just a roof, after all," Thomas Fraser said.

"Not just any roof!" Shanks huffed. "A roof on a nine-hundred-year-old building that we are attempting to save from collapse!"

Fraser sighed. "I understand your concerns. I will report them to the full committee," he promised.

There was a sudden disturbance downstairs, and Forsyth excused himself. Within minutes, Janet popped her head into the reading room. "Master Shanks? Master Forsyth asked if you would join him downstairs for a moment."

Shanks offered his hand to Fraser. "We have kept you late. My apologies. Janet will help see our friend Grant to his room."

In the parlor, Shanks found Forsyth talking with Morrison.

"We may have an intruder in the ruin," Forsyth said.

Shanks could hear Janet helping old David Grant down the winding staircase, followed by Fraser and the lord provost. "Say no more until our guests have gone." He quietly closed the parlor door before anyone passed by. "We will say our goodbyes to our guests in the morning," he whispered to Shanks. "Now, Morrison. Tell Shanks what you just told me."

20

Locked In

Elgin was a quiet place after the last church bells chimed.

Will had never been alone in the ruin this late in the day. But, of course, he was not truly alone. Johnny was there, too.

The autumn sky turned red and gold as the sun winked out in the west. The sudden sound of faraway gunshots startled Will. A second volley echoed in the distance and his heart settled back into place. Grouse season was underway and the best hours to hunt them were at sunset and dawn. Locals still dreamed of bagging a black grouse or an elusive capercaillie. The roasted flesh of such birds could spark poetic descriptions from Elgin's old-timers.

Then Will heard a different noise. Scraping sounds of moving rock coming from the direction of the Pans Port. His first impulse was to investigate, but it seemed unwise to leave the Pictish stone.

Once there had been four gates in the old cathedral wall. The West Port faced the road into Elgin. The North Port led to the bishop's palace, and the South Port opened to the hospital. Now the old walls and the three once-grand entrances were mostly crumbled. Only the Pans Port was somewhat intact.

Will lit the peat fire for warmth. His night vision was better without it, but his eyes would adjust. Nighttime in Elgin was truly black. There were no outdoor lights in town save for moonlight and stars. "As black as the Earl of Hell's waistcoat," some would say to describe the night. Events in Elgin were mostly scheduled so folks could get home before dark. Everyone retired early except on special occasions. Keeping to a road or track after dark was extremely difficult. Those out late were usually accompanied by a young servant carrying a glass lamp hung at the end of a long stick. Without such guiding lights it was impossible to find your way after dark. Elgin had lately considered outdoor gas lamps for the center of town. There were good reasons to back the project and start a local gas company. Such progress might, once and for all, dispel the lingering tales of things that go bump in the night.

Elgin's town elders supported modernization. They had even backed the teardown of the medieval Muckle Kirk to build its replacement—despite pleas not to destroy the ancient building. The decision to tear down the old kirk puzzled Will. How could town elders feel so passionate about saving a cathedral ruin while demolishing an equally ancient church?

The sound of a struck match, the smell of lit tobacco. A cough, and then another disrupted Will's sleep. Someone was outside the wall.

"Don't be a fool, Clachan. I knew you were awake when the snoring stopped."

"Christ!" Will whispered. It was Johnny.

"A shame there's a wall between us. This whiskey we buried last year near the Pans Port is worth sharing." Will heard Johnny gulp from the bottle, and then a loud belch. "Wasn't that our plan?"

A bad combination of alcohol and anger made Johnny's voice edgy. "But now you're in there and I'm out here, so I'll drink your share." Will stayed quiet. He remembered the evening Johnny had appeared at the ruin with that fine bottle of liquor. Pinched from the distillery outside of town. Together, the boys had decided to bury it. Davie, Walt, Will, and Johnny made a pact to dig it up when there was something to celebrate worthy of such a bottle.

"What's your good news?" Will asked, knowing the sound of Johnny's voice was too irritated to be celebrating anything. The bottle smashed against the wall and Will recoiled.

"Me? Not a damned thing. But now you, Will Clachan. You have plenty to celebrate, looking and acting like a damn dandy today."

"Why are you here, Johnny? What do you want?" Will heard the unmistakable sound of another Lucifer match igniting.

"I hate you, Clachan! And I want you as miserable as me."

"Who goes there?" Now it was Morrison's voice.

"It's Johnny Murray and he's drunk!" Will shouted "Oi! Let me out!"

"Keep your hair on, Will." Shanks opened the door in the wall and together they found Morrison near the wagon. Forsyth's servant girl was leaning into the warm horse. She held a lamp and tightly clutched her cloak over her petticoats.

"I've run him off!" Morrison's voice was furious. "The scoundrel tossed a lit match on the keeper's hut roof. I put out the flames with water from the cistern, but it charred the thatch. I will hunt that devil by daylight if he's still in Elgin."

"The Pictish Cross is safe," Will assured Shanks. "Johnny never got near it."

"It has been a long night," Shanks said wearily.

Morrison helped Will move his belongings back into the hut,

and Shanks locked the ruin. Then the wagon departed.

Will collapsed onto his bed, grateful to Morrison for saving the hut. With the odor of burned thatch in his nostrils, Will fell into an unsettled sleep.

"Hungry, Will?"

Morrison jumped down from the wagon and hauled out an enormous basket filled with bread, potted meats, cheese, and fall fruits. "There's a serviceable waterskin in there, too," Morrison said carrying the basket into the hut.

Will held an apple to his nose before taking a bite.

"I'll leave you to it." Morrison winked, helping himself to a roll. "Master Shanks and Alanna are on their way. Come help me load the chairs into my wagon once the ruin is unlocked."

Will quickly filled his stomach and stowed the remaining food. Dressed in his work clothes, Will made certain the carved creature was tucked safely in his pocket. He tried not to dwell on all that he might have lost if the keeper's hut had caught fire.

His tailored clothes from the previous day had been quickly discarded in his rush to guard the ruin. But now he carefully folded them away. He gave the trousers a good shake. To his surprise a coin fell to the floor. It was heavier than any coin Will had ever held. One side showed the laurel-wreathed head of King George. The reverse was a handsome horse mounted by a caped rider with sword in hand. And below the horse, a beast whose scales and tail resembled Will's own stone carving. He had clutched pennies and farthings and groats while running errands, and they, too, bore images of King George. But Will had never held a crown before. He turned it over in his palm and wondered who had left it in the trousers and who it rightfully belonged to. Certainly not him.

Will heard another wagon and knew this was a mystery that would have to keep. He scanned the hut for a safe place to hide the coin and decided the best place might be back in the pocket of the suit trousers. Checking to be certain there were no holes in the pockets, Will discovered something odd. A flap of fabric that turned out to be a tiny cloth envelope stitched inside the pants pocket. Just the right size to fit a coin. He tucked the money back where it belonged.

Outside the hut Will greeted Shanks and Alanna. "Thank you for the food basket, sir. And the waterskin, too." Shanks waved a hand and nodded. It was clear his mind was on other matters. After unlocking the ruin, Shanks went off to find Morrison. Alanna stepped toward Will with something folded over her arm. "Your jacket," she said, holding it out to him. She blushed a little, her eyes downcast.

"Glad to be useful, miss. About the clothes—I spoke with your grandfather before having them altered, but I am still unsure if you wish to have them back."

Alanna looked surprised. "Oh. Of course not. They were meant for you to keep. To wear when Grand-Dey has visitors in the ruin."

"Thank you, miss." Will dropped his eyes. "About the trousers…"

"Say no more," Alanna quickly touched his sleeve and then turned away.

"I should get to work," Will replied.

After stowing the jacket, Will joined Morrison and together they hauled the chairs and podium to the wagon.

Later, when Forsyth arrived at the ruin, Alanna and Shanks were nowhere in sight. "Hullo!" he called loudly.

"Over here!" Morrison waved.

Dressed in white corduroy trousers and a fine jacket, Isaac Forsyth smiled and touched the brim of his hat. With his long legs and sturdy boots, he had no problem maneuvering the ruin's rubble.

"They are in the chapter house, sir," Morrison offered, although Forsyth had not asked a question.

"Thank you, Morrison." Forsyth nodded without stopping.

"What are they doing in the chapter house?" Will wanted to know.

"Mistress Alanna is sketching," Morrison explained.

"On the walls?" Will squeaked.

"No, Will. Not on the walls." Morrison laughed. "Go see for yourself. Just stay out of the way is all."

Will hesitated.

"Go have a look. Then get yourself back to work."

Tentatively, Will approached the chapter house. It was quiet inside. He peered around the edge of the doorway so as not to disturb whatever was happening within. To his surprise, Alanna was seated on a low stool with her back to the door, a sketchbook in her lap. Shanks and Forsyth stood to each side, looking over her shoulders as she sketched. Although Will did not have a clear view, Alanna seemed to be drawing the center pillar and the wall beyond.

Shanks sensed Will's presence and motioned him in. Alanna did not seem to notice. She was absorbed in her work. After a few minutes Shanks turned to Will and said quietly, "Let's go outside." Will was worried he had done something wrong, but Shanks seemed pleased enough.

"Why is she sketching the chapter house?" Will asked.

"Last evening, the Works Committee members presented a letter to us from Robert Reid.

"The King's Remembrancer?"

"Aye, among other things," Shanks laughed.

"What was in the letter?"

"Reed is asking for architectural drawings of the chapter house. He believes the drawings will help him determine the best materials to use for the roof repairs."

"Couldn't he just come see for himself?"

Will's question made Shanks laugh a little. "Aye, Will. I have asked the same myself. But Robert Reid is a very busy man. If he wishes to see drawings of Elgin's chapter house, he shall have them."

21

THE VIEW FROM EDINBURGH

Robert Reid *was* a very busy man.

His colleagues often speculated how there must be two of him, to accomplish all he had done and continued to do. In truth Reid had no twin. He did, however, have a very capable staff who made it seem as though Reid was accomplishing the work of several living souls. Reid employed the best young architects in Scotland. Together they were redesigning the face of a city. Edinburgh desperately needed modernizing. For decades he had worked to rebuild a new government city in Edinburgh. Now Reid was redesigning the Palace of Holyrood while overseeing extensions to Parliament House and the Supreme Courts of Scotland. Meanwhile, his architects were planning new city neighborhoods and renovations to the city's great cathedral. Reid had set aside smaller projects. He was no longer a young man, and he worried about running out of time before finishing all that he had begun in his beloved Edinburgh.

Mindful of his mortality, Reid delegated most day-to-day decisions to the Scottish Office of Works. Especially those matters concerning historic properties outside of Edinburgh. Mostly administrative in nature, the office reviewed the requests for repairs to historic buildings scattered across Scotland. It seemed every municipality in the nation could sense a new era on the horizon. It was a time for decisions about Scotland's aging antiquities. The Office of Works was methodical, if not quick, in responding to requests for funds. For the most part, Reid had successfully detached himself from these procedurals. The only remaining demand on his time was his authorizing signature to approve or deny funds for projects recommended by the committee. Important work, but not part of his beloved Edinburgh.

Reid no longer wasted precious time traveling around the countryside examining decaying properties. The members of the Scottish Works Committee were now charged with that task. It was a great relief to Reid. He considered the time saved might eventually allow him to take on another project or two in Edinburgh—perhaps the Royal Botanical Garden, or the university.

Despite best intentions, Elgin's ruin was one remote property Reid had failed to distance himself from. For all the castles, priories, kirks, and monasteries moldering into decay across Scotland, Elgin's ruin was like none other. Reid remained fascinated by what it had once been. But he needed a way out of the time-consuming correspondence with the newly appointed keeper, John Shanks. The man was becoming a pest. Shanks had been sending the Scottish Works Committee a stream of letters and reports for the better part of a year. After meeting with the committee in Edinburgh, Shanks now wrote directly to Reid concerning his comprehensive plan for the ruin. Reid forwarded Shanks's letters to the committee, unopened.

Reid had conducted his own research on Elgin Cathedral's chapter house. The medieval structure fascinated him. The octagonal building was designed as a meeting place for the church's powerful college of canons. It resembled others built in England throughout the thirteenth century, suggesting an exchange of architectural design between the two regions. The fact that Elgin's chapter house was still standing was remarkable, when all that remained of the cathedral around it was now rubble on the ground.

It was Reid's concern for Elgin's chapter house that pulled him back into discussions about the ruin. Reid worried that a misstep in replacing the roof on the ancient building might unintentionally result in its destruction. There were certain load-bearing matters to take into consideration. He had combed through medieval documents in Edinburgh's private libraries, attempting to discover the types of materials originally used to roof other octagonal chapter houses in the realm. His findings narrowed the possibilities, but he was not ready to make a final decision. He needed more information. Now it was his turn to ask for something. Reid sent word to Elgin requesting architectural drawings of the chapter house. He believed the drawings would enlighten his decision on roofing materials.

Now on Reid's desk was a letter from a dear friend, Isaac Forsyth. A good and brilliant man who knew better than to waste Reid's time. Their friendship extended far back to when Reid was a young surveyor with a modest reputation. Forsyth's letter to Reid had been written at John Shanks's bidding. Shanks was displeased by Reid's failure to correspond with him directly

Forsyth's letter was apologetic and concise. He confirmed which repairs in the ruin were most urgently needed and advised Reid that the requested architectural drawings would be prepared. "You and John Shanks share the same vision for what the cathedral ruin might one day become," Forsyth assured Reid.

Reid heaved a sigh. Requesting professional scaled drawings

was asking a lot from a small burgh like Elgin. But without them he refused to sign off on a project that might collapse the centuries-old chapter house. It was a unique property, and he did not want its survival dependent on the whims of a stubborn old man. It was not a gracious thought, but it was an honest one.

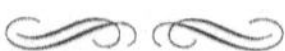

Weeks passed without Shanks looking at the slash marks in the notebook.

The old ruin keeper was preoccupied with Alanna's sketching. Occasionally she spent hours in the chapter house, but most of her visits were short. She did not keep to a particular schedule, but she was always accompanied by Shanks or Forsyth—a result of Johnny making trouble at the ruin. And despite Morrison's efforts to find him, Johnny seemed to have disappeared from Elgin.

Will stayed busy wheeling rocks to the Witches Pool. In his worn work clothes, he was once again easy to ignore. He was slowly reducing the landslide of rubble where the West Port once opened toward town. Shanks had chosen the precise spot for Will to work without explanation. What was clear to Will was that Shanks was anticipating more visitors coming to see the Elgin Cross.

"Word of such discoveries can spread quickly," he told Will. "All sorts of people are curious about unusual antiquities with in-teresting stories. It is only a matter of time."

One afternoon, with just the two of them in the ruin, Shanks leaned on his shovel and watched Will work. "Did I ever tell you about the great fire? The night the cathedral burned?"

Will glanced up, but there was no need to answer. Once a story was on Shanks's mind, he would tell it. The burning of the cathe-dral was an old, old story. The evil deeds of the Wolf of Badenoch were widely known, and anyone in town could recite some version of the tale.

Shanks cleared his throat. "The night the Wolf of Badenoch set fire to this great cathedral must not be forgotten. The year was 1390. Elgin Cathedral had stood strong for one hundred and sixty-six years."

Will shoveled another pile of cathedral wreckage into his wheelbarrow. He felt invisible whenever Shanks used his speechified storytelling voice. All he could do was listen. He wondered whether this recitation was inspired by Johnny's attempt to torch the keeper's hut. Or if Shanks was simply practicing for future guests.

Noticing Will's inattention, Shanks paused. "I'll wager you don't know that Lord Badenoch was the son of King Robert II." His voice was back to normal, meaning Will was expected to answer.

"I did not, sir. Only that he was angry at the church, and it had something to do with a woman."

The ruin keeper's face bloomed red. "Aye. There were complications with a wife to whom he no longer wished to be wed. And the Catholic church stands firm on the sanctity of marriage. No matter his reasons, Badenoch was a Highland savage who repeatedly took up against the Church. Even before the fire, the brute had seized church lands and refused to give them up. So, the bishop excommunicated him."

"Ah. The excommunication." Will nodded, now leaning on his own shovel. "That's the part I heard was about the wife."

Shanks ignored Will's comment. "In those days, excommunication was the highest punishment in the land. It doomed a soul to hell without any chance of salvation. After he was excommunicated, Badenoch asked the bishop to change his mind, but the bishop refused. Angered by this news, the Wolf set about wreaking havoc across Moray. Seeking to avenge the injustice he felt had been done to him, Badenoch and his armed men attacked Elgin." Shanks paused. He lowered his voice. "The June night was warm, and the hour was late. The notes of the last vesper hymn had died away…"

Shanks now possessed Will's full attention. "It is difficult to consider the recklessness of such a violent attack upon the cathedral and the innocent inhabitants of Elgin. Imagine the ferocious cruelty. To descend on the bishop—a defenseless old man—and the cathedral's sleeping household. Consider, too, the sacrilegious nature of such an act. This was a time when all crimes against the Church were looked upon with horror and indignation."

"And the Wolf of Badenoch?" Will asked, attempting to guide Shanks back to the exciting part of the story.

"Aye. You know the rest well enough." Shanks removed his kerchief and wiped his neck. He could have used a swig of cider, but the jug was empty. "The peace-loving citizens of Elgin prayed that the Wolf and his men were destined to some other place. But that was not to be. Any last moments of calm were fast replaced by shrieks of despair and chaos. Men, women, and children hurried into the streets seeking safety in flight. The growing crowd pressed onward, scarcely daring to look back as screams and shouts rang in their ears. Through the intense darkness the flames shot skyward in fitful jets. Those who escaped quickened their speed. Feeble old parents, tottering wives, and helpless children all were dragged onward."

"Did the townspeople know it was the Wolf of Badenoch?" Will asked.

"A few suspected, but most did not. For all they knew it was the end of the world."

Will put down his shovel and sat on the edge of the wheelbarrow.

Shanks wiped his face. "No one dared to stop until they were well-hidden in the neighboring woods. Few possessed the courage to look back. Those who did witnessed the destruction unfolding in Elgin. The college, the church of St. Giles, and the hospital of the Maison Dieu all in flames. But those blazes paled against the dire spectacle of the cathedral. All its beautiful Gothic windows and towers were illuminated by a furious fire raging high within the walls."

Will's eyes were wide, his breathing shallow.

"Wailing and lamentations filled the air. The vault of heaven began to redden in the glare of the spreading flames. The sounds of the fire mixed with cries of terror. The destruction was relentless." Shanks fell silent for a long moment before continuing, "And to this day, some still say the Devil himself rode with the Wolf of Badenoch that night." The old ruin keeper closed his eyes and lowered his head.

But Will could not bear to let the story end there. "And eventually, the cathedral was rebuilt," Will offered, attempting to finish the story with some bit of cheer.

"Yes, Will." Shanks sighed. "It took another generation to save what was left. A larger and more glorious cathedral was designed to replace the Gothic masterpiece lost that night. The tall spires that gave the cathedral its name 'Lantern of the North' were erected as part of that reconstruction."

"Whatever happened to the Wolf of Badenoch?" Will wanted to know.

Shanks solemnly shook his head. "Strangely, out of fear or perhaps some divine intervention, he humbly submitted in the Blackfriars Church at Perth. He received full absolution of his crimes on condition of his making peace with the Bishop of Moray. Likely some financial restitution was involved. After his death, a flattering monument was erected. The plaque at its base says he died in full reconciliation with the Church he had attempted to destroy."

"No! That can't be true." Will frowned.

"I'm afraid it is," Shanks sighed.

"How could he be forgiven?" Will needed a reasonable explanation.

"Sometimes history can take a long view of itself." Shanks shrugged.

"I do not understand what that means, sir."

"Sometimes people are judged differently with the passage of time."

"Even for such a monstrous crime?"

"So it seems. I confess, I cannot put sense to it. But do not fret, Will. Your morals are in a good place if you cannot forgive such a man."

Will thrust his shovel into the compressed rubble at his feet. "May I ask one more question, sir?"

Shanks nodded.

"I have heard many people tell stories of the cathedral's burning, but they are never exactly alike." Will hesitated. He needed to take care with what he was about to say. "None of the others contained so much detail. How do you know all the small bits of this story, Master Shanks?"

Will's question surprised Shanks but he answered quickly. "There is a history book I have read titled *The Wolf of Badenoch*. It is in Isaac Forsyth's library and was written long ago. The details of the night are captured in that volume."

Will imagined holding that book and turning its pages. He wondered if such a thing could happen if he truly learned to read. "Is the book written in our language?" Will asked.

"Yes. In English not Latin, if that is your question. It contains some Old English words we no longer use, but it does not require a translator."

Not a translator, Will thought, but the ability to read a book. He pictured himself in Forsyth's library holding *The Wolf of Bade-noch* and reading every word.

22

Unexpected Visitors

Shanks read the brief message and then read it again.

Three members of the Scottish Works Committee were in the region inspecting properties. Before returning to Edinburgh, they planned to stop for a night in Elgin.

Shanks could not decide if the last-minute notice was a blessing or an insult. Clearly Elgin was not on the gentlemen's original itinerary. Although it was highly likely the men were coming to see the Elgin Cross, Shanks hoped this unexpected visit might bring good news. Even though Alanna's sketches were still unfinished.

"We have guests arriving tomorrow," Shanks informed Will as he unlocked the ruin. "Likely they are coming to inspect the chapter house and to see the Elgin Cross."

"Would you prefer me not to shovel when the guests are here?"

"Hmm," Shanks paused. "You should accompany me as I guide the gentlemen around the ruin and lend a hand if needed."

"Yes, sir." Will lowered his eyes.

"To work with you now." Shanks waved Will away. The ruin keeper had his own plans to ponder.

Will finished filling his barrow and left for the Witches Pool. When he returned, Alanna and Isaac Forsyth were in the ruin. The girl was seated outside the chapter house sketching. Forsyth nodded to Will, but Alanna did not look up.

Will could not resist the occasional glance in the girl's direction as he shoveled. Pausing for a drink of water, Will ran a hand through his hair and along his chin. He would need to clean himself up for the visitors. In his dirty clothes he considered how invisible he must be.

Alanna and Shanks were talking together when Will next returned from the pool. The girl's face was mostly hidden by her bonnet, but he could clearly see her sketch.

At the end of the day, Shanks asked to see Will's notebook. The old ruin keeper's lips moved silently as he tallied up slash marks. "I will keep this for now," Shanks told Will, "since you have no need of it tomorrow."

The members of the Scottish Works Committee arrived in Elgin on the early coach. To everyone's relief the three gentlemen appeared agile, inquisitive, and were not hard-of-hearing. The tour proceeded as Will imagined it might. Shanks began with the Elgin Cross, allowing his guests ample time to examine the carved stone. He pointed out its subtle features and repeated much of what the Pictologist had said.

Douglas, MacDonald, and Blair, the three committee members, proved a good audience. They spoke politely, seemed intelligent, and were acquainted with Shanks's reports. They were fascinated by the walls inside the chapter house and happily lingered as Shanks talked. There was no need to rush. The gentlemen had been well fed at Forsyth's table before their tour. When they were ready to move on, Shanks stressed the importance of buttressing the remaining choir and transept walls. Will watched the men's faces while Shanks related a shorter version of the cathedral's destruction. "The great fire was the end of our magnificent Gothic cathedral, inferior to few in Europe. Yet the ruin of that great church was not the end of the story. Over the years, Elgin Cathedral was rebuilt more glorious than ever. It was the only cathedral in the country with five aisles." Amazed by this small fact, the men exchanged meaningful glances.

"There was a good reason why this cathedral was once called the Lantern of the North," Shanks continued. "It possessed a unique central tower." Shanks looked skyward, imagining the tower, and his guests did the same. "It was capped by a spire two hundred feet tall. Nearly the height of the York Minster." Impressed, the men nodded.

"It may surprise you to learn the greatest single disaster here was not caused by fire but by wind," Shanks continued. "In 1711, a strong wind collapsed the central tower, taking with it the greater portion of the nave. That collapse caused a massive caving-in that accelerated the cathedral's ruination to a point of no return. Unlike other disasters that struck this cathedral throughout its existence, this time was different." Shanks had the gentlemen's full attention. The point he was about to make was relevant to the Scottish Works Committee's mission. "This time when disaster struck, no one was seeing to the maintenance of this building. The Reformation left it abandoned as it slowly decayed into unsalvageable ruin. Only the chapter house was kept in a reasonable state, to be used as a meeting place for Elgin's tradesfolk."

Will listened carefully, absorbing the facts Shanks shared. His mind flashed to the past and then to the future. Seeing this place as it once was, and then imagining himself one day giving such a tour.

Shanks shepherded his guests as close to the ruined west wall as the cascaded rubble allowed. "The cathedral's west towers were originally capped with wooden spires and measured eighty-five feet from the floor of the church."

The men looked up again, and then surveyed the wreckage around them.

"It is backbreaking work, gentlemen. Sorting and hauling away so much wreckage." Heads nodded appreciatively.

"In recent months, I have personally seen to the removal of more than three hundred barrows of rubble." Shanks squared his shoulders. Then he pulled the notebook from his pocket and flipped it open. "And I have the records to prove it!" Shanks never once looked in Will's direction.

Will's face flushed and he quickly stared at his boots to hide his reaction. He supposed he might have foreseen this moment and reminded himself that nothing here was his to claim. Not even the suit of clothes he wore.

"We cannot yet know what might lie beneath all this rubble. What we might discover next week, next month or next year," Shanks said. "It is my plan to one day make this glorious ruin widely accessible to those who wish to visit here."

Will scanned the visitors' faces for some small doubt about the old shoemaker's claims but saw none.

"And there is yet another reason for this work." Shanks paused. "To uncover what might be awaiting discovery." With a flourish, Shanks pulled from his coat pocket the white marble hand Will had saved from the Witches Pool. "Look here, gentlemen. This western front once had a large portal and two tall towers. See the empty arch-shaped opening above the portal?" He pointed toward a blank surface high on the remains of the ruined west wall. "Visualize a religious tableau dedicated to the Holy Trinity. Now consider the hand of the baby Jesus." Shanks held the broken hand high above his head in the direction of the west wall. "The hand of the Christ child in the arms of the Virgin, surrounded by angels. Gleaming radiantly down upon all who entered here." Shanks carefully passed the fragment to MacDonald, and encouraged the men to examine the piece of shattered art. "We have only begun to discover the mysteries buried here."

Shanks was a master at holding his audience's attention. Will was certain the old ruin keeper could help even a blind man see the majesty of what once stood on this spot. Will was certain the committee would provide the funds Shanks sought.

Will thrust a hand deep into his pocket and protectively gripped his small carved stone. He tried not to imagine what Shanks might say while holding Will's creature aloft for all to see.

When the works committee members left Elgin, Will had more questions than answers.

Could all the stories Shanks told be true? Not that Will thought Shanks was a liar. But he questioned how the old shoemaker knew such small details—even with the help of a book. It was a tricky question, and Will was unsure who to talk with about such things. Asking his father would be time ill-spent. And Mam would be unlikely to share her thoughts. Morrison seemed to know Elgin's history, but he would never question Shanks.

Staring into his nearly dry rain barrel, Will thought of James Thompson. A teacher might know how to sort facts from myths, and what a person might learn from a book. Having only met the man once, Will decided to leave a message at the Free School asking if Thompson might meet for a reading lesson. To his surprise, the teacher appeared at Will's door early the next morning.

"You are kind to come so soon," Will welcomed Thompson.

"When someone asks for a reading lesson, I am fast to reply. But my time is short. I must be back for morning classes. I thought we might make use of this early hour to read together. I brought books."

As the reading lesson progressed, Will gathered his nerve to ask Thompson his question about the old ruin keeper's stories. "Do you think it is possible that everything Shanks tells visitors about the cathedral is true? Surely, not all his stories come from books."

"There is much to be learned from books and people both," Thompson counseled. "You could continue wondering, or you could simply ask the man if all the stories he tells are true."

Embarrassed, Will squirmed.

"Ask him respectfully, of course. He might stretch the truth when telling a tale, but John Shanks is unlikely to lie about it."

Thompson was gone long before Shanks arrived to unlock the ruin, and Will was glad of it. He had time to mull over Thompson's advice. It was a quiet morning. Will and Shanks were deep in their own thoughts while shoveling up large chunks of rubble along the cathedral's collapsed west wall.

"Take this load," Shanks muttered, wearily stepping back from his barrow. "And the notebook, too," he continued, pulling it from his coat.

"Sir?"

"Yes, Will?"

"I was wondering, sir," Will fidgeted. "May I speak with you about the cathedral stories you told our guests?"

"Aye, boy, I could use a sit-down. We'll take our meal and talk when you return from the pool."

Pushing the barrow, Will worried over asking Shanks his question. It was more than facts Will was wrestling with. He did not understand how Shanks could suggest to the committee members the possibility of treasures hidden under the rubble, after laughing at Will's discovery of the marble hand.

Months ago, Shanks had told Will the same story about the collapse of the cathedral's towers. "It was the singular point of no return," Shanks claimed. There was no one responsible for the cathedral's maintenance. Not even a watchman or a caretaker. No one to notice cracking walls and wood rotting. The removal of the lead roof had not done as much damage as decades of long-term neglect. Shanks had been adamant. The collapse of the towers had turned the cathedral into an unsalvageable pile of rubble. Yet if that were true, what was Shanks searching for now?

At the Witches Pool the air was clear and still. Will leaned over the water's edge to find his reflection. Since he first shaved, he had become curious about the appearance of his face. He was looking less like a boy. Will blinked hard and stared at the water, trying to see past the surface. Looking for evidence of all those rocks he had dumped. "Bottomless," he whispered. It was a curious word. How deep must a pit be for it to be bottomless? Will dumped the wheelbarrow. He opened the notebook and made a mark.

When Will returned to the ruin, Shanks had their meal ready in the chapter house. Seeing Will's exhaustion, Shanks handed him the cider. "I am pleased you have questions. It shows you were listening on the tour."

Will took a long drink. "What I was wondering, sir. About what you said to the guests…"

The old man met Will's eye and cocked his head.

"With respect, sir, is it all true? All the stories you told the Works Committee, and all the stories you told me?"

Shanks sat up, the corners of his mouth dipped and rose again. Here was the stonemason's boy he had chosen to provide labor and protection. But now Shanks saw a glimmer of something more. *He is bright*, Shanks thought. Not book smart, but commonsense smart. The boy was a good listener and fast learner. More intelligent than he first considered. Shanks finished his cider before answering Will's question. "Most every story I tell is true. Yet for all we know about the history of Elgin Cathedral, much remains a mystery. For example, we know the original cathedral was a magnificent Gothic building. But all the records and history of that first cathedral were burned in the fires lit by the Wolf of Badenoch. Pieces of the story are missing. We must assume what might have been, in between what we know. Does that make sense, Will?"

Will hesitated. "I'm still not sure."

"Let me try again." Shanks stood and paced a bit before turning back to Will. "When I am here in the ruin alone, thinking about the cathedral's magnificent history, I begin to feel the invisible people who once inhabited this space."

"Ghosts?" Will asked, eyes wide. "I thought you did not believe in ghosts, Master Shanks."

"No. Not ghosts. Not some specter—but our imagined version of real people who lived and worked here. The Italian carvers, the stonemasons, the monks, priests, bishops. The cooks and distillers and candlemakers, seamstresses, scribes, bakers, butchers, gardeners, and physicians. All of them serving the church clergy and going about their daily routines. The sounds of choir voices, the bells, the chanting. The smells of baking bread, melting candle wax, soap, and sewage," Shanks closed his eyes and smiled. "Sometimes, Will, we must imagine history. Not invent it but imagine it." Shanks opened his eyes. "We can only speculate about the missing pieces that join what we already know. Do you understand?"

"I am beginning to, sir." Imagining invisible people sounded a bit like conjuring ghosts, but Will kept that thought to himself.

"Many different people lived here, visited here, pillaged here. Not everyone loved the cathedral. Certainly, Cromwell's men did not. Nor the Wolf of Badenoch. But those are not the people I normally think of when I stand in the ruin." Shanks smiled. "Do you understand?"

"I am beginning to," Will repeated.

"Good, good." Shanks seemed pleased. "At times this ruin may be a quiet place, but no history is entirely mute."

23

West Wall Discoveries

Shanks turned his attention to clearing the landslide of rocks that were once the west wall.

After days of digging, Will and Shanks began to see changes in the broken rock and mortar. They even uncovered fragments of ancient wood as hard as the rocks. "Petrified," Shanks called it. "Part of the ruin's buried secrets."

"Secrets? What secrets, sir?"

"The secrets we hope to discover by digging."

Aware of his own small secret, Will thrust a hand into his pocket and rubbed the stone creature's scales. Something about the place they were digging niggled at Will's memory. There were things he knew about the ruin that Shanks did not.

That night a deep loneliness settled upon Will and he could not sleep. His mind churned through conversations he wished to have with the people in his life. He had not chosen to be alone, but here he was. He missed his family, his dog, and his friends. Especially his good cousins. He missed being with people his own age. He had not seen Morrison or James Thompson in some time, and Alanna was busy at home, finishing the chapter house sketches.

Will was unsure how to go about solving his loneliness. "I need to go home," he finally said aloud, trying hard not to cry.

When at last Will fell asleep, he dreamed of the past. He saw the little stone creature he had discovered in the ruin resting in the small hand of his younger self. In the dream, his hand became Alanna's hand gently holding the little carving.

Three days later, Will's shovel struck something metal.

"What's that?" Shanks dropped his shovel and moved closer. "Dig it out carefully."

Will pulled a piece of iron from the pile. It was nearly two feet long, bent and broken off at both ends. He handed it to Shanks, who examined it carefully. "Keep digging," Shanks instructed. "Maybe there's more of it."

By noon Will had barely filled a single barrow, but he had dug out three more pieces of iron.

"Look at the hammer marks, here and here," Shanks pointed out. "These were all part of something—but what it is I do not know. Keep digging, Will!"

Will did as he was told, but he was unsure what all the excitement was about. Over the years, the stonemasons had uncovered all manner of broken things buried in the ruin's rock piles. Another hour of digging revealed more of the same.

"I wonder how it all fits together," Shanks mumbled, rearranging the pieces on the ground.

"Look here, sir." Will lifted his shovel for Shanks to see what was on it. The old shoemaker removed his glove and carefully picked up what appeared to be a thick piece of broken glass. Its wavy surface was etched and marred.

"Forsyth needs to see this!" Shanks exclaimed. "You stay here. I will take the wagon and fetch him." Shanks made his way to the door in the wall faster than Will had ever seen the old shoemaker move. "Keep digging!" he called over his shoulder.

As the wagon sounds faded down the lane, Will's stomach grumbled. The excitement had not curbed his appetite and their midday meal was still in the wagon. From his inside coat pocket, Will removed a stale bun. He stared at the iron pieces on the ground while he chewed. There were short ones and long ones. He tried to see how they might fit together with the piece of glass Shanks had taken with him.

When the bread was gone, Will continued scraping into the pile. He knew what he was looking for now. It made the digging more interesting. But there was a difference between digging with a purpose and finding something unexpected like his stone creature. Will pushed the thought away. Right now, he needed to focus on what was here at his feet.

When Shanks returned with Forsyth, there were three more lengths of twisted iron on the ground and two small slabs of thick glass. Shanks excitedly gripped Will's shoulder. "Well done, boy!"

Forsyth had brought a large book, a folio of some sort. He passed his book to Shanks before squatting to handle the finds. The stack of wooden pieces caught his eye. "All these were in this same location?"

"Yes," Shanks said.

Forsyth moved the pieces around like a puzzle. "Let me see the book." He leaned against the nearest wall and Shanks joined him.

On the pages Forsyth was turning Will saw large drawings and sketches of the cathedral next to the printed text.

"Look here," Forsyth said pointing. The two men huddled

over the open folio. "And here." He turned another large page.

Shanks nodded, squinting.

"Keep digging, Will," Shanks instructed. Then he returned to his conversation with Forsyth. The men lowered their voices, but in between the scrapes of his shovel Will could hear them discussing the found bits. Something about a debris field and the collapse of the great tower.

Will's shovel never stopped. The sounds of rubble spilling into a wheelbarrow punctuated the men's words. Most of what they were saying seemed unimportant to Will—until they mentioned something that touched a memory.

"We must take into consideration that we may not be the first to rearrange this rubble," Forsyth said.

"And yet—if what lies here at the west wall includes larger finds…"

Will sensed Shanks was hesitant to say more, concerned Will might be listening to their conversation. He yawned and stretched. "Sir? Might I help myself to the food basket?"

"Goodness, boy! I forgot. It's still in the wagon."

Will left the ruin, but not before he heard the words, "…carved figures…colossal statuary…burial tombs."

Before the day was done, Will uncovered a thick flat iron disc with a rusted-out section in the middle. Its shape might have once been circular or octagonal. It was impossible to know its original size and shape. Shanks came with his shovel to help lift it from the pile.

The men spent a long time examining the pieces of glass. They were not like the fragments of glass from the cathedral that showed up in church windows in nearby townships. Pieces that everyone assumed were originally from the cathedral's now-ruined rose window.

As Will made a last trip to the Witches Pool, Shanks locked the ruin and Forsyth carted off the collection of finds.

Shanks and Forsyth were gone when the last load of rubble slid from Will's wheelbarrow into the Witches Pool. But something caught Will's eye, and he quickly righted the load, scattering rocks at the water's edge. On the ground at his feet lay another worn piece of iron, but this one was distinctly recognizable. A single link from a chain that must have been magnificent in size and strength. Will ran his hand along the length of the link. He closed his eyes and let his imagination take over. "A massive chain strong enough to hold…" He hesitated, considering the other finds of the day. "Strong enough to hold the Lantern of the North."

Will wondered how he failed to notice the large chain link.

Luckily, it had not gone into the Witches Pool. He was in no hurry to show the link to Shanks. Never again would he anticipate praise for his finds. Shanks's words still stung. "It is not your job to decide what is worth saving." Now here was another discovery. This time he did not question his instincts.

He dumped the heavy link outside the hut. Shanks and Forsyth could cart it away whenever they liked. Will was curious if anyone else would see what he saw. Or they might imagine something entirely different from Will's conclusion.

The following day, after examining the iron link, Shanks feverishly continued excavating the site. Excitement drove the old shoemaker to dig at a frantic pace.

Will was returning from the pool when he heard Shanks cry out. He assumed Shanks had made another discovery, but the cries sounded more like a wounded animal. He ran back to discover Shanks on the ground, grabbing his leg. Will had seen stonemasons injured and recognized the old man's expression of pain. Something was seriously wrong.

"What's happened, sir? Where are you hurt?"

"My ankle, I think, and my foot. Hurry, boy. Come help!"

Will knelt next to Shanks and grimaced at the sight of the twisted leg. He hoped there were no broken bones, but he was no physician.

"You need a doctor, sir. I will fetch Master Forsyth and he will bring someone to see to your leg."

"You will do no such thing!" Shanks demanded. "You cannot leave me here alone!" he wailed, clenching his teeth in pain. "Help me up," he pleaded.

"Let me look first, sir. If it is broken, you do not want to stand on it." Will carefully lifted away the rubble touching Shanks's ankle and foot. He considered removing the man's boot but thought better of it. "We need help, sir. I cannot do this alone."

"Just get me to the wagon," Shanks said with a grimace.

Will shook his head. "I do not think—"

"You are a strong boy! You must find a way." Shanks sprawled back on the ground, closed his eyes, and moaned.

"I am strong, sir, but I doubt I can carry you to the wagon. We need to splint your leg before you try to move. We do not want to make the damage worse." Will selected two short pieces of wood from a pile nearby. He measured them on either side of Shanks's ankle. "This will have to do," he muttered. Then he removed his jacket and began to take off his shirt.

"What are you doing?" Shanks wailed.

"I need a bit of cloth to secure the splints to your leg. My shirt will do."

"Wait," Shanks said. He pulled at the scarf wrapped around his neck. "Use this."

It had been some time since Will had seen someone splint a limb, but he felt sure of himself. Without bending the leg any more than necessary, he secured the wooden braces with the scarf. But Will still did not know how to get Shanks out of the ruin. "I cannot carry you to the wagon," Will said, "and I cannot bring the wagon into the ruin."

Shanks moaned but was no longer arguing.

"I have an idea, sir." Will touched the man's shoulder before running to retrieve the empty wheelbarrow.

It took some time for Will to lift Shanks into the barrow, but he realized he was stronger than he thought.

Shanks was breathing heavily. His limbs spilled over the sides of the barrow and Will folded the man's arms across his chest.

"Not dead," Shanks grumbled between groans.

"I'm only trying to center your weight, so you do not fall out if we hit a bump. And there may be a few bumps, sir."

Shanks resumed his moaning.

Will did his best to keep the wheelbarrow on the cleared paths and tried not to think about what came next.

By the time Will got Shanks into the back of the wagon, both men had sweated through their clothes. But the old shoemaker remained conscious through it all.

"Do you know how to drive a wagon?" Shanks asked.

"I do, sir." Will had never driven a wagon himself, but he had watched others do it. Seeing the door to the ruin standing open, Will asked, "Do you want me to lock the ruin?" Will climbed into the wagon bed and took the key from Shanks. After locking the door, he returned the key to Shanks's coat pocket.

"We are going to the doctor," Will announced, feeling himself in charge now that he was holding the reins.

Shanks mustered a last protest. "Not the doctor. I want to go home."

Will shook the reins and the horse stepped off. "To the hospital, then."

"No. Home is closer," Shanks insisted. "Alanna can send for a doctor."

The mention of Alanna swayed Will's decision. He would do as his master demanded.

Shocked by her grandfather's condition, Alanna moved quickly to comfort him. She set the household into action and sent for the doctor. Will went to find Morrison who lived in the small apartment above the shoemaker's shop. Thankfully, Morrison was there. They returned to find Alanna fussing over her grandfather in the sitting room. She was arranging him on a divan, her hands full of pillows. Will noticed the tears in her eyes as she kept repeating, "Oh, Grand-Dey! What have you done?"

Shanks's face was frighteningly pale, and his breathing did not sound normal. The cook came with a cup in hand. Alanna lifted her grandfather's head to help him sip the whiskey. Anything to help ease the pain.

The concern on Morrison's face matched Alanna's. The old shoemaker looked bad off. Morrison could not bear to see his employer in such a state. "I'll go find the stable boy and see to the horse and wagon," Morrison told Will. "You stay here in case Miss Alanna needs anything. If the doctor does not come soon, I will go drag him here myself."

By the time Shanks finished his second whiskey the doctor had arrived, accompanied by Isaac Forsyth. Dr. Randall was John Shanks's personal physician and friend. He quickly shooed everyone from the room.

Randall's examination of the patient did not take long. He quietly addressed his comments to Alanna. "I am sending for Dr. Calder. He is the best practitioner in the parish, specializing in bones."

"Do you think it is broken?" Alanna whimpered.

"It may well be just a very bad sprain. With all the swelling, I cannot be certain. That's why we will call in the specialist."

Alanna nodded, thankful to have a doctor present.

"Who brought him home from the ruin?" Dr. Randall asked.

Will was afraid to answer, worried that he might be accused of some wrongdoing. It did not take much for him to imagine others judging his decisions.

"Will did!" Alanna said, an expression of sincere gratitude on her young face.

"Well done, son," the doctor nodded. "If he had been alone, he might still be lying there in the ruin."

Will blushed, unaccustomed to kind attention from anyone other than Mam.

"And I must say," the doctor concluded, "I cannot fault the splinting work."

Relieved when the doctor turned his attention back to Shanks, Will looked for Morrison. He wanted to tell someone exactly what had happened in the ruin. Thankfully, Morrison was willing to listen. After recounting the morning's events Will added, "I thought someone should know that I locked the ruin before we left. I returned the key to Master Shanks's coat pocket."

"I will let Miss Alanna know."

"Should I plan to work tomorrow?" Will asked tentatively.

"Let's assume not," Morrison said.

"Then I will go see my mother."

"I think that will be fine, Will," Morrison replied.

As Will opened the front door to leave, Alanna called out. "Will Clachan. Wait!" She joined him as he stepped out onto the porch. "How can I ever thank you, Will? If you had not been there…" Alanna began to weep again. "You must come visit Grand-Dey when he feels better. I am sure he will want to thank you himself."

"I will return when the time seems right," Will assured her.

As Alanna reached for Will's hand, he was suddenly conscious how dirty he was compared to everyone and everything around him. Alanna did not seem to mind, but Will did, and he pulled away, embarrassed. "No time to wash up," he mumbled.

This made Alanna giggle. "Of course not. You were too busy rescuing my grandfather."

Will lowered his eyes. "At your service, miss." Then he quickly walked away. He resisted the temptation to glance back over his shoulder. But he sensed Alanna's eyes watching him until he was out of sight.

24

A GIFT OF TIME

"Time is a gift," Will's mother liked to say.

Until now Will was never certain what that adage meant. Released from work with many hours remaining in the day, he was unexpectedly free to do as he pleased. This was the gift of time his mother talked about. And there was something Will wished to do before heading home.

At the edge of the woods, not far from the Bishop's Well, stood an ancient apple tree. So weather-beaten, if you saw the tree in winter, you would think it was long dead. The variety was called Red Devil. It survived in the shadow of the ruined cathedral. These apples were sweet and tart and perfect for dumplings. Will picked up some nice windfallen fruit. It would be a good surprise to carry home to Mam. After the events of the morning, a quick wash in the spring would be pleasant, too.

As Will made for the woods, Mam's adage spun round in his head. There was one more thing he would like to do with this gift of time. He would examine the moss-covered rocks in the glade near the spring. The ones James Thompson had claimed were the skeletal remains of an ancient tree.

While filling his waterskin at the spring, Will heard young voices nearby. After washing up, he followed the sounds. To Will's surprise, Thompson and several young students stood in the center of the nearby glade. The boys were gathering leaves and examining the autumn greenery. Will smiled and raised a hand in greeting.

"Will!" Thompson said. "A pleasure to see you. What brings you into the woods this morning? A trip to the spring, I presume?"

"I was filling my waterskin and thought I might look at the remains of the ancient tree you mentioned."

"Come see." Thompson motioned Will to one of the large mounds in the ring.

"I always assumed these were rocks."

"Let's take a look," the teacher said. With a pocketknife Thompson scraped some moss from the hard surface beneath. A young student held out a small glass jar. "We will take the moss back to school and look at it under a microscope." Thompson winked at the child. "Look here." He turned his attention back to Will. "Take this knife and carefully make a cut where I've cleared away the moss."

Will ran his fingers over the newly uncovered surface. "It feels like rock," Will insisted.

"Yes," Thompson agreed. "Now press the blade tip firmly into that spot."

Will worked the knife tip back and forth until it exposed something more pliant. He touched the spot with his fingers and leaned down to sniff the exposed surface. "It smells like old wood." Will walked to the center of the glade. He turned slowly, looking hard at the circle of moss-covered mounds he had long believed to be an old stone circle. He was not alone in that assumption. But now, with a gift of time, he had learned these mounds were the remains of an ancient tree. In his mind's eye, the size of the thing was staggering.

He looked skyward again. "Heavens," he murmured.

"Exactly," Thompson said. "Can you imagine how high the top branches must have reached? All the way to the heavens."

A small boy stepped up beside Will. "Can you come back to school with us for supper?"

"Not today," Will replied kindly. The child's face turned sad. Will ruffled the boy's hair. "Maybe another time."

"I'm surprised to see you here in the middle of the day," Thompson said.

"It's a long story." Will shrugged. He briefly explained Shanks's injury, minimizing his own role. Good practice for later when he would tell his father about the day's events. "I will not be working in the ruin for the next few days," Will concluded.

"Perhaps tomorrow would be a good day for a reading lesson," the teacher offered.

"I would like that," Will said, "but I am on my way home to visit my family. It has been too long since I have seen my mam."

"You have a mam?" the littlest boy asked wide-eyed.

"I do." Will nodded.

"How lovely," the boy sighed wistfully.

"Then perhaps Saturday for your next lesson?" Thompson persisted.

"Yes," Will agreed. The teacher's offer was too kind to refuse.

"I have a book here you might find interesting." Thompson bent to the bag he carried. "You can return it when we meet."

Will studied the book's title as the teacher said it aloud. "*Theory of the Earth* by James Hutton. He's a Scotsman. He writes about the importance of rocks and what they tell us about natural history."

"Rocks." Will laughed, carefully placing the book in his own sack. "My specialty."

Will had a lot on his mind on his way to the Clachan croft. Out of all the day's events, the one he could not shake was the wistful look on the young schoolboy's face when he learned Will had a mother. It made Will walk all the faster toward home.

Mam was just hanging up her bonnet and cloak when Will arrived. He might have cried at the sight of her, but Mam took no notice.

"Your brothers are off snaring rabbits, or so they said." Her eyes smiled at Will. "And your father is working on the lord provost's new home. I expect him by nightfall."

Will was pleased to have Mam to himself. He considered how to talk about Shanks's injury, and his role in the rescue.

"Come," his mother said, looking closer at her son. "Let's talk while I cook."

Will had planned to wait until his father returned before relating the day's events, but he could not help himself. His mother's solitary attention was comforting. His story spilled out as he watched her set a batch of dough near the oven to prove.

"You should be proud of yourself, Will." She draped an arm around his shoulder, careful of her floury hand. "It was good you were there. I hope Master Shanks was appreciative."

"He was in a lot of pain, Mam. I cannot say he was in the mind to express his appreciation. But his family seemed grateful."

"Family?" Mam asked.

"His granddaughter."

Mam knocked back the dough. "It sounds like you did all the right things, Will."

"The doctor said so."

"Can you stay the night?"

Will grinned. "Will the boys mind my company?"

"They may resent Jock sleeping with you instead of them."

Will laughed softly. "And Da?"

"Your da should not care. Especially with your news about Shanks. Your father has been working so hard. He is often asleep in his chair before the boys are down for the night."

"Oh, I nearly forgot!" Will removed the six nearly perfect apples from his sack and placed them on the table. "From the Red Devil tree." He grinned.

Mam rolled each one between her hands inhaling their scent. "How lovely, Will. Thank you."

Mam turned her back to Will and reached for a bowl. She did not want him to see her tears. She already knew how he had rescued Shanks and she was proud of her boy. In town, the story had quickly spread from domestics to merchants and customers. A shopkeeper had shared the news with her. "If it wasn't for your son, Shanks might have lain injured in the ruin all day."

Will heard his brothers outside the door and quickly ducked out of sight.

"Mam! Mam! We have two rabbits for you!"

"Wonderful!" Mam said. "Guess what I have for you?"

"Is it something to eat?" Luke asked hopefully.

Will jumped out from his hiding place, making Ross squeal. "Will's here!" the boys shouted, and Jock barked to be let in.

"Everyone outside," Mam ordered. "Take these rabbits and see how quick you can dress them. After you've washed up, I'll give you each a nice slice of cheese and bread.

As Mam predicted, an exhausted Tom Clachan arrived home before dusk. He greeted Will and the rest of his family before heading outside to wash.

At dinner, Will watched his father's face, eyes drooped as

though he might fall asleep any moment. At the end of the meal, Da turned to his oldest son. "What brings you home to us in the middle of the week, Will? Did Shanks decide he doesn't need you, after all?"

"No, sir," Will replied.

His youngest brothers wisely excused themselves and slipped out the back door. They knew too well their father's moods.

Will keep his story short. "Shanks injured his leg in the ruin today, Da. He could not walk, and he was in a lot of pain. I splinted his leg and got him into the wagon. I drove him home and stayed until the doctor came. I will not be working for the next few days, so I came home for a visit."

His father stared silently at the table. "Are they not feeding you in the meantime?"

The implication hurt—that Will was only home because he needed fed.

"Everyone was pleased I had rescued Master Shanks. Even the doctor said I did a fine job splinting his leg."

Will's father remained silent.

"I learned how to splint a leg from you, Da." Will blinked back tears.

"Did Shanks not give you the key to the ruin? Does he not trust you to work while he recovers?"

"No! It's not like that."

"The man still does not trust you, Will. Even after you rescued him."

"I do not believe—" Will tried to explain, but Da slammed a fist on the table.

Will had hoped for his father's change of heart. He thought the key to the ruin might be less important now. Especially with his father building a house for the lord provost. But Will was wrong.

Da still wanted access to the ruin. And he wanted Will to secure the key.

His father pushed himself up from the table, mumbling a mild curse. Without a backward glance, he went out the back door with his pipe in his hand.

Hot tears crept into the corners of Will's eyes.

After a moment, a tiny grin played across Luke's face. "Wish I had been there to see you put Shanks in that wagon. How did you manage it?"

Will just shook his head.

Luke touched his brother's arm. "It's not just you, Will. He's mad at the world."

"Why does he think Shanks will ever give me the key to the ruin?" Will seethed. "Shanks thinks me a good worker. He even likes me a bit. But that does not mean he will hand over the key, no matter what Da wants."

Mam kept still, powerless to change her husband's black mood. It broke her heart to see Will's earnestness overshadowed by the expectations of his father.

In the morning Mam made apple pancakes, and everyone ate heartily. Even Da seemed to enjoy his food before heading out. Will lingered, helping his mother with the dishes. She handed him four bannocks wrapped in a towel. Placing the parcel in his sack, Will remembered Thompson's book and showed it to his mother.

"Where did this come from?" Her look of concern was at odds with the excitement in her voice.

"I have made a new friend. A young teacher at the Free School of General Anderson's Institute. His name is James Thompson, and he is helping me improve my reading. He loaned me this book. Shall we look at it together before I go?"

Mam carefully wiped her hands dry and spread a clean cloth on the table for the book.

"Why is this teacher helping you?"

It was a good question, but Will was uncertain of the answer. "He is new to Elgin. When I met him, I told him I wanted to improve my reading. He offered to help. Like me, he does not have time to spare. He comes to read with me before I start work and his classes begin. He will visit again on Saturday, and I will return the book to him then."

"This seems a very scholarly book, Will," his mother observed.

"I think he loaned it to me because I spend my days moving rubble and rocks."

Mam opened the book and slowly read aloud. "In Scotland there are two great tracks of mountainous country, each of which reaches from sea to sea."

Turning the pages, she came to a drawing.

"Rocks." Will grinned. Interspersed with the text were illustrations of rock formations.

His mother read the descriptions. "Fig. 1. – Granite veins traversing limestone. Glen Tilt."

The illustrations were different from any drawings Will had ever seen. And there was this: "In matters of science, curiosity gratified begets no indolence but new desires." Mam read that passage aloud very slowly.

"He teaches boys about nature and history, and he thinks I should know about the rocks in the Earth." Will paused. "Also, the book is written by a Scotsman."

"Ah," his mother smiled. "Now I understand."

25

ALANNA AND THE KEY

A lanna unlocked the ruin so Will could return to work.

As Will and James emerged from the keeper's hut, Alanna stepped from her pony cart and removed her gloves. Smoothing her skirts, she turned to see two young men smiling at her.

"Goodness!" Alanna exclaimed, surprised by the presence of a stranger.

"James Thompson," the schoolteacher introduced himself. "I am just leaving."

Alanna blushed, but not as much as Will when Thompson added, "Will and I have been reading together." Thompson's tact was a kindness.

"What book?" Alanna asked.

"The Complete Angler, written a long time ago by Izaak Walton. Most people think it is about fishing, but it is truly about the joys of nature. Do you know it?"

"I believe my grandfather owns an old copy. And I have seen the book in Master Forsyth's library. Isaac Forsyth is a good friend of my family." Alanna paused. "Mostly, though, I spend my time with Sir Walter Scott." A small grin masked her girlish cleverness. "His works, of course. Not the actual gentleman."

"I see." Thompson stared down at his shoes. It was a safe place to look when veiling one's true thoughts. "I must be off," James said. "My students will wonder where I am. Same time next week?"

Will hesitated. He glanced at Alanna and then back at James.

"If it does not interfere with your work, of course," Thompson added.

Will looked at Alanna.

"Oh!" She suddenly realized they expected her to comment. "I am certain it will be fine with Grand-Dey."

Will shook the schoolteacher's hand. "Thank you again, James. See you soon."

As Thompson strode off in the direction of the Free School, Alanna watched him go. "He seems a nice young man. I am surprised I have not met him before."

Will recognized the look on her face as female interest. The idea of competition for Alanna's attentions unsettled him.

"James Thompson is new to Elgin. He arrived at the start of the school term," Will explained. "He teaches sciences and history."

"And reading?" Alanna asked.

Will nodded. "That, too." He was acutely aware he and Alanna were now alone together. He politely inquired about her grandfather's recovery.

"Dr. Calder says we must have patience, but Grand-Dey is already restless." Alanna reached for the key to the ruin dangling from a green ribbon around her neck. She did not see Will blush when she inserted the key into the lock. Her small hands looked soft and pink but not particularly strong. There was a blemish inside the first joint of her right middle finger where she grasped her pens. Alanna leaned into the heavy door.

"May I help, miss?" Will asked.

She moved aside and tucked the key away while Will pushed open the heavy door.

"I have brought a food basket in my cart. Can you fetch it while I go inside the ruin? I need another look at the chapter house for my sketches. If you would bring my sketchbook, too, please."

"Yes, miss." After Shanks's injury, Will was relieved that someone had remembered his meals. When he returned to the ruin, Alanna stood at the entrance to the chapter house. He handed her the sketchbook.

"A fascinating place," she said stepping inside.

"A wonderful place," Will agreed.

"Making my sketches, I have been astonished by what remains."

"I spent long days here with my brothers and cousins. We each had a favorite image on the walls."

Alanna stepped inside and sat on the nearest stone bench. She opened her sketchbook and produced a pencil from the little bag hung on her wrist. "Which image do you like best?" she asked without looking up.

Will blushed, thinking of the heart on the wall nearby. He would not tell her the truth, just as he never confessed it to his cousins. "You first," he said.

She scanned the walls in the morning light. "I have always liked that wing," she said as her hand began sketching the worn feathery image on the wall. "I imagine an angel's wing, but we will never know to what it belonged."

"I wonder about the small bits of colored paint on the ceiling." Will pointed up. "The remains of something unknown."

"Umm." She nodded.

Standing behind her, Will watched Alanna finish sketching the wing. Noticed how she gently bit her lip and the concentration on her face.

"The ear has always been a puzzle," he said, squinting high up the wall.

"Ear?" Alanna looked where Will pointed.

"It's easier to see when the light is from the west."

"Oh, I see it! I never noticed that before." Alanna set to sketching the ear on the same page as the wing.

"I have a theory about those flecks of paint up there," Alanna said. Finishing the ear, she began sketching a skull and crossbones.

Theory. There was that word again. The same as in the title of the book James lent him. "What is your theory?" Will asked Alanna.

"I believe there was once a giant mural painted on this chapter house ceiling. A mural depicting God and the Savior and angels and saints."

Will strained his neck looking up. "I cannot see it."

"I cannot see it either, but I can imagine it. There is a book in Isaac Forsyth's library with images of such murals that still exist in some great cathedrals. And I have seen such things in a great house I visited in Edinburgh with Grand-Dey." Alanna shifted to face a different wall and began sketching a halo.

Will was enjoying the girl's imagination. In that small moment she had made him feel special. Then Will sighed and the spell was broken. "Time for me to start work."

In Shanks's absence, Will continued digging where they had found the metal and glass. He carted rubble to the Witches Pool and diligently marked in the notebook. He did not total up the slashes spilling across the pages. He would leave that to Shanks.

"Grand-Dey says to remind you not to loaf about in his absence," Alanna told Will on the third morning she unlocked the ruin.

"Ask him if he would like to see the notebook," Will replied, offering it to the girl.

Alanna waved it away. "I will ask, but try not to be angry with him. He is just anxious to return to work."

Will cherished the few moments each day when Alanna unlocked the ruin. Their brief exchanges eased Will's loneliness. He found himself thinking of small things he could say to the girl. All the while knowing he should be keeping his distance. There were days when Will wondered if they might ever be friends.

In his digging, Will came across a few more pieces of metal, but nothing as significant as their earlier finds.

Will had not visited Shanks at home. He could not see himself making a social call while Shanks was still on his back. And Will believed Shanks would soon return to the ruin. Even if he could not work, he would supervise. In truth, Will's primary interest in such a visit—to see Alanna—was happening almost daily at the ruin.

"Today you get Scotch broth and Howtowdie. That's what Grand-Dey is having, too," Alanna explained, handing Will his food basket. "He wanted mussel broth, but I cannot stomach the odor. Grand-Dey will be having a hot toddy with his meal. None of that for you." She giggled. The smell of the roasted chicken was enough to make Will wish Shanks might stay abed forever.

Alanna continued to unlock and lock the ruin for Will. The key remained in her possession hung around her neck. Just the thought of that key, warmly nestled in the girl's bosom, made Will's heart quicken.

Most days, Alanna arrived without an escort, but Morrison frequently accompanied her safely home. Will always made one last trip to the pool as Alanna locked the ruin. When he returned with his empty barrow, the girl would be gone.

James Thompson's early arrival at the ruin took Will by surprise.

He had been expecting Alanna but not the teacher.

"Are you all right, Will?" Thompson asked anxiously. "Is all well with you and yours?" Thompson was wearing a black arm-band—a thin piece of cloth knotted over his jacket sleeve. His expressions of concern made Will uncomfortable.

"Yes. I believe so. Why do you ask?"

"I received a message from Mistress Shanks requesting my presence at the ruin this morning. The message instructed me to wear mourning clothes." James glanced down at the armband. "It was the best I could do."

Will knitted his brow. "I have had no word. Certainly, it cannot be Shanks! Someone would have told me."

Before they could say more, a carriage appeared down the lane. Morrison was driving, with Alanna and Isaac Forsyth inside. It was one of Forsyth's nicer conveyances, kept mostly for special guests. Both Forsyth and Morrison wore dark jackets, but it was the sight of Alanna as she stepped down from the carriage that made Will feel suddenly ill. She was dressed all in black with her face covered by a lace veil.

"Is it Master Shanks?" Will asked, his eyes anxiously searching the faces.

"Goodness no!" Forsyth replied. "Don't even suggest such a thing."

"Have you not heard?" Alanna sniffled.

"Heard what, exactly?" James asked.

"Sir Walter Scott is dead!" Alanna moaned. She swayed as though she might faint, whether from the sad news or the weight of her clothes, it was uncertain.

Forsyth took Alanna's elbow. He glared at Will and James. "Alanna wishes to have a small memorial in the chapter house. We will read a few lines and perhaps have a quick prayer."

Alanna extracted the key to the ruin and passed it to Morrison. He quickly undid the lock and the small group filed into the chapter house.

"Please, everyone be seated," Alanna instructed. The men moved to the benches lining the walls. She stood before them, sniffling under her veil. "Isaac, if you would be so kind." She moved to a seat and Forsyth stood, taking a folded paper from his pocket.

"Yesterday the news arrived. Sir Walter Scott has died. His funeral in Edinburgh was a grand memorial to a great man. I have here a bit of what was published. Part of what was read and said at his funeral. I thought I might share a small portion." Forsyth cleared his throat and began:

"Dust unto dust,
To this all must;
The tenant hath resign'd
The faded form
To waste and worm-
Corruption claims her kind.
Through paths unknown
Thy soul hath flown,
To seek the realms of woe,
Where fiery pain
Shall purge the stain
Of actions done below.

In that sad place,
By Mary's grace,
Brief may thy dwelling be
Till prayers and alms,
And holy psalms,
Shall set the captive free."

Forsyth looked at his small audience. "Those were the man's own words, read at his own funeral. First written for the mourning of a friend gone before him." Forsyth hesitated and glanced at Alanna. "And now, Alanna will read from the great man's works."

James leaned into Will's shoulder and whispered almost silently, "Do you think this will be long? I have classes."

Forsyth took a seat and Alanna stood. She began reading from the weathered book in her hands.

"Oh heavens," James quietly hissed into Will's ear, "not *Ivanhoe*!"

Morrison made eye contact with James and scowled.

James closed his eyes and kept them closed throughout the reading, which seemed exceedingly long. He was unsure how Rebecca's trial and sentencing to die as a witch held any meaningful relevance to the author's death. Apart from the fact that Scott had written the atrocious drivel. It was to everyone's relief when Alanna finished reading, swaying, and gulping, and took a seat.

Forsyth rose one more time and shared a final quote from the paper. "Alas for Scotland! Her highly gifted, her beloved, her idolized Sir Walter has yielded his mighty spirit into the hands of him who created it. He is gone from us forever!"

Alanna let go one last sob.

"Amen!" Forsyth added.

"Never again will there be a new Walter Scott novel to read!"

Alanna moaned.

James and Will quickly made their excuses and said their farewells before bolting from the chapter house. There was no time for Alanna to execute the dramatic faint she so carefully rehearsed.

26

Alanna Maria Oglethorpe Shanks

Alanna carried her completed sketches to the chapter house one last time.

She wanted to see her finished work in its setting before the drawings went off to Edinburgh. The building's measurements appeared in a lower corner where she had neatly penned them: thirty-four feet at its apex and thirty-seven feet from wall to facing wall. In the opposite corner were the words: Drawing by A.M.O.S. Centered below the sketch, neatly printed: Chapter House Elgin Cathedral, Elginshire.

Will stood behind Alanna, looking over her shoulder at the sketch she held. It perfectly mirrored the wall beyond.

"I spent so much time with these sketches, I am sad to see them go." She sighed.

Will bent to see the printed words. "What is A.M.O.S.?" he asked.

"That's me," Alanna said, grinning. "It was Grand-Dey's idea. He thought I should have credit for the sketches. And using my name might be…difficult."

Will wondered whether it was the use of her surname, or the fact that she was not a man, that could present the larger problem.

"I know what the *A* and *S* stand for—what about the other letters?" Will asked.

"Alanna Maria Oglethorpe Shanks," she said slowly.

"That's a lot of names."

"It is." She hesitated. "They are part of my story. That's what Grand-Dey says."

Will kept still, hoping she might tell him more.

She ran a clean finger lightly over the letters.

"May I sit down?" Will asked.

She glanced at Will. "Of course. Oglethorpe was my father's surname. Shanks was my mother's maiden name. Grand-Dey and Grand-Mere were her parents who raised me." She paused as a tremor of emotion crept into her voice. "My father died at sea. I was too young to remember him." She let the sketch settle flat on her lap and stared at the wall. "He worked for the East India Company. The suit of clothes I gave you belonged to him. I have a silhouette of his profile. We have the same nose."

Will kept still, sensing the importance of what she was telling him.

"My grandmother Shanks always said my father died at sea, and my mother died of a broken heart. I remember my mother. I was seven when she died suddenly from a fever. My mother's parents, Grand-Dey and Grand-Mere, took care of me and raised me as their own. They were old for raising a child, but kindness was their strength. My grandmother died when I was twelve." Alanna's voice quavered and steadied again. "She taught me many things. And she loved me so much." Alanna paused.

It was a lot to tell, Will thought. So many people to lose in a short life. Especially people you loved.

"I remember leaving the graveyard holding Grand-Dey's hand, after my grandmother died. 'What did she die of?' I asked him. 'Old age,' Grand-Dey told me. 'Your good grandmother died of old age.' It was the only time I ever saw Grand-Dey cry."

Will was tempted to touch the girl's shoulder to comfort her. He thought better of it and remained completely still.

Alanna gave the smallest laugh as she hiccuped and wiped away a tear. "I knew four things a person could die from: old age, a fever, a broken heart, and lost at sea. But my grandfather never wavered in raising me. He simply took over where Grand-Mere left off. Grand-Mere taught me how to read. She trained me in fashion and manners and society ways. She arranged piano lessons and tutoring in Latin and French. But it was Grand-Dey who taught me history and architecture and art and nature. How to think for myself and how to ask questions. He taught me about the world around me."

Alanna grew still. She would not say any more aloud. Her tears might overpower her. Grand-Dey was so good to her. He took her along with him when she was too young to be at home alone. He took her to meetings, and to see art collections in Edinburgh, and recitals and plays. Took her on fishing boats and larger ships so she would not be afraid of the sea. He hired the best tutors and music teachers. Put books in her hands and dancing shoes on her feet. Shoes made with his own loving hands.

Streaks of golden sun breached the west window of the chapter house. Soon they would lose the light. Alanna turned to Will. "I have told you all my dearest secrets. Now you must tell me one of yours."

Without hesitation Will removed the carved creature from his pocket. He presented it to Alanna in the palm of his hand. The streaks of sunlight animated its features.

Alanna leaned closer. "I have never seen anything like it."

Will's heart raced.

"Who made this for you?"

"It's a long story. Part of the secret I cannot tell. Would you like to hold it?"

Alanna opened her tiny hand and Will carefully put the little creature in her palm.

"Such fine workmanship," Alanna cooed.

Will held his breath in joy and terror. Here was the image from his dream. The creature perched in Alanna's small hand.

"A griffin? No. The feet are wrong for a griffin. A dragon perhaps? And the wings…" She tilted her head closer to Will.

Alanna's fragrance was intoxicating. She smelled of damask roses and wild thyme. Will felt light-headed, alone with Alanna so close.

"This is remarkable, Will." Her face was near to his, her expression smitten.

Will closed his eyes for only a moment to steady himself. Then he reached to retrieve his possession. His nearness to the girl made him light-headed. He slowly inhaled through his pursed lips to steady himself.

It was the look on his face that startled Alanna so suddenly. A mistake of proximity, crossing some invisible line. When Alanna turned toward Will, she saw his bow lips and heavy lids. With a gasp Alanna was quickly on her feet and the creature left her hand as though taking flight. Before it hit the stone floor, Will caught the carving single-handed. He turned in time to see Alanna disappear through the door, her sketches held tight in her hand.

As Will considered what to do next, he heard the heavy door to the ruin bang shut. "Wait! Alanna! Please wait," he yelled, running through the ruin. When he reached the door he could hear her pony cart moving up the lane. He yanked the door handle, but it did not budge. She had locked him in the ruin. Will felt ill. He sank to the ground and leaned against the locked door. He had made a great mess of things, just as it seemed he and Alanna might become friends. Will groaned to think what she would tell her grandfather. He might even lose his position.

The last light in the sky faded fast. Only a sliver of moon hid among the clouds. Will looked around. He did not want to spend another night locked in the ruin. Nor suffer the embarrassment in the morning when someone would come to let him out. If Johnny could find a way to escape, so could he. Will had an idea how Johnny managed it. And if Will was right, he would sleep in his own bed that night.

Back in the keeper's hut, Will was unable to sleep. If not for the circumstances he would have felt good about finding the hidden way out of the locked ruin. Instead, he lay awake considering what to do next.

Come morning, he could wait for someone to return and unlock the ruin. Or he could clean himself up, put on fresh clothes, shave his face, and present himself at John Shanks's front door. For what purpose? He could claim he was there to check on Master Shanks's recovery. He would take along one of his recent finds—a small piece of prismed glass. He might be able to offer a quiet apology to Alanna, should she make an appearance. But such a thing was difficult to imagine. Whatever the outcome, Will was certain of this—he was not going to wait at the ruin wondering when someone would return.

Will carefully chose the time of day for his arrival at John

Shanks's home. Too early would be unacceptable. Too late and he might encounter Alanna. Midmorning would have to do.

Shanks's house girl answered the door and let him in. When Will explained he was there to see Master Shanks, a concerned look crossed the girl's face. Will could hear Shanks's voice from the other room.

"How many times must I tell you? I do not require your wishful prayers for my healing. All such matters are in the hands of the Almighty, whose divine wisdom should not be questioned. God's plan cannot be altered by your supplications, nor mine. Man must trust that God knows best and will act accordingly in the world. If Dr. Calder does his best and I mend well, we shall offer our prayers of thanksgiving. Now get out. And do not come back unless I call for you!"

A red-faced clergyman shot past Will and out the front door. Will considered leaving, too. It seemed a bad time for an uninvited appearance. But the girl was already announcing his arrival.

"Will," Shanks called loudly. "Come in!" His voice was no longer gruff. Will could only assume Alanna had yet to tell her grandfather about locking him in the ruin. "Sorry to disturb you, uninvited," Will began. "I only wished to see—"

"I am improving every day," Shanks interrupted. "Thoughtful of you to come visit. It will not be long before I am back in the ruin again. Sit a minute. Tell me, have you found anything new while digging?"

Will was just taking a seat when Alanna burst into the room. "Grand-Dey? What do you prefer for lunch today? Some broth, or a bit of the leftover…oh!" Alanna froze. Will stood up and lowered his eyes, embarrassed.

"Will is here to visit me. Isn't that thoughtful? Yes, I will have the broth today. And bring enough for Will to join me."

"No, I cannot possibly…" Will began.

"I insist," Shanks said.

Alanna blushed. "Yes, Grand-Dey," she replied without looking at Will. "I'll see to it myself. Then I have errands to run." Clearly, she had not discussed Will's behavior with her grandfather.

Will wanted to apologize. Or at least let Alanna know there had been no ill intentions. He only wished to be her friend. *Only.* The word seemed misplaced. He was in awe of the girl. In the chapter house he was intoxicated by Alanna's closeness. It had stirred unfamiliar feelings—painful and otherworldly. Could a person survive a friendship with someone who made them feel that way? Will wished to be back in Alanna's good graces as quickly as possible. But now the fate of their friendship seemed entirely in her hands.

Isaac Forsyth was a veteran traveler.

After Shanks injured his ankle, Forsyth volunteered to deliver Alanna's sketches to the Works Committee. He knew the road between Elgin and Edinburgh and did not mind long coach rides. He would happily lose himself in a book for the duration of the journey.

Forsyth's message about the change in plans pleased Robert Reid. He enjoyed Forsyth's company much more than the old ruin keeper's.

Once in Edinburgh, Forsyth personally delivered the sketches to Robert Reid's offices. Although Reid was not in, he had left word about meeting for supper at his favorite tavern.

Though neither man drank strong spirits, they both enjoyed a good piece of beef, properly prepared. They spent the evening discussing old friends and the latest news from abroad. They talked about books and art. Only after the pudding arrived did Forsyth return to the purpose of his visit. "It is kind of you to entertain me, Robert. I know your time is precious."

"Oh heavens. Every man's time is precious," Reed replied. "Although some are more aware of that fact than others."

Forsyth dabbed his napkin at the corners of his mouth. "If you have questions about the architectural sketches once you examine them, do let me know. I have other business here in Edinburgh before returning home."

"There is a new book shop opened on the High Street," Reid volunteered. "The owner possesses some interesting volumes. But I suppose you already know that."

Forsyth nodded and smiled.

"I wish you better luck than I had purchasing books from his collection. It remains unclear whether the man is more booklover or bookseller."

Forsyth laughed. "I fear I am just such a man myself. It's how I amassed my library. That inability to let loose of any book I truly love."

"And you have many loves." Reid smiled.

Forsyth cleared his throat. "About the drawings—we hope they provide the committee what they need to approve the work."

"Agreed." Reid nodded. "It would be good to start on the chapter house roof before winter arrives in Elgin."

"The sooner the better." Forsyth smiled at his friend. "None of us are getting any younger, and that includes the chapter house."

"Speaking of just that"—Reid motioned to the server and ordered two small glasses of brandy. "May I speak plainly about John Shanks?"

"Of course, Robert." Forsyth leaned closer. "If you are concerned about his work in the ruin, I can assure you…"

"It's not that." Reid sipped his brandy. "I know he is a feisty old goat. I do not mean to insult your friend. There is no question of his passion for Elgin Cathedral ruin. Yet what I find myself questioning is…" Reid knew what he wanted to say but worried Forsyth might think it harsh.

"His judgment?" Forsyth guessed.

Reid sighed. He could feel the bags under his eyes drooping. "We are all getting older. And for some, judgment gives out with age."

"At present I'd say the man's bad leg is his primary weakness," Forsyth replied.

"And I am sorry for that. Truly I am." Reid sighed. "Please convey my best regards for his fast recovery. But let me say this, Isaac. I am very glad you are in Elgin to give guidance when needed."

"And keep an eye on things?"

"I did not say it. But yes, that, too."

Forsyth considered the liquor still in his glass. "I am certain you and Shanks share a greater vision of Elgin Cathedral, although you do not always see eye to eye."

Later that evening, Reid stood alone at his desk and unrolled the chapter house sketches. Although he had no preconceived expectations, he was surprised by what he saw. He had not thought to ask Forsyth who prepared these sketches. Reid just assumed the town had employed someone from Aberdeen or Inverness. Not the best talent, but good enough. Everyone knew the best draftsmen in Scotland were in Edinburgh, and most were employed by Reid.

Yet there was something impressive and different about these drawings. He judged them to be equal parts art and craft. There were exterior elevations of the chapter house, and interior views of the center column and windows. Even thumbnail sketches of selected images from the interior walls. Reid had handled more draftsmen's sketches than he cared to recall. But never had he seen the likes of these. Everything he expected was there on the page, in the proper placement. The measurements were neatly penned and so was the label: Chapter House Elgin Cathedral, Elginshire, along with the year.

After appreciating what was spread before him, Reid adjusted his glasses. He ran a finger down the sketch to find the name of the draftsman. Instead of a name there were initials: *A.M.O.S.* It was puzzling. His office was filled with sketches from all around the country, but Reid was certain this was not the work of anyone he had seen before. Which meant the sketches were the work of a novice. Fascinated by the renderings, Reid made up his mind to meet the man who drew them.

27

A Tourist in the Ruin

Will wisely kept his distance when Alanna returned to unlock the ruin.

Aside from her cold-voiced "Good morning," the girl remained silent. Clearly, she had not spoken ill of him. His food baskets remained generous, and he could not imagine Alanna intentionally poisoning him.

When Morrison unlocked the ruin, he shared news with Will about Shanks's mending leg. James Thompson was good company, but his visits were always short. Otherwise, Will's life was quiet and lonely without Shanks in the ruin. Isolation gave Will too much time to think. Visits home were equally difficult since his father was no longer speaking to him.

Will jammed his shovel into the rubble. "What is wrong with me that I am no longer on speaking terms with two people I care for?" He knew he could not be a ruin keeper's assistant and keep his friends. And he could not work for Shanks and be the son his father wanted him to be. Will was thinking about running away from his problems when he heard a voice outside the wall.

"Hallo?"

Before Will could reply, a man stepped into the ruin. "Oh! There *is* someone here. Am I in the right place?"

"That depends. How can I help?" Will offered.

The stranger was a nervous-looking fellow, tall and thin, with a neck and head that reminded Will of a turtle. "I have come a long way to see the Pictish pillar." He glanced around and his Adam's apple bobbed. "The Elgin Cross I believe you call it. I was hoping for a tour?"

Will removed his work gloves and rolled down his sleeves. Some part of him wanted to shoo this man away. Tell him to come back some other time. But it fast occurred to Will this was an opportunity he should not squander. He ran his left hand through his hair and wiped his right hand on his trousers. "Where do you hail from, sir?

"I came from Aberdeen, on my way to Inverness. From there I will head home to Oban on the west coast. Have you heard of it? No matter. The important thing is I am in the right place!" He let his eyes travel around the ruin, his mouth agape. "Just as it was described," he murmured.

Will offered his hand. "My name is Will Clachan, sir. I am the assistant ruin keeper. I would be glad to give you a small tour."

"Excellent! My name is Daniel MacLean." He circled the Elgin Cross before squatting down for a better look. "The detail is amazing!"

Will proceeded to tell MacLean everything he knew about the Pictish pillar, from its recent discovery to its placement in the ruin.

"Any idea how old it is?" MacLean asked.

"Not exactly sir. Most likely it dates to before Christianity came to this region."

"And the expert you mentioned. I am fascinated to learn there is such a profession as a Pictologist. Do I have that correct? The name you used just now?"

"Aye." Will nodded.

"I had no idea," MacLean murmured. "In the Western Hebrides where my people are from, we have our share of these stones, although nothing quite like this. And I daresay, to the best of my knowledge, we have not been visited by a Pictologist. But I have been away from home too long." MacLean knit his bushy brows in consternation. "For all I know my daughter might have married a Pictologist by now."

Gauging the man's interests from his questions, Will guided MacLean through the ruin. He told the story of the Wolf of Badenoch and saved the chapter house for last. MacLean sat on a stone bench and gazed up, slack-jawed.

"May I ask, sir, how you came to find us?" Will inquired. "How you first heard of our Pictish Cross? Was it in Aberdeen?"

"No. It was in London. My business took me there and I stayed for some time. Not long ago a colleague showed me a pamphlet. It was a register of historic ruins scattered throughout the countryside. Your venerable cathedral ruin was on the list, and it mentioned the Pictish pillar. Elgin was the only Scottish ruin listed in the pamphlet. I made up my mind there and then—when I finally left London for home, I would find Elgin and see this Pictish stone. I am not disappointed. I'll have you know, there was no mention of this chapter house in the pamphlet's description. Can you imagine?" MacLean gawked at the ceiling.

Out in the ruin grounds, Will related the story of the cathedral's purloined roof, and the eventual collapse of the Lantern of the North. "I am sorry I have no refreshment to offer, sir," Will said. "The town is just down the lane. There is a hotel and a boardinghouse where you might find a meal and a place to stay."

"I was in town earlier and will return for the night. I'll have you know I plan to write my associates in London and tell them what an amazing ruin this is." MacLean shook Will's hand and thanked him. But at the door he hesitated. "I was wondering"—he looked around the ruin. Then he pointed at the ground. "Might I have a small souvenir to take with me?"

"A souvenir, sir?" Will was unsure what the man had in mind.

"Just one wee rock from the ground would be nice."

Will thought MacLean might be drawing his leg, but the man was serious. Will shrugged. "Take your pick."

MacLean hesitated. "Um, would you choose one for me?"

For a moment Will thought the man daft. But MacLean's expression vouched for his sincerity. Will scanned the ground. He took a few steps and picked up a piece of rubble small enough to hold in a hand. Before presenting it to MacLean, Will examined it. It was nothing special. Destined for a barrow ride to the Witches Pool. Except now it would be leaving with a man bound for Scotland's west coast, where he would likely show the piece of Elgin Cathedral ruin to his family and friends. "This looks like a fine one," Will said, handing over the rock.

MacLean rubbed his thumb over the stone's surface.

"If you have no further questions, sir, I should be getting back to work."

MacLean reached into his pocket and produced a coin. "For your trouble. Many thanks. I shall not forget this day."

As MacLean left, Will considered telling Shanks about the visitor. But for now, he would keep his thoughts to himself.

Will heard voices in the ruin.

Returning from the Witches Pool he hurried to see who was inside. Although he would gladly welcome another tour-seeker, he was in no mood for intruders. To Will's surprise it was his father and the lord provost, Peter Nicholson. They stood talking near the transept wall.

"Father!" Will called, relieved to see familiar faces. "I was not expecting you."

"Yet here we are." Da's voice was calm. "Today we are cutting the cornerstone for the lord provost's new house." Nicholson smiled and stepped away. "The stonecutters will be here soon," Da added. "But do not let us interrupt your work, son."

"I need to fetch my barrow," Will replied and quickly left the ruin. Will's heart raced. He could not believe his father had put him in such a difficult position. "I must tell someone," Will murmured. It would take time to cut and remove the stone once the workers arrived. But there was no reason for Will to delay. No reason to tell his father where he was going. He would run all the way to John Shanks's house.

Will had not gone far when he met Morrison's wagon in the lane.

"I am relieved you are here. I was on my way to see Master Shanks," Will blurted, "but maybe you can help. My father and the lord provost are at the ruin and plan to cut a cornerstone for Nicholson's new house. What should we do?"

"Nothing," Morrison said. "Master Shanks knows about the cornerstone. The town council gave their approval last evening."

Will stared at Morrison in disbelief.

"I was surprised, too, Will. Shanks said to continue your work as best you can, but do not hinder theirs."

A dumbfounded expression crept across Will's face.

"I imagine this is not easy for you." Morrison hesitated. "Shanks does not wish to come between you and your father."

Will nodded.

"It's good the work will be done while Master Shanks is out of the ruin," Morrison added. "To that end, how would you like to run errands with me for the rest of the day?"

Without comment, Will climbed into the wagon.

Much later, after dropping Will at the keeper's hut and locking the empty ruin, Morrison stood in Shanks's parlor. Hat in hand, he nervously tried not to toe the carpet. Until Shanks's injury, Morrison had rarely stepped inside the shoemaker's home. His business with Shanks was routinely conducted elsewhere. At the ruin, or in carriage houses, stables, and shops. But the old ruin keeper's immobility changed all that, and it was not a change Morrison enjoyed. He would be glad when Shanks was back on his feet.

"Well?" Shanks stared hard at Morrison. "Will they be finished and gone tomorrow?"

"I believe so, sir. The stonecutters are making good progress. But there is one more thing you should know."

"Some new problem?" Shanks sighed.

"No, sir. Something good, I believe. Worth the telling."

"Go on, then. What is it you want me to know?"

"When I was on my way to the ruin, Will came running down the road. He was nearly halfway to town."

Shanks cocked his head. "Where was he going?"

"He was coming here to tell you that his father and Nicholson were inside the ruin preparing to remove a stone." Morrison watched Shanks consider this news.

"The boy continues to surprise me," Shanks said softly.

After Morrison's departure, Shanks thought about Will's decision to put his work ahead of loyalty to his own father. Shanks would not have thought such a thing possible when he chose Tom Clachan's son as his assistant. Will had proven himself—guarding the Elgin Cross, rescuing Shanks when he injured his leg, and reporting a perceived transgression. Shanks felt a new respect for the boy and the emotion was not unwelcomed. It seemed Will Clachan was becoming his own person.

The day the last cut stone was carted out of the ruin, a rush of emotions stirred Will's heart. The stonecutters had returned for one last job, bringing with them the workaday sounds of their trade. There were plenty of familiar faces, but Will no longer felt like he belonged.

The cornerstone was strapped to a sturdy wagon, ready to be hauled away.

The last stone cut from the ruin was escaping its ancient origins to become part of something new. "Just like my cousins," Will mumbled. "Off to some new purpose while I'm left with the rubble."

"Will!" Tom motioned his son to join him. His clothes and boots showed evidence of a hard day's work. But his back was straight, and his shoulders squared.

The happy look on his father's face surprised Will. It was an expression he thought he might never see again. Yet here it was, now that his father had what he wanted from the ruin—without Will ever possessing the key to let him in.

Tom grasped his son's arm. "I want to show you something."

Near the Pans Port Tom trailed his rough hand along the wall's masonry until he found what he was looking for. "This is what I want to show you, son. Right here."

Will scanned the perimeter wall, unsure what he was meant to see.

"This fragment of wall. See where the mortar changes? It's from the medieval precinct wall. Centuries ago it was part of a much taller curtain wall protecting the cathedral."

Will stroked the rough stones. "How old do you think, Da?"

"It might be the oldest remaining part of the cathedral," his father reflected. "More than five hundred years, I suspect."

"And the rest of it?"

"Carted away to build new structures. Not so different than what we did here today. Carting off a bit of history." He patted the ancient piece of stonework and smiled at his son.

Will wondered where this version of Da had been hiding these many months. He watched his father run his hand over the stonework—the old part, the new part, and the connecting mortared joints.

"Almost no one knows about this piece of precinct wall. That's why I'm showing it to you, Will. We found this ancient section while building the new wall, and I decided not to knock it down. Instead, I added it to the new wall so it wouldn't be lost. It may be the most important work I've ever done."

Will ran his hand over the old stones.

Tom touched his son's shoulder. "This bit of wall was likely built by one of your distant relations. Always remember. We were builders. That is what my father and my father's father and his father's father have been. Stonecutters and builders all. Our ancestors built and rebuilt this great cathedral, and the town of Elgin, too. Never forget that, Will."

"I will remember, Da."

The stonemasons loaded the last of their equipment and moved off down the road. Soon after, Morrison arrived with Alanna to lock the ruin.

"How is Master Shanks?" Will asked politely, expecting Morrison to answer.

"Improving, thank you," Alanna replied. "His physicians visited today. They believe he will soon be back on his feet. It was welcome news for Grand-Dey, as you would expect. Still"—she exchanged a meaningful look with Morrison—"the doctors have cautioned him not to overdo."

"I look forward to seeing him as soon as he is able." Will wondered how Shanks would navigate the terrain in the ruin with a gimpy leg.

"Miss Alanna," Morrison said, "I promised your grandfather I would inspect the ruin after the stonemasons left. But I will be quick about it." As Morrison disappeared into the ruin, Will turned toward the keeper's hut.

"Please wait," Alanna whispered. At arm's length, she offered Will a folded paper dangling from her gloved fingertips. "It's for you," she said, her eyes lowered. "I am truly sorry." Her cheeks flushed. She was still not looking at him.

"Why?" Will's question hung in the air. He considered stepping near enough to retrieve the paper.

"I am sorry it is not perfect," she said quietly. "The best I could do from memory."

But before Will could retrieve the paper, Morrison stepped out of the ruin and Alanna retracted her hand.

"All's well, miss. We can lock up now."

Will stayed as Alanna locked the ruin.

"See you tomorrow, Will," Morrison said.

"Oh wait. I nearly forgot," Alanna said. "Grand-Dey asked me to bring an extra basket of sweet buns for Will. I left it in the wagon." Moving more like a girl than a young lady, Alanna bounded away and returned with a small basket. "Grand-Dey said to thank you for taking care of the ruin while he's been abed. And he looks forward to everything returning to normal when he comes back to work." She gave a little nod and passed the basket to Will as though it held something special.

The basket sat on the table in Will's hut, tempting him with fresh-baked smells. The rolls were uncovered but still untouched. In his hand Will held Alanna's folded paper. She had tucked it beneath the napkin, between the rolls. For some reason he could not bring himself to unfold it. He kept thinking through what had happened while Morrison was in the ruin. He wanted to understand what Alanna was trying to tell him when she first offered him the paper. But he could not quite remember all she had said: "Wait…for you…not perfect." And "…thank you…sorry…back to normal…." As much as he wanted to open the paper, he feared what might be inside. Words written to break his heart all over again.

As night fell, Will lit the lamp and snatched a roll from the basket. The folded paper made him angry, but with whom he could not say. There was much in his day to be thankful for, especially his conversation with Da. And if he left the paper folded, he just might sleep. Will kicked off his boots and lay on his bed. He recalled his father's smiling face telling him about the old precinct wall. But the folded paper was not going to let him be. A little voice in his head chanted, *What if, what if, what if…*

"Enough!" Will whispered, grabbing up the note and quickly

unfolding it.

To Will's surprise, there was nothing written on the paper. Only a small sketch. A right-size sketch of his stone creature, or something close to it. *Not perfect,* he could hear Alanna's voice in his head. *The best I could do from memory.*

28

THE BACK END OF THE YEAR

Daylight waned and twilight thickened.

Autumn escorted a North Sea chill into Elgin. Even in Will's young bones he could feel the seasons changing. He did not need a calendar to tell him All Hallows Eve was at hand. He had startled several young boys at the Witches Pool bearing burlap bags. Stuffing down their fears, the boys foraged for frogs and toads and salamanders. They lay on their bellies, arms outstretched into the reedy shallows. Will had once done the same, faking fearlessness in the company of peers. It was a boyhood custom to brave a trip to the Witches Pool and capture some unfortunate toad. The creatures were used to startle unsuspecting siblings and grannies on All Hallows Eve.

Absorbed in gigging a frog or catching a salamander bare-handed, the boys jumped and squealed when the rubble from Will's barrow hit the water. Will was keeping an eye out for his youngest brothers. Even though Ross and Andrew were forbidden by Mam to visit the Witches Pool, those same rules had never kept Will and Luke from coming here.

"Anyone seen a great crested newt?" Will asked the boys. "Black with yellow stripes on the belly. I might trade you something for it—if it's still breathing." Young eyes grew wide, imagining such a creature. Will enjoyed teasing these boys. Although they were easy to startle, they were not afraid of Will. Even if he was dumping cathedral rocks into the Witches Pool.

When the boys were gone, Will stood near the pool listening. The wind swished the reeds making them whisper and dance. A toad croaked rhythmically, filling the air with news that he had not been caught. The breeze in the trees was like a hushed conversation. But there were no incantations. No mumbles from ghosts or hags. For that, Will was grateful.

Returning from the pool at the end of the day, Will saw Alanna locking the ruin. He nearly called to her, but she seemed eager to be on her way. They had not talked since she gave him the tiny sketch. He hung back as Alanna turned her pony cart toward town. He liked the way she squared her shoulders and held the reins in her gloved hands. He watched her go—until he sensed someone else was watching, too. At the edge of the woods Will caught sight of a man in a raggedy kilt disappearing into the shadows under the wych elm trees.

"It's Johnny," Will hissed. Will broke into a run. By the time he reached the woods there was no one in sight. It was disquieting to think Johnny was back in Elgin. Where had he been and why was he wearing an old kilt? An uneasy feeling spurred Will to run down the lane. If he could not find Johnny, at least he could assure Alanna's safe arrival home.

It did not take long for Will to have Alanna's pony cart in sight. What he saw next chilled his heart. Something Alanna had not yet noticed. Coming out of the woods, a man was running full-out toward Alanna's cart. It was Johnny alright, although his face seemed haggard.

Will called to Alanna, but he was too late. Johnny grabbed the pony's reins and the small beast jumped sideways, nearly tipping over the cart.

Alanna shrieked and the pony twisted in its harness, whinnying and wild-eyed.

Will lunged for the cart, trying to protect Alanna. But the sudden appearance of both Johnny and Will confused the girl. She pulled away, unable to trust anyone.

Johnny grabbed at Alanna's skirts as he tried to climb into the cart. She whipped the pony, then snapped the whip in Johnny's face. He scowled and fell to the ground. Regaining control of the reins, Alanna did not look back. The pony moved out fast with Alanna leaning in the direction of home.

At the side of the road, Will lunged at his cousin. Johnny rolled to his feet. A line of blood trickled down beside his eye—Alanna's doing. Will successfully ducked a punch and missed with a swing of his own. They were both breathing hard, grunting and cursing. Intent on tearing each other apart. Will tried to push Johnny to the ground. His cousin kept his balance, only losing a shoe. Johnny kicked Will's feet out from under him, landing Will facedown in the road. Will got up in time to see Johnny disappear into the woods. A quick flash of color as the late-day light caught Johnny's kilt among the trees. The faded red grid on a green field of cloth, the old Murray of Atholl tartan.

Will needed to know Alanna was safely home. On any other day he would not have hesitated, but this was All Hallows Eve and the light was fading fast. "Be quick about it," Will muttered. He wiped his nose on his sleeve, ignoring the smear of blood. Then he plucked Johnny's muddy shoe from the road. Evidence of his attempt to protect Alanna. It was no more than a thin piece of tanned hide punched with holes for a length of leather lace.

Will arrived at Shanks's town house in time to see a gray-haired stable groom leading away Alanna's pony. Will tapped the man on his shoulder and the groom yelped. "Heavens, boy! You should know better than to scare a soul like that on All Hallows Eve."

"Is Miss Alanna safely home?"

"And what would you know about that?" The groom looked Will up and down, assessing his appearance.

"I fought off the scoundrel who attacked her."

"She went straight into the house and was very upset," the groom said.

"Is she unharmed?"

"As best I could tell."

A sudden loud noise from the center of town startled Will. The groom glanced at the sky. "I need to be about my business, and home safe before dark. I suggest you do the same." He tugged on the pony's reins and hurried toward the stables.

Will lingered in front of the town house just long enough to see a lamp lit in a corner room upstairs. He turned away. He wanted to find Morrison before returning to the ruin. Will took a last glance over his shoulder. He thought he saw someone at the edge of the curtain in the upstairs window. It might have been Alanna, or the house girl. He could not be certain.

Will was anxious to talk with Morrison about Johnny's attack on Alanna. He stopped at Morrison's rooms, but the man was out. Catching sight of a familiar-looking errand boy, Will left word. "Tell Morrison I saw Johnny today right here in Elgin." No last name was necessary. Morrison would know.

In the street men were piling logs and brush into barrels, preparing to set them afire at dusk. Will had no interest in lingering. A head full of twice-told tales about the goings-on after dark on All Hallows Eve was sufficient to fuel his imagination. With the possibility that Johnny was abroad in Elgin, he felt compelled to hurry back to the ruin.

Inside the keeper's hut, Will barred the door with a chair. Johnny's presence in Elgin on Hallowe'en unsettled Will to distraction. It was not a fear of spell-casting fairies that frightened him. It was the people who believed in witches, and devils, and demons. In Elgin, good people knew better than to be out-of-doors on All Hallows Eve. Good people stayed home. Tonight, the bonfires would be lit to keep evil spirits away. Some folks would dance in the streets, others would tell tales. Many would make mischief—some of it innocent, some of it not. For others, it was a night for courting—if you believed in such folk stories, which Will did not. Mam and Da had taught him better. A hidden frog in a drawer to scare Mam was the extent of All Hallows Eve. The holiday made Da grumpy. "Folk should have better things to do than revisit the old Samhain rituals." And although Mam enjoyed Robert Burns's writings, of his poem "Halloween" she had said, *He did us no favors with that one.*

Davie and Walt stood at the edge of the crowd on the High Street.

Alcohol-fueled voices cackled and howled. The noise and the bonfire smoke were disquieting. The boys craned their necks to see what was happening. But mostly, they were looking for girls.

Davie yelled into Walt's ear, "I thought there would be girls our age."

"We've been misled, brother. Believing we might meet a fine lass here on All Hallows Eve. Ha! There's no one here but old folks scheming and screaming and getting drunk."

"I definitely thought there would be more girls," Davie repeated.

"I thought there'd be food," Walt sighed.

A smelly old sot wobbled toward them. He began to speak, then turned and vomited into the street.

"That's it," Walt said. "Let's get out of here."

"Which way?"

Davie pointed past the crowd. "I wonder what Will is up to tonight."

"Do you think he's at the ruin?" Walt asked.

"I expect so."

"I've got an idea." Walt waded into the crowd, motioning his brother to follow.

"Walter!" Davie hollered over the noise, using his brother's full name to gain his attention. Their mother had named him for Sir Walter Scott in a dreamy maternal moment. Walt hated that name, so most everyone called him Walt. "What are you up to, brother?" Davie wanted to know.

"Follow me." They navigated through the crowd and reached the road to the ruin. "Let's go pay Will a visit," Walt said. "Give him a scare. Just for fun. What do you say?"

Davie shrugged. "Better than staying here."

Walt grabbed an unattended candle lamp as Davie pinched a mostly empty whiskey bottle from the fist of a sleeping drunk. "I think he's had enough, don't you?" Walt laughed. With their backs to the bonfires, they left the crowd behind. Where the road skirted the woods, Walt retrieved a downed tree branch and stripped its leaves. He hung the lamp from the stick to light their way. As the bonfire glow receded their eyes began to adjust.

"Next year there will be no need for bonfires in town," Walt said. "Gas lamps will be lighting the streets."

"Do you think it might happen?" Davie asked as they walked.

"Da says it's for certain. The town council has passed a resolution."

"That will change things."

"Aye," Walt agreed. "Can you imagine Hallowe'en with gas lights?"

"Spoil all the fun." Davie glanced over his shoulder. "If you can call that mess fun."

Walt tended the lamp to make certain it did not gutter and go out. "Speaking of fun, how should we give Will a scare?"

"We could pull our coats over our heads and pretend to be disembodied spirits," Walt suggested. "Or use our shirts to look like ghosts haunting the ruin."

"I can laugh like a witch." Davie demonstrated his cackle, and something took flight from a nearby tree. The boys startled. Then they laughed and shoved each other.

"Careful! We have no way to relight this lamp if it goes out."

"We should find some sticks to beat against Will's hut while we make ghostly sounds," Davie suggested.

"As many spooky noises as we can," Walt agreed.

"We'll give him a good scare!" Davie laughed.

"All good fun, no harm done. The three of us will laugh in the end," Davie insisted.

"And we can offer the whiskey to calm his fright." Walt gestured to the bottle in Davie's hand.

"And then," Davie's voice softened, "we'll have a good visit. I miss our cousin."

"Aye, it will be fun to be with him again," Davie said sincerely.

"Right after we scare the wits out of him!"

Deep in the grove of wych elm trees, not far from the keeper's hut, someone else was making plans. A harvest moon played hide-and-seek behind the clouds, but it did not illuminate Johnny. He was well hidden. Mangled as he was, it did not matter. Johnny touched the pouch hanging round his neck. Empowered by hate, he felt invincible. The past would always be the past. The future was unknown. He could only own the present. He patted his pocket. All was well. The source of his power was there—a flint and a fistful of Lucifer matches. No light was necessary for what came next. Raising a full bottle to his lips he took a long swallow. The rest would fuel the flame.

Taking no chances, Will barricaded himself inside his hut, intending to stay put until daylight. Tomorrow he would find Morrison. He would visit Shanks to be certain Alanna was unharmed. The night was quiet. Will's All Hallows Eve vigilance soon melted into exhaustion. When his lamp burned low, he fell asleep leaning against the barred door.

Davie and Walt paused behind a large tree. They could see the keeper's hut. "Would you say he's asleep or awake?" Davie asked.

Walt hesitated. "Does it matter?"

"Suppose not."

The brothers tried not to snicker. With sticks at the ready to beat on the hut, the boys paused. "Should we put out the lamp?" Walt asked.

Davie looked at the sky. The clouds were bright, the moon hidden. "We can see well enough. The lamp's nearly out anyway." As the brothers moved toward the keeper's hut, a sudden high-pitched yell shattered the quiet. A chill of fear shot through both boys as they saw a great fireball emerge from the woods. It was moving fast.

"What the...?" Davie yelled. Then he saw the figure. Someone was running full-out toward the keeper's hut, the fireball swinging faster and faster. Before Davie and Walt could think what to do next, the fireball arced through the air and landed hard on the roof of the hut. On impact, the flames burst skyward as the dry thatch caught fire.

"Run!" Walt yelled.

"Which way?" Davie screamed.

"You get Will! I'll go after...*that*!" He pointed at the runner.

As Davie reached the hut Will yanked open the door. Bits of spark and flame were raining down inside. "Get out, get out!" Davie pulled Will through the door.

Will grabbed his bucket and ran to the rain barrel. Frantically he tossed water onto the roof making the flames dance and hiss.

A sudden painful cry came from beyond the ring of firelight. "That would be Walt," Davie explained. "He's chasing down the demon who did this."

"Go help him!" Will insisted.

Davie shook his head. "First we've got to put out this fire!" There was no time to argue. The roof was still aflame. Will and Davie filled the bucket again and again, dousing the burning roof.

"Will!" Morrison's cry startled the boys. They had not heard him arrive. He had grabbed a horse blanket from his wagon and was climbing onto the burning roof. He beat down the remaining flames with the blanket. Will used the last of the water in the rain barrel to douse the tiny embers dancing on his bed.

Morrison spied a shadowy figure in the darkness approaching the hut. "Who goes?" he hollered.

Will grabbed Morrison's arm. "Wait!" The harvest moon slid from behind the clouds. Limping slightly, Walt emerged from the darkness with a big stick grasped in his fist. His nose was bloodied and his clothes torn.

"I beat him off," Walt said to Will. "Tried to capture him, but he got away," he told Davie. "He ran into the woods." Walt was breathing hard.

"Who ran into the woods?" Morrison asked.

"Johnny Murray!" Walt said, spitting blood from his mouth. "The bugger," he added under his breath.

Morrison was still confused. He looked from Walt to Davie. "What are you two doing here at this hour?"

"Good question," Will agreed. "Though they may have just saved my life."

"Is the fire out?" Walt asked, looking at the roof.

"It is," Morrison assured him.

"What brought you two here tonight?" Will asked his cousins.

"We came to visit you," Walt said.

"Sort of," Davie added.

"On the way here, we thought it might be fun—"

"Being Hallowe'en and all," Walt put in.

"We thought it would be fun to scare you a bit first. Make some ghost sounds outside your hut."

Morrison gave the two boys a stern stare.

Walt picked up the story. "But just as we reached the lane, we saw a fireball moving through the darkness. It came out of the woods, flying toward the keeper's hut."

"It nearly scared the shite out of us!" Davie put in.

"Then we saw a figure throw the fireball onto the roof of the hut, and that's when I rushed to rescue Will, and Walt ran off to catch the devil who torched the hut."

"I had no idea it was Johnny until I knocked him to the ground," Walt added. "I bloodied him good, before he got away from me."

"Are you certain it was him?" Morrison needed to know.

"I am," Walt said, "and here is proof of it." He held out his clenched fist. Dangling from Walt's bloodied hand hung a small leather pouch at the end of a broken cord.

Will took it from Walt. All three boys nodded knowingly. "It's his alright," Will said. "If you do not mind, Walt, can I keep this for now?"

"I suppose. Though it would make a fine trophy to go with the telling of my story." Walt looked up at the burned roof. "But you can have it."

"Thanks, Walt." Will wrapped the cord around the pouch and tucked it away.

"How did he do it? The fireball, I mean," Davie asked.

Morrison hoisted himself back up onto the roof and looked around. "This," he said, cautiously toeing something with his boot. It was heavy and still steaming when it rolled off the roof and hit the ground with a thud. The boys gathered around for a close look. Pieces of a burned shirt were stuck to the fire-blackened rock.

"He must have wrapped the rock in the shirt and lit it on fire," Walt said. "Then used a hammer throw to launch it up on the roof."

"Christ!" Morrison cursed. He took a last look at the roof to assure the fire was truly out before climbing down again. Morrison pointed at Will. "We're lucky the whole hut didn't burn to the ground with you inside! Let's make certain nothing is still smoldering. Then I'll take you boys home." Morrison motioned to Davie and Walt. "And Will, you'll come along, too. You can sleep on my floor until morning. We'll clean up this mess tomorrow."

"What about Johnny?" Will asked, wishing for his own moment of revenge.

"He'll not be back tonight. The damage here is done. But tomorrow I'll hunt that devil all the way to the sea if I must!"

Will took one more look inside the hut. He quickly found what he was looking for, pocketed it, and shut the door. Weary beyond words, everyone climbed into Morrison's wagon and headed back to town.

29

Ruination and Reflection

The smell of smoke jolted Will from sleep.

He looked around, confused. Then he remembered. He had spent what was left of the night sleeping on Morrison's floor. The smell was coming from his clothes piled nearby. Morrison had provided a clean shirt and a blanket so Will would not have to sleep in burned clothes.

Will was eager to sort out the condition of his belongings back at the keeper's hut, and anxious about his own fate. As he started putting on his smoky clothes, he noticed a shirt and a pair of corduroy trousers folded on a chair. Even a clean pair of stockings.

"Are you up, Will?" Morrison called from the other room.

"Aye, sir. I am," he answered, running a hand through his singed hair. "Can you tell me..."

"You need to wash up before you put on those clean clothes." Morrison seemed impatient. "I've arranged for you to have a bath at Mrs. Hendry's boardinghouse."

"What?" Will started.

"I've just come from there myself." Morrison was clean and

groomed. A far cry from the man's appearance only hours earlier.

"No, wait. I…"

"No arguing now. Your condition is bad enough to merit a bath. Put on your singed clothes and carry these others with you. The boy who helps me now and again—the one you left the message with yesterday—is waiting outside. His name is Jimmie. He will escort you."

"I do not need an escort," Will insisted.

"Fine." Morrison said. "Jimmie will go with you to Mrs. Hendry's."

"Is this truly necessary?"

Morrison was undeterred. "Jimmie will stay until you are done. Mrs. Hendry will give you some breakfast before you bathe. Now get going. Master Shanks will be waiting for us by the time you return."

Will felt suddenly ill. What would the old ruin keeper say about the events of last night? Will had good reason to fear whatever might come next. But first, he was about to have a proper bath in a boardinghouse. Something he had never done before.

Will walked to Mrs. Hendry's in silence. Jimmie carried the clean clothes. He stayed a few paces ahead of Will, who looked and smelled bad enough that even the errand boy preferred not to stand too close.

The boardinghouse door flew open when Jimmie knocked. "Merciful holy hell!" a beefy woman exclaimed, staring hard at Will. Her form filled the doorway. She smelled of bleach and starch, and something unpleasantly sweet. Her hands remained lost among the folds of a skirt that covered her wide hips. "You look like something the Devil belched out!" she said.

Will stepped back, but the woman took hold of his collar and propelled him inside.

"Wait!" Will tried to pull away, but he was no match for this woman's powerful arms. Firmly she guided him deeper into the house. At the entrance to a room with an open door, he was pushed inside with firm instructions. "Everything off!" she told Will. "And you!" She pointed at Jimmie. "You wait right here with those clean clothes and do not move until I say."

With the boy stationed just outside the room, the woman gave Will some last instructions. "When I say everything off, I mean everything. Breakfast is there on that table. Eat up fast. Then into the tub before the water gets cold."

The woman seemed old enough to be Will's mother, but much bigger and scarier. He turned his back as she stepped out, and he heard the lock bolted. In the center of the room stood the largest tin tub Will had ever seen. A fire was lit in the hearth, making the room cozy. A white sheet was draped across the narrow end of the tub and neatly turned back just enough for Will to step into the water. A few pottery jars and a large bar of soap sat on a table close by. Two breakfast buns and a mug of cider were laid out on a tray. Will ate the food with minimal chewing. He carefully removed his trousers and Morrison's shirt, along with his stockings and boots. Then he stood contemplating the tub. A loud rap on the door made him jump. His heart raced.

"Are you in?" came the woman's gruff voice.

Will heard the lock slide open and saw the door handle turn. "Wait!" he hollered. Quickly, he slid into the water, exhaling from the pain and pleasure of immersion. Before Will could think what to do next, the door began to open. Embarrassed, he squeezed his eyes tightly closed so he would not see the woman looking at him.

"Give me those clean clothes," she snapped at Jimmie. Then the door banged shut. Her heavy step crossing the room shook the tub, even with the weight of the water and Will sitting in it. "Lean back and keep your eyes closed," she ordered. Will obeyed. She draped a warm, wet cloth over his eyes. "Now arms up. Show me your hands." Will did as he was told, and she placed the cake of soap in his palms. "Now wash. I want you to wash yourself good and clean. Be quick about it! Then we'll wash that hair." The soap held the same scent as the woman, along with other herby smells. Scents he would prefer not to reek of if he had a choice—which he did not. "Use this cloth to wash your face and neck and all. And keep your eyes closed."

"May I sit up?" he asked.

"Aye, but no peeking."

He wondered what difference it made if his eyes were opened or closed, seeing as how he was the naked one. Anyway, he preferred not to look at his torturer. After following her instructions, washing every inch of his skin, the smoky smell began to fade. Even if the herbal scent lingered, it was an improvement. Will leaned back in the tub again. A fresh cloth was placed over his face. A new fragrance filled the room. Will heard someone fiddling with the pots on the table.

"Thank you, Martha. I will take over now," the voice was sweet and young.

"You're welcome, ma'am," the large woman replied. The door opened and closed.

Will jumped at the sound of the new voice. He tried to sit up, but soft hands now held his head firmly in place. "Not so fast. We need to do something with this hair."

The hands began gently massaging his scalp. "Who are you?" Will sputtered.

"Mrs. Hendry, of course. Be still now and let me finish. Your hair is badly singed."

While Mrs. Hendry quickly snipped and clipped his hair, Will tried to solve the puzzle he had created, mistaking the large woman for the proprietress.

"There, that's better. Now give me your hand." She touched a metallic handle to Will's palm, and he grasped it. She removed the cloth from his face. "You can open your eyes now." Will obeyed. He held a woman's hand mirror reflecting his scrubbed face and trimmed hair. Sharing his reflection was the very young Mrs. Hendry. One of the prettiest women Will had ever seen.

Will was left alone to dress. After pulling on the clothes Morrison had provided, he discovered his own clothes were missing. Rushing from the room he ran into Jimmie.

"About time," the youngster grumbled. "Thought you would never come out."

"I'm looking for my clothes," Will urgently appealed to the boy.

"You have them on," Jimmie answered.

"Not these clothes. Never mind, where's Mrs. Hendry?"

"Saw her go out the back."

Will ran toward the rear of the house. "Mrs. Hendry!" he called. "Mrs. Hendry?"

In the kitchen, the mountainous Martha blocked his way. "Yer not supposed to be back here."

"I'm searching for my trousers. Have you seen them?"

Hands on hips, Martha looked Will up and down. "You have them on," she pointed out as though he might be daft.

"Not these corduroy trousers!" Will seethed. "The singed ones I was wearing when I arrived."

"Those rags? I tossed them in the garbage heap out back. Nothing worth saving but the buttons." Martha produced two buttons from her skirt pocket as evidence.

"Show me!" Will pushed past Martha.

She pointed out the back door. Will took the rear porch steps two at a time. He found the reeking bin and held his breath to reach inside.

"What's all this?" Mrs. Hendry had joined Martha on the back porch. "Come away from there," she ordered Will. "We just got you clean."

"Not until I find my trousers." He did not need to dig far. The discarded clothing was beneath the morning's kitchen garbage. But it was not the rotting smells that made Will feel sick. He snatched the trousers from the bin and thrust his hand into the pocket.

"Whatever are you doing?" Mrs. Hendry asked.

Will's hand found the folded paper and the leather pouch. He quickly stuffed both into a pocket of the corduroys. He searched the old trousers for his creature, but it was not there. Will went weak in the knees and his stomach sickened.

"We need to go," Jimmie called to Will. The boy stood with the women on the porch. "Morrison will be angry."

"You're going to be dirty again before you have a chance to be clean," Mrs. Hendry insisted.

Will rooted around in the garbage as his eyes filled with tears. At last, beneath a scattering of hair clippings, his fingers found a familiar friend. Will tightly squeezed the carved creature in his fist where it stayed until long after he hurried from the boardinghouse.

Will was out of breath when he climbed into Morrison's wagon.

Morrison shook the reins. "Took you long enough." Will was in no mood to talk. They had not gone far when Morrison sniffed the air between them. "Are you certain you got a bath?"

"I did," Will mumbled, "but I did not care for the soap."

As they made their way through town Will asked, "Are we not going to see Master Shanks?"

"Forsyth might bring him to the ruin later."

Will was surprised. "Is his ankle mended? Is he up and around?"

"I have not seen him standing."

"Later is good." Will nodded.

"It will give us time to check the damage," Morrison agreed.

"And clean things up before Shanks arrives."

"We will do what we can," Morrison said.

Morrison's assessment of the damage to the keeper's hut was straightforward. "The roof looks worse than it is," he told Will. Plenty of black singe, but the thatch did not burn deep—except where the flaming rock landed. It's a small enough hole. If it cannot be repaired, you might find another flagstone in the ruin to cover the worst of it."

Will wasn't convinced. The damaged door would need to be rehung, and the inside of the hut still stank of smoke. While Morrison busied himself outside, Will inventoried his losses. He would need to repair the chair damaged during his escape, and the globe for his lamp was shattered. Unfortunately, the burn hole in the roof was directly over his bed. His blanket and bedding were badly singed. Will had kept the suit of good clothes carefully bundled in an old clean cloth and tucked under his mattress. He was relieved to find the clothes had survived.

Then Will remembered Alanna's sketch and pulled it from his pocket. His heart ached. The tiny drawing was damp and badly damaged by sparks and soot. There were stains from Mrs. Hendry's garbage pile. It made Will sad to see the sketch in its present condition, but he would not throw it out. It was, after all, a gift from Alanna.

Shanks was not a man who could sit and do nothing.

When his convalescence dragged on, he drafted a treatise about Elgin Cathedral. A collection of stories interspersed with ruminations on life, religion, and society. When his eyes grew weary, Shanks kept Alanna and the housekeeper busy setting his home to rights. By the end of his convalescence the sitting room had been repainted, the cushions restuffed, and new artwork hung on the walls.

Shanks wrote regularly to the Scottish Works Committee and Robert Reid. Instead of answering Shanks directly, Reid wrote to Forsyth requesting patience. "Elgin Cathedral is among many properties needing funds," Reid explained. "And Shanks is like a wasp I cannot swat away. I plan to visit Elgin, but I cannot yet say when." Reid did not mention his burning curiosity about A.M.O.S. and the chapter house drawings.

When the pain in his foot subsided, Shanks had planned his return to the ruin. He designed custom-made crutches and sent for a trusted woodworker. To assure a proper fit, the woodworker asked Shanks to stand. With help from Alanna, he complied, but it was still painful to put weight on his foot.

The doctors were summoned. The swelling was down, and it appeared his ankle was mending, but the physicians remained concerned. "The persistent pain in your foot is likely from a small crack in one of the bones," Dr. Calder informed Shanks. "With time, it may mend on its own. More likely, it will remain difficult to ignore."

Morrison had been sent to fetch tools and supplies from Shanks's workshop. The old shoemaker knew a thing or two about customizing a boot. There were ways to support a bad ankle and pad an insole to reduce pain. Shanks was determined to get back on his feet sooner than later.

On the morning after All Hallows Eve, the news of the keeper's hut fire spurred Shanks into action. He sent word to Forsyth and called for Alanna. Nothing would stop him from returning to the ruin. Supported only by the crutches, Shanks felt faint. Alanna encouraged her grandfather to sit awhile longer. "Sip some broth. There's no need to rush," she told him.

"Take your time," Forsyth agreed, troubled by Shanks's frail appearance.

After a few trips around the room with the crutches, Shanks prepared to leave the house. With the help of Alanna and Forsyth, he made his way down the front steps and into a waiting carriage.

The afternoon was nearly gone when Morrison and Will heard Forsyth's carriage approach. When Shanks attempted to climb down, everyone jumped to lend a hand, even Forsyth. Shanks was pale and shaky. Will wondered how long the old man would last before needing a proper place to sit down. And Will's only chair was broken.

Shanks sniffed the air. His eyes settled on Will. "What's this I hear about a fire?"

"It's good to see you, sir," Will offered.

"Yes, yes. Go on. Start from the beginning," Shanks insisted.

Alanna's eyes darted between the roof of the hut and her grandfather's face.

"It was very late, and I was asleep." Will looked to Morrison for confidence. "I was awakened by a commotion outside the hut. Something heavy landed hard on the roof. Sparks flew in all directions. The door was stuck closed. Then someone pulled me out."

"Was it Morrison?" Shanks asked.

"No, sir. It was my cousin, Davie."

"What was your cousin doing here in the middle of the night?" Shanks demanded.

"He came to visit—"

Morrison interrupted, "His cousins were in town for All Hallows Eve and stopped to see Will on their way home. It was lucky timing, indeed. They were helping Will put out the fire when I arrived."

"And they chased off Johnny Murray, who set the fire," Will added.

"Johnny Murray?" Shanks asked.

"The boy who hid in the ruin, Grand-Dey," Alanna gently put in. "Remember the one I told you about?"

"Yes, yes. Of course."

"He is also a cousin of mine," Will confessed. Morrison surreptitiously stepped on Will's boot to silence him.

"Who chased off this devil of a boy?" Shanks wanted to know.

"My cousin Walt," Will said. "Walt tried to capture him, but Johnny escaped into the woods."

"And this Walt. Who is he?"

"Another cousin," Will said. "A good cousin."

Morrison stared hard at Will, discouraging him from saying anything more. "In the end," Morrison concluded, "Will's two good cousins chased away the man who committed this crime. And they also helped put out the fire."

"How did the fire start?" Forsyth asked.

"He wrapped a large rock in an alcohol-soaked shirt," Morrison explained. "Lit it, and then flung it up onto the roof."

"Heavens!" Forsyth exclaimed.

"When I arrived, the fire was nearly out, thanks to the boys' fast work. The roof will require repairs, and the furnishings in the hut will need replacing."

"Goodness! The fire was inside the hut, too?" Alanna asked.

"Yes, miss. I'm afraid so," Will replied.

Shanks was beginning to sag. He took a few steps and repositioned himself closer to the carriage. "Morrison, what were you doing out here at that time of night?"

"Will had left me a message. He thought he had seen Johnny earlier in the day and wanted me to know the boy might be back in Elgin. That Johnny might…" Morrison hesitated. "That he might be following Alanna with ill intentions."

"Heavens," Alanna whispered, retreating to her grandfather's side. "It was that dreadful boy who tried to steal my pony cart."

"I believe we owe Will our gratitude," Forsyth said. "It seems he has proven to be a vigilant keeper."

"Yes," said Alanna. "Thank you, Will."

Morrison added, "I have already alerted the sheriff. Word is out about Johnny Murray. If he remains in Elgin, he will not be on the loose for long."

Will earnestly hoped to never see Johnny again.

"Meanwhile, miss," Morrison said to Alanna, "it would be wise not to drive or walk alone. Please let one of us escort you."

"Very good advice." Forsyth nodded.

"Yes, my dear," Shanks agreed. "And now that I am back on my feet, you will not need to venture out on your own."

Forsyth circled the keeper's hut and briefly stepped inside. When he emerged, he quietly said to Will, "I have an extra mattress and bedding going unused. I will have them sent out in the morning."

"Thank you, sir. I will do my best to repair the hole in the roof."

"We will see that things are put to rights," Morrison added.

Will had feared he might be cast off by these people after the events of the previous night. Instead, they were treating him like a friend.

30

ROBERT REID, MASTER OF WORK

The Master of Work to the Crown of Scotland was in an ill-tempered mood.

A letter lay on Reid's desk from the Inverness City Council, a group that regularly tried his patience. The letter concerned a few unexceptional antiquities found in some shopkeeper's window. The council alleged the items had once belonged to the medieval Blackfriars—religious men who left Scotland at the time of the Reformation and never returned.

When the Blackfriars departed Inverness, they entrusted their land and all earthly belongings to their patrons, the Cuthbert family. In due time, the assets were claimed by the Inverness City Council. In the sixteenth century the council created a comprehensive list of these assets. Three hundred years later, the list was still used to identify and reclaim items the council considered stolen property. It came in handy whenever some long-missing item resurfaced.

As head of the Scottish Works Committee, Reid was responsible for adjudicating these claims, forcing him to travel to Inverness. Reid cared little about the Dominicans' chalices, crucifixes, and altar candlesticks. Although he did find it curious that these items of gold and silver were once owned by religious men who took vows of poverty. What Reid cared about were the last remains of the Blackfriars, buried in a patch of ground in the center of Inverness. Only a small plot survived from what was once a larger cemetery.

The last item in the council's letter was the cause for Reid's irritation. Evidence of digging in the Blackfriars' burial plot, and speculation about grave robbers. Reid was infuriated. Clearly the Inverness Council was not taking good care of the ancient burial ground. He worried someone might damage the fifteenth-century gravestone of Alexander Stewart, Earl of Mar. It was a life-size stone carving of a knight in armor, an important piece of Scottish history. The news of encroachment and failed grave robbing fired Reid's anger. For this he would drop all else and make a trip to Inverness before the weather grew cold.

Reid tossed the letter onto his desk and turned to the cubbyholes lining his office walls. They held drawings for dozens of building projects. Reid knew the exact location of the plans he wanted. The Elgin chapter house drawings always made him smile. After Inverness he would journey on to Elgin.

Reid dreaded the road—the endless uncomfortable carriage rides, poor accommodations, and bad food. The scenic countryside no longer awed him. There was just too much of it. The possibility of adventure or some fascinating discovery no longer enticed him. The city of Edinburgh had spoiled the great architect. "I must be getting old," Reid muttered.

In Inverness, Reid wanted the Blackfriars' property sorted as quickly as possible so he could move on to Elgin. But it proved to be a weary week in the company of the town council. Reid loathed these men. Imbeciles, the lot of them, waving their tattered parchment lists in his face. It took days to convince them of what he had come for. "I will sign off on these acquisitions under one condition," he firmly informed the council. "Sell these candlesticks and use the proceeds to pay for an iron fence and a locked gate around the Blackfriars cemetery."

The councilmen stalled and grumbled.

While waiting for the council to see things his way, Reid caught cold in the rainy damp of Inverness. When his business was concluded, Reid contemplated going home instead of traveling on to Elgin. He decided to see how he felt in the morning. Suffering chills and congestion, he did not venture far for supper. A strong drink and a bowl of soup in a nearby tavern were all he wanted. Bent over the steaming bowl set before him, Reid overheard a fellow patron.

"Aye, I've just come from Elgin," the man told his companion, "and I should have stayed. The weather in Moray is lovely right now. Sunny and cool."

"Sunny," Reid wistfully sighed. He pulled a handkerchief from his pocket and gingerly blew his sore nose. *Maybe,* Reid thought, *if I go to Elgin all the decisions about the ruin can be addressed, and the work will begin.* Reid was desperate to end the river of correspondence from Shanks flowing across his desk. He hoped his visit to Elgin would settle matters once and for all. But there was one more thing. He might meet the mysterious A.M.O.S. And if A.M.O.S. was all that Reid imagined him to be, he planned to offer the man a position with his firm in Edinburgh.

Before leaving Inverness Reid dispatched three messages, each with the same news—he was on his way to Elgin.

Reid arranged for a carriage from Inverness to Elgin. The rest of his plans could wait. With his messages on their way, Reid went back to bed to nurse his cold. One more day and night in Inverness. He hoped he might feel better by the time the carriage to Elgin arrived.

Forsyth, Shanks, and the lord provost were each surprised by news of Reid's imminent arrival. That was Reid's intention. The short notice would work to his advantage.

Forsyth set about arranging a comfortable stay for his friend. It was not long before John Shanks and Peter Nicholson appeared at Forsyth's door with their own messages in hand. Together they discussed the importance of Reid's visit.

"If only we had known sooner," Nicholson said.

"He may not want us to make a fuss," Forsyth speculated.

"But he is Master of Work to the Crown," Nicholson insisted, knowing firsthand that titles came with expectations.

"Robert and I are old friends," Forsyth stressed. "I will offer to lodge him here. If he prefers the hotel, I will assure the best room is available."

The lord provost was concerned about protocol. "Shouldn't we have a reception? A welcoming committee? Certain people must be notified. The Earl of Fife, the Gordons, and the Innes family. He must be properly welcomed."

"Reid was very deliberate in who he notified," Forsyth insisted. "If Robert intends to meet with the earl, no doubt the earl received his own message. I believe Reid is coming on business and we should act accordingly. Clearly his intention is a meeting with the three of us."

"He will want to tour the ruin," Shanks insisted. "Inspect the walls and examine the chapter house. Hopefully he will have news about a new chapter house roof."

"That is my assumption, too," Forsyth agreed. "When Reid arrives, we will make him welcome." Forsyth looked hard at Shanks, and continued, "Before riddling him with questions."

"Precisely," Nicholson agreed. He pointed at Shanks. "And if it must be a dance, for heaven's sake, John, let the man lead."

Reid slept through most of his trip to Elgin. Although the journey seemed long, the carriage was new, and as comfortable as the roadbed allowed. Tucked up with warm woolen blankets and a flask of hot tea and whiskey, Reid continued to sleep off his cold. When at last he arrived in Elgin, his symptoms were mostly gone.

It was a welcome relief when Forsyth invited Reid to be his guest. "You have no idea how pleasant your invitation is, my friend. I have come from rainy Inverness, lodging in a leaky hotel, and I am just over a bad cold. Your hospitality is appreciated."

"Would you like to go straight to bed?" Forsyth asked kindly. "Supper is planned for just the two of us, and I will take no offense if you prefer to rest."

"I cannot pass up supper with you, Isaac. It will give us time to talk. Then I will retire. Sleeping in a carriage is no substitute for a bed."

Forsyth gently guided Reid to a seat by the fire. "Tomorrow we will tour the ruin with Nicholson and Shanks. And discuss other matters that brought you to Elgin."

Will was surprised when Shanks announced Robert Reid was coming to the ruin. "During his visit I want you working as you normally do," Shanks said.

"Are you certain, sir? Wouldn't it be better if I wore my good clothes and stood close by in case you need anything? Or might it be best for me to be out of the way altogether?"

"No. I want Reid to see our accomplishments and be reminded of the rubble we have cleared. I want him to know our work is very deliberate. Not just some old man's hobby."

"Yes, sir. I will keep working and stay out of the way."

"Excellent!" Shanks patted Will's shoulder. "I know I can count on you, boy."

Robert Reid smiled as he entered Elgin Cathedral ruin. The air was brisk, and the sun warm. Pausing to take it all in, Reid felt a familiar shudder of awe. It was just such a moment that led to his life's work. There was nothing like the beautiful remains of what was once an architectural wonder. Even the presence of John Shanks could not ruin his day. Reid was immediately drawn to the Pictish Cross. Focused as he was on the chapter house project, he had nearly forgotten about the pillar. Reid had inspected numerous Pictish stones but none quite like this one. He closely examined the ancient masterpiece, running a hand over its surfaces. "Well!" Reid exclaimed, "this is quite a find."

"It was a joyful day when we moved that stone into the ruin," Nicholson said.

"We were sorry you could not join us," Shanks chimed in.

"We are very pleased you are here now," Nicholson added.

Following a fine night's sleep and an excellent breakfast, the unexpected pleasure of seeing the Pictish Cross added to Reid's good mood.

"Shall we examine the choir and transept walls?" Nicholson suggested.

They made their way through the ruin on recently cleared pathways.

Reid ran his hand along the old stone walls.

"We had these walls plumbed and they appear to be stable," Nicholson noted.

"For now," Shanks added. "After your inspection, we would appreciate your thoughts on adding support buttresses."

"I would like to talk with the mason who plumbed these walls. Can that be arranged?" Reid asked.

Nicholson replied, "We will send for him at once."

"Must we?" Shanks countered.

"That is my preference," Reid said.

Returning from the Witches Pool, Will saw the group of men as he entered the ruin. They stood close by the landslide of rubble near the remains of the west wall. Shanks, Forsyth, Nicholson, and another man that Will presumed was Robert Reid, were deep in conversation

Will took up his shovel and went straight to work. He purposely positioned himself with his back to the men. He was close enough to hear much of what was being said without appearing to eavesdrop.

Robert Reid looked nothing like what Will imagined he would be—the Master of Work to the Crown. Reid was tall and broad-shouldered. He wore the trousers and shirt of a workman, yet his wool coat and boots were very fine. His head was bare, and his hair was thinning. His nose was rather large. His chin was square and without whiskers. But it was the man's hands that surprised Will most. Large hands as rough as any workman's. If this was the famous architect, clearly the man did more than sit in an office with ruler and compass.

"With so much broken masonry piled against these walls, it is difficult to judge how much buttressing might be necessary," Reid said. "Hard to say whether the rubble is putting stress on the walls—or helping hold them up."

The other men nodded.

"Much has been done since I was here last," Reid said to Shanks. "Clearly, you have been hard at work."

Leaning on a shovel, Shanks stood straighter. He had abandoned his crutches that morning, not wanting to appear weak in Reid's presence.

"Most likely these walls will require additional support when more wreckage is cleared," Reid said. "In the meantime, I suggest you continue your efforts, especially along this west wall. I will be anxious to see what remains to be discovered here. I remember in my research some mention of bishops' tombs. That was some time ago and I do not recall the source. The truth is none of us knows what is buried here."

Now we have a new purpose, Will thought. He wondered if he alone would continue digging out the west wall. Or if someone might suggest more men to speed the process. But no one did.

"We can discuss funding for the buttresses once we know the scope of the work," Reid concluded. And with that the group moved on to the chapter house.

It surprised Will that Shanks seemed satisfied with Reid's answer regarding the buttresses. But with his back to the conversation, Will had not seen the stern look the lord provost gave Shanks, ending further discussion.

Nicholson hailed Will and sent him off to fetch his father. "You will find him working on my new house. Take my wagon. Find him and bring him back here forthwith."

Will did as he was told.

Reid led the way into Elgin's chapter house. It had been years since his last visit. After examining the A.M.O.S. sketches he was eager to see the actual structure once more. He was in Elgin because of the chapter house roof, but first he needed to satisfy his artistic eye. Reid scanned the interior walls and admired the beautiful column. The late morning light illuminated the space. He would take his time and not be rushed. Before the day was over, these men would learn to be patient with him.

Although Shanks was eager to get on with discussing the new roof, the expression on Reid's face kept everyone quiet. What thrilled Reid most was the confirmation that A.M.O.S. had captured the magic of this place in a set of architectural drawings.

At last Shanks cleared his throat.

Without looking at Shanks directly, Reid began to talk. "I have done extensive research on the octagonal chapter houses from this period. As you may know, the cathedrals at Wells, Salisbury, Truro, Liverpool, York, and Westminster were all built with octagonal chapter houses. Elgin is the only one north of Hadrian's Wall. It is most likely, but impossible to prove, that the thirteenth century master mason Henry of Reyns, designed them all."

The Elgin men nodded enthusiastically.

"Given the dimensions of this building and the apparent condition of the walls, I believe the best material for a new roof should be flagstone shingles. However, before committing to a final decision, I wish to have a closer look." Reid turned to Shanks. "I assume you have ladders that we can use for such a purpose?"

Reid's question caught Shanks by surprise. He had not considered a man like Reid would climb up to the rooftop. When Shanks stammered, Forsyth came to his rescue. "We can arrange for ladders to be brought out."

Reid frowned. "Let's move outside."

"Later we will retire to my home for supper," Shanks offered. "The ladders can be delivered to the ruin while we eat. We can return before the light is gone. Then you can climb up and see for yourself the poor condition of the roof."

The huffiness in Shanks's voice amused Reid. "I do not doubt the roof needs replacing, John. But I need to see its condition firsthand. That is what I came for—an accurate assessment. We must be certain the walls are not bulging near the roofline, which is often the case with buildings this age. The next step will be to have workmen deconstruct a small portion of the remaining roof to look for wood rot."

"Can't that wait until the project begins?" Nicholson asked.

"It could," Reid replied. "However, since I am here, I would like to see for myself. Then I will have a better idea how much needs to be cut away and what needs to be reinforced. We will reuse as much ancient oak in the roof's structure as possible." Reid had everyone's full attention. He had ventured into a discussion of detailed matters none of them had considered.

"Reusing pieces of the ancient oak is an extra expense, but well worth it," Reid told them. "It takes time to select and cut suitable blocks from the old timbers. Ancient oak becomes extremely hard as it ages. It takes longer to cut than new oak."

Nicholson asked, "Isn't there an easier, less expensive way?"

Reid laughed. He wanted to think the lord provost's question was not seriously asked but knew better. "This will make for an interesting conversation, gentlemen. No need to rush bringing the ladders," he told Shanks. "Tomorrow will be soon enough. If you could arrange for a workman to assist me up on the roof tomorrow morning, it will speed things along. My hands are not as nimble as they once were." He smiled at the lot of them. Only Nicholson was younger than he, and all of them had the hands of gentlemen. To his surprise, even Shanks. Then he recalled Shanks had been nursing an injury, which explained the lack of fresh blisters on his hands.

"Here is the mason you asked to speak with," Nicholson told Reid, as Will and his father entered the ruin. To Shanks's surprise, Tom Clachan offered his hand and introduced himself to Robert Reid. "At your service, sir. My son tells me you asked to speak with me."

"Are you the mason who recently plumbed these walls?" Reid asked.

"I am," Clachan confirmed. "I have plumbed them regularly over the past many years."

Tom looked down the length of remaining transept wall. "For a structure of this age, I can assure you, sir, it has fared well. There has been some settling as sandstone falls from the exposed mortar."

"I see." Reid realized this man with the Pictish features was a mason who had previously worked in the ruin.

"Unfortunately, I cannot say the same for the choir walls," Clachan continued.

"Are they as fragile as they appear?"

"Yes, sir, I would say so."

It was not Reid's place to give a history lesson. He could contain his words, but not his thoughts. Since the abolition of bishops within the Scottish Church in 1689, ownership of this abandoned cathedral fell to the Crown. But no attempt to save the building took place until the Scottish Works Committee was formed. Now, here he was surveying the remains of what was once an impossibly splendid cathedral city. The fantastic structures were built in Moray when there was nothing else remarkable in the region. Reid could visualize the towers, the walls, and the village within the cathedral grounds. All built to glorify God.

Reid pointed skyward. "The cloisters were supported by a double row of pillars. The original design was unlike any other cathedrals in this country during that period. It is assumed the plans for Elgin Cathedral must have come from France or Italy where such designs were already in use. My assumption, as a scholar and an architect, is that the architectural plans for this cathedral were brought by the Italian Freemasons of that time."

"If I may, sir." Tom Clachan looked to Reid for permission to speak and Reid nodded.

"My ancestors were likely among the stonecutters working during that era. Constructing walls and foundations that lasted for centuries here in Elgin."

Reid's hosts were uneasy about a common workman addressing the esteemed architect. But Reid seemed comfortably engaged in his conversation with Tom.

With a smile the stonemason said, "Our hands were not designed for the beautiful workmanship the Italians brought to our shores. Lifelike angels and bishops emerged from the stones under their skilled hands."

Reid nodded, and Clachan tilted his head deferentially. "Those are the stories I was told as a child, by my grandfathers."

John Shanks squirmed at being outdone by a stonemason.

"I cannot deny Elgin Cathedral was once unmatched in form and ornamentation," Reid said to Clachan.

Later, when the four men took their seats around Shanks's table, they seemed an odd group. Although Reid and Forsyth were old friends, their conversation did not reflect it. Reid spoke about the reason for his trip to Inverness, and his insistence on building a locked fence around the Blackfriars graveyard. "You were wise to build the wall around the ruin when you did," Reid noted, "although I recall it was not a popular decision."

"True," Shanks said, "but it has served us well."

"I hear more frequently of city dwellers traveling to visit ruins all across Britain," Forsyth offered.

"So I have heard," Nicholson agreed. "Gentlemen in the cities are coming to realize they can experience ancient wonders without a trip abroad."

"True, but Moray is no Tuscany," Reid assured them.

"Something to consider." Forsyth smiled at Shanks. "Before long, you might be both ruin keeper and tour guide."

As the first course was taken away and the second delivered, Alanna entered the room carrying a silver basket filled with hot rolls. The cook followed with the fish course.

"Thank you, my dear." Shanks smiled. Noticing Reid's look of surprise at his familiarity with the girl, Shanks explained by way of introduction. "This is Alanna, my granddaughter. Alanna, this is Master Robert Reid from Edinburgh."

Alanna curtsied. "A pleasure to make your acquaintance, sir." She nodded to the rest of the gentlemen before returning to the kitchen.

"A blessing to have a fine girl who can cook," Reid attempted a compliment.

"It is the least of her talents, if you must know," Shanks replied.

"She is a smart and talented girl," Forsyth added.

"Speaking of talent"—Reid dabbed his mouth with a napkin—"there is another matter I wish to discuss."

"Do tell us what is on your mind," Shanks offered, glad for a change of subject.

"I must be honest. I have much admired the sketches of the chapter house you supplied. I know the names and talents of most every draftsman in Scotland. But I have never heard of your A.M.O.S. While here, I hope to meet the man."

Shanks choked on his wine. In the kitchen, a plate clattered to the floor.

"That may not be possible," Forsyth replied lightly.

"Does he not reside nearby?"

"Aye," Nicholson said.

Forsyth recovered quickly. "We can inquire about A.M.O.S.'s availability."

"Is A.M.O.S. the man's actual name?" Reid wanted to know.

"The one used for work," Shanks explained.

"Can you tell me his given name?"

Alanna reentered the room carrying a full carafe of wine. She refilled the men's glasses, starting with Robert Reid. "I sincerely hope you are enjoying your visit to Elgin, sir. I have heard so much about you from Grand-Dey and Master Forsyth. It is an honor to have you as our guest." She batted her lashes and Reid was charmed.

"Why, thank you. Alanna, is it?"

"Yes, sir. That is my name." Everyone looked at Alanna. The expression of intrigue on the young girl's face was priceless, but she gave nothing away. She curtsied and slipped back into the kitchen.

Shanks endeavored to change the subject. "Robert, might you share with us your thoughts on a start date for the chapter house roof?"

31

REVELATIONS

Robert Reid was perched at the top of a ladder propped against the chapter house.

He took a moment to appreciate the view. Compared to Edinburgh, the Moray countryside was pastoral bliss. The trees were taking on autumn colors and the air was crisp and clear. He had spent the morning locating the damaged sections of the roof. Two young workmen on ladders followed Reid's instructions. They carefully cut samples from the ancient wooden beams. Reid needed the samples to determine the extent of rot and decay caused by the passage of time. He had seen worse.

While pulling away a rotted ceiling brace, something captured Reid's attention. He had exposed a section of wall that had been hidden from sight. It took Reid a moment to realize what he was looking at—the top of a beautifully sculpted little head. It was the head of a stone angel peering down into the chapter house. She was peeking from behind feathery wingtips that covered most of her lower face. The angel's eyes were impishly sweet, as though she were eavesdropping on conversations below. Positioned as it was, the small sculpture could only be seen from the acute angle Reid now held. It was difficult to contemplate why such a fine piece of medieval work had been purposely hidden from view. A petite bowed head in a shadowed recess. Reid could imagine the carver intentionally concealing his small masterpiece, existing for its own sake to the glory of God. Such unusual finds added to the wonder of Reid's work. One never knew what might be revealed when deconstructing an ancient building.

"Gentlemen!" Reid called from his perch. "There is something here worth climbing a ladder to see!"

The ladders remained in use throughout the day. Reid was not one to rush things. From his vantage point, he had noticed the roof on the keeper's hut just outside the wall. Some sort of fire had blackened the thatch. Then the boy who had carted rubble all day stepped inside the hut. "One more project to discuss," Reid mumbled.

That evening Reid and his hosts gathered in Forsyth's parlor. Each man had a glass in hand, although not all contained the same liquid. Over a light meal, Reid had walked them through his findings. He shared his proposed plans, along with his intentions for the Scottish Works Committee to fund the new chapter house roof. "Flagstone shingles from the nearby quarry are the material of choice for this job," he told them.

"How can you be certain?" Shanks wanted to know.

"What I saw today assured me the structure can support flagstone roof shingles. They are lighter than granite and less likely to chip than slate. With tiles we would need to worry about their weight. That is why we will use the thinner shingle. The central column and the interior vaulting both appear sound, stable, and in good condition," Reid explained. "That's one more reason I do not believe the chapter house roof was ever covered in lead. Its medieval roof appeared to use shingles made from ancient hardwoods. That is what saved the chapter house for us. If its roof had been covered in lead like the rest of the cathedral, it would have been removed at the same time. And the chapter house would have met the same fate as the collapsed cathedral. At some point the shingles were repaired and a second layer added."

"You could tell all that from peeking under the roof?" Nicholson asked.

"Yes. The work we did today assures me that a new flagstone roof will not collapse the ancient walls. Many of the supports are still as firm as stone. Those that are not can be replaced during the project."

"That's a relief to hear," said Forsyth.

"The two young men working with me today were familiar with the challenges of removing the rotted sections and replacing them with new timber. They told me they recently worked on the roof of St. Giles. Their skills are fresh and will come in handy once our project begins."

"Labor is a topic we need to discuss," Shanks put in. "I for one would prefer to employ the very best skilled labor. Shouldn't such a piece of history be repaired by the most experienced laborers? Certainly, the best ones are working for you in Edinburgh."

Reid did not appreciate the direction Shanks was leading the conversation. "I thought you would want to use local workmen from Elgin," Reid said to the lord provost. "I cannot imagine the masons and carpenters of Elgin taking kindly to imported labor."

Shanks did not give Nicholson an opportunity to answer. "My concern is for the quality of the repairs, and I would like us to have the best."

"Were there labor problems with the work on St. Giles?" Reid wanted to know.

"No, sir," Nicholson replied. "We have plenty of capable workmen here in Elgin. As lord provost, I feel I must state the obvious. Who better to hire than the stonemasons who quarried the ruin for generations?"

Always the peacemaker, Forsyth quietly added, "John, I am certain an important issue here is timing. We have waited years to begin this project and now we are ready to start. It is likely…" he paused to look sidelong at Reid, "very likely, if we use Elgin men for the work, we can get a quick start and begin before the first snow flies. With the St. Giles project completed, we have men available right now here in Elgin. If you insist that we use workmen from Edinburgh, where Robert has more projects underway than he has laborers to keep up…" Forsyth shrugged. "Robert, am I correct in assuming it might be some time before you would have men available to send to Elgin?"

"I must be honest with you, John," Reid said in his kindest voice, "if you insist on using laborers from Edinburgh… Well, let us just say that you and I will likely be in our graves by the time that happens."

Shanks startled.

Reid pressed on, "Let us commit to a swift beginning, and I will see to it the funds for the roof are expedited through the committee. Hire your men, let us secure the best materials, and begin. There are such treasures on the walls inside the chapter house. We should move quickly to protect the interior from further exposure to the elements."

Reid, Forsyth, and Nicholson raised their glasses. Begrudgingly, Shanks joined in. "To a new roof!" Reid toasted. "Which reminds me, John. While I was up on the ladder today, I noticed the hut with the singed thatch. The place looks a bit of an eyesore. What happened?"

"Some All Hallows Eve mischief," Shanks grumbled. "It needs more than a new roof, but all in good time."

"Who lives there?" Reid wanted to know. "The young man working in the ruin?"

"Aye. Will is a good and bright boy," Shanks said.

"Then why not fix the hut and the chapter house at the same time?" Reid suggested. "The boy could help. He seems eager enough."

"I need him clearing the ruin," Shanks objected.

"A never-ending job," Reid sighed. "A roof should not be left in ill repair, especially if you intend for that boy to guard the ruin all winter. What say you, John? A few improvements and some shingles to replace the straw?"

"As you wish." Shanks was too weary to object, if Reid was funding it.

"The two stone shingles on that singed roof—where did they come from?" Reid asked.

"From the rubble in the ruin. I plucked them out myself," Shanks replied.

"Well, there we have it!" Reid said as though a mystery had been solved. "Evidence that flagstone shingles were once used somewhere in the cathedral."

"Shall we call it a night, gentlemen?" Forsyth asked, sensing all that could be accomplished was done for the evening.

Reid held up a hand and his hosts resumed their seats. "There is one more thing." Reid lifted a portfolio into his lap. He undid the clasp and carefully removed a set of sketches. He held them out for all to see, keenly watching the tired faces around him. "I would very much like to meet this A.M.O.S."

The men's expressions alerted Reid to some mystery he had not contemplated.

Shanks was the first to reply. "That will not be possible."

"Not presently," Forsyth added, attempting to soften Shanks's stern response.

"And why is that?" Reid pressed.

Forsyth tried again, "Is there a problem with the sketches?"

"Not at all. Just the opposite. They are exceedingly good, as anyone can see. But I do not recognize the work. I would like to meet the man who made these sketches."

Reid waited. Only the crackling fire disturbed the silence in the room. "Tell me, friends, how would I go about contacting this A.M.O.S.? I would like to send a message."

Reid had raised his voice just enough for Alanna to hear every word. Ensconced in Isaac's library, she was reading while waiting for her grandfather. She had not been paying much attention to their conversation until she heard the famous architect talking about her sketches.

As Alanna tiptoed down the stairs, carefully avoiding the squeakiest steps, Reid was speaking again. "These drawings are remarkable. I am curious where this draftsman learned his technique. I just want to talk to the fellow. Tell me something about him. Where he studied, perhaps. But let's begin with his name. Who is he?"

"To what end?" Forsyth asked.

"I would like to see more of his work. If he is all I have imagined, I may offer him employment in Edinburgh."

John Shanks was shaking his head when Alanna appeared in the doorway. She stood calmly, staring directly at Robert Reid.

"Oh. Hello, child," Reid said kindly. "I apologize if we disturbed you."

With hands clasped behind her back and eyes downcast, Alanna spoke slowly in a strong, clear voice. "My name is Alanna Maria Oglethorpe Shanks. I am who you seek, sir. I am A.M.O.S. And I am a *she*, not a *he*."

Reid was astounded by the facts newly presented. "Impossible!" was the first word out of the architect's mouth. "Come here, girl, let me see your hands."

Alanna walked shyly into the room to stand before Reid. She presented her hands for his inspection. There, on the skin of her right-hand middle finger was the evidence he sought. An artist's bump stained blue-black.

Alanna locked eyes with Reid and said softly, "I wish to sketch the angel. The one you discovered in the roof of the chapter house."

"If that is your wish, Miss A.M.O.S., I shall make it so."

32

Mirth

In the ruin, scaffolding was quickly raised outside the chapter house.

"How will she get up there?" Shanks wanted to know.

Confronted, Reid explained his plan. "I have customized a sturdy chair for her to sit in with a tray in front to serve as a small drawing desk. When she is seated securely in the chair, we will hoist her up to the platform. I will anchor the chair close enough for her to see and sketch the angel."

"Have you ever done this before?" Shanks wanted to know.

"Yes, I have," Reid assured him. "One of my best draftsmen was thrown from a horse last year. For a time, he could not walk. He wanted to finish the project he was working on, but he was unable to climb the scaffolding."

"She is a girl," Shanks felt the need to remind Reid, "and she is my granddaughter. You must understand my concern for her safety."

"I will be beside her the entire time she is sketching. And I will not let her do anything perilous."

"Hoisting her to the rooftop seems perilous enough to me," Shanks muttered. He knew he could forbid Reid from taking Alanna up the scaffolding, but there was no stopping the girl once she set her mind to something.

Alanna was not concerned about her safety. If she had her way, she would climb the scaffolding just like the young workmen. She was certain she could do it, if only she could wear the right costume. A pair of her father's old breeches would work nicely, belted tight at the waist and cinched at the ankles. Up in the attic she dressed in his clothes and imagined herself as Rosalind in Shakespeare's *As You Like It*, traveling safely through the Forest of Arden. But Grand-Dey's face turned purple when Alanna appeared before him, wearing the outfit she made for herself.

"Absolutely not!" he sputtered. "Change out of those clothes at once, and do not let me see you in men's breeches ever again!"

Begrudgingly, Alanna complied. Donning men's clothing in private was not the same as being seen dressed that way in public. She decided to wear the breeches hidden under a skirt, without extra petticoats to get in the way.

When all was made ready, Shanks and Forsyth brought Alanna to the ruin. Reid and the lord provost were already there. As were the muscular workmen who would hoist Alanna to the roofline. Shanks gave firm instructions for the young men to keep their eyes to the ground as they hoisted.

"And how will we know when she's at the top? Compared to heaving pallets of stone, the girl is as light as a feather."

"I will instruct you." Shanks's face was stern. He did not want these boys looking up his granddaughter's skirts.

Reid carefully climbed a ladder to the top of the scaffolding. Once Alanna was belted into the chair, the workers quickly hoisted her up. Reid reached out to guide Alanna's chair onto the platform.

He secured it and released the hoist.

"How was your ride, Miss A.M.O.S.?" Reid asked quietly. He had taken to calling her by her pen name from the moment she introduced herself. His familiarity disturbed everyone except Alanna.

Down below, the others watched and waited. Will was there, too. They could not hear the conversation between Alanna and Reid, but they could see. Alanna shifted her position. Reid helped her adjust the chair. She opened her sketchbook and a passing breeze ruffled the pages. Reid and Alanna laughed quietly as she pegged the paper under her left forearm. Reid said something that made the girl giggle. She craned her neck to see into the chapter house. Only Reid heard Alanna's tiny gasp when she saw the angel sculpture for the first time.

Shanks was displeased that he could not hear Alanna's conversation with Reid. He felt omitted from his granddaughter's joy, and Reid's proximity to Alanna was making Shanks uncomfortable.

Alanna sketched and time passed. The men grew tired of looking up and talked among themselves. But Shanks never took his eyes from Alanna.

As Alanna sketched, Reid kept still. It was a joy to watch this gifted young artist at work. From the moment her pencil touched the paper, it was as though nothing else existed beyond herself and the sculpture below.

Reid remained mesmerized by Alanna's face, hands, and eyes. He was surprised by where she began her sketch and how she viewed her subject. For Reid it was like watching a street magician. He could not afford to look away for fear he might miss the moment when the magic happens.

Will joined Shanks and together they stared at Alanna. One sketch appeared. Then another. Alanna wanted a different angle.

The girl and the architect tipped their heads together while conversing.

Will knew what it felt like to watch Alanna's hands as she made an image come alive on blank paper. Shanks leaned on his shovel, but he was not thinking about his granddaughter's art. He was busy watching Robert Reid watch Alanna. What he saw, he did not like. "What are they doing now?" Shanks suddenly cried out.

Alanna and Reid were slowly exchanging places. Only Will had seen Reid unhook the strap holding Alanna in the chair.

Shanks began to cry out, but Forsyth hushed him. "Don't, John. You might startle her." In an instant the two had switched places.

"She is going to ruin my heart," Shanks gasped, pressing a hand to his chest.

"Best breathe, man," Forsyth told Shanks. "They need to change seats one more time before she can come back down."

"Oh, Lord," Shanks moaned.

Alanna was unaffected by the commotion below. A third sketch was underway. This one from an angle that let her see the expression of impish devilment in the angel's smiling eyes. Without looking away from her page, Alanna said quietly, "I wish I were a hummingbird. I would fly around this angel's face as though she were a flower and draw her from every possible angle."

Except for the brief conversation about swapping seats, Reid remained silent. That was their agreement. He was not to talk while she sketched. It disturbed her concentration.

On the final sketch Alanna printed the word *Mirth* beneath the angel's face.

"Mirth?" Reid could not help himself.

"Hush!" she scolded. Adding another curl to the cherub's head Alanna whispered, "Mirth is this angel's name."

Forsyth was relieved to have his house to himself again.

A confirmed bachelor, he enjoyed conversation in reasonable doses. Now he only wanted to sit in his library reading a delightful book about birds. But first he must open the letter in his hand. Reid had discreetly left it on Forsyth's desk before returning home. Forsyth broke the wax seal and began to read.

"Thank you, my friend. Without you, John Shanks and I would have never overcome our differences.

What I write here is for your eyes alone. Shanks and the lord provost will receive formal letters from the Office of Works Committee approving the work to be done in the ruin. My official seal should provide John Shanks some satisfaction. Although we are both committed to conserving Elgin's cathedral ruin, he and I seldom agree on matters of approach and timing. To that end I will do my best to summarize our salient decisions.

First. Remains of the transept and choir walls will require bracing. Digging out the west wall should begin promptly.

Second. Reroofing the chapter house should commence immediately, before winter sets in. I will see to the prompt dispatch of funds, including a supplement for labor costs. The stonemasons and carpenters of Elgin are perfectly capable of completing the work required. If concerns about qualified labor in Elgin persist, I will reply to Shanks with one word: *A.M.O.S.* If his granddaughter's skills are good enough for the Master of Work, the stonemasons of Elgin should be given the same opportunity.

Third. I shall make good on my personal commitment to fund repairs to the keeper's hut. These include a flagstone roof and a stone fireplace, hearth, and chimney. New windows, plank flooring, and a door that locks properly. Work on the hut should be concurrent with roofing the chapter house.

Last. I came to Elgin to meet A.M.O.S. with a mind to hire a new draftsman. Instead, I discovered a delightful young woman with an exceptional artistic eye. I believe she would flourish with some time abroad. I have friends who manage a small art school in Florence. I am certain they would be delighted to have her join them.

I am not asking you to be my intermediary on this matter. I am making you aware of my intentions for one reason only. If I convince Shanks to let the girl go abroad, might you serve as her escort to Florence? I anxiously await your response.

Please know that I respect Shanks and all he has done in the ruin. So it is in confidence that I share my concerns. I fear that Shanks's stubbornness may reflect his advancing years. He was not a young man when this project began, yet his diligence and dedication reflect the efforts of someone younger. Still, we must acknowledge our limitations. I pray the day never comes when John Shanks is unable to walk the grounds of Elgin Cathedral with a shovel under his arm. But in truth, we all know that day is approaching.

Your friend and confidant,

Robert Reid

Master of Work to the Crown of Scotland"

Reid kept his word. The formal documents arrived swiftly from Edinburgh. All was in order—with one not-so-minor modification. In the official letters Reid named himself as architect of the chapter house project.

Shanks was infuriated.

"It is pro forma," Forsyth tried to soothe Shanks, fully aware of the territorial battle scaling up between the two men. Forsyth dreaded the day when Shanks would receive his next correspondence from Reid concerning Alanna and the art school in Italy. He contemplated escaping to London for a time, but he had promised Reid he would watch over the keeper's hut project. And Forsyth was a man of his word.

Will was glad when Robert Reid departed for Edinburgh.

Reid's presence made Shanks angry with everyone. It puzzled Will how Shanks and Reid could both love the ruin yet dislike one another.

Will now had more company in the ruin. The masons and carpenters working on the chapter house roof frequently whistled and called to him. It was nice not to be lonely, but he wished he could join them on the scaffolding. Will's father and the lord provost frequently checked on the progress of the work.

Alanna had not returned to the ruin since Reid left Elgin. When Will asked Shanks if Alanna was well, he explained she was busy sewing and sketching. But with so many young men in the ruin, Will assumed Shanks was purposely keeping her away.

One cold afternoon Forsyth paid a visit, watching the work underway. Will's father arrived and the men stepped outside the wall together. When Will pushed his full barrow out of the ruin, his father hailed him. "Master Forsyth has a proposition, son. Come hear what he has to say."

"How may I be of service?" Will asked politely.

"Robert Reid wishes to be your benefactor, Will. He believes you are an asset to the work in the ruin," Forsyth explained. "To that end, he has decided to personally pay for repairs to the keeper's hut."

Will was speechless. His father nudged his elbow. "What say you, boy?

"Thank you, sir. Thank you."

"I am only the bearer of the news," Forsyth said. "It is Robert Reid to whom you owe your thanks. Your father has been hired to oversee the work, and you will need to help with the repairs. I have spoken with John Shanks and he has agreed."

"I am to work in the ruin and on the hut at the same time?"

"Yes." Forsyth nodded.

"It's a small hut," his father said. "We will be done before they finish the chapter house."

"When will we begin?" Will looked from Forsyth to his father.

"As soon as possible," Forsyth replied. "With hopes of finishing before the snow."

"Materials will be delivered in a few days," his father added. "Tomorrow we can start tearing off that roof."

"Will we be thatching again?"

"No, Will," Forsyth answered. "Reid has insisted on shingles, just like the chapter house. And a new stone fireplace, as well."

Will's father smiled. "Apparently you made a good impression, son."

The next morning, Will's father arrived at the keeper's hut with Luke and two workmen from the quarry. Will was surprised to see his brother.

"I guess someone did not care for our thatching work." Luke smiled, pointing at the singed roof. "Da says we get to have another go at it." The brothers embraced. Will had not felt this happy in some time. Shoulder to shoulder the Clachan men began transforming something dilapidated into something useful and new.

33

SAINT ANDREW'S DAY

The posters went up weeks before the event, as was the annual custom.

"The Earl of Fife graciously invites the citizens of Elgin to the Saint Andrew's Day celebration on the thirtieth of November with a dance and refreshments, to observe the national Scottish holiday."

The elite members of Elgin society received engraved invitations to an exclusive banquet preceding the dance. The earl and his family were honored guests, being the largest property owners in the region. It was a grand affair held in the banquet hall of Elgin's Assembly Rooms. The provost, magistrates, and town council were invited to the dinner, along with the most respectable inhabitants of Elgin. The dinner was a formal occasion with speeches followed by a haggis feast where the finest French claret was served. The dinner was followed by the dance, to which all of Elgin was invited.

On this last night of November, the citizens of Elgin were in a festive mood. The annual dinner was a great success where the lord provost delivered a memorable speech.

"It has been a most productive year in Elgin. As we celebrate our accomplishments, and remain grateful for the roofs over our heads, let us not forget the past that brought us to this place and time. We all know the story, yet it bears repeating. After the Reformation in 1560, Elgin Cathedral was abandoned for the town's parish church. The cathedral's roof was dismantled for its valuable lead. The bells were taken away, the choir screen used for firewood. The stones continued to be plundered. Only the chapter house survived fully intact, thanks to its usefulness as a meeting place for the incorporated trades of Elgin."

"Here, here!" someone called out among the otherwise quiet guests.

The lord provost cleared his throat and adjusted his cravat. "Thanks to Robert Reid, Master of Work to the Crown of Scotland, and the Scottish Works Committee in Edinburgh…" Again, the lord provost was interrupted by cheers and approving shouts.

"…and with sincere thanks to Isaac Forsyth and the town council, I am pleased to report that Elgin cathedral's chapter house is getting a new roof."

Everyone stood and applauded. The boisterous nature of the assemblage was likely due to the claret.

"And last, but not least, Elgin will forever be indebted to John Shanks, keeper and watchman of the ruin, for helping make the impossible happen."

It had taken nearly four hundred years of neglect, but at long last the effort to preserve a piece of Elgin cathedral had finally come to pass. For that alone, everyone had reason to celebrate.

In the ballroom the musicians began tuning their instruments. Those dining in the elegant supper room on the floor above brought their event to a close. The townsfolk were gathering on the High Street. Elgin's young men arrived early. They were willing to brave waiting in the cold to be the first in line at the punch bowl.

To pass the time, one among them lifted his voice. Others joined in. Half chanting, they sang a refrain from a not-so-old verse. "The Bachelors of Elgin" by William Hay was the talk of the town. With enough whiskey, it became a drinking song.

"We could weep when we think of the woes that befall

The poor married serf—the bonsman—the thrall,

A burden which never shall fetter or gall

The necks of the bachelors of Elgin—

the unmarried men of the North."

Others joined in, making a cloud in the cold night air.

Elgin's women arrived, swishing along on the arms of husbands, uncles, and sons. The unattached ladies dreamed of linking arms with the perfect dance partner.

As the crowd waited to enter the hall, it was more than fate that placed John Shanks next to Tom Clachan. Both their womenfolk were off to one side, talking with their own kind.

"Evening, John." Tom nodded. "I was wondering—what do you think about the redevelopment in the center of town?"

Shanks seemed reluctant to engage in a battle of words. "Are you referring to the recent destruction of ancient buildings on King Street?"

For a moment the two men glowered at one another, each with their own point of view. An aspiring master builder bantering with a keeper of a ruin.

"You must admit, this is the way it has always been in Moray," Tom said. "It is a resourceful practice."

Shanks tried to ignore Tom, craning his neck to keep a close eye on Alanna among a clutch of young women.

"Time and the elements alone have seen to the destruction of those buildings," Tom continued. "Like the cathedral, we cannot save it all."

"But we can damn well try!" Shanks growled.

"If left to you, John, would we have never fixed the roads in town? Never discovered that Pictish Cross you cherish so dearly? Would you have just left the old kirk to fall down around the worshipers?"

"Of course not," Shanks answered curtly. "Old St. Giles was built as solid as the Pyramids. It would have never collapsed. It lasted for eons. But men like you are too impatient, Tom. Itching for progress instead of valuing history."

Alanna returned to her grandfather's side as Tom moved off to find his wife.

The Assembly Rooms' doors opened and music floated out. The wind danced a swirl of snowflakes and wisps of frost graced the air. Elgin's citizens soon filled the hall.

The town's ballroom was the talk of the region. An enormous dance hall with ceilings twenty-one feet tall. Most amazing was its tension-sprung dance floor that was adjusted according to the number of dancers expected to attend. The surface offered a noticeable give that seemed to please everyone on the dance floor, young and old alike.

Inside the hall guests milled about, sampling refreshments and awaiting the first dance. It was a time to greet friends and neighbors and introduce the new faces in town. Will watched the stream of arrivals. At last, the person he was waiting for appeared.

Alanna arrived on the arm of her grandfather. Her green velvet cape trimmed in fur was flecked with a scatter of frost. Her hair was done up with combs, her cheeks red from the cold. She slipped out of the cape and Shanks draped it over his arm. He smiled with pride at his granddaughter, happy to be her escort. Beneath the cape Alanna wore a celery-green dress of finest silk. A beautiful wool shawl draped her shoulders. She seemed to glide across the floor. Will could not look away.

"You best close your mouth, son," Will's mother whispered in his ear. Smiling, he followed her suggestion. His mother was beautiful, too. In a silver-gray dress with delicate lace, she was the loveliest mother in the hall.

Will caught sight of his father. Tom Clachan was conversing with a small group of men. They were discussing secondhand news about what had been said in the room above during the private event. Although uninvited, they were interested in what Elgin's upper crust had to say.

This was Will's first time inside the ballroom for the annual Saint Andrew's Day celebration. The first time for Luke, too. Younger children played outside the Assembly Rooms during the dance. This year, Andrew and Ross were among them. Peat fires kept the chill away. The boys played tag and chase while the girls played peevers with pebbles for markers. Now and then they peeked through the door to watch the dancing.

For Will those times did not seem so long ago. It felt remarkably sudden to be invited inside with his own beautiful mother on his arm. She had made him a new vest and a handsome cravat to wear with his altered suit of clothes. His boots were shined, and his hair trimmed, and he smelled of clean shaving soap.

When the musicians announced the first Scottish reel, his mother winked at Will. "Let's see if you remember what I taught you."

"I'm not ready yet, Mam."

"Ready enough!" she assured him.

Will took his place in the line of men across from his mother in the line of women. The music began fast and loud. No time to think—only dance. His mam put him at ease. She danced like a girl and laughed like one, too. He was not the only one watching. When the reel ended Will took his mother's arm. They were both winded and laughing together.

Standing nearby, John Shanks caught Charlotte Clachan's eye. She nodded politely in Shanks's direction, lifted her skirt modestly and pointed her toe. Just enough for him to see the beautiful green slippers he had made for her. Will noticed his father across the room near the punch bowl. He was frowning in their direction.

Shanks stepped nearer. "Good evening, Will. Madam."

"Good evening, John," Charlotte Clachan replied. Will looked away, embarrassed at his mam's familiarity with his employer.

Shanks was dressed in a wool suit and a festive velvet vest. He leaned heavily on the silver handle of a polished wood cane. He tapped the cane against his right boot. "If not for this bad foot, I would ask you to dance." His eyes glimmered playfully.

"Might I suggest instead," Charlotte Clachan offered, "that Will ask Alanna to dance?"

"Mam!" Will cringed, but she pinched the back of his arm where she held it.

Shanks glanced behind him. Alanna waited with interest to see what might happen next. The musicians were tuning up. Alanna took a step in Will's direction. "May we, Grand-Dey? Since you cannot dance with me this year?"

"I suppose…" Shanks's eyes scanned the crowd for an alternative but found none.

Alanna took Will's arm, and he guided her onto the dance floor.

From across the room, Tom Clachan watched his wife. John Shanks watched his granddaughter. Charlotte Clachan watched her son. And Alanna and Will could not keep their eyes from each other as they danced the next two reels.

At the break, Will noticed James Thompson on the far side of the hall, looking in his direction. He was with a group of young men. Fellow teachers at the Free School, Will guessed by their manner and dress. Will smiled and Thompson raised a hand in greeting.

"Is that your friend from the Free School?" Alanna asked. "Are those other young men teachers, too?" For a moment Alanna wondered what it might be like to marry a teacher. She had not considered the possibility, having never read a love story about a teacher.

"Alanna!" Shanks put a hand on his granddaughter's arm, interrupting her thoughts. "I have someone I would like you to meet."

Suddenly, a commotion erupted near the door. Will's young brother Andrew pushed his way into the hall and headed straight for Da and Luke. By the look on Andrew's face Will knew something was wrong.

"You are not supposed to be in here, son!" Tom Clachan said sternly. "Now turn yourself around and go…"

"It's bandits, Da! Breaking into the Assembly Rooms' storehouse!"

Tom gripped Andrew firmly by the shoulder and pointed across the room. "See the sheriff there in the blue coat? Quick, go tell him exactly what you told me. Tell him I've gone outside."

"Yes, Da!"

Tom and Luke ran for the door. As Will attempted to follow, James Thompson touched Will's shoulder.

"Something is happening outside," Will explained.

"I'll come with you."

From the outside steps Tom and Luke spied men moving through the shadows below. Bandits had broken into the locked storeroom and were rolling whiskey barrels toward their wagon.

"Stop!" Tom yelled. "Move away from there!" He jumped from the steps and tackled one of the bandits. Luke blocked the storehouse door, fending off the intruders with a hefty piece of firewood. Sheriff Cunningham and his men rushed from the hall to join the fray while the schoolteacher shooed the children into the ballroom. Will ran to his father's side and knocked a fleeing bandit to the ground.

Outnumbered, the bandits were quickly subdued. Sheriff Cunningham made his arrests, and his deputies proceeded to march the bandits up the street to the jail.

Tom patted his sons on the back. Only then did they notice the blood. "You're cut!" Luke said, grabbing Will's hand.

"I didn't feel it."

James offered his handkerchief and examined Will's hand. "Not too deep," the young teacher said as he skillfully wrapped the wound. "That should take care of it. Along with a cup of punch. Let's go back inside."

"Aye," Cunningham agreed. "You boys deserve my thanks." The sheriff posted a guard at the doors and accompanied the Clachan men and the schoolteacher into the hall. The music and dancing stopped. Conversation fell to whispers as everyone turned to stare.

Sheriff Cunningham stepped forward. "Good evening!" he bellowed. "Before the next dance, I want everyone to know that all is well in Elgin tonight!"

The crowd, into their second or third cups of punch, cheered the good news.

"And before we resume our celebration, I want to recognize these fine folk! Most of all"—the sheriff put an arm around Andrew—"we owe a debt of thanks to this young man. Three cheers now for Andrew Clachan, who saved our Saint Andrew's Day celebration!" Andrew turned red and smiled while everyone applauded.

The sheriff nodded for the musicians to call the next dance. Before Will could catch his breath, someone tapped him on the arm.

"That seemed quite a lot of excitement," a sweet voice said.

Will turned to see Mrs. Hendry. If he had thought her beautiful in her day clothes, the young woman appeared angelic dressed in blue satin. Her blond hair was swirled into a gracious twist of curls, and a small fan hung from her wrist. Will was speechless.

"I was hoping…" she glanced at the dance floor and extended her hand.

"Oh. Of course! Might I…" As he offered his arm, they both looked at the bloody handkerchief tied around his hand.

"Goodness!" Mrs. Hendry said but did not turn away. She grabbed Will's wrist. "Let me take a look at this," she ordered him. Before Will could excuse himself, she had unwrapped his hand. "Peter," she called to a tall man nearby. "Let me have your flask."

"But—" the man began to protest.

"Now," she ordered. "I only need a splash." Mrs. Hendry batted her eyelashes. "You will not miss it a wink."

With a firm grasp on Will's wrist, she poured a trickle of whiskey into the cut. Reflexively, he tried to pull away, but the woman possessed a powerful grip. "Hold still now," she cooed, dabbing the wound with the soiled handkerchief. She blew gently on the cut, and he flinched. "It's begun to clot. The whiskey will ensure good healing." Mrs. Hendry let go just long enough to extract her own handkerchief from her bosom. "Let's tie this up again so we might dance." She smiled as she efficiently bound Will's hand. The blood-soaked handkerchief was passed to Peter. "Take care of this, please," she said.

"It belongs to a friend," Will interrupted.

"He'll need a new one, I fear," Mrs. Hendry said with a shrug. The musicians were calling the next dance. "Shall we?" She took Will's arm.

"Mrs. Hendry—I do not even know your given name."

"Dance with me and I'll tell you," she said coyly. "Or maybe I'll have you guess."

"I am poor at guessing," Will told her as they took their places in the lines.

On their first pass she offered, "It's Davina. As a child I was called Ina."

"Davina is pretty," Will said.

"Now you know why I go by Mrs. Hendry," she laughed as they changed partners.

The reel continued, and Will was cautious with his bandaged hand. The floor bounced gently under the weight of so many dancers.

Two partners later, Alanna was on Will's arm and clearly displeased. "Why are you dancing with that woman?"

"I could ask the same of you. Why are you dancing with my friend James Thompson?"

"Because I asked him!" Alanna declared.

Will looked down the line. James appeared agitated.

"He does not like my dress," Alanna pouted. "I did not know he was a naturalist." She nearly hissed the word. "He asked about the fur on my cuffs and was appalled when I told him it was vair."

"Why?" Will asked.

"He said *vair* is just another word for red squirrel fur. Which, of course, anyone knows who has read *Ivanhoe*! I do not understand what the fuss is about!"

When the dance ended, Will escaped to find his family.

"How is Ross?" Will asked his father. Mam was seated nearby with an arm around her youngest son.

"We might leave early and take the young boys home. Although it will break your mother's heart to miss the last dance," Tom Clachan muttered.

"Luke was hoping to come back to the keeper's hut with me for the night. Do you approve, Da?"

"A good idea. This is not a night for anyone to be abroad in the dark alone. Promise you will stay alert along the way."

"We will, Da. I promise. We have had enough excitement for one night."

"Good citizens!" The lead fiddler called out. "It is time to circle round!"

Will saw Mam give Da a meaningful look. Ross appeared to be nearly asleep beside her. To Will's surprise, Da smiled at Mam and crossed the floor to hold out his hand. He helped her to her feet. Ross was too tired to mind.

Will moved quickly across the room to take Alanna's hand. Her grandfather stood on her other side.

Mrs. Hendry gently lifted Will's bandaged hand into her own. "Where is your husband? Peter, was it?" Will asked quietly.

Mrs. Hendry laughed. "Peter is not my husband. He works for me. He has gone to fetch my wagon. I have asked him to take your family home this night. That is the least I can do."

"But your husband?" Will was still confused.

"Is of no concern to you or anyone else, my new friend." Her eyes danced in a way that did not match the sternness in her voice.

Everyone was busy joining hands to form an expanding circle. Looking at Will from across the room, James Thompson appeared sullen. While Will had a beautiful woman on each arm, James was flanked by the McKay sisters—two very large girls painfully squeezing his hands.

Mam and Da were in the circle, too. Happier than Will had seen them together in some time.

"Step back! Spread out, now!" The fiddler instructed the crowd. "Remember, left hand over right. Cross your arms across you, just like our dear Scottish flag! Join hands on your right and your left. No breaks now! We do not want any bad luck!"

The fiddler began by playing the last measures of the song. There was a long pause before everyone joined in and sang. The familiar words were always touching, especially after enough punch was consumed. Some swayed to the music, others stood rock still. More than a few tears rolled down cheeks.

They sang nearly all the verses. And then came the final chorus. Even the children, drowsing in the corners of the room, stirred enough to join in.

"And there's a hand, my trusty fiere!

And gie's a hand o' thine!

And we'll take a right guid willy waught

For auld lang syne.

For auld lang syne, my fiere!

For auld lang syne.

We'll take a right guid willy waught

For auld lang syne!"

With the fiddler's final prolonged note, everyone rushed to the center of the circle still holding hands now raised overhead, cheering and shouting, laughing and giggling. Just as it was intended, Saint Andrew's Day had left all those present with feelings of goodwill—despite the earlier disturbance. Underscoring the importance of preserving old friendships and looking back over the events of the year. The future would do what it will.

Alanna squeezed Will's uninjured hand. She gave him a meaningful look. Then John Shanks draped her cape over her shoulders and pulled his granddaughter toward the door. If Will could trust his instincts, he felt certain he knew what Alanna was thinking. It was the end of a meaningful year for each of them. The end of childhood. They had shared experiences no one else had shared.

And whether as friends, or as something more, their relationship remained undefined.

34

CRUST

Despite the calendar, the weather held.

The early weeks of December remained mild while a team of good men made quick progress on the chapter house roof.

Shanks took advantage of the limited daylight hours. He cleaned along the west wall where Reid had told them to dig. Will helped work on the keeper's hut, and ran barrows to the Witches Pool.

"Are you ready for me, sir?" Will called out.

Shanks was leaning on his shovel watching the workmen remove the scaffolding. "On this date in December 1637, a gale force wind blew down the cathedral's rafters." Shanks sighed. "It was as though history was a living thing seeking its next victim." Until this grim story, Shanks had lately been quiet. Within the week, Will learned what was occupying the old shoemaker's thoughts.

One dark morning Morrison arrived alone to unlock the ruin. "Shanks said to keep working," Morrison grumbled to Will.

"Is Shanks unwell?"

"What makes you ask?"

"He's been unusually quiet."

Morrison furrowed his brow. "Ye'll know soon enough, I suppose. Miss Alanna is going to Italy."

"Italy!" Will echoed. "Why?"

Morrison examined the key in his hand. "That story is not mine to tell."

"Who else will tell me if not you?"

"Shanks, most likely. When he is ready."

Will refused to plead for more news. It seemed too childlike. "I will ask Master Shanks myself." Will assumed there must be a good reason if Morrison was unwilling to share what he knew.

"I will be back at dusk to lock up." Morrison flipped the key in his hand. "I'll let you get to it." But still Morrison did not move. "That run-in with the bandits on Saint Andrew's Day. You were all very brave."

Will looked away. "Family, you know. There wasn't a choice."

Morrison shrugged.

"Why do you suppose there aren't more stories with pleasant folk and happy endings?" Will asked.

"Because no one would remember them. Nobody ever remembers the good folk except when they're preyed on by evil ones."

"I will have to think on that. Of all the books in Master Forsyth's library there must be some stories about good people who are more than victims."

Morrison was still looking at the key in his hand. "You know, Will. If it were up to me, I would hand this key to you and be done with it."

Morrison's words were unexpected. Will kept still.

"Unfortunately, that decision is not mine to make."

It had been some time since Will was alone in the ruin.

Repairs to the hut were nearly done and work on the chapter house would resume in the spring. Da and his men were working at the quarry.

Will was estimating the number of barrows he might cart to the pool before dusk. A short six-hour window of light was all this December day would offer. After a run to the Witches Pool and back, he paused to add a slash mark in the notebook. Soon he would run out of pages.

"I recognize that," Alanna said softly.

Will flinched, dropping the notebook. "You startled me! Where did you come from?"

Alanna retrieved the book. "This was once mine," she said coolly, as though she had been standing there all morning.

"I did not see you arrive."

"I was in the chapter house. With the workers gone, I wanted to look for the angel up in the ceiling." She shook her head. "It was wishful thinking. I still like knowing she is up there even if I cannot see her."

"I thought you were not supposed to be out alone," Will remarked.

"Heavens, Will. It's midday."

He wanted to remind her that danger was not restricted to darkness, but he held his tongue.

"I brought you some shortbread," Alanna said proudly. "I made it myself."

"Shortbread? Before Christmas and Hogmanay?"

"I'm practicing."

Will laughed.

"While I'm here, I have a favor to ask."

Will could not imagine what the favor might be.

"I was wondering if I might see the little carved figure once more."

Will nodded, unsure how showing her the carving might be perceived as a favor.

"I would like another chance to draw it."

Will bit his lip, weighing her request. His hand was already gripping his little good luck piece in his pocket.

"I would like to sketch it in the chapter house while the light is good. It will not take long."

Stalling, Will asked, "Were you very young when you took up sketching?"

"When I was a little girl, I saw a traveling artist sketch sections of the ruin. Grand-Dey and I came to watch him work. I had to promise to be quiet. I was captivated by how the artist made the pictures. That was when my interest in sketching began. But I really had no desire to sketch the ruin until Robert Reid requested the drawings. Others had already drawn the ruin, so why should I?"

Will pulled the carving from his pocket. It had been a long time since he admired the lovely creature in full daylight. Something about its appearance, lit so well and sitting in his hand, produced an unexpected tug at Will's heart.

"It is like nothing I have ever seen," Alanna whispered.

"You mustn't tell anyone," Will cautioned. "Anyone who looks at your drawing, I mean. You cannot tell them who the carving belongs to, or where you saw it. I would not want it taken away from me. It is my good luck piece. Do you understand?"

"Yes. I promise." Alanna's eyes were sincere.

"You won't be long?"

"Not long at all."

As he had done once before, Will gently set the carving in Alanna's small hand. Alanna disappeared into the chapter house and he was not invited to follow.

Will returned to his digging near the west wall, but his thoughts were elsewhere. He recalled what Reid had said about focusing their efforts with hopes of future discoveries. Seeing his little good luck piece in full sunlight had brought back old memories. Will felt unmoored. He closed his eyes and leaned hard on the shovel. He could not ignore his sudden recollection: the carved creature caught in a shaft of light, sitting in a child's small hand—his hand. A memory of the moment he had rescued the creature from a rubble pile somewhere in the ruin. Will sensed there was something more. A bit of lost and found, winning and losing. He shook his head and opened his eyes. He needed to stop thinking about the past and get back to work. The carving was safe with Alanna. Nothing bad was going to happen.

Will stabbed his shovel into the rubble and a second flash of memory overtook him. The image was not entirely unfamiliar. It had lurked in his dreams for years. But this was different. He was fully awake with a new perspective on a nearly forgotten occurrence. A memory that evaded recollection until now. Carved figures. Burial tombs. Those vague feelings he occasionally experienced while working in the ruin. A sense that he knew things about this place that John Shanks did not. The murmurs he had overheard among Forsyth, Shanks, and Reid. Educated men seeking finely carved figures, tombs, and colossal statuary. Amazing sculptures created by skilled carvers from Italy and France—surely something must have survived among all this wreckage. Yet without firsthand evidence, they were just old men with old documents, making new assumptions about what they might find. Hoping for some proof of the cathedral's lost magnificence. Wishfully certain it could not all be gone.

Will thought he might be sick. His memories illuminated an incident he had nearly forgotten until now. While looking for a hiding place in the ruin during a childhood game of All Hide, he had discovered the little carved creature he still carried hidden in his pocket. The rest of what he saw and felt in the darkness that day seemed unimportant. Until he recalled that the tiny shaft of light streaking through the ruin had landed on…the nose of a sleeping stone man.

Will had never found his way back to the hidden figure. As time passed, it was likely he had grown too big to fit into the spaces he had squeezed through on that day. And the older he got, the more that day seemed dreamlike. A possible creation of his young imagination. He never told anyone what he had seen, fearful no one would believe him. Or worse, that he might land in trouble for venturing somewhere he wasn't supposed to be, or for taking something he wasn't supposed to have. The only physical thing that gave these memories credence was the carving. Now years later, his memories had come full circle.

Will put his head down and did his best to calm his heart. He felt suffocated and trapped, even sitting out in the open. He did his best to shake off the dreamlike memory.

"Will?"

He looked up. It was Alanna, her face a map of concerns.

"Will?" she said again. "Are you unwell? You look…"

"It's nothing," he said, getting to his feet. He ran a hand through his hair and dragged a sleeve across his eyes.

"I have been calling to you from the chapter house door. Did you not hear me?"

He shook his head.

"There was the most beautiful shaft of light coming through

the chapter house windows. It seemed magical the way it lit your tiny carving. It almost looked as though the little thing might come to life and take wing." Alanna placed the carving back into Will's hand. He gripped it tight enough to leave an imprint of wings in his palm before slipping it into his pocket.

"May I see the sketch?" Will asked.

Alanna grinned and her dimples bloomed. "Not yet. But I promise, you will see it when it's done. Before I go—"

"Go where?" Will knew the answer but wanted to hear it from her.

"I am not supposed to speak of it."

"And yet you have," Will pointed out. "Shall I guess?" Simply looking at Alanna made Will feel grounded again, recovering from his daydream by the minute.

Alanna clapped her hands together. "Yes! You may have three guesses." Suddenly she was a child playing a simple game.

"Three guesses. Hmm. Let me see." Will looked skyward, feigning deep thought. "Are you going to Edinburgh to celebrate Hogmanay?"

"No!" Alanna said boisterously. "Guess again!"

"Wait! What do I get if I guess correctly? More shortbread?"

"Quite possibly."

"The sketch in your hand?"

"No."

He was feeling a bravado that surprised even him. "A kiss?"

"Absolutely not!"

"Are you going to London to see the king?"

"I am not!" She crossed her arms. "Last guess!"

Will scratched his head and squinted at Alanna, "Hmm…I wonder. If I try hard enough, do you think I might read your mind?"

"Never!" she giggled.

"Italy!" he said.

Alanna gasped. "How did you…?"

"I read your mind, miss," he answered smugly. "What I do not know is when and why you are going."

"Who told you?"

"I guessed, remember?" He was being difficult, but he did not care. "Why are you going to Italy?" he asked sincerely.

"I am not supposed to talk of it," she said primly. "Not yet."

"Fine. But I still get my kiss."

"I never said—"

"Ah. I suppose I must settle for shortbread."

She laughed. "Alright. I will tell you. But you must act surprised when Grand-Dey shares the news. He is not happy about it."

He's not the only one, Will thought.

"Robert Reid believes I have artistic talent. He told Isaac that if I were a young man, he would hire me to apprentice in his offices in Edinburgh. Since I am a young woman"—she swished her skirts—"he believes I should master my talent at a small art school in Italy."

"Goodness. Couldn't you study in Edinburgh or London?"

An expression crossed Alanna's face, suggesting she had not thought of those possibilities. "No. I do not believe so. The best architectural artists study in Italy. And Robert Reid has friends there with an art school in Florence. Master Reid is going to be my benefactor and assume the cost of my studies."

"How long will you be abroad?"

"I have no idea. Until I am an artist of merit, I suppose."

"Will you not miss your grand-dey? And your home? And Elgin?" He wanted desperately to add himself to the list but knew better.

"I suppose so. But those aren't sufficient reasons not to go."

"When do you leave?"

"Sometime after Hogmanay. Isaac is accompanying me to Florence. He has promised to see me safely there. I do not believe Grand-Dey would have agreed, if not for Isaac's influence."

Will was speechless.

"I had best get home. Before Grand-Dey sends someone to look for me."

"And I had best be back to work. Before Morrison arrives to lock the ruin."

In a fearless mood, Alanna gave Will a flirty little wave as she left.

Will picked up his shovel. With Alanna gone, his mind reverted to the flood of childhood memories. Instead of shoveling he walked slowly along the edge of the collapsed walls. He tried unsuccessfully to find any opening like the one in his memory. Most likely, the entrance he had discovered was now blocked entirely with rubble. He shook his head. Had he truly seen all that he remembered? The only evidence was tucked safely back in his pocket. No, Will thought suddenly. Not the only evidence. Now there existed a drawing of his tiny creature in the pages of Alanna's sketchbook

35

WILL LEARNS TO WHISTLE

Alanna's looming departure did not stay secret for long. Shanks returned to the ruin with emotion to burn. He grabbed a shovel and began digging. He had decided to wait until the end of the day to tell Will the news about Alanna.

"I suppose you will go home for Christmas," Shanks mumbled.

Will sensed Shanks's mood and gave a silent nod.

"It is good to have family at Christmastide," Shanks added.

"Aye, sir. I am grateful. Although sometimes it is good to live under a roof where fewer people are snoring."

Shanks laughed. "You do entertain me, Will. Which reminds me, did you enjoy Saint Andrew's Day? I always appreciate the music. There's nothing like a good tune. When I think of the joys this cathedral once offered, I often wonder what the music must have been like. The chanting and vesper song. It is nice to hear the occasional tune. Do you whistle, Will?"

"A little. A few ditties my father taught us boys."

"Have you ever heard this one?" Shanks stopped shoveling,

licked his lips, and puckered, offering a dozen melodic notes.

"I cannot say I have," Will replied. "Where did you hear it?"

"From the lips of a fair-haired young tinker passing through El- gin last year. He did not sound Scottish at all. Seemed nice enough, though. And he repaired the bottoms of two pots Alanna burned clean through."

Will struggled not to laugh.

Shanks repeated whistling the short musical phrase.

"Does the tune have a name, sir?"

"Something about a good king. I can teach it to you, if you like."

"What I would most like to learn is how to whistle through my fingers. I have never been able to do it." Will shrugged.

Shanks nodded and put down his shovel to wipe his hands against his coat. He examined the cleanliness of his fingers and shrugged. "It's not so hard, if done right. I taught Alanna."

Will could not see why a girl would whistle. It seemed unlady- like. Yet it offered him a new image of Alanna. The girl knew how to whistle.

Shanks explained, "If she ever needed help, she could whis- tle." Will tried to imagine Alanna whistling. Not something she could do with gloved hands holding the reins of her pony cart when Johnny attacked her.

"Pay attention now," Shanks instructed. "Do what I do."

Will followed Shanks's lead and wiped his dirty hands on his coat.

"Draw back your lips over your teeth." Shanks demonstrat- ed. His teeth were not pretty, but at least he still had them. "Your lips must fully cover your teeth. Now, form the letter A using the first two fingers on both hands. Use your fingers to raise the tip of your tongue and point it up and back. Next, blow air through the gap between your fingers. You must blow hard, like blowing out a candle from far away. No air should escape from the sides of your mouth. All the air should be blown out hard and fast between your fingers." Shanks slowly did each step one more time. The last step produced a sharp, piercing whistle.

"Amazing!" Will was impressed that someone so old could whistle so loud.

"You try it," Shanks insisted. "I will do it with you."

Three times Will tried and failed.

Shanks shrugged. "Keep practicing. You'll manage it soon enough."

"If only I could practice and shovel at the same time." Will grinned.

The whistling had made Shanks jollier. But the ruin keeper's good mood did not last. Shanks's shoulders soon slumped. "Sorry, Will. I need to go home." He hesitated, attempting to control his emotions. "Alanna is going away," Shanks said at last. "She is leaving Elgin to live in Italy and study art."

Will could see the muscles in Shanks's jaw working.

"Robert Reid has made introductions. She seems so happy, but I cannot imagine life without her. And when I do imagine such a thing—" Shanks let out a tremulous sigh. "I have said too much. I will see you in the morning."

Will watched Shanks lock the ruin.

"One more thing, Will. The locksmith from town is coming to fit a new lock for the door to your hut. Please ask him to make us two keys."

With a new key to the keeper's hut in his pocket, Will headed home.

He carried small gifts for his family. River stones shaped like snail shells for Ross and Andrew. A fine rabbit's foot with an extra toe for Luke. And for Da, a bit of pipe tobacco Robert Reid had left behind in the keeper's hut. The flower seeds he had gathered for Mam were carefully tied up in a piece of gauze.

In the Clachan croft, Christmas was less about gifts and more about Mam's cooking. Will's stomach rumbled just thinking of the pudding and the roast, and her delicious bawd bree with stuffing balls. A bite of her ginger cake, hot from the oven served with butter, could make grown men cry.

Will's arrival home was a happy one. Even Da seemed in a pleasant mood. Mam was busy cooking. The smells made their stomachs growl, a chorus of hungry souls.

Will felt at ease with Da, as though the fight with the bandits had brought them a mutual respect. No one talked about the fight. They were too full of good news and great joy. His father greeted Will with a slap on the back. "Have you heard? The town council is increasing Shanks's pay!" In the face of such news Will held his breath, anticipating a display of his father's temper. Instead, Da smiled. "That means you get a raise, too. Shanks came to tell me himself. He is happy with your work."

Will was glad for his family, but it was difficult to feel happy when he was not receiving the pay. He had spent the past year living on his own without any money. Plenty of people survived this way, but the stress of it, even with Shanks and Alanna feeding him, was something he hoped to outgrow.

As though reading Will's mind, his father produced three coins and placed them in Will's hand. "For you, son. You've earned a share."

"Thank you, sir," Will was surprised.

"My work is going well, with more projects to come," Da explained.

A peaceful relief settled on the faces of Will's family. For now, it seemed safe to be happy.

"I have gifts, too!" Will reached for his bag.

"Wait!" Ross demanded. "First, we have a gift for you that you need right now." He and Andrew stepped closer. Each in turn reached to hug Will hard around the neck. Andrew placed a small leather pouch in Will's hand. "It's a purse!" Ross said excitedly. "For your coins."

"So that you don't lose them," Andrew added.

"Thank you, boys." With a bit of exaggeration, Will dropped the coins into the purse one by one and pulled the leather string tight. "Perfect," he said, tucking the purse into his sack. Then Will distributed his own gifts with a wish for a "Happy Christmas!"

"My turn," Mam said, wiping her hands on her apron. She opened a dresser drawer and one by one presented five pale gray sweaters. The look of joy on Mam's face as each of her men slipped a sweater over his head reminded Will how much she loved them.

"Mine's so soft," Ross cooed. "Not scratchy like my old sweater."

"Lamb's wool," Mam explained. "And lots of wool carding."

"Goodness, Charlotte. How did you manage to make these without us seeing?"

She raised a brow and smiled. "Timing and hard work."

The five Clachan men rubbed the chests of their sweaters. "They are very handsome, Mam," Luke said. "Thank you."

"Thank you, Mam!" the other boys echoed.

"Yes. Thank you, Charlotte." Will saw a twinkle in his father's eyes.

"All this and a pudding, too!" Ross exclaimed.

"And pudding, too." Mam smiled.

When all the Christmas pudding was eaten and the bowls licked clean, Da asked Will, "How are you liking the new hut, son?"

"It has more new parts than old now. All thanks to you, Da. And Luke, and the men, too."

"You are welcome, son. But we were well paid for our efforts. Reid saw to that."

"He saw to many things," Will agreed. "Most of all a new roof and a chimney. It is a relief to have a well-fitted door and windows." Will reached into his bag. With a look of pride, he displayed his new key. "And now the hut has a lock."

"You'll want to hold tight to that," Mam said. "Find a safe place to carry it."

"In your new purse," Ross suggested.

"Good idea." Will smiled.

"Thanks to Isaac Forsyth I should be warm and comfortable this winter." He touched the sleeve of his new sweater. "And thanks to you, too, Mam." Will was tired of talking about himself. "Da and Luke have seen the place. Some time you should come see it, too, Mam, with the boys." Will clapped his hands together. "Now. Who wants to play a game?"

Later that evening, after the young boys were asleep, Da sat with Will and talked about his new projects. "Last week I learned Unthink Manor ruin is to be torn down to make way for new buildings. I have been asked if I would like to harvest the ancient stones in exchange for hauling them away. Another man wants me to use those stones to build him a new house on King Street. And the Earl of Fife has agreed to give us access to the remaining odd stones at Pluscarden Abbey. Last week I met with the earl himself. The old monastery has been done up nicely with a little chapel. There's talk of a small Presbyterian congregation using it."

"That's good news, Da." It seemed his father's dream of being a master builder might come true.

"Yes, and good for Elgin's stonemasons. Everyone has work. And there is still much work to be done." Da massaged a muscle in his neck. "I have a question for you, Will, and I would appreciate a forthright answer."

"Yes, sir." Will tried to guess what serious matter was about to be discussed.

"I was wondering…" Da waited for Will to meet his gaze, "… if you might come work with me building houses. Now that I have plenty of work and resources."

The question was unexpected, and Will froze. Too many feelings were vying for consideration. Did he wish to be done with the ruin? How would he get news of Alanna if he were no longer working for Shanks? Did he want to be one of Da's men? Give up his newly repaired hut and move back home? Or would he rather keep shoveling rubble? He had seen himself making more discoveries in the ruin and giving tours to the visitors Shanks insisted would soon be coming. "If I say I am unsure," Will's voice quivered, "will you be angry with me, Da?"

His father looked disappointed. "Surprised but not angry."

Will knew it was a privilege to be asked. Da could have easily told Shanks their agreement was over and ordered Will home. Now he felt guilty for not giving his father the answer he wanted. "May I think on it, Da? I do miss working with you and Luke."

"Let us say no more for now." His father reached for the pipe in his pocket. "It's time for me to try that new tobacco." Da paused before stepping out into the cold to smoke. "I am not worried, Will. I know you will make the right decision."

36

FIRST LOVE LAST

There was a knock on the new keeper's hut door that had never been knocked on before.

When Will opened the door, there was Alanna wearing her fur-trimmed cloak and carrying a large basket. All around her the air was filled with tiny flakes of sparking snow.

"May I come in?" Alanna asked, stepping over the threshold.

Will looked to see who had accompanied her, but there was no one.

Alanna appeared concerned. "Are you unwell?"

He opened his mouth to answer, but no words emerged. *Lovesick,* he thought—but he would not say the word aloud.

"Nothing contagious, I hope."

"No. Not contagious," he assured her. The girl was headed to Italy looking as healthy as he had ever seen her.

Alanna placed the basket on the table. She shrugged out of her cloak and laid it on a chair. Beneath the cloak she wore a sheath dress of the thinnest fabric, fastened with tiny buttons. Finely embroidered morning glory vines bloomed and twined down the placket. Her clothes seemed suited for some dressy occasion. Likely, she was dropping off his provisions on her way elsewhere. It occurred to Will this might be the last basket she would bring him. "You did not have to…" He stopped and began again. "Why are you here? Your grandfather said you were packing."

An odd expression overtook Alanna's face. She stood erect, slowly removing her gloves. When at last she made eye contact her words were deliberate, "I do not wish to go to Italy a virgin."

The last word hung in the air, neither of them certain of its true meaning. Will stared slack-jawed.

"Having not lain with a man," she explained in a practical voice. She knew that phrase from reading books. It had something to do with loving. A complete set of details were still unclear to her. Will knew less than she. Alanna moved closer and he took a step back, nearly tripping. He caught himself and managed to exhale.

"Have you ever lain with a woman?" she asked him directly.

"No," he answered too quickly. "Not yet." Will searched her face, for what he did not know. And then they were kissing. His brain grew fuzzy, his heart raced.

Alanna stepped out of her shoes and stretched out on his bed. In a position of love or death, it was difficult for Will to determine. He removed his boots and his jacket, and carefully laid down beside her, and they faced one another. She threaded her cold fingers through his warm ones. For a moment they each stared at the other. The full length of their bodies side by side, knees and noses nearly touching. Will placed a hand in the small of her back, watching her face. She moved, and he gasped, breathing shallow.

"Oh. My—" she said in a whisper tickling his ear. Her breasts pressed firmly against his chest. Only her shift and his shirt and trousers stood between them. He could smell her perfume, and under that the essence of the girl. Will's ears began to buzz. There was more movement and shifting about. They kissed again and clasped together. Will's body convulsed and he moaned. Alanna gasped and pressed herself into him, holding firm.

When at last Will opened his eyes, Alanna was still beside him, watching his face. A euphoric feeling swept through him, far exceeding the normal release he experienced when his body burst on its own. Will felt the dampness, but Alanna seemed not to notice. The ecstasy quickly melted as he looked at Alanna with new desires. Fully aware that very soon she would be gone. On her way to Italy.

"I think we have done it," Alanna whispered, smiling triumphantly. "Lain together. But we must tell no one. Swear it!"

Her voice was commanding, and he answered at once, "I swear."

"Happy Christmas," Alanna grinned devilishly.

"Happy Hogmanay," Will replied.

Alanna raised up on one elbow. "Are you Catholic, Will? Or Presbyterian?"

"Neither," he replied. "We are Congregational Church members," he explained. "And you?"

"Lapsed Presbyterians, I suppose. Grand-Dey is more interested in science and history books than reading the scriptures. He still gives generously to St. Giles."

The mention of John Shanks broke the spell. Alanna climbed off the bed and lifted the cloth on the basket. She recovered more quickly than he.

"I've brought you something," she told him.

Will's stomach growled and he sat up at the thought of food. "Is it something delicious?" He was suddenly famished.

She found what she was after and returned to the bed. In one hand she held a large piece of shortbread. In the other, something small and shiny.

Will finished the shortbread in no time. "A well-tidy biscuit," he told her. "Your baking skills are improving."

"It's not mine. Our new kitchen maid banished me from the kitchen after I burned my last batch." Alanna perched on the edge of the bed beside him. Her small hands covered the item she held in her lap. "I've brought you more than just shortbread." Her voice had gone quiet as she looked down at her hands.

Will wiped crumbs from his fingers as Alanna presented her small gift. "For you," she said solemnly, opening her hand to reveal a small locket. "To replace the ruined one."

Will was confused by the locket Alanna placed in his hand. He searched his memory for what this gift might replace.

Seeing the confusion on Will's face, Alanna reached to open the locket. Inside was a very small sketch. The one she said she would make for him someday, after the first sketch was ruined in the fire. Now here was the finished drawing. Along the bottom edge, penned in tiny letters, were her initials and the year. Above the sketch were the words, "Creature. Elgin Cathedral." Will removed the little carving from his pocket and they examined the two side by side. The drawing was perfect.

"Thank you," Will whispered, his emotions swelling.

"Take good care of this one." She reached for her cloak. "I must get back."

"Wait. I have something for you." Will crossed the room to where he kept his good suit of clothes. He reached into the trouser pocket and returned to the bed. "You should have this," he said, carefully placing the gold King George coin into Alanna's hand.

"I do not understand."

"It was in a secret pocket in the clothes that belonged to your father. It must have been his."

Reflexively, Alanna clutched the coin.

"Take it with you to Italy. For good luck!"

Alanna opened her hand and turned the coin over, examining both sides. She raised it to her lips and kissed it gently. "You must keep this safe for me until I return. A good luck charm for the both of us."

"I do not think…"

"I insist. Give it to me when I return from Italy."

Alanna placed the coin in Will's hand and closed his fingers around it. She covered his hand with her own.

"Your wish is my duty, mistress." It was something he once heard Da say to Mam.

"You are my young squire, Will Clachan. Promise you will always be chivalrous."

"I promise." He wanted to kiss her again.

Before Will could imagine how to prolong her stay, Alanna was into her cloak and out the door. Away toward home one last time.

When he could no longer see her, Will placed his fingers between his lips and tried to whistle. He failed on his first attempt but tried again and miraculously succeeded. In the brief silence that followed, Will imagined Alanna removing her gloves. Carried on the wind, her whistle was loud and clear.

Will kept out of sight.

It was difficult to watch, but he needed one last glimpse of Alanna before she left Elgin. The driver was struggling to load her huge trunk into the coach. Will tried to imagine its contents. Shanks was there, wearing a handsome coat. He kissed his granddaughter on each cheek, holding both her hands, not wanting to let go. Murmuring some last instructions, he wiped at his face to stall his tears. She was leaving sooner than expected, hoping to avoid the onset of winter weather.

Will saw Alanna disappear into the shiny black coach. Shanks shook Isaac Forsyth's hand and thanked him profusely, wishing him a safe journey. Forsyth climbed in and the door banged shut. Painted boldly on its side was the name of the coach, known for its reliability: the Defiance. With a crack of the driver's whip, they were away. The coachman had a schedule to keep and a reputation to uphold. For an instant, the steam from the horses' breath lingered in the cold morning air. With a last echo of clopping hooves on cobblestones, the coach was down the road and gone.

What a fool I have been, Will thought. He knew there were wiser men than he who experienced heartbreak. It did not change his feelings. He longed to possess the power to somehow reason it all away. Escape the emotions he now suffered in the wake of Alanna's departure. He could never pretend she left him with his heart intact.

37

First Footer

This was no ordinary snowfall. No ordinary Hogmanay.

The storm was a "doonlay." Thick and heavy and drifting, there was nothing picturesque about it. Not the kind of snowfall a child might call a "katty-clean-doors." This snow was useless for sledding, or sliding, or snowballs.

There are so many words and names for snow, Will thought. So many types of frozen precipitation in Moray. Morrison had recently taught him a new one while telling a story from back when he was a boy. About a friend who died of "snaw-smoor."

"Of what?" Will had asked.

"Have ye never heard of snaw-smoor? Suffocation in a snow-drift. Just a boy, he was. Walking home alone. The storm was fierce and the drifts large. He tripped and fell headfirst into a great snow pile and could not get up. He suffocated, and then froze solid. It took a thaw before he was found."

Will shuddered. The storm was reason enough for him not to venture home for Hogmanay. The light was gone from the sky by midafternoon and would not reappear for eighteen hours. Earlier, when he was in town, Will had sent word so Mam would not worry. Now with the storm blowing in, Elgin would soon be under the weather. He would miss Mam's black bun cake, but she would save him a slice. In a house not filled with hungry boys, the end of a rich and dense Hogmanay black bun might last 'til spring.

Will stoked a generous fire and gave thanks for its warmth. The stone chimney meant there was no longer a hole in his roof, and the tight-fitted windows and door mattered on a night like this.

Not a day had passed and already Will missed Alanna. How could he not? The smell of her clung to his bed. It was difficult to convince himself she was truly gone. And equally hard to believe she was not gone forever.

After first learning of Alanna's plans, Will had shyly asked Forsyth if there were books about Italy in his library. With Shanks's permission, Will had paged through a volume about Florence. It was filled with drawings of amazing buildings and works of art. Will could not imagine Alanna returning to a place like Elgin from someplace like Italy.

Loneliness made Will want to smash something, but instead he gorged on food from the basket. He emptied a cider crock and opened another. After all it was a holiday, even though it did not feel like one. "Hogmanay and another new year," he muttered. He needed to be thankful for his family, his possessions, his situation, and all he had recently been given. He wanted to be less angry, less sad.

Will wiped his hands clean before opening the clasp on the locket, revealing Alanna's gift. The detail in the tiny sketch was breathtaking. Sighing, he closed the locket and tucked it away.

How many secrets was he now keeping from Mam? From Da? Eventually they were bound to find out. It was no longer solely about Alanna, the locket, and his creature. Will opened his shirt and removed a small chain hung round his neck. He stared at the key he had failed to show his father on Christmas day. A key of his own that opened the door to the ruin. He had intended to tell Da what a surprise it had been. How, after the locksmith had come and gone, Shanks handed Will two keys. A key to the keeper's hut, and Will's own key to the cathedral ruin.

The ruin key had come with a lecture from Shanks. "It's not just a key I'm handing you, Will. I'm giving you new responsibilities." Will had been too surprised to reply. "This decision is a matter of convenience. It is only logical to give you a key. But I insist on two things: never give this key to anyone unless I instruct you to do so. And under no condition do you allow someone into the ruin without my permission. Unless it's someone requesting a tour."

Will's own key to the ruin—what his father so anxiously longed for. He had intended to tell Da about it on Christmas. But once Da mentioned coming back to work with him, the timing felt wrong. The news that Shanks had entrusted him with a key could wait.

Will poked at the fire and wished he owned a book. Even if he didn't know all the words. Some little diversion telling someone else's story. Instead, he returned to the basket on the table. Alanna had emptied out the larder for him. So many crocks and jars and breadstuffs wrapped in cloths. He rearranged the contents searching for more shortbread. At the bottom of the basket the fulfillment of his prescient wish startled him. In his hand he held Alanna's page-thumbed copy of *Ivanhoe*.

With a book in his lap and an empty cider crock at his feet, Will dozed until the bells of St. Giles woke him, ringing in the new year. He tossed a last dead branch of heather into the fireplace and watched it burn down to ash. Its scent offered some comfort despite his low mood. He regretted his choice not to go home, where his brothers would be laughing and beating pans to mark the new year.

His remorse did not last. Moments after the bells stopped ringing, a fierce wind shook the keeper's hut. Snowflakes were already finding their way past the shutters and piling up against the new windowpanes. Will put the fire to bed and extinguished the lamp. He was ready to let sleep find him. Until he heard scraping and whimpering outside his door. The noise was too pitiful to be frightening, and too persistent to ignore.

"Who's there?" Will called. No one replied, but another wretched whimper trailed off in a moan. He could not bear the sounds. "Please God, do not let this be a witch," he mumbled, opening a small crack in the door. Before he could peek outside, a burst of fur shot through the opening. In a shower of snowflakes, whatever it was disappeared under the table.

"What in the name of…?" A wind gust nearly yanked the door from Will's hand, and he fought to slam it shut. He had no idea what had invaded his hut. But he wanted it gone. Will grabbed the fire poker. He heard the thing but could not see it in the darkness under the table. It was breathing hard in short puffs. The sounds could have belonged to a wild creature, or a young child with a stuffy nose. Will circled the table trying for a better look. "Come out now, ye wee beastie, whatever you are! You're too small to be a witch, that's for certain. Unless you're disguised as a cat!" Will raised the poker and waited, but nothing happened. Just hard breathing and the warming smell of something wild.

Will crept closer. He plucked a bit of dried bacon from the basket and stepped back quickly. If he opened the door and threw the bacon outside fast enough, the beast would surely go after it. He put down the poker. "On the count of three," Will said aloud, one hand holding the bacon and the other on the door handle. "One! Two! Three!" Will yanked open the door and tossed the bacon outside. A small wet furball leaped from its hiding place and jumped into the food basket on the table. Will leaned hard on the door to shut it against the wind. Cursing his failed plan, he turned to face the intruder.

Frozen in fear, two brown eyes stared up at Will. A morsel of bacon hung from its mouth.

"What are you?" Will bellowed. Frightened, the furball jumped from the table and skittered beneath a chair. It quickly swallowed the stolen morsel. Will squatted down for a better look. The fur was wet from melted snow, and the smell was familiar. "Are you a dog?" Will asked.

The small beast yipped in reply. Then it shook itself, releasing a fine spray before it set to trembling. Will reached into the basket and picked out another small scrap. Kneeling on the floor, he set the tidbit halfway between them. "Let's see what you look like, you little thief," Will said in a kinder tone. Slowly, a small wet pup crawled from under the chair, never taking his eyes from Will. His V-shaped ears quivered. His black nose wiggled toward the crumb of food on the floor.

Will considered grabbing the dog and tossing it back outside. But it was so small. Already Will's uninvited companion was working its way into his heart. An effective magic most dogs possessed. "Alright then, ye wee thief. Like it or not you are my First Footer on this New Year's Day. You best be bringing me good fortune."

Long before the sun was up, the pup woke Will with its whining.

The storm was over. Empty of snow, the fast-moving clouds blew out to sea on a wild wind. All was quiet in Elgin at the start of another year. In the dark there was no telling the hour.

Will donned his warmest clothes, including his new sweater.

Carrying a shovel and a small lamp to light the way, he ventured outside with the anxious pup to see what the storm left behind. Man and dog relieved themselves in a snowbank. There were patches where the snow had blown away. Ice-sheathed blades of grass poked up from the frozen ground. Will discovered the remains of a stale roll in his pocket. He waved the bread for the dog to smell, tempting the pup to follow close. "Come on, ye wee beast," Will called. They bounded through the drifts toward the ruin. The little dog tumbled along, sniffing and tunneling into the snow. "Are you a ratter?" Will asked.

The dog sneezed in reply.

At the door to the ruin Will removed a glove to retrieve his key. He felt the significance of the moment as he unlocked the ruin for the very first time. It was a week of firsts with no need to list them.

He watched the clouds sweep the dark sky, illuminated by the moon they were hiding. He set down the lamp and blew into his hands for warmth. The dog bounded off to explore. Despite the snow there were scents to discover. As the pup romped and tumbled, it occurred to Will that he had already broken one of Shanks's rules—bringing someone into the ruin. Except it wasn't exactly a someone. Will attempted to sort out the pup's age and breeds. It was a very young male, a terrier of some sort, with a bit of retriever. The rest he could not guess.

Will watched the sky. The clouds were too swift to ignore. Moonbeams peeked through as the clouds broke apart. The light splashed across the snow-covered ground, making shadows and shapeshifters. Will tried not to think about magic and witches. He looked for the dog, but it was nowhere in sight. Will removed his gloves and wet his lips. With no one to judge his success or failure, he whistled. Short bursts. Once, twice, three times he practiced his new skill. The pup was too young to know a whistle meant come.

Will picked his way carefully through the ruin, picturing the pathways he had cleared, now covered by snow and ice. Not far off, the dog snuffled and sneezed. Will made his way toward the sounds. Behind the choir wall he spied the dog. Digging furiously, it was tossing up snow like a whirlwind, nearly hidden in a shower of white. Something was demanding the dog's attention under all that snow. Will imagined it might be a frozen rat.

"I wish I could teach you to move rubble like that," Will called to the dog. "What's that you're after?" Will asked the pup. The dog ignored him, focused on its own buried treasure. The clouds parted and the moon emerged. Full and fat, it lit the breasts of new snow.

Will watched the little dog's frantic digging for a while before moving closer. He was curious what the pup might find. Whether it was something dead or alive, the dog would soon uncover it or wear itself out with the effort. A scatter of dirt, gravel, and grass mixed into the flying snow. The dog stopped digging and sniffed excitedly at the hole he had made. He looked up at Will with a happy puppy grin. Will approached slowly. Something in his gut encouraged hesitation. The dog sat down opposite Will on the other side of the hole. It cocked its head as though listening to something. The dog sniffed the air, then the hole, then the air again.

Will peered into the hole. A bit of moonlight took command of the sky. Something caught Will's eye under the rearranged bits of rubble. Next to a small frozen field vole, an object shone in the moonlight. Will reached into the hole with his shovel and dished up the vole for the dog. He carefully scraped away the dirt and gravel. Under it all there appeared to be something solid. Some sort of decorative rock. Will squatted for a closer look at the bottom of the hole.

The pup abandoned his prize—the vole was too frozen for the dog to eat. Instead, the little beast moved next to Will and leaned against him for warmth. They studied the hole. Will cleared away a bit more dirt with his gloved hand. He was uncertain whether he was looking at metal or stone. But what was clear were the bits of letters appearing under his fingers. Will grabbed a handful of clean snow and swiped away the filth of ages. He lifted the lamp for a better view. An image and a few letters appeared. Texture and forms. "A grave marker," Will mumbled. On his hands and knees, he did his best to uncover what he now knew was there.

In the strengthening moonlight, Will lost track of time. He worked to reveal as much of the object as possible until his fingers lost their ability to feel. He knew the dog was cold, too, even with its thick fur.

"When Jock smells you on me, he is going to be furious," Will muttered.

The pup yipped in reply.

Will got to his feet. His lamp had gone out. He began to imagine what Shanks might say when he saw this grave. It seemed to be an effigy of some sort. By the light of the moon Will could see the words *de la Hay*, and an *M* and *CCCC* all in a row. Will was certain there was more to uncover, but for now he was too cold and exhausted to continue. "Patience now. Excitement later," he mumbled.

No bells had chimed from St. Giles since the mark of the new year at midnight. Will stepped out from behind the choir wall. He stood stock-still and stared. Filling the empty oculus of the long-demolished stained-glass window, a Wolf Moon glowed as golden as the sun.

38

UNEXPECTED NEWS

Four years had passed. The dog was no longer a pup, and Will no longer a boy.

Will was a creature of the sun. His life was dictated by length of days and seasons of the year. The lack of daylight in midwinter could be forgiven once summer solstice approached. In Elgin the light now lingered long past midnight, barely escaping the western sky in time for dawn.

Will went to the river to bathe. The dog tumbled through grasses and wildflowers. He chased moths and snapped at bugs, pounced on small lizards and large grasshoppers, eating them whole. Mice, too, were fair game. At the river the dog splashed about, chasing small fishes. Feeding himself made Brodie happy. Swimming and fishing were pure joy. Having Will in the water with him was the best. Brodie's survival depended upon his self-sufficiency. Will's contribution to the dog's diet was sparse. Brodie did not eat Will's precious food, except for stray bits of dried bacon. A taste acquired on a long-ago Hogmanay morn.

With time the dog had grown, but he would never be large.

His personality was as mischievous as ever. Although now the tiny terror of fur was Will's friendly companion. Brodie's V-shaped ears tipped forward whenever Will spoke. He paid attention with his soulful brown eyes. His fur was coarse, thick, and short, good for cold weather and swimming. His color was a mix of golden browns with a scatter of red hairs gracing his expressive ears.

In the beginning, Will had called the wee beast "Dog." After watching him in the river, Will considered naming him Lossie. But instead, he settled on an old Pictish name given to a castle far up the road, and the mysterious man who lived there. Will named the dog Brodie. "I suppose this means you'll be staying," Will had sighed. "Once I've named you, I cannot kick you out."

Will was in the water playing with the dog when he heard Shanks call his name. The old man stood at the water's edge motioning Will to come out of the river. He waved a paper over his head. "We have urgent news!" he hollered.

Will's first thoughts were of Alanna. Her letters to Shanks had been less frequent of late, and Will knew how Shanks worried. At the shoreline Will quickly pulled on his clothes. Clearly something was wrong. He could see it in Shanks's expression. "What is it, sir?" Will asked, stepping into his boots and ascending the bank.

"A death! A funeral!" Shanks declared.

Will felt his stomach twist. *Oh God*, he thought, *let it not be her.*

Shanks seemed in a frenzy. "We've work to do!"

"Who's funeral, sir?"

Shanks handed Will the letter. "It came by express messenger early this morning. All the way from London! The same messenger took news to Gordon Castle. The messenger said both letters told the same story."

Will carefully scanned the contents of the letter. He now understood Shanks's urgency. "What is today's date?" Will asked. He rarely kept track of such things unless it was a holiday.

"The eighth of June. We have barely two days!" The old man's voice made it sound as though Judgment Day was approaching. The letter carried news of a ceremonial funeral to be held in the ruin for the last Duke of Gordon. Will now understood Shanks's concern.

"Most likely a member of the Gordon family will arrive soon to give us our instructions," Shanks said hopefully. "Unless they expect us to call on them at the castle. We need to alert the town council and the lord provost. Goodness, I do not know where to begin."

Will reread the long message. The carefully penned letter reported the death of the duke at his London home in Belgrave Square on May 28. His body was taken aboard one of the king's ships accompanied by his grieving widow and a party of close friends and peers. The late duke would arrive by sea with the ship docking near Gordon Castle, his ancestral home. There the late duke would lay in state. A funeral was scheduled for June 10 in Elgin Cathedral ruin, where his body would be placed in the family vault. A funeral procession was to be expected from Gordon Castle all the way to the ruin. After which the widow and family would retire by coach.

"Where will the rest of the procession go after the funeral is over?" Shanks wanted to know. "Might they be staying in town, or returning to the castle? Has anyone thought this through?" Shanks pulled at the sparse tufts of hair on top of his head.

"I am certain…" Will began, but Shanks cut him off.

"How can we be certain of anything?"

Will did not argue. His stomach grumbled. Whatever ideas he and Brodie might have had about a frolic and feast to start their day, the dog was about to be disappointed. "I will change into better clothes and you can send me to talk with the lord provost or to Master Forsyth. Then we can make plans. It is possible the lord provost has also received word."

Shanks nodded. Will knew what the old man would say next. "If only Alanna were here..." Shanks sighed.

Word from Gordon Castle soon reached Elgin's town elders. It was a healthy mix of fact and gossip. Forsyth shared what news he had with Will. "Although he was a Scotsman to the core, the duke and his wife preferred the society of London," Forsyth explained. "He also owned property in Bath where the couple were married. When he died, his colleagues in London were surprised by his funeral directives. They had assumed he would be buried in London's prestigious Highgate Cemetery. As we now know, that is not to be. Nor will he be laid to rest in the chapel at Gordon Castle. Nor at Brodie Castle, his wife's family home. Instead, the duke chose the family tomb on the grounds of Elgin Cathedral."

"Are we to assume his decision was a surprise to the family?" Will asked.

"Quite possibly," Forsyth replied. "The Gordon tomb in the ruin has long been ignored by the rest of the family. However, it seems the duke wished to lie among all the Dukes of Gordon who preceded him into the kingdom of death. Seeing as he is—was—the last of his line."

"I know the tomb," Will said. The Gordon tomb was located along the choir wall. Close by one of the oldest tombs in the cathedral, the tomb of William Hay of Lochloy. A stone chest supporting a recumbent knight in armor with a lion sleeping at his feet. The same tomb uncovered by Brodie on the pup's first Hogmanay. The year on the tomb was still readable in old Roman script: M CCCC

XXII. It was widely believed that William Hay had served with the Knights Templar before escaping persecution in France and taking refuge in Scotland.

"Aye," Forsyth said quietly, "nearly three hundred years of their lineage rests in the Gordon tomb. And the duke's last will and testament confirmed his intention to join them."

Later, Will found Morrison, and the two discussed what they knew. "Already the hotels and boardinghouses are filling up," Morrison said. "The number of Gordons milling about on Market Street is fast outnumbering the locals."

"Think what the town will look like by tomorrow at this time," Will agreed.

"If you don't mind, Will, I need you to run an errand. Do you think you can secure a large drape of black crepe? A piece of cloth big enough to cover the Gordon tomb."

"I'll do my best," Will replied. "Maybe from St. Giles?"

"A good thought. If not there, perhaps the dressmaker. If you find one, take it to the ruin straightaway and cover the tomb."

"I'll see to it, but what is the reason for the cover?"

"To dissuade gawkers until after the funeral."

"I understand." Will nodded.

"When I saw Shanks earlier," Morrison continued, "he told me there would be no ruin tours until after the funeral. People are already pressing him to let them see inside."

"I will be watchful, and assure the ruin stays locked," Will said.

"Once the funeral is over and the duke's remains are interred, it will be up to the widow to decide how long the tomb will remain covered," Morrison explained.

These protocols were new to Will. Although there were many graves and markers in the cathedral grounds, he had never witnessed the funeral of a nobleman.

"Most likely members of the family and his peers from London will request a private tour," Morrison suggested. "Others paying their respects will want tours, too. You and Shanks will be busy."

"I should be off, then. Where did you see Shanks last?" Will asked.

"He was headed for the ruin."

Shanks was relieved when Will arrived carrying a folded black cloth. Together they secured the drape over the Gordon tomb. Shanks looked skyward. "Let's hope the rain stays away. Nothing worse than a funeral procession in the rain."

Will surveyed the ruin. "What else needs done?"

"Let's smooth the pathway," Shanks said. "I have talked with the lord provost. He and the council will see to the arrangements with the family. A tent will be erected with a few chairs beneath it. Generally, people only linger but so long following a funeral. I suspect the immediate family will take their leave promptly after the final amen. Return to the castle and begin to grieve."

"How shall we handle the tours?" Will asked.

"No tours on the day of the funeral unless the immediate family asks to be shown around. The following day we will open. If the crowd is large, we will each take a group.

"That seems reasonable," Will agreed.

"I suppose those coming from London will be fascinated by this ancient ruin where the duke chose to be buried," Shanks said. He turned to admire the recently installed gates at the now-grand entrance. It had taken more than two years to clear after Shanks and Will discovered four ancient steps under all the debris. For centuries the entrance had been hidden under layers of rubbish and rubble. The new gates gave the entrance a majestic appearance. It was not difficult to imagine a funeral procession passing into the ruin.

As had become his new habit when admiring the grand entrance, Shanks removed the snuffbox from his pocket. It was a fine little memento presented by the town of Elgin. A beautiful thing made especially for Shanks by an Elgin silversmith. The front was inscribed with an image of Elgin Cathedral, and on the reverse a note of thanks: "From the inhabitants of Elgin as a reward to John Shanks keeper of the Cathedral. For his attention and care of it generally, and in particular for discovering the grand entrance now restored to its just proportion."

Will did not mind being excluded from the recognition. But he did think the message etched on the snuffbox might have been shorter.

39

FUNERAL FOR A DUKE

Will wore his best suit to the funeral.

He had long outgrown the altered clothes once belonging to Alanna's father. These days both Morrison and Mrs. Hendry contributed to his small wardrobe. None of it was new, but none of it was patched. And although most of the clothes were thirdhand, everything fit him properly.

Will and Shanks stood waiting at the entrance gates. It was rare for either of them to be so well-attired. The morning was warm but not uncomfortable, even dressed in dark clothing. Days like this were all about waiting. At the edge of town where the road to Elgin met the road to Aberdeen, Elgin's town elders patiently watched for the funeral procession. When it arrived from Gordon Castle, they escorted the cortege to the ruin.

Will heard the procession before he could see it. "Look!" he cried, pointing down the road when at last they came into view. It was unlike anything he had ever seen before. The pipers led the way dressed in full regalia. In their wake followed a caisson carrying the casket of the last Duke of Gordon. It was draped in black and pulled by a team of handsome horses. They were perfectly groomed and shiny as ebony. The immediate family followed close behind. All wore the Gordon regimental tartan along with their mourning clothes. Will believed the Gordon Highlanders tartan was among the most beautiful of the highland plaids. Its Scotland sky blue and forest green were the colors of the Moray countryside. Behind the family trailed the more distant relations. And behind them, a seemingly endless stream of the duke's peers who had accompanied his body from London. When the bagpipes ceased the sounds of grief were unmistakable. Horses' footfalls, jangling reins, human whispers, and muted sobs.

The duke had not died young, but his wife was twenty-one years his junior. She held the full attention of anyone who could see her. A handsome and dignified woman, she possessed something many widows did not—her own identity. She had been a Brodie before marrying the duke. And she brought her own small fortune into the marriage, allowing the duke to pay off all his debts, gambling and otherwise. Although she was not the duke's primary heir, she was enough of a businesswoman to assure her own comfortable destiny after her husband's death. They had no children together, but the late duke recognized three illegitimate children. Now adults, they processed behind their father's statuesque widow.

With both Gordon and Brodie family estates just up the road from Elgin, the confluence of relatives parading into the ruin was the largest gathering of people Will had ever seen. It required an extravagant amount of time for the procession to enter the ruin. Will and Shanks bowed their heads solemnly as each clutch of souls passed by.

"I believe we may be almost out of room, sir," Will whispered to Shanks.

Shanks looked down the road. "We will close the gates soon."

"How will we know when?" Will asked.

"The minister is the last to be admitted. See him there with the Bible in his hand?"

"What about the rest of the people behind him?"

"Curiosity-seekers, outcasts, black sheep, and pretenders," Shanks muttered. "Be ready to close the gates fast behind the man of God."

A familiar face appeared not far back in the crowd. "Wait! There's Morrison." Will pointed.

"Here to help us," Shanks said. "Do let him in after he stems the tide. We will lock the gates from within."

Shanks cleared the way as the pallbearers bore the casket into the ruin and rested it on a bier close by the Gordon tomb. Without the pipers there was only the silence of an ancient place. And the breathing of more people gathered in the ruin than anyone living could recall.

Morrison and Will positioned themselves where they could keep an eye on the gates. But they were still close enough to see the widow's auburn hair tucked beneath black lace. Near enough to hear her sniffle and sigh. She briefly glanced in Will's direction with a hint of a smile.

"This might be the largest concourse of gentry and nobility Elgin has ever seen," Morrison whispered in Will's ear.

The minister called for a prayer and then read from the Bible. A senior member of the Gordon clan spoke of the dead man's life. Followed by praise and recognition from one of the duke's peers who had traveled from London to have his say. And like all funerals, it was what went unsaid that was most interesting about the late duke. He had been a strikingly handsome man right up to his death at age sixty-six. The last male descendent of the ducal family. A ladies' man, truth be told, but well-liked by his friends and family. The duke's life offered nothing much to object to. Other than the existence of the three illegitimate children, spawned before his marriage.

There was less to say about him, and more to say about his wife. Elizabeth Brodie was the duke's primary asset in life. By paying his sizable debts when they married, she earned the duke's life-long gratitude and love. Some said she was the richest woman in Scotland. She was an only child, the niece of the Brodie of Brodie, an heiress of great wealth. She had made the duke very happy.

The service ended and the bagpipes resumed their lament. Will stepped quickly to unlock the gates. Morrison, close on his heels, made a way for the departing family. As the widow left the ruin on the arm of her uncle, she gave Will a sidelong glance, and swished her widow's weeds over his polished boots, close enough to brush his pants leg.

As the mourners continued filing out, Morrison leaned in close to Will. "You cannot deny she was flirting with you!" Morrison whispered excitedly.

"Ridiculous," Will mumbled, blushing all the same.

"I would not discount it entirely if I were you. She may not be the most handsome woman, and she's older than you for certain. But they say she is worth one hundred thousand pounds!"

Never had there been so many people waiting outside the ruin for a tour.

Gawkers, visitors from London, and Gordon relations all lined up to see what was locked inside the walls. The morning after the funeral, Shanks and Will escorted tours through the ruin. Shanks recited his most beloved stories and Will polished his own favorite tales. The Gordon tomb remained covered, despite repeated requests for a quick peek. "Not until the widow so orders," Shanks explained, using noble tones as watchman and keeper and shower of Elgin Cathedral ruin.

Eventually the crowds diminished. The basket of small rocks kept by the entrance for souvenir seekers was empty. Although plenty more still littered the grounds.

After so many tours, Shanks needed a day of rest. He locked the gates telling Will, "If any more Gordons bother you, tell them to come back another day." The old ruin keeper produced a few coins from his pocket and handed them to his assistant. Shanks knew visitors sometimes gave Will coins directly, but Will and Shanks were long past discussing how the small gratuities were shared. It was entirely up to Shanks and how generous or grumpy he was feeling.

When the visitors dispersed and Shanks was gone, Will unlocked the ruin. He stepped inside with Brodie at his heels. "No digging," Will ordered. The dog snorted and trotted off. A breeze stirred the black drape.

Will considered how much he and Shanks had accomplished. All the old graves and tombs uncovered, cleaned, cataloged, and repaired. The extensive pathways winding through the cathedral yard. The massive task of digging out the grand entrance. And an assortment of carvings Shanks displayed in the chapter house. Yet Will was still making barrow runs to the Witches Pool. They were still rearranging rubble, searching for what remained undiscovered. Will now thought of it as a grand treasure hunt that would likely never end. At least not in his lifetime. That realization fascinated Will, but frustrated John Shanks.

There was talk of a museum in Elgin. A Scientific Society had recently formed with an interest in cataloging and displaying collections and specimens from the region. The group could not move fast enough for Shanks. He believed his discoveries in the ruin deserved to be prominently displayed.

Will thought the broken statuary, decorative carvings, fused glass, and metallic remnants seemed insignificant compared to the historic graves they had uncovered. Many dated back hundreds of years. The ruin was once again becoming a place people in Moray wished to be buried. That fact disturbed John Shanks. He wanted the ruin to be appreciated for its history, not for its use as a graveyard. Although Will was certain that when the time came, Shanks would be interred here, too. Presently however, despite the man's advanced age, John Shanks was showing no signs of dying. And no one knew that more intimately than Will Clachan.

Will wandered past the more prestigious tombs to a small, unadorned gravestone. It remained his favorite. He enjoyed showing it to visitors and watching their reactions. He had uncovered this lowly marker not long after Brodie dug up the knight's tomb. The contrast between the two memorials seemed a good reminder of the equalizing power of death. No decoration, no name, and no dates were etched into the flat stone. Just this:

The World is a Cite full of streets
And death is the mercat that all Men meets
If Lyfe were a thing that monie could buy
The poor could not live and the rich would not die.

Will tried to ignore the early-morning knock at the keeper's hut door.

A gentle knock and then another produced a groan from Will and a muffled "woof" from the dog. Will called out, "Sorry! No tours today. Come back another time." The only reply was another knock. Will opened the door just wide enough to shoo away who-ever was there.

"Hello?" a soft voice asked.

The dog commenced barking. "Hush, Brodie!" Will ordered.

"Pardon?" the voice outside asked sharply, "How do you know my maiden name?"

Will flung the door wide. The widow Gordon stood outside frowning. "I am a Brodie by birth, but most people refer to me as Duchess, unless they are a close friend. Then they may call me Eliza."

Will made a quick courtly bow. "My apologies, Duchess. You see, my dog's name is Brodie."

"I am certain my uncle, the Brodie of Brodie, would find that amusing." The duchess chuckled.

"How may I be of service?" Will offered meekly.

"I'll be returning to London soon and I was hoping I might visit the Gordon tomb before I depart. Would that be possible?"

"Now, do you mean?" Will asked meekly.

"Yes. Now would be best." She glanced at Will's shoeless feet and grinned. "If it's not an imposition."

"Of course, Duchess. Just a moment." He was unsure about leaving her standing outside.

"I'll wait right here," she said, as if reading his mind.

Will stepped into his boots and pulled on his jacket. He combed a hand through his hair and told the dog to stay. The duchess was perfectly dressed in many less layers of black than she wore to her husband's funeral. Will had never seen such an attractive widow. He noted the delicate pair of slippers on her feet and offered his arm. "My name is Will Clachan. I am the assistant ruin keeper."

Her eyes danced. "So I have been told." She gave a small wave to the waiting coachman, assuring him all was as it should be. At the entrance to the ruin, Will unlocked the gate. The duchess took his arm again and he carefully escorted her to the Gordon tomb. "I would like a moment with my husband. Do not go far. I will not be long."

Will moved far enough away to still hear her soft voice, but he could not distinguish the words. She might have been reminiscing, or praying, or a little of each. When she called to him, Will quickly returned to her side. "What else might I do for you, Duchess?" he asked as she took his arm once more.

"I understand the ruin's chapter house is a sight many come to see. Will you show it to me?"

"Of course." He walked her carefully along the paths and paused at the entrance to the chapter house. Will began to wonder whether it was appropriate for them to be alone together. "Shall I fetch your driver, Duchess?"

"Am I making you uncomfortable?" A small smile sneaked into her expression. "Fear not. I do not bite."

Will blushed and diverted his gaze as he helped her through the doorway. As her eyes adjusted, the duchess softly gasped. A common reaction for first-time visitors to the chapter house. There was so much to look at all at once.

"Shall I leave you for a moment?"

"No. Please do stay. I would like you to tell me a story about this place. I have been told you are a very fine storyteller." She settled onto one of the stone benches and looked up. The black lace scarf draped over her head slid away as she leaned back, exposing her beautiful features and her gorgeous hair. Then she released her shawl, revealing a lovely bodice and its contents.

Will did his best not to stare. She looked too young to be the widow of an old man. He sensed she was aware of his eyes. He cleared his throat. "You wish for a story, madam?"

"Yes, please. A story but not a history lesson."

Will smiled. "I have just the one." He proceeded to tell the story of the angel sculpture hidden up in the ceiling. About Alanna and Robert Reid ascending the scaffolding. How Alanna was hauled up to the roof with her sketch pad, and the beautiful sketches she made. How she had named the angel sculpture "Mirth."

"If I cannot see the sculpture, where may I see this drawing?" the duchess asked.

Will hesitated for a moment. "In Italy." He did not elaborate.

"Italy?"

"Yes. Mistress Shanks took her drawings with her when she left Elgin to study in Florence."

"What a shame. I would have liked to see her work."

Will remained quiet. He had not intended to discuss Alanna.

"Maybe someday I will travel to Florence." The duchess sighed softly. "In truth, I have no idea what to do next. Of course, I am ob-ligated to return to London and see to my late husband's estate. Meet with his solicitors and oversee the disposition of property and assets." She paused and looked directly at Will. "I am needing an assistant. Would you care to accompany me to London as my com-panion? Once my husband's affairs are settled, I will likely return to Moray. After that, who knows? I have always dreamed of traveling to Italy." The duchess gazed directly at Will. "What do you think?"

Flustered, Will blushed. "Oh. I do not think…" Questioning the duchess's true intentions he looked away, unable to control his face. "I have responsibilities here, you see. My work in the ruin. My family…"

"Are you married, Will?" she asked. "I was already married to the duke by the time I was your age." She stared at the ceiling, thinking aloud, "And now I am nearly the same age the duke was when we wed."

"I am not married. But my parents and brothers live here in Elgin."

"Ah, well. You cannot blame me for trying. You seem such a competent young man."

"Thank you, Duchess."

"Please. Call me Eliza." The duchess stood and casually replaced her shawl and veil. "Thank you, Will. You have been most kind."

Will offered his arm. She ran a gloved hand down his sleeve before taking a firm hold of him. He walked her carefully out of the ruin to her waiting carriage. The driver jumped down to open the door.

"Maybe we will see each other again when I am back visiting my relatives." She looked up into Will's face and gave him a most attractive smile.

"Come for another tour and I will tell you more stories." He returned her look with one of his own.

The coachman helped the duchess into the carriage and closed the door. She leaned out the window. "A favor, Will."

"Anything, Duchess."

"Please. Do not name any more dogs after me."

40

THE MAIL COACH

Four summer solstices had passed since Alanna had departed for Italy. During those years an unbelievable amount of work had transpired in the ruin. Will did not count slashes in the notebooks as frequently as he once did. The last time he tallied up, the notebooks showed 983 barrows of rubble carted to the Witches Pool. He also kept a list of new discoveries he and Shanks had made. Graves, mostly. But other bits, as well.

Waiting for mail from Alanna was like picking at a scab that never healed. The mail coach made weekly stops in Elgin, and it was a regular reminder of how much Will missed the girl.

Will disliked his memory of the last time he had seen Alanna. That cold winter day she left Elgin. He preferred to remember her in sunlight, reading and sketching out of doors. Spring was a more reasonable time to dwell on lost love. In springtime his thoughts of Alanna glided past the solstice and lasted into summer. It was a time when the Moray region imitated the Garden of Eden. It became a lush and fragrant land bursting with beauty and the goods of the Earth. Enough to keep even the poorest fool physically fed right through autumn. But feeding Will's emotions was another matter.

He worked hard not to dwell on his first love. He even revisited the duchess's offer, and the possibility that she would soon return to Moray. Thoughts of the duchess still made Will uncomfortable but not without wondering what he was missing in London. Meanwhile, he accepted invitations to social gatherings and attended the town's celebrations. But regardless of other women who passed through Will's life, Alanna still haunted his dreams.

Mrs. Hendry regularly insisted on Will's company. She refused to allow him to mope. "You are much too young a man to have a broken heart," she informed him.

"Tell that to my heart," was Will's customary reply.

Davina Hendry was good company. She taught Will about social manners as well as matters of the heart. Took over from his mam in seeing to Will's appearance. "You are much too handsome a young man not to look your best," Mrs. Hendry insisted.

Will's hut did not have any form of running water. Only a pitcher and washbowl perched on a stand with a porcelain chamber pot. Except for an occasional bath in the river, Will was bathed and groomed regularly at Mrs. Hendry's boardinghouse. In winter months he ate his meals there, as well. But Mrs. Hendry was not fond of Brodie. "I will not have a dog sitting under my table while people are dining," she told Will. "Not even your dog. No matter how charming he may be." So, for most of the year, Will and Brodie fed themselves. Will eventually became Mrs. Hendry's friend, after serving as something more ill-defined. An entertainment, or perhaps a dalliance.

For Will, there was a difference between living a solitary life and being lonely. He wished for neither. Which was why Brodie was such a blessing. And why Will was always pleased to have one of his younger brothers visit him at the keeper's hut. Only his mother had not come to see him there. During a visit home she confided, "It would put a crack in my heart to see you living so lonely an existence."

"But Master Shanks is fine company, Mam. He's a good talker."

"There's no denying that," Mam laughed.

In the months after Alanna's departure, a flurry of letters arrived addressed to Shanks. Long letters, full of all her news and excitement about Florence. Some included tiny sketches. Miniatures of the view from her window. A statue in a square. Garden paths. Even a sketch of what looked like a bowl of worms that she labeled pasta and noted it was her dinner. Shanks had shared most of those letters with Will, reading them aloud in the chapter house. They found joy and solace together in hearing from Alanna and missing her. It was not long before the initial flurry of correspondence trailed off and settled into a less frequent report. The letters soon became much shorter. Although the old ruin keeper wrote to his granddaughter faithfully, her letters to him arrived further and further apart. A fact that weighed heavy on Shanks. But the sparseness of correspondence did not keep him from meeting the mail coach no matter the weather. When there was no letter from Italy, Will could read the old man's face and his slumped shoulders. He was bereft after the mail coach rolled out of town.

Will had his own correspondence from Alanna. Four letters addressed only to him. Each now dog-eared and smudged, tucked away with his other treasures. His first letter from Alanna was written soon after she arrived in Florence. He could read most of it, but some words he did not know. He asked James for help, and he was happy to assist. "Florence is a magical place, Will," the letter began. "So much to see all at once. At times Italy can make a person feel dizzy with the beauty of it all. I do not know if you would like it here. It is very warm and very crowded. I am already sketching everything in sight. My teacher wants me to slow down and focus on one subject. Otherwise, a person might become ill surrounded by so much beauty." There was more. All of it about her new life. Nothing about missing him or Elgin. She did not sign it "Fondly," or even "Your friend." Only "Alanna." By the time her fourth letter arrived, it was signed "A.M.O.S." That was when Will knew he had lost her.

Will was removing his boots when he heard a terrible wailing outside.

His youngest brother was sobbing on the doorstep of the keeper's hut.

"What is it, Ross? What's happened? Has Da been injured? Is Mam unwell?" Ross buried his face in his brother's chest and cried uncontrollably.

Will lifted his brother's chin. He tried but failed to recall how it felt to be neither man nor boy. Only a fleeting recollection of freedom and misery. Ross's face was smeared with snot and tears. Will offered his kerchief. "Dry your eyes and wipe your nose. Then sit beside me and tell me what has happened." Brodie trotted over and rested his head in the boy's lap. Ross's tears began anew as he buried his face in the dog's thick coat. In sympathy Brodie let out a baying howl.

"Enough!" Will got the attention of both boy and dog. "Brodie!" Will commanded, "Go lie down! And you, Ross Clachan. Stop weeping and tell me straightaway what has happened." Will was rarely stern, which made his orders effective.

"I've run away," Ross moaned, wiping his nose on his sleeve.

"What's happened?" Will asked once more. "Does Mam know where you are?"

The tears reappeared. "It's Jock. Jock died!" The boy's distraught face and the news he brought lanced Will's heart. "When? What happened?" Will needed to know.

Ross could not make eye contact with Will. "We played ball and went for a walk to look for rabbits. When we came home, Jock lay down in the yard and fell asleep. Then Mam tossed a bone into the yard for him. Jock didn't move. That's when Mam noticed he wasn't breathing."

Will felt as though someone had ripped away a piece of his heart. "Oh, Ross, I am so, so sorry." Will hugged his brother and wiped at his own tears. After Ross assured him that someone knew where he had gone, Will sat still and listened to the boy without interrupting.

Quietly, Ross said, "I do not know if I can live without Jock because I never have before. Jock has always been there. For my entire life. And now he's not."

Will whispered, "I loved him, too. He was my dog first, you know."

"He was your dog first, and you left him. He was my dog last."

"I remember the day I brought him home," Will told Ross. "Da said I could not keep him, but I hid him in my blankets. Da found out and threatened to make us both sleep in the yard."

"What happened?" Ross asked, eyes now wide.

"We slept out in the yard. But it was summer and not a difficult thing to do. In the morning Mam had words with Da and the next thing I knew, Da said the dog could stay. But it would have to sleep outside because there were already too many breathers under one roof. That didn't last long. Jock howled to be let in, and Mam convinced Da that Jock would be a better guard dog sleeping inside the house."

Ross's eyes grew misty. "Mam is wonderful."

Brodie crept close to Ross and put his snout on the boy's leg. The dog raised his concerned eyes to the boy's face. Ross hugged the dog hard around the neck.

"Believe me, Ross. I feel your sadness."

Ross looked up at Will and nodded.

"I will not tell you that the sadness will go away. It will always be there whenever you think of Jock. Eventually, you will think of him less and less. And when you do think about him, it will be to remember what a good dog he was for such a long time." Will's eyes filled. "It will take time, Ross, but time heals wounds of the heart. I know you do not believe me, but eventually it will not hurt so much."

He glanced out the window, gauging the hour. "It's too late to walk home now. You'll need to spend the night. Hopefully, Mam will not worry."

"Can I sleep with Brodie?"

"I'll get you a blanket. But we'll be up early to walk you home.

There was work to do in the ruin, but first Will would walk his young brother home.

"Can Brodie come with us?" Ross pleaded.

"Not today. He needs to stay and guard the ruin." There was only a kernel of truth in Will's excuse, but Ross nodded respectful-ly. Together the brothers set off for the Clachan croft. While Ross fretted over his likely punishment for running off, Will feared his parents might be sick with worry. Luckily, Luke had discreetly followed his young brother, and once he realized where the boy was headed, he returned home reporting that Ross was with Will.

When the oldest and youngest Clachan brothers arrived home, Da was the first out the door to greet them. He placed a firm hand on Ross's shoulder. "Glad you are home, son," he said. The men patted backs while Mam hugged and kissed Ross. The resemblance between Da and Ross was more striking than ever. Those similarities, along with his status as the youngest child, helped Ross escape punishments the older boys had sustained at his age.

Will overheard Da whisper to Mam, "I am finding it difficult to punish someone who looks so much like myself."

Mam replied, "*Spareth the rod* is just fine by me."

"Ross," Da said kindly, "we have made a place for Jock. His favorite sunny spot by the garden wall."

Ross was doing his best not to cry. He squared his shoulders but remained close to Mam.

"We thought we might have a little service for Jock," Mam said. She placed a hand on Ross's back, but her eyes were on Will. He had spotted the small bundle wrapped in a clean cloth lying by the back door. Luke carefully carried the shrouded dog outside, and everyone followed. With great care Luke laid the dog in the hole Da had dug.

"I thought you might say a few words, Will. Since he was your dog first. Maybe something from the duke's funeral," Da suggested.

Will closed his eyes and tried to recall the duke's service. "Blessed are those who mourn," Will recited, pulling the minister's words from his memory. "For they will be comforted. Do not fear, for I am with you. Do not let your hearts be troubled." Will felt his own heart aching. "There is a time for everything. A time to be born and a time to die. A time to tear down and a time to build."

"Aye. Amen to that," Will's father whispered.

"A time to weep and a time to laugh, a time to mourn and a time to dance. Amen."

Will opened his eyes and looked at his family. "Let's each say something we liked about Jock. I'll go first. What I loved most about Jock…" Will paused. The words stuck in his throat. He began again, speaking more quickly. "What I loved most was how he would follow me anywhere. No matter what else might have his attention—a rabbit or a bird to chase. He would always go with me. He was the happiest dog I've ever seen." With tears in his eyes, Will looked to Mam.

"He appreciated my cooking, even when I only gave him the burned bits," Mam smiled and swiped away a tear.

"He was never my dog, but he was a darn good fisher. He could catch a fish nearly twice his size," Andrew offered in admiration.

"I never knew another dog who liked me no matter what," Da mumbled. "And that's saying something."

Luke's eyes twinkled. "I'm going to miss his snoring. How will I ever sleep at night without that dog snoring in my ear?"

Everyone laughed and sniffled.

"And he sure could chase a ball," Luke added.

Ross stepped away from Mam and disappeared around the side of the croft. He returned with the old rag ball and placed it in the hole next to the bundle. He did his best not to cry.

"Are you sure about that?" Andrew asked Ross. "You might wish you still had that old ball if you get another dog."

"There will never be another dog like Jock," Ross lamented.

"You never know." Mam patted Ross's shoulder. "One day another dog might become your new friend."

"But not like Jock," Ross repeated.

"No. Not like Jock," Mam agreed.

"He knew all my secrets," Ross whispered.

Ross's words grabbed Will's heart. "Mine, too," Will whispered.

As Da gently patted dirt on the little grave, Mam led the boys back inside. "I've a fine broth simmering with plenty of lovely vegetables. The baps are in the oven. Why don't you eat with us, Will?"

Will smelled the food and his belly pleaded. "Aye. Alright, then," he said, taking a seat at the table. "But I cannot stay long." As Will spoke he looked at Mam's face. She was busy stirring the pot. Mam did not seem herself. She was pale and there were circles under her eyes. There was something about the way she was standing. Maybe it was Ross running off or Jock's death. Maybe she was just tired. He noticed the veins in her hands and neck as she placed a full bowl before him.

"There," she said softly, gently touching the back of Will's neck. Even her voice sounded weary.

Will carefully took Mam's hand and met her eyes. The others were still outside. "Are you unwell, Mam? You do not look yourself."

For a moment she laid her cheek on the top of his head and gently removed her hand from his grasp. "I am just tired," she offered.

The rest of the Clachan men came through the door. Andrew's arm was draped around Ross's shoulders. Luke and Da were talking about quarry work.

Will listened to their latest news. Then he told a few stories of his own. "There's talk that Elgin Academy might be adding another building. Have you heard that, Da?"

"Aye, I have." He winked at Will. "I might have to barter some schooling for Ross in exchange for foundation stones."

"What's that?" Ross's eyes grew large at the mention of school. Everyone laughed.

"Do not worry your head, Ross," Luke said. "You'll not be needing classroom learning as long as Mam is our teacher."

Only Will saw the shadow pass over Mam's face before she joined in the laughter.

41

Sketches of the Past

Will and Shanks enjoyed giving tours to visitors.

Yet Shanks never stopped talking about the unfinished work in the ruin. Only Will foresaw a time when a stack of notebooks filled with slash marks would gather dust in some Elgin attic. But removing the rubble might go on forever.

When they were clearing the ruin's grand entrance, Shanks had unearthed a trove of medieval stone carvings. Broken faces and figures, cracked grotesques and gargoyles. In ages past they had decorated the cathedral's columns. Shanks found them amusing and displayed these capitals and cornices inside the ruin. But Will thought the nightmarish figures were a distraction from the beauty of the chapter house.

After the duke's funeral, Will and Shanks made an important decision. They would stop their random digging and focus their efforts, just as they had done when clearing the grand entrance. Hopeful for another glorious discovery they discussed removing the largest remaining mounds of rubble in the ruin. The great pile was wedged between the choir walls and the chapter house. "I am fearful it could bury us if we disturb it," Shanks told Will. "Or worse, create a landslide and damage the chapter house."

"We will be cautious," Will assured Shanks. And with great care they began carting away the immense stone pile. Shanks was quick to lose interest in the project. But Will believed there was something more to discover. Something more striking than a carved goblin with an evil grin, flaunting bare buttocks. Will understood that tourists expected something more than a tidied ruin. Very few visitors could appreciate the removal of tons of rubble as a tangible accomplishment. To take credit for what was no longer there was meaningless. It was easier to point to the grave markers Will and Shanks had uncovered as evidence of their work.

The discoveries in the ruin were largely credited to Shanks, but most were found by Will. He had saved the carved white hand and dug up the bits of fused medieval glass that were remnants from the great fire. He had uncovered the first ancient graves inside the choir. (Although, credit for finding the knight's gravestone belonged entirely to Brodie.) And it was Will who rescued the massive brass key that once opened some remarkable cathedral door. But it was the little carved creature Will still secreted away that offered hope of more wonderful discoveries.

Shanks speculated on how the great pile might shift as they pulled it apart. Both men were anxious for progress.

The pile's first landslide followed a week of careful digging. The falling rubble moved slowly, giving Shanks and Will time to retreat.

"I believe this pile was part of the central tower that fell during the great windstorm in the 1700s," Shanks told Will one morning. The speculation fit the stories they recited to visitors. Here was some last vestige of the tower that earned the cathedral its nickname as the Lantern of the North. "Thinking we will find anything here—anything more than handsome rubble…" Shanks shook his head, not bothering to finish his thought.

"It's still too soon to know, sir," Will insisted.

The next morning Will was up early and went to the river to wash. Recently, he was paying more attention to his cleanliness. Brodie tagged along. Being a dog who loved rolling in stinking dead things, he was never one to judge good company by bad smells. By the time Will arrived at the ruin, the door was already opened. He walked inside expecting to see Shanks. To his surprise, his father and Shanks stood side by side with their backs to Will. They were looking up at the large rubble pile where Will and Shanks had been working.

Will was about to speak when he saw what had their attention. Another large landslide of rubble had fallen to the ground. Emerging from the pile was a colossal stone statue of a bishop. From the chest up it seemed mostly intact. "Heavens!" Will exclaimed.

"Will!" Shanks grabbed Will's shoulder. "Why didn't you come get me? How did you dig this out?"

His father was also awestruck by the mammoth sculpture. "To think it's been here all this time waiting to be uncovered."

Will was amazed, too. Not only by the statue but by the inexplicable sight of Shanks and Da cheerfully standing side by side. The two men Will sincerely wished to impress seemed to believe that he, Will Clachan, had dug out this giant stone bishop on his own. The sum of those facts left Will speechless.

As it turned out, Tom Clachan was there because Shanks had sent word. The Office of Works Committee had at last approved funds for the buttresses, with one stipulation. Robert Reid had designated Tom Clachan to supervise the work. But that topic of conversation was quickly lost when the two men entered the ruin and saw the larger-than-life stone bishop. From the statue's midsection down, the rubble pile remained.

"How did you do it?" Shanks pressed Will.

"I didn't. The rubble must have slid away on its own."

In slack-jawed silence, Shanks could only gape in wonder. The figure was carved from beautiful white stone that reminded Will of the blocks his father was cutting at Pluscarden Abbey quarry. For a while longer, the three men stood and gawked.

Then Will moved closer, carefully picking his way through the rubble. He looked up at the bishop's face, especially the nose. He reached to touch the smooth stone made to look like flowing folds of cloth decorated with carved religious symbols. Will's sensory memory took him back to the sleeping man he had seen when he was a child. There was no doubt. Will was certain the same artisan had chiseled them both.

James Thompson paced the courtyard outside Isaac Forsyth's home.

When he saw Will, his face lit up. "At last! There you are."

"An unexpected visitor to the ruin." Will shrugged. "I came as fast as I could." Will rapped the door knocker. The ancient house had a history. It was once a haven for the Knights Templar fleeing persecution in France. Forsyth used the unusual tower room for his circulating library, the first of its kind in the region.

"If I could be anything at all, I might like to be a bookseller like Forsyth," James said wistfully as they waited.

But Will knew better. James Thompson was becoming a scholar. He was helping Hugh Miller search for fish fossils along the Moray Firth coastline. Miller had been a stonemason before becoming a self-taught geologist and corresponding with Charles Darwin. James was so focused on geology that he trained Will to watch for fossils on the headstones unearthed in the ruin. Will was certain James would soon be off to Edinburgh or London to study and teach.

Forsyth's girl opened the door, blushing at the sight of two handsome young men.

"We are here at the invitation of Master Forsyth." James smiled shyly.

"He is out this afternoon," the girl explained as they stepped inside. "The books you requested are on the table in the library. Stay as long as you like." She opened the heavy wooden door leading to the tower room. "My name is Margaret. I will show you out when you are done."

"Is she new?" James asked, once out of earshot.

"I've not seen her before," Will replied as they climbed the circular staircase.

James and Will were now regular visitors to the library. Forsyth offered it for Will's reading lessons when he learned the young teacher was volunteering his time.

James removed a science book from his worn leather bag. "I borrowed this when I was here last."

The two pulled up chairs side by side at the long table where several books were laid out. "These are the most comfortable chairs I have ever had the pleasure to enjoy." James closed his eyes and shifted his slight frame into the ample leather cushions.

Will laughed. "I know to put on clean clothes before coming here."

"Can you imagine the Knights Templar meeting in this room?"

"Do you think they could read?" Will asked.

"Unlike most knights trained solely in the art of warfare, the Knights Templar were well-educated. Their duty was to guard the Holy Sepulchre. Beyond their vows of knighthood, they were bound not to marry."

Will reached for the book closest to him. *The Pictures of Scotland* by Robert Chambers. "I know of this book. Shanks and Forsyth have brought it into the ruin to compare its descriptions with our finds. Only recently have I been included in those conversations."

"What's changed?"

"Shanks is showing his age. Recently, Forsyth has come to me about matters concerning the ruin."

"Are you familiar with the story of Elgin's favorite son, Andrew Anderson?" James asked. "A lieutenant-general who worked for the East India Company. He brought his fortune back to Elgin and built the Free School at the start of the century."

"I have often heard his story," Will nodded. "Told by visitors to the ruin looking for the place where he and his destitute mother took refuge when Anderson was an infant. There are so many versions of that story. Shanks claims Anderson never visited the ruin after he returned to Elgin."

"I have been told he was a recluse," James said. "He wanted little to do with public service in Elgin, beyond the school he funded and its students." James thought for a moment. "So which version of his story do you tell?"

"The one where Anderson's destitute mother sheltered in Elgin's chapter house to suckle her infant son. There's no way of knowing the truth of it. So we let people decide for themselves."

James reached for a different book. "I was told by the school librarian that the man who wrote this book borrowed heavily from Chambers's *Pictures of Scotland.* Have you seen this one before?"

"I have not," Will replied.

"*Sketches of the Past and Present State of Moray* by William Rhind," James read the title aloud. "Published in Edinburgh in 1839. Rhind has a lot to say about the history of Moray. The man is quite a windbag."

Will chuckled.

"This book is a collection of excerpts from many sources, including some very old texts. Rhind claims the book is his attempt to record the history of Moray from its origins to the present."

"That sounds like an impossible undertaking," Will said.

"There are some lovely bits scattered throughout. I know you are searching for new stories to entertain visitors to the ruin. This book is filled with tales about the history of the cathedral. Yet the best parts are the lovely drawings." James continued turning pages until he reached the first sketch. "All the sketches were drawn by one D. Alexander. Here, near the start of the book, Rhind says, 'The object of this work has been to collect and preserve all that remains of the antiquities of the County of Moray.' He is referring to the sketches that make this book so special. I am not certain that one hundred years from now anyone will care much about Rhind's thoughts on the weather in Moray. But I do believe people will be forever fascinated by Alexander's etchings of the county's antiquities."

James slid the book in front of Will, opened to the first sketch. A black-and-white pen and ink drawing of Pluscarden Priory, beautiful even in its ruined state. Will stared at the sketch. It made him think of Alanna's drawings.

James read aloud from the facing page, about the era when the Cistercian monks were run out of the priory by Cromwell's men. "'The Cistercians were how the records of Christianity were transmitted to present times. Through centuries of darkness and desolation. In those days there was no law in Scotland; save for the great man oppressing the poor man, and the whole kingdom was one den of thieves.'"

"No! Does it truly say that?" Will asked wide-eyed.

"Here. You read the rest." James slid the book in front of Will.

Will continued reading, "'Slaughters, robberies, fire raisings, and other crimes went unpunished, and justice was sent into banishment beyond the kingdom's bounds.'" Will whistled. "Sounds like a version of hell. Hard to imagine Elgin could have ever been that horrid a place."

"Then try imagining the beauty of the cathedral," James said, "and the surrounding priories at that time, sitting in the midst of a small population of illiterate, fearful, and unclean people, living in hovels and shacks, scavenging a meager existence."

"And I would have been among the scavengers, while you would have lived among the literate," Will replied seriously.

James turned more pages. He slid the book back to Will. "See the very long poem, written by William Hay?"

Will began to read. A seemingly endless verse about the old Muckle Kirk, likely meant to be sung as a drinking song. Will rolled his eyes at James.

"I know. An impossible poem." James paused. "Take a look at the first paragraph after the end of the poem."

Will did as he was told. "What's this?"

"Read it aloud," James urged.

"It says: 'We would request of our friend John Shanks to send us the whole of the inscription. He will find the tombstone lying about six or eight yards from the southeast corner of the Gordon family's tomb. The stone lies flat on the ground, much covered with moss. The words of the inscription are very difficult to decipher as they are arranged, not in lines, but instead encircle the stone without stop or pause.'"

Will could only stare at James.

"Do you know this stone, Will?"

"I do not. But if it is where the author says, I should be able to uncover it. But whose stone is it?"

"Here is my guess. And it is only a guess," James offered. "I think someone placed this stone in the cathedral grounds as a memorial to the old Muckle Kirk."

"But when, I wonder. And why?" Will shook his head. "Tomorrow I will look for it. If it is there, I will uncover it. And then I will ask Shanks what it all means."

"Do you think he knows about his name in this book?" James asked.

"Can you imagine he doesn't?"

"I believe you may have a new story to tell." James smiled. Then he flipped more pages and pointed to a sketch labeled *The Lantern of the North*. It showed the ancient cathedral with its central tower still standing—long before it became a massive pile of rubble. The sketch showed the tallest spire adorned with four large statues. Will thought it seemed possible the recently discovered stone bishop was one of them, but the drawing was so small he could not be certain.

"To think you might yet find the rest of them," James said.

Will took a closer look at the drawing and thought the other statues might be a king and a knight.

As James turned the page, Will kept thinking about the statues surrounding the tall spire. He wondered what the odds might be of finding another one, not broken to bits.

"The next time I visit the ruin, I want to take a closer look at that knight's tomb," James said. "Have you ever considered that your knight might have lived in this house?"

"I suppose it is possible. Even Forsyth talks about his home once belonging to the Templars," Will said.

Later, standing together outside Forsyth's house, Will asked James, "Would you like to join me for supper tonight at Mrs. Hendry's?"

"Thank you for the invitation," James replied, "but I am saving my coin." He shrugged. "I eat for free at the school."

"True." Will smiled at his friend. "Although the conversation is sure to be more interesting at the boardinghouse."

"Next time," James promised, and they went their separate ways.

42

Mrs. Hendry

It was not the first time Will awoke in Mrs. Hendry's bed.

It was, however, the first time he awoke in her bed without her in it. Usually, she shoved him out in the middle of the night. Pushed him through the side door with his boots and his clothes in his arms. Even on cold nights she could be merciless.

Typically, he left the boardinghouse before daylight. But now he could hear Davina talking with the cook in the hallway about the day's meal plans. A line of weak daylight leaked through the shutters. Although his stomach rumbled with hunger, he thought it best to quickly and quietly step out the side door.

For quite some time the boardinghouse had been Will's refuge. Mrs. Hendry offered clean rooms and good food at reasonable prices. Supper was served at four thirty sharp throughout the year. A modest breakfast was provided to boarders. Meals came with the price of the room. Those not staying the night could pay a few coins for a chair at the supper table. Mrs. Hendry maintained few but strict rules. No alcohol was permitted at her table. Her boardinghouse was neither a pub nor a club. It was neither a brothel nor a bawdy house. Absolutely no hanky-panky. If you stayed in her rooms, you stayed alone. She offered four rooms for single men and kept one room for single women boarders. Couples who crossed her threshold were pointed out the door and up the street to the hotel.

She expected intelligent conversations at table and no cursing. Political discourse was discouraged. And you had best not reek. Her side businesses did well. Hot baths, haircuts, and laundry services offered at reasonable prices.

Of course, these rules applied only to Mrs. Hendry's guests. After all, this was a business. But her relationship with Will was pure pleasure. And an entirely different set of rules applied to Mrs. Hendry's special guest.

Behind her bedroom door, Will was expected to call her Davina. He was to be discreet and quiet while in her company. Lastly, he was to do whatever she told him. It did not take long for Will to figure out the extent of that last rule.

The first time had been a surprise. He was in her bed and out the side door before he knew what he was about. The second time involved a lot more conversation.

"Here's everything you need to know about good lovemaking, Will. It is not just one thing. It is many things. But it must always include a beginning, a middle, and an end. Most people don't know this, especially men. They think a lot about the end, and sometimes about the beginning. But men often skip over the middle. Which is unfortunate because the middle can be the best part."

"But last time we just—"

"Hush! I know what we did last time. It was lovemaking, but it wasn't the best lovemaking." Her eyes twinkled.

"So how do I...?"

"Stop talking and I'll show you." She had continued showing

him—off and on—for quite some time. Until her birthday arrived.

Will worried about the weather as he waited for James to arrive.

Bitter cold had moved into Moray at the start of the month. First came the chill rains, then the sleet. A true hoarfrost left a skin of ice on every tree limb, fence post, and blade of grass. The sleet even stuck to strands of Will's hair. The storm clouds passed, and a Black Moon emerged. The landscape glittered. The empty moon hung over the Witches Pool, daring anyone to challenge the magic in the air. The sight of it had tickled Will's scalp. But Will did not believe in the devil, any more than he believed in a modern witch. Both were symbols of the past. And although Morrison insisted it was impossible to believe in God without believing in Satan, Will disagreed. There was enough evil in the world without inventing more. A man of this new Victorian Age should be allowed to embrace the goodness of a loving God, without the need to believe in a demon. That was Will's choice.

He understood the workings of the Church, enough to know men of God created stories of both gods and monsters. It helped the clergy reign power over people. At least, so said the boarders at Mrs. Hendry's table.

Will was now a man of facts. There was no room in his imagination for demons. However, the potential for evil wrought by humans kept Will cautious. In the years since the keeper's hut was set afire, he made it a practice not to be alone on All Hallows Eve. With his responsibilities to keep watch over the ruin, he could not leave. But this year, with the enticement of Mam's cake and a half-bottle of sherry, Will convinced James to keep him company. He had sweetened the offer by mentioning a fossil recently unearthed in the ruin. It was not a very large fossil, but when it came to such things, James could not resist.

"We can eat cake and read books and play checkers and talk about fossils to your heart's content," Will promised his teacher friend.

At the sound of a knock on the keeper's hut door, Brodie barked just once, telling Will it was a friend.

The wind blasted James into the hut. His cheeks and nose were bright red. His warm hat was pulled down tight, with two scarves wrapped around his neck. Will guided his friend to a seat near the fire and handed James a hot toddy. "It's the least you deserve for coming out on a night like this," Will said. "You are a true friend."

"You'd best have your mam's cake, or I'm leaving." James shivered with a grin.

"I would never have asked you…"

"I know. You despise this holiday."

"I truly do."

James settled by the fire, petting Brodie's warm coat. The dog yawned. "Halloween is the bane of the educated man," James declared.

"Which I most certainly am not."

"You are not exactly illiterate," James insisted.

"Then what am I?"

"Like the rest of us." James smiled. "Works in progress."

"Progress." Will sighed the word.

"A difficult thing to perceive," James assured him.

"I wonder what Shanks might say about my progress in the ruin," Will muttered.

"How is the old man?"

"He's not been himself lately. I cannot tell if he is unwell or just getting older. He keeps falling asleep in the chapter house. The noise of his snoring bounces off the walls and he wakes himself up."

"Goodness. When did you see him last?" James asked.

"Several days ago. Before this cold weather set in."

"Maybe he needed a rest. That happens when you get old. How old do you think Shanks might be?" James wondered.

"I have no idea." The two young men sat quiet, trying and failing to imagine what it must be like to be old.

James removed a small book from his bag. The book looked new. "I sneaked this from the teachers' shelves in the school library," he explained. "There's good news for you in this book, Will, despising Halloween as you do." James carefully flipped pages. "This is the part I want you to hear." He took a sip of his drink and began: "'At the start of this century, it was common practice on winter evenings to sit round the fire and relate the most marvelous stories about witches, the evil one, ghosts, and fairies, all which were once confidently believed.'"

Will interrupted. "How is this supposed to settle my fears about All Hallows Eve?"

"Just listen," James chided. "This is a recent commentary written specifically about Elgin and Moray." He sipped his wine and read on, "'There has existed a charm about these old superstitions that appears to be fading from society. With the increase of education in the region, superstition has much declined. In recent years the belief in the power of departed spirits, witchcraft, fairies, and demonology has receded from society.'"

"Enough!" Will shuddered. "I do not want to think about this."

"Believe it or not, Will, those words were published earlier this year. It seems we are progressing away from such beliefs here in Elgin." James raised his glass and toasted, "Death to the Knock of Alves!"

Will and James clinked glasses.

"I have an idea," Will said. "Let's eat my mam's cake and pretend it's Christmas."

"Fine by me." James smiled.

As Will cut the cake, James examined a shelf of small items discovered in the ruin, including a triangular-shaped padlock and several keys of different sizes. One could only imagine what they once unlocked. "Those heavy old keys make me appreciate the new ruin key around my neck all the more," Will told James.

The bits of medieval stained glass reminded James of broken butterfly wings. The carved hand was there, too.

"All of it is destined for the new museum when it opens. In the meantime, they are here for safekeeping. We've learned the hard way that small items displayed in the chapter house disappear during tours. I cannot decide if I will miss all these bits or be glad to have them gone."

"In the museum they will be behind glass," James observed, touching a finger to the beautiful etching on a worn padlock.

"True, but who knows when they will finish the museum."

"First they need more funds," James added. "The age-old problem of running out of money before the work is finished."

"Shanks is losing patience. He cannot believe the museum is taking so long."

"What's this?" James picked up an odd bit of rock nestled among a few ancient stone plumb bobs.

"That's your fossil." Will smiled. "A snail, is it? Anyway, come eat your cake."

"I might make a scientist of you yet." James pocketed the fossil and took a seat. "I recently read that the Queen's new prince has an interest in the sciences."

"Another advocate for progress." Will grinned.

"You and Shanks are not the only ones eager for the new museum to open. Hugh Miller is also anxious. Elgin's Scientific Society long ago agreed to accept his fossil collection for the museum. But his fish fossils now number in the hundreds. He's run out of places to store them." James took a bite of cake and moaned with pleasure. "Your mam needs to give cooking lessons to the kitchen staff at the academy."

Will grinned.

James pointed to a large feather next to Will's hat. "Osprey feather?"

"Aye." Will refilled their glasses and served James another slice of cake. "It looks like the feather carved on the chapter house wall."

James nodded with his mouth full of cake. "Heavens, this is tasty! Do thank your mother for me." He wiped the crumbs from his lips. "I used to make pens out of feathers. Did you know the word *pen* means feather? It's from the Latin *penna*."

"This is why I believe you are bound for some greater purpose, James. You know so many facts!"

"I do not approve of killing birds, unless it's to eat them," James stated.

"Why is that?"

"It's such a waste. Recently, a speaker visited the school to show the students his rare stuffed birds. Some were from as far away as the West Indies. They seemed like impossible creatures. And I thought it sad that someone had to kill them to show them off."

"Da has told me about shooting parties at Gordon Castle. They shoot a lot of birds, but I think they eat them."

"Maybe," James said, "but in the school library is a notebook filled with lists of birds of prey destroyed on one estate alone. Hundreds of eagles and osprey and hawks and buzzards, magpies and kestrels, crows, ravens, owls—such a waste."

"Why do they keep lists?" Will wanted to know.

"Something to brag on, apparently."

Will shook his head. "I could never kill an owl or a golden eagle."

"Not even for the feathers?" James asked.

Will reached into his pocket and rubbed the feathered wings on his little carving. "Not even for that. There are other ways to appreciate such creatures," Will said softly.

"How's that?" James asked, sinking farther in his chair. The wine and warm fire had put both men at ease.

"Imitation and art," Will replied quietly. Then without another word he placed his small carving on the table between them.

James gave a small gasp.

Will could read his friend's mind. He knew the question James would ask first.

"May I...?"

Will lifted the carving and carefully placed it in James's open hand.

"What is it?"

"It may well be many things," Will said slowly, "but it is one thing for certain."

"Which is what, exactly?" James asked as he studied the winged creature.

"A secret," Will whispered.

James raised an eyebrow. "Who else knows about it?"

Will pulled a locket from around his neck and opened it. "Only Alanna."

To have a birthday, to know your age, you need a mother, or a family Bible.

Davina Hendry had neither. She had chosen her own date of birth—November 1. She liked the symmetry of the first day of the eleventh month. She could only guess at the year, which she had done long ago. This year would be her twenty-fifth birthday. A full quarter century. She considered it an accomplishment for someone without family.

Davina had been talking about her birthday for weeks and planning an elaborate celebration. "A festive meal by invitation only," she informed Will and the rest of her regular guests. She made no secret that she expected gifts.

At twenty-five, Davina believed she would be much too old for Will. Never mind that the difference in their ages would be unchanged on her birthday. That rationale escaped her.

If Davina had been at all hesitant about ending her relationship with Will, his birthday gift sealed her decision. It was not that she had a particular gift in mind. She knew Will's situation—the impoverished life of a young ruin keeper. Her issue was with the gift itself. She had no words for how his choice made her feel. He might as well have given her a broom.

"You have to admit, it's a clever gift," Will said proudly presenting Davina with his offering. "You are always looking for new ways to eliminate rodents in the kitchen." Will stopped talking about his gift when the happy expression on Mrs. Hendry's face disappeared. He had brought her a tiger-striped wildcat—a male kitten with tufts of fur on the tips of his ears, extremely long whiskers, and a tail too large for his body. Both its claws and teeth appeared sharp.

"His name is Tommy. I thought you might—" Before Will could pass her the kitten, it scratched his hand and escaped with a mighty yowl.

"See?" Will said meekly, "he's already a mouser."

As more guests began to arrive, Will considered leaving quietly. He reached to retrieve his coat, but Mrs. Hendry stopped him. She grabbed his wrist and squeezed, leaned in, and whispered in his ear, "Do not dare to leave this house until I say."

Mrs. Hendry's dinner party was a gathering of favored patrons and people she regarded as friends. The wonderful meal was like a holiday feast with cakes and a lovely wine. There were toasts and well-wishes. Everyone drank to Mrs. Hendry's good health, and a happy birthday. There were gifts of flowers and sweets, books, and small amusements. Things Will never considered. Even Morrison, who had long tried to hide his feelings for Mrs. Hendry, brought beautiful colored ribbons for her hair.

As Will stood to toast Mrs. Hendry's happiness, something in a far corner of the dining room caught his eye. The kitten was lifting a leg. Hoping to keep everyone's attention diverted, Will made his toast more animated. Davina scowled quietly.

At the end of the evening, as the guests said their goodbyes, Will lined up with them. Then he saw the displeasure on Mrs. Hendry's face. "Do not dare to leave," she threatened him quietly.

After seeing off her last guests, Davina silently led Will into her bedroom. "If you cannot bring me a proper birthday gift, I will have to claim what I want."

In the wake of Davina's displeasure, Will was unsure what to do—but his body did, and so did Davina. She proceeded to slowly and silently undress him. By the look on her face, Will knew she was still displeased. "Maybe I should take your boots for my birthday gift." She considered their condition before dropping them to the floor. "Or this scarf. I've always liked this scarf."

"You gave me that scarf," Will said.

"Exactly my point." After removing her blouse and skirt, she wrapped the scarf around her neck. "I understand you are a man of no means, Will Clachan. But a *cat*?" She removed the rest of his clothes, and most of her own, before shoving him down on the bed and following him in. Without another word, Davina proceeded to have a long and angry intercourse with Will.

He lost track of the hour. Knew better than to ask if she had enjoyed her birthday. "Sorry about the kitten," he whispered into the darkness, but she put a finger to his lips.

"No matter," she whispered. "As of today, I am too old for you anyway."

"But..."

"Hush. No more words." Davina climbed atop Will one last time. A shudder of quenched desire traveled through him before the two fell apart and asleep.

Will was unsure where he was when he awoke in Davina's bed the next morning. Then he heard her voice. She was in the hallway talking to the cook. Without a moment to lose he was out of her bed and into his clothes. As he struggled to pull on his boots Davina walked into the room.

"I think you have the hang of this now"—she gestured toward the bed. "You are ready for whatever comes next."

On his walk back to the keeper's hut, Will could not decide which woman he would miss most—Davina or Mrs. Hendry.

Upset and jealous, Morrison left Mrs. Hendry's birthday party an unhappy man. For many months he had been unsuccessfully trying to court her, but Mrs. Hendry had failed to notice him in the same way he noticed her.

Mrs. Hendry's adoption of Will as her favorite had made Morrison angry. It had taken some time for Will to work out what Morrison was moping about. But he did not know how to make things better. After all, it was Mrs. Hendry who had chosen Will, not the other way around.

Will made it a point never to discuss Davina in Morrison's presence. He might mention "Mrs. Hendry," but not "Davina." Like the time Mrs. Hendry had gone to nurse Will's mam. When Morrison eventually asked after his mother, Will told the man what he already knew. "It's only thanks to Mrs. Hendry that my mother is on the mend." Then Will lowered his voice to whisper, "Mrs. Hendry said it was women's ills."

With her case of tonics and remedies and her insistence on bed rest, Davina had made Charlotte Clachan well again. She had given Will firm instructions. "She will be fine, but she must rest. The men in your family will need to fend for themselves for a while. That's the least you can do, after all the years she's taken care of the lot of you," Mrs. Hendry paused, "with no daughter in the house to help out."

Without another word, Davina had swished away, leaving Will to ponder several matters he had never considered before. Not the least of which included "women's ills" and "daughter."

When she was well again, his mother took Will aside. "She is a very capable and hardworking young woman, Will. You could do worse, you know."

Will did know. Unfortunately, his relationship with Davina faced greater challenges than his poor taste in birthday gifts, or the modest difference in their ages. Neither could afford to give up their livelihood to live under the same roof with the other. And then there was the matter of Will's unspoken longing for Alanna.

The night of her party, Morrison brought Davina Hendry more

than hair ribbons. He had taken her aside to share important news. "Isaac Forsyth is discreetly writing to Alanna Shanks concerning her grandfather's health. He's counseling her to return home from Italy." Morrison did not want to see Davina's heart broken.

Davina patted Morrison's hand and thanked him for the information. She always knew Will was still in love with Alanna and was happy to overlook that fact while Alanna remained in Italy. But Davina had never been a wait-and-see kind of woman. The news Morrison brought was the true reason Mrs. Hendry graduated Will from her bed.

43

JOURNEY HOME

Alanna's first meal of the day was delivered to her studio. Everything was prepared to her liking. It had not always been that way. When she first arrived in Florence, she had tried and failed to instruct the cook regarding her food preferences. Alanna's inability to speak Italian contributed to the problem. She struggled through her Italian lessons. Shopping on her own quickly taught her useful words and phrases. *Una tazza di tè*, a cup of tea, was essential in a culture that thrived on strong black coffee.

The pleasant sunshine lighting Alanna's studio seemed more like spring than winter. On her breakfast tray lay four sealed letters. She placed a hand over the small stack and sipped her tea. Outside her window the city beckoned. She could only imagine the cold air in the places these letters originated. One thing was certain. Only bad news came in abundance.

Alanna poured more tea. Sitting next to the window gave her a fine view of the garden.

She recognized each man's handwriting on the first three letters. The last one she could only guess at. One by one she read the news from Scotland.

Dearest Alanna,

I sincerely hope this letter reaches you in time. Your grandfather is declining. Two weeks ago, he took to his bed. We are doing all that we can to keep him comfortable. His physicians have seen to him and ordered rest. They can find nothing that requires treatment, seeing as how old age has no remedy.

If you wish to hold his hand once more in this world and talk with him again, I encourage you to return home in haste. We look forward to your homecoming.

Kindest regards,
Isaac Forsyth

My dear Alanna,

I hope this letter finds you well and able to travel. I have received word from Isaac that your grandfather is unwell and has taken to his bed. I have made arrangements for your return to Elgin as quickly as possible. How long your grandfather will last in his present condition no one can be certain. For all I know, he may be rising from his bed as I write these lines and pulling on his boots to go to the ruin. We are all acquainted with his determination. Nevertheless, I suggest you make haste.

Your patron,
Robert Reid

My dear friend,

It hurts my heart to write this letter. Your grandfather has not come to the ruin in many weeks. He has not been out of bed. When I visited him, he asked for you. Please come home.

Your servant,
Will

Dear Miss Shanks,

Come home. He needs you. They both need you. Do not delay.

Davina Hendry

Alanna was sad to leave Florence.

The start of Advent season was a magical time in the birthplace of the Renaissance. The trip home would be arduous. The weather harsh. And it was quite possible that she could suffer the journey and arrive too late to see Grand-Dey alive. It was nearly as disheartening to imagine she could make the trip and discover her grandfather was back in the ruin leaning on his shovel. She felt guilty for her selfishness. Her feelings would nag her all the way home.

When Alanna finally came ashore at Aberdeen, a cold wind greeted her without mercy. Her body had fallen in love with the Mediterranean climate. Although she was wearing her warmest clothing—the same she had worn when she left Scotland—she felt defenseless in the frigid air.

Robert Reid had arranged for a private carriage to meet Alanna's ship and transport her to Elgin. Unfortunately, the ship arrived a day late. Along the docks snow swirled through gray Aberdeen skies. As Alanna considered what to do, a familiar voice called her name. Robert Reid was dressed for the weather, his face nearly obscured by his hat and scarf. "There you are, my dear." He threaded her gloved hand through his arm as though no time had passed since they last saw one another. "I have a carriage waiting. Your trunk will be delivered to Elgin once it is off-loaded from the ship. It is too cold for us to wait."

"And Grand-Dey?" Alanna asked anxiously.

"When I left Elgin two days ago, he was frail but stubbornly alive."

"Does he know I am coming?"

"He knows we wrote to you, asking you to return. He was not pleased with me about that. But he is anxious for your safe arrival."

They might have been wiser to remain in Aberdeen. Big fat flakes of snow had begun to fall and stick to everything. Reid's plan was to make haste to Elgin with as few stops as possible. But the ship's delay and the blowing snow discouraged progress. By the time the carriage reached Banffshire, drifting snow covered the roads. Stopping in the village of Keith, Reid arranged for a message to be carried ahead by a young rider on horseback.

They pressed on in the carriage. The road rattled through them. Far into the evening, they crossed a bridge and passed through a large stone gate. "I have friends here," Reid told Alanna. "I've sent word. They will be expecting us."

The large pile of a house was ablaze with lights. Before Alanna could ask where they were, the carriage stopped. The door was opened by a footman who offered a gloved hand. "Welcome to Gordon Castle, madam, sir."

Alanna wanted nothing more than to be in Elgin and have this journey done. But as she sank into the soft mattress on the four-poster bed, she was ever so grateful not to be aboard a rocking ship or a teeth-rattling carriage. Her clothes had been discreetly whisked away as she prepared for bed. Exchanged for a silk dressing gown and slippers.

In the morning, before Alanna arose, a maid delivered tea to her room. She offered to brush Alanna's hair and help her dress. Her traveling clothes, miraculously cleaned and pressed, had reappeared in her room. Without her trunk, they were the only clothes she possessed.

Alanna was dressed when the housekeeper knocked at her bedroom door. "The duchess would like you to join her in the sunroom for breakfast." Alanna knew nothing of the Duchess of Gordon. She had appeared briefly the night before, welcoming them to the castle. But the hour had been late, and Alanna exhausted.

It was midmorning when the two women were settled in the sunroom. Alanna thanked the duchess for her kind hospitality and for rescuing them from the weather. She tried not to gape at her surroundings. After all, Florence had introduced her to the grandeur of great homes. Alanna inhaled the smell of fresh flowers and wondered, with all the snow outside, where they had come from.

"The men have ridden out to the front gates to check the road conditions," the duchess told Alanna. "There is no sense packing you into a carriage, only to discover the road is impassable."

Alanna cradled the warm cup of tea in her hands. She was anxious to see her grandfather. But she had no reason to burden the duchess with her family concerns.

The two women exchanged pleasantries. The duchess was curious about Florence, and Alanna politely answered her questions. At length, the duchess tilted her head and said softly, "I must confess. I have been looking forward to meeting you." Her expression changed in a way that made Alanna uncomfortable. "We have an acquaintance in common. Some time ago, when I was in Elgin for my late husband's funeral, I met the young ruin keeper there. I believe he works for your grandfather?"

In the wake of her rigorous travels, it took a moment for Alanna to realize who the duchess was referring to.

"He told me about your artwork, and when I asked where I might see your sketches, he explained that you had moved to Florence."

"Are you referring to Will Clachan?"

"Yes, I am, my dear," the Duchess paused, studying Alanna's face.

Alanna struggled to imagine Will discussing art with a duchess.

"He told me about your sketch of a lovely little angel carving in Elgin's chapter house. That one I would like to see someday."

"I'm afraid all my belongings are still in Aberdeen."

After a brief pause the duchess asked, "If I offered you pencils and paper, could you draw something for me now?"

It seemed an odd request for a duchess. But as a guest in the woman's home, Alanna felt she could not refuse. The duchess rang for the housekeeper. Before Alanna could invent an excuse, she found herself sketching the duchess sitting in the sunroom with a vase of lilies over one shoulder.

Once the sketch was completed the duchess was delighted with the result.

"I cannot decide if I should keep this or send it with you to Elgin to give to that handsome young ruin keeper to remember me by."

Alanna was lost for words. At the duchess's insistence, she signed the sketch, "Kindly yours, A.M.O.S."

When at last she arrived in Elgin, Alanna's reunion with her grandfather was bittersweet. He burst into tears at the sight of her. She did the same, sobbing harder as she tenderly hugged his fragile body. He felt all skin and bones.

"You shouldn't have come, but I am glad of heart to have you here," he whispered.

Alanna settled into her old room. The view from her windows

could not match the view she left in Florence. But here under this roof was her only family. On her bed lay an unsent letter, sealed and addressed to Alanna in Florence. Without hesitation she opened it. It had been dictated long ago by the man now sleeping in the next room. She recognized Isaac Forsyth's handwriting. In his letter, Shanks instructed Alanna not to come home:

My dearest Alanna, my only family and kindest confidant,

I loved you in this life and I will love you in the next. Under no circumstances should you return to Elgin on my account. We will see each other again by-and-by.

Your loving Grand-Dey

She sobbed wildly at his selflessness. And she was glad that whoever decided not to mail the letter had left it for her to read here and now.

44

Tea for the Ruin Keeper

Will did his best to stay out of sight following Alanna's return to Elgin.

In his visits to see Shanks, Will would slip quietly past the housekeeper, up the back stairs, and out again. The first time Will and Alanna crossed paths was in Shanks's presence. Their greetings were brief and formal. It seemed neither could abide the sight of the other without feeling a need to flee.

Eventually Alanna and Will came face-to-face in the doorway of the town house. She was headed out with a shopping basket on her arm. He was going in. Will silently nodded. Then he opened his fist to display two small fragments of amber-colored glass. "He still likes to see what bits I've dug up."

"It's good to know some things in Elgin do not change," Alanna said.

"Change is the only thing that is certain in Elgin these days." Will looked down the High Street. He considered all that was different here since Alanna left for Italy, including himself. "I would gladly give you a tour."

"That's kind but unnecessary," Alanna replied. "Compared to Florence, Elgin is the size of Queen Victoria's new postage stamp." Alanna was pleased with her analogy. "Is he expecting you?" she asked.

"Always"—Will fought a smile—"as long as I have something to show him."

"Have there been many new finds in the ruin?"

"You should come see—when the time is right."

"I was wondering…" before Alanna could finish, a gust of wind caught her hat. "Goodness! In Florence one can easily forget about such wild weather," she muttered. "I was wondering," she tried again, one hand holding tight to her hat, "if you might have tea with me. Here in the parlor next Wednesday? I should be settled in by then."

"Certainly, miss." Will made a small bow.

"Please, Will. Call me Alanna." She hurried away before either was tempted to say more.

After Alanna's invitation, Will made himself scarce. If he was need-ed in town someone would send for him. It seemed like old times— distracted by thoughts of Alanna while carting rubble to the Witch-es Pool. How she had changed! She was taller and her features no longer childlike. She seemed beautiful to him in a completely new way. Alanna was no longer a girl. She was a woman who looked every bit a lady.

Based on recent experience, Will knew not to take lightly Al-anna's invitation to tea. His good suit of clothes was clean and he would shine his boots. He needed to look his best—but the idea of going to Mrs. Hendry's for a bath, shave, and a haircut to impress another woman made Will shiver. He could almost imagine Davina slitting his throat with a razor.

Will decided to ask Mam for help. She might even have suggestions for an appropriate gift. He had learned his lesson with Davina. As Mam cut Will's hair, they discussed what gift he might bring Alanna.

"You need to take her something personal." Mam tilted his head to trim the back of his hair. "But not too personal. Something useful."

"Definitely *not* something useful," Will insisted. "I've learned my lesson about useful gifts and women."

"Be still." Mam placed a hand firmly on his head. "I mean useful in a personal way. Something to remind her of home. Something she would appreciate and use." Clearly Mam was simply thinking aloud. "Hmm. And you need it by Wednesday? Leave this to me, Will."

When Will arrived at the town house for tea, Alanna showed him to the parlor. She settled on the divan across from him. She wanted a good view of his face. The better to read his thoughts. "I have given most everyone the afternoon off. We have the house to ourselves." She rearranged the spoons on the tea tray.

"Except for your grandfather."

Alanna did not raise her eyes from the teapot. "Isaac is sitting with him. He reads to Grand-Dey on Wednesday afternoons. Did you not know that?"

"I did not. But then I still spend most days in the ruin." Will bit his tongue, recalling Forsyth's generous spirit. It wasn't the bookseller's fault Will was born the son of a stonemason. It wasn't anyone's fault.

"Sugar?" Alanna asked. "Milk?"

"Both, please."

"You cannot imagine how I have missed a good cup of tea. How Italians can ruin tea, I have no idea. It never tasted as good as tea tastes here." She turned the saucer and graciously passed Will his cup. He noticed she was wearing gloves.

"My hands haven't been warm since I left Italy." She began fixing her tea.

"A warm cup of tea cannot hurt," Will replied. "Or this might help." He smiled and handed Alanna a pretty little sack tied with ribbon. Mam had outdone herself.

"What's this?" She undid the bow and removed a small fur muff, soft and warm.

Mam had made it herself from two rabbit pelts she had been saving. It was a beautiful little thing. Practical, too. Mam was truly a genius.

Alanna slid her hands inside the muff and sighed with delight. "Oh, Will. Thank you! This is perfect." She let out a tiny laugh, happy with her gift.

Alanna looked lovely. Everything about her seemed flawless. Her hair, her clothes, and her posture. The soft scent of something springlike tickled his nose with every move she made. It all felt a bit formal until Alanna lifted the cloth from a tray of sandwiches and sweets—enough food to serve a half dozen guests.

"Likely many things about you have changed since we last met," Alanna said with a devilish smile. "May I assume your appetite isn't one of them?" She offered the tray with a lighthearted giggle, and he laughed along with her.

"It is difficult to look at you and not recall the last time we were together—before I left." She lowered her eyes.

Will's face reddened. She spoke softly but still. He glanced pointedly in the direction of the stairs. Shanks's room was at the top of the landing.

"No need to fret. The door is closed, and Isaac is reading aloud. I asked that we not be disturbed."

Will was not a tea drinker, but he needed something to wash down the sandwiches.

Alanna chose her words carefully. "It is difficult for me not to laugh with embarrassment when I think of our last encounter."

Will was not about to let Alanna brush past her farewell visit to the keeper's hut. He sensed she perceived him as unchanged since her departure for Italy. "Are you referring to the night you insisted we lay together?" He stared at her without flinching, making her blush.

"I was rather hoping you had forgotten." She laughed softly into her glove. Will wondered if she had rehearsed this conversation. "My misunderstanding of such things did not last long, once I was settled in Florence and allowed to be on my own." Alanna paused, watching Will's face.

He had leaned back in his chair. If she thought she was about to shock him, she was wrong.

"My first lover in Italy set me straight," she said lightly.

Will sipped his tea. "An Italian, was he?" Will asked. He could play at this, too.

"Oh, goodness no. A Frenchman." She offered him the plate of sweets.

With a small wave of his hand, he declined.

"And you, Will? Have you experienced true love?"

Wisely, Will decided against mentioning Davina. "Love?" he replied calmly. "No. Nothing like that." Their eyes met for a moment and he blushed and looked away. Will quickly turned the question back on Alanna. "Why not an Italian?" he wanted to know. "Do they prefer only Catholics?"

"Of course not. It's because Italians do not bed virgins. Unless they have married one. Frenchmen are much more suited for that sort of thing."

Will tried to cover his shock while Alanna chattered on. He was unsure how he had been drawn into this gossipy conversation about lovers. And to what end? Was she trying to shock him? Will held his tongue, but his expression gave him away.

"Oh, Will!" Alanna laughed softly. "You are so provincial."

He did not care for the sound of that accusation. Clearly, she had outgrown him. Outgrown the whole of Elgin, considering the way she now talked and dressed.

"Do not look so sad, Will," Alanna said matter-of-factly. "You know I will always love you best." She spoke in a sisterly tone, certain that he was not otherwise engaged.

"As a good friend, perhaps. As a brother," Will muttered.

Alanna kept still. She could not imagine Will attracted to anyone other than her. But in fairness, she knew that men married for many other reasons.

Will could not read Alanna's true feelings. Not like when she was younger. At last, he said what was on his mind. "How could I ever again hope to vie for your affections, Alanna? For all I know you have already married."

Alanna locked eyes with him. "I will have you know I have not! I am many more things than when we last met, Will Clachan. But a married woman is not one of them." Indignantly, she pulled off her gloves. Her hands were still as fair as ivory bone, save for her artist's bump. No wedding ring sparkled on her finger.

Alanna reached down beside the divan and produced a roll of paper fastened with a beautiful purple ribbon. "I, too, must consider how I might compete for *your* attentions. She handed the roll to him in a way that made it clear this was no gift.

"Should I open this now or…"

"Now." It was a command more than a request. She wanted to see his face, gauge his reaction.

Will slowly slid the ribbon from one end of the roll. He unscrolled the paper and sucked in his breath. In his hands was a sketch of the Duchess of Gordon, bearing Alanna's distinctive signature. The shock on Will's face was priceless. It told Alanna everything, and nothing.

"She asked me to deliver it to you."

"When? Where?" He could not finish a single question.

"I might ask you the same. When and why? And how, for heaven's sake! A duchess, Will?"

"It's not what you think."

"So I have heard…"

He cut her off. "Rumors. That's all they are. Just rumors," he claimed. "Wishful thinking on Morrison's part, if that's who you've talked with. But no. The duchess and I only talked together. Nothing more." Will heaved a great sigh. "That woman does not give up," he muttered.

Alanna's laugh was not a happy one. "And yet I remain ever so curious how a…"

"How a young man like me could be known to the not-so-young Duchess of Gordon? Have you never heard of friendship, Alanna?"

"Her face told me different. She asked me to give this to you. She wants you to keep it for her until her next visit to Elgin."

Will rerolled the drawing and handed it back to Alanna. "Her imagination is no match for reality." Staring at one another they paused to gauge the volume of their voices. "It makes no difference, Alanna." Will shook his head. "Whether you are married or not. Whether a duchess is unsuccessfully courting me or not." He stopped, caught her eye, and began again. "Tell me true, Alanna. How could I ever compete for your affections in the shadow of your lovers?" He rose to his feet and went to the window.

"Because…" Alanna hesitated, waiting for the emotional tension in the room to subside.

Will stood staring out the window. His profile was lit by the waning winter sun. She waited for Will to shed his boyish attitude and show his true self. The remarkable young man who stood before her. The most handsome and loving face she had ever known.

Alanna made a small throat-clearing sound. "Infatuation is a very different type of relationship," Alanna's voice was gentle and slow. "It is nothing at all like true love," she whispered. She went quiet, waiting for Will to catch up.

He turned to face her. Clearly, he was moved by her words but still doubting.

"You will always be my true love, Will."

"I do not doubt you will always love me as a brother, because I stayed and took care of your grandfather."

"Of course, I love you for all you have done in my absence. But you were not peerless in that regard. Isaac and Morrison also watched over Grand-Dey while I've been away. And I'm not in love with them. Let us be honest, Will. Gratitude is not what we are discussing." The pair stared hard at one another, as people whose hearts have been squeezed often do. "I know you have been waiting…"

"I have not been waiting," Will lied.

"…waiting for me to return. To take care of Grand-Dey. So that you could get on with your life. I can only imagine what the waiting has cost you."

"Cost me?"

"I see you are angry with me, and I am sorry for it. Feel free to go if you like."

Will shook his head. "I am not going anywhere," he whispered. "Go sit with your grandfather. I have work to do. I will return in the morning." In two strides he stood before her. Lifted her hand and bent over it. His lips barely brushed her knuckles before he released her. A quiver unlike any other slipped through her, making Alanna wish for something more.

45

SOMETHING OLD SOMETHING NEW

Will fingered the gold coin.

"Heads I ask her, tails I wait." He tossed the coin at the same moment someone called his name. Will snatched the gold piece in midair without giving it a chance to land.

"Are you Will Clachan?" The man standing at the entrance gate wore a crooked smile. He had witnessed Will's small sleight of hand.

"I am, sir. And who do I have the pleasure of addressing?"

"My name is Hugh Miller. I am a geologist—a fossil hunter. We have a friend in common. James Thompson?"

"Yes, of course." Will moved to unlock the gate. Opening the ruin to visitors had not been his intention. He had planned to present himself at Shanks's town house as soon as the hour was reasonable. Now it seemed he might be delayed. It did not matter. His intentions were set, and the delay could not be helped.

"Would you like to tour the ruin?" Will asked. "Inspect the fossils in some of the headstones, perhaps?"

"Thank you. Maybe another time. But I was hoping to speak

with you about the museum."

Will quickly tucked away his key. "What about the museum?"

There was a puzzled look on Miller's face. "I have come to town this morning at the request of Isaac Forsyth, to attend a meeting with the Scientific Society. To discuss plans for the display of my fossil collection." He glanced over his shoulder in the direction of the new museum. "When I arrived, the doors were locked."

"I know work is still underway inside. Might they have moved the meeting to another location?" Will asked. "Or possibly they did not hear you knocking. Some of the gentlemen are a bit hard of hearing."

"That's the thing," Miller said. "There are no lights on inside, and there is a large chain and a lock on the doors."

Will accompanied Hugh into town. He believed what the geologist told him, but he wanted to see it himself. Will and Hugh were peering through the windows of the locked museum when they heard their names called. The members of the Scientific Society had emerged from the bank up the street.

Forsyth led the way. "So sorry!" he said as the group joined Will and Hugh on the steps of the museum.

"What's happened?" Hugh asked.

Forsyth ran a hand through his silvering hair. "The bank has locked us out! They insist we produce the money to pay off the remaining loan before they allow us back inside."

"I do not understand," Will said.

"The bank loaned the funds for the building, but the project has taken longer than expected," Forsyth explained.

"And cost much more than planned," mumbled another committee member.

Forsyth continued, "Now they are insisting on payment in full or they will take legal possession of the building."

"Can they do that?" Hugh's face turned ashen. "Wait! Is my collection inside?" he asked anxiously.

"No," Forsyth assured Hugh. "Your collection is safely stored elsewhere."

The geologist was only mildly relieved. "What will you do?" Hugh asked.

The members of Elgin's Scientific Society glanced from one to the other, but no one said a word. Forsyth cleared his throat. "I suppose the Society will adjourn to my library and discuss our options."

Will wondered if Elgin's new museum might be the man's downfall.

As the group retreated, Forsyth hung back to talk with Hugh and Will. He shook Hugh's hand and said, "My apologies, sir. I am certain the project will be underway again soon." Forsyth turned to Will. "Do not let John Shanks hear of this. It would be his undoing."

But word spread quickly around the small town. Elgin Museum was in financial trouble. By the time Will arrived at Shanks's town house that afternoon, Alanna had already heard the news.

"You did not tell him, did you?" Will whispered to Alanna as they stood together in the parlor. "Isaac was very clear. He instructed me to make certain your grandfather did not learn of this setback."

"Of course not," Alanna said. "It would break his heart."

At the mention of heartbreak, Will became acutely aware of one unspoken truth. The future of Elgin's museum was not the topic he had planned to discuss with Alanna this day. But the matter of the museum's financial woes seemed sufficiently pressing. Will frowned. "Everyone thought the museum would be finished by now."

Alanna patted the seat next to her. "Tell me what you know. I want to understand what's happening. Maybe I can help."

Will stifled a smirk. The idea that Alanna might know how to remedy the museum's fiscal woes seemed laughable. But he quickly reconsidered. After all, Alanna had successfully accomplished most everything she had set her mind to do.

"I will gladly share what I know," Will assured her. "But first I must ask you something. It's an important question, Alanna. It's the true reason I came to see you today." He had her attention and for a moment Alanna's rapt expression flustered him. Will reached for her hand. "I wish to court you, Alanna," he began. "I would ask your grandfather's permission, but I do not want to upset him. For all I know, he might be pleased. But last night it occurred to me—you may feel sufficiently independent to decide for yourself about my offer of courtship." Will reached into his pocket for the gold coin. "Before you left for Italy, I wanted to give you this coin for good luck. You insisted I keep it until you returned. So here you are." Will placed the coin gently into the palm of Alanna's bare hand. The warmth of the coin surprised her. "This is the coin I found in your father's suit of clothes. Tucked into a hidden pocket. It's time you had it back."

Alanna protested, but Will put a finger to her lips. "I want you to keep it—until you are ready for me to have it made into your wedding ring."

The tears in Alanna's eyes brimmed and fell. Will kissed the woman, with no regrets for the loss of the girl she had been.

Alanna was determined to rescue the museum project for Grand-Dey.

She had come home to Elgin for only one purpose: to care for her ailing grandfather. Now it seemed she had also come home to Will, and to Isaac, and Elgin. And ultimately to Scotland—to the soil where her parents lay. Most important of all, Alanna had returned home to her own true self.

Taking up the cause of the unfinished museum seemed right for Alanna to do. Involving herself on behalf of her grandfather. He had been among the first to envision a museum in Elgin to preserve collections of scientific value and display specimens from the region. She wanted this for her grandfather who was growing weaker every day. She needed his dream completed before he died, if such a thing were possible.

Forsyth had donated the land for the museum and some building funds were raised, but most were borrowed. Alanna soon learned about the Scientific Society's grand plans that had run into trouble. It was not long before Alanna was introduced to the source of that trouble, a captivating young architect named Thomas Mackenzie. Elgin Museum was his first commission and he had seized the opportunity to impress. Unfortunately, the man's inexperience and overreaching plans had outstripped the funds for the project. His Italianate designs were repeatedly scaled back. Unpaid workmen walked away. And now, close to completion, it seemed the Scientific Society might lose the museum building to the bank.

Isaac did not take Alanna seriously when she offered her assistance. "How do you think you might help us, my dear?"

She gave Isaac her best beguiling smile. "I have a few thoughts. Show me the plans, introduce me to the architect, and tell me how much money is needed, and when."

"You should be taking care of your grandfather."

"I am. But I can also help make his dream of opening a museum come true."

Before long, Forsyth understood that the adult Alanna Shanks could be every bit as persuasive and charming as her younger self had been. Much to Forsyth's displeasure, Alanna insisted on a private meeting with the young architect.

"I believe I should be present," Isaac informed her.

Alanna politely declined. "I will meet him in your library, and you can join us later." It was a meeting Will wished he could have witnessed. Alanna was experienced in dealing with charismatic men, a talent she brought back from Italy. And she knew all about the skills required to design and draw buildings, and about young men with inflated self-esteem.

Mackenzie, of course, knew nothing of her.

In a modest amount of time, Alanna had met with and managed the ambitious architect. When Alanna was done with Thomas Mackenzie, he had agreed to forgo all further payments for his work. She had scolded him, knowing just what to say to bruise his pride. "Would you want it known that a young woman easily took over and completed your maiden project?"

Alanna set to work scaling back Mackenzie's ornate interior plans for the museum. She convinced the Society members that simple interiors were preferable for the wonderful collections and displays. The architect begrudgingly supported her decision.

Will was concerned about the time Alanna and Mackenzie were spending together. But Alanna assured Will, "Mackenzie is in love with only himself. I could never be charmed by such a man. Besides," she whispered in Will's ear, "I have a gold coin from the most attractive young man in Elgin. And he has asked to court me."

After setting Mackenzie straight, Alanna asked Isaac to assemble the members of the Scientific Society. "I have a proposal I wish to present," she informed him.

"Can you share it with me first?" Isaac asked.

"I don't think so," Alanna answered kindly. "But no need to

worry, Isaac. I promise, I will not embarrass you."

Awaiting her audience with the Scientific Society, Alanna remained busy. Sitting with her grandfather, she dashed off correspondence to a select group of Elgin's citizens. All of them with one thing in common—they wore skirts.

When the responses swiftly arrived, Alanna knew her plan would work. She quietly gathered information and secured goodwill, asking her contacts to keep matters confidential for a bit longer.

On her way to meet with the Scientific Society, Alanna carried several neatly hand-lettered broadsheets. She intended to post them around town on her way home. Time was of the essence.

She was ready for her meeting with Isaac and his society members, including Rear Admiral Duff, banker John Lawson, and town clerk Patrick Duff. Only her grandfather was absent. When the men were seated, Alanna began, "Gentlemen! Thank you kindly for your presence, and your willingness to receive my proposal to rescue Elgin's Museum—before it defaults to the bank." She made eye contact with each gentleman, wisely reminding them of their own shortcomings to successfully fund the museum. "This proposal comes not only from me, but from the ladies of Elgin. We propose to hold a charity bazaar. All funds raised will benefit the museum."

"Bazaars take months, sometimes years to plan," Isaac interrupted. "You cannot hold a bazaar soon enough to meet the bank's demands. Certainly not this time of year."

The men nodded, muttering a chorus of "Aye."

"We believe we can. And we shall. Committees have been formed and plans are underway." Alanna continued with confidence, "On behalf of my grandfather, John Shanks, your peer and friend, who grows weaker every day."

The gentlemen quieted. They listened respectfully while Alanna shared her plans. She had secured a location for the bazaar on a date soon enough to meet the bank's deadline. Volunteers were already knitting and baking and organizing. She handed around one of the broadsheets she planned to post, announcing the bazaar.

"Do you truly believe you can do all this?" Patrick Duff asked sincerely.

Alanna replied, "Do you doubt the diligence of the women of Elgin?"

The room fell silent.

Forsyth quietly asked, "And what if the bazaar fails to raise enough funds to pay the bank? It will all be for naught."

Alanna paused. Her eyes twinkled. "Have you arrived at a better solution?"

No one said a word.

"With the Scientific Society's endorsement, the women of Elgin are ready. All that remains is to secure the Society's approval."

Alanna stepped into the next room while the gentlemen deliberated. It did not take long. With no other ideas, they agreed to be swayed. Though the men did not truly believe a group of women could raise the sum owed to the bank before the deadline—they came around to the idea of not saying no.

"Oh, why not, my dear?" Isaac offered when Alanna returned to hear their decision. "Why not let the ladies of Elgin lend a hand? What can it hurt?"

"Hurt?" Alanna scowled at her friend. "I think you have misunderstood. The women of Elgin are about to save your museum." Her face softened. "And give hundreds of fish fossils a permanent home." Laughter filled the room. Her cleverness was winning them over. Alanna started for the door, reconsidered, and turned around. "One more thing. The committee of women will have complete control over the bazaar's plans." The gentlemen began to object, but Alanna kept talking, "Let me be clear. The bazaar's committee oversees this event. And you, the Scientific Society along with the citizens of Elgin, will be the beneficiaries of our good works. Every penny raised will go to pay off the museum's debt."

"Nevertheless—" Isaac began, but Alanna swiftly raised her hand.

"No exceptions," Alanna said softly. "No interference will be necessary."

With Alanna at the forefront of the effort, and the ladies of Elgin close behind, Forsyth began to believe. For a moment he allowed himself to imagine the day when Elgin Museum would finally open its doors.

46

ELGIN'S CHARITY BAZAAR

Come One and All
to the
End of Winter Charity Bazaar
"A Fancy Faire"
Hosted by the Women of Elgin
Saturday, March 27
Ten in the morning until dusk
All funds raised for the benefit of Elgin Museum
Performances & Contests
Puppet Shows & Fortune Teller
Jumble Sale
Knitwear, Leather Goods, Baked Goods
All forms of domestic and decorative artistry offered for sale
Women's Whistling Competition
A choral performance and a play given by students
from the Free School
Grand Auction!!!
Drawing for a lifetime of free admissions to Elgin Museum
Everyone Is Welcome to Attend

Isaac and Will peeked in at the door. The meeting was underway. So many female voices talking at once, more than either man ever imagined.

"A conspiracy of women," Isaac whispered to Will.

"Make no mistake," Will whispered back, "for all their apparent differences, they are in this thing together."

The first official meeting of Elgin's women volunteers met with great success. The ladies were enthusiastic. It was winter, and most townspeople felt housebound this time of year. An opportunity for something new excited the community. There had never been a women's charity bazaar held in Elgin.

"Ladies! Listen carefully!" Alanna spoke over the happy chatter of women full of ideas. "We have exactly seven weeks before this bazaar opens. We will not, we cannot, change the date. The museum must have the funds we raise by the last day of March. We cannot delay. Whatever we plan, we must be able to accomplish by that deadline."

The women whispered among themselves.

Again, Alanna asked for quiet. "Please! If I might have your attention just a little longer. Some of you know me. Many of you only know of me. Some of you have asked why I have taken on this challenge. It is important to me that you know one small part of my story. I am the granddaughter of John Shanks, the ruin keeper of Elgin Cathedral. This winter he took to his bed. It seems old age has finally caught up with him. He is not well—" Alanna broke off and wiped away a tear. "For years, it has been his wish for Elgin to have ·a museum that was open to everyone. A place to display pieces of the past. All manner of collections and unique scientific discoveries. Although that wish is within reach, there are still funds that must be raised before the museum can open. If we do not meet the deadline, the bank will take possession of the building and there will be no museum. I cannot allow that to happen. There is nothing I want more than to see my grandfather's dream fulfilled. A dream he retains, even on his deathbed." Alanna let the tears spill down her cheeks.

The room fell silent.

"Although we would all wish for more time and warmer weather to hold this bazaar outdoors, we must work within our circumstances," Alanna pressed on. "Which means we need to be knitting and baking and planning starting right now. We do not want to lose our museum."

The ladies applauded Alanna's earnest words and took them to heart. Plans for a successful bazaar were quickly underway. Excited volunteers got to work. Over the next several weeks, there was no place in Elgin where there wasn't a woman knitting or crocheting or stitching—even in church. Donated goods were collected for the jumble sale. There was nowhere the smells of baked cakes and breads did not permeate the air.

Alanna had read about church fairs and women's bazaars. Similar events had been held in small towns throughout England and Scotland to raise funds for local schools and hospitals. She had been to large church fairs in Italy, and she was convinced Elgin's bazaar would be a memorable event. Without much else happening in Elgin this time of year, Alanna was certain the attendance would be high. Especially if the bazaar offered something for everyone. And she would make sure news of the event traveled far and wide—all the way down the road to Gordon Castle.

March 27 dawned cold and bright. In the Assembly Rooms all was made ready. Elgin's women had transformed the grand ballroom into a delightful destination. Attractive stalls were piled high with goods, and the attendants were ready to sell an assortment of lovely things. The smell of foodstuffs was intoxicating. Even Alanna found herself anxious to taste a ginger cake. At the appointed hour the doors were opened, and people streamed in.

When Elgin's lord provost took to the stage, he greeted an assembly of citizens already overflowing the hall. "Welcome one and all! Let us give our thanks and appreciation for the ladies of Elgin who have made this fair possible." The crowd applauded enthusiastically. "Everything here today has been donated. And every penny raised will go to fund Elgin's new museum. With your goodwill we hope to repay the loan from the bank—" A few boos and jeers briefly interrupted the speech. "I am told by the Scientific Society that if we successfully raise funds, the museum could open in June."

Everyone cheered.

The lord provost looked at the paper in his hand. "In just a wee bit, the choir from the Free School will sing. Later members of the school's upper grades will entertain us with a short play. After that, there will be a whistling contest—for women only!"

Laughter and applause filled the hall.

"Raffle tickets are now on sale near the doors. See the two lovely ladies standing there waving? They are ready to sell you a ticket. The drawing will be at three o'clock sharp. Only one ticket will be chosen. And the winner will receive free lifetime admission to Elgin's new museum!"

The crowd applauded, but they were growing restless.

"Last but not least. Immediately after the raffle drawing, a very special auction will be held on this stage. If you have not seen the list of amazing objects to be auctioned, it is posted near the punch bowl. All items will be displayed when the auction begins. Even if you do not plan to bid, you will want to be present to witness this exciting event."

The smell of food was distracting everyone.

"Thank you for coming! Please do not go home empty-handed. And finally, beer goes on sale just outside the doors at noon. Enjoy!"

Alanna could not have been more pleased by the size of the crowd. Throughout the day people continued to arrive. The mountains of baked goods and handmade woolens grew smaller. The pile of items on the jumble sale table seemed to melt away.

The puppet show drew all ages, and the puppet masters repeated their skits until they could no longer move their hands.

Alanna was surprised how the crowd hushed during the short play performed by upper-grade students from the Free School. A short version of *The Comedy of Errors*.

Although tempted to enter the whistling contest and show off her skills, Alanna thought it best not to outdo anyone. Will was disappointed. "I might have given my last penny to see you whistle onstage."

"I'll whistle for you later." She grinned.

Will turned pink as Alanna moved off through the crowd.

Outside the hall, men drank watered-down beer on sale for pennies a cup. They stood close by the warming fires gossiping like women. Some began to sing, entertaining the crowd.

"He was a braw gallant, and he played at the ball,

An' the Bonnie Earl of Moray was a flower among them all.

Lang may his Lady look from the Castle Doune,

Ere she see the Earl of Moray come soundin' through town.

Ye Hielan's and ye lowlan's, O where hae ye been?

They have slain the Earl of Moray and laid him on the green!"

As the call was made for last-minute entries in the raffle, Alanna could not tear her eyes from the door. The individual she most needed to arrive remained absent. If the day were to be a success, Alanna needed that person to appear. Time was running out.

"If I might have your attention." Isaac Forsyth had taken the stage and held the small barrel containing the raffle tickets. "We are about to hold the raffle drawing. If you have not yet purchased tickets, this is your last chance. I will be drawing one ticket at precisely three o'clock. The winner of today's raffle will receive free lifetime admittance to Elgin's new museum and will be the first person to walk through its doors on opening day. I cannot wait to see whose ticket is pulled from this barrel."

A few stragglers came forward to deposit their tickets.

Forsyth removed his pocket watch to check the time. "I would like to invite to the stage the one person who convinced us all we could hold a fancy faire in March!" The crowd's laughter was warm and kind. "Alanna Shanks, will you please come draw the winning ticket?"

Alanna stepped onto the stage and with a bit of coquetry she carefully rolled up her sleeve. She pulled the winning ticket and handed it to Isaac. Squinting, he fumbled unsuccessfully to find his glasses. Then handed the ticket back to Alanna with a shrug.

"The winning ticket number is…126! If you have ticket number 126, please raise your hand and come to the stage!"

Everyone looked around. No one seemed to be moving forward. Then Alanna noticed a shuffling motion to her right. An ancient little man was carefully picking his way through the crowd.

She took his arm and helped him forward. He placed his ticket in her hand. She let Isaac check the number. He had found his glasses.

"We have a winner!" Isaac called out.

A grand smile appeared on the man's face, displaying his lack of teeth. Isaac did his best to cover his own amusement. A lifetime membership for a man who looked every day of eighty years old. "Do you have a grandson?" Forsyth whispered loudly into the winner's large ear.

"I do," the man replied.

"Wonderful. We will make sure your membership goes to your grandson after you are done using it."

As Forsyth helped the elderly gentleman from the stage, Alanna introduced the last event. She did not want to lose her audience. "And now," Alanna said, beaming, "it is time for the grand auction!" The room broke into applause. Clearly everyone was enjoying the day. "Many of you have seen the list of items we are about to auction. Each one is special in its own way."

Alanna looked to find Morrison. He was ready to begin. He had agreed to serve as auctioneer for the event, having had some experience with such things.

"Let the auction commence!" Morrison's voice carried nicely throughout the crowded room. One by one the auction items were brought to the stage, each carried by a member of the auction committee. Alanna had purposely chosen the most attractive volunteers. She felt confident in Morrison's skills and knew he would keep things moving. But she continued to steal glances in the direction of the hall's entrance.

"This beautiful woolen lap blanket was kindly donated by Johnstons mills," Morrison announced. The young woman holding the blanket stepped to the edge of the stage and Morrison began the bidding.

Alanna checked the crowd to see their reaction. She could barely stand to listen. Already the bidding was underway.

"Going once, going twice. Sold!"

Alanna's heart was beating fast. They needed this auction to be a success.

The next presenter stepped forward. "This handsome Speyside fly casting rod was graciously donated by the estate manager at Gordon Castle," Morrison announced. Whistles came from men in the crowd. Whether in appreciation of the rod, or the young woman carrying it, Alanna could not be certain. "And with it comes a beautifully tied fly—the Lady Caroline."

Alanna watched as several men navigated forward for a better look. The bidding began and grew fierce. A sense of relief made Alanna feel slightly nauseous. They might raise enough money, after all.

"Next, we have a magnificent silver hand mirror." A mixed reaction from those present prompted Morrison to improvise. "There are rumors concerning whose reflection might once have appeared in this looking glass. But I am not one to name names."

Morrison's speculation prompted a stir of whispers. Alanna detected many in the hall considered the item too expensive. Morrison sensed it, too, and quickly announced, "Remember, there are no minimum bids! Each of these wonderful items will go home with someone here today."

"I'll give ya' a farthing for it," a voice called. Everyone laughed. To Alanna's relief the bidding continued. Then she noticed a shifting of heads and shuffling of feet near the door.

"Here is something I would not mind bidding on for myself," Morrison cooed. He carefully lifted the object from the presenter's hands as though it were a newborn babe. He held it high for all to see. "A fine bottle of Macallan single malt whiskey, donated by Alexander Reid himself."

There were shouts from men in the crowd and groans from the women as the bids for the whiskey exceeded the bids for the fly rod.

"Patience now, we're nearly finished," Morrison assured everyone. "The next item up for auction is a beautiful gown from Italy. Now imagine some fine Elgin lady wearing this to the next Saint Andrews Day ball!"

The dress had been one of Alanna's favorites, but she felt no regret parting with it. When the winning bid came from Davina Hendry, Alanna felt a pang of jealousy. Her reaction, if she ever saw Davina wearing her gown, was a matter to ponder another day.

The final auction item brought onstage was covered with a red velvet cloth. Alanna still enjoyed a flair for the dramatic. "This piece is one of a kind," Morrison announced. With a practiced motion the attractive young presenter revealed what was beneath the cloth—a simple frame holding a singular sketch. Alanna's own copy of her *Angel Mirth*.

Morrison had suggested Alanna say something about the sketch, but she had declined. "Are you certain you wish to part with it?"

"I have others," Alanna assured him. "Even so, it is not an easy thing for me to do. But there is a good reason to do it, and I've made my decision."

Now, Alanna's good reason had arrived. Morrison presented the sketch to the crowd, but Alanna was no longer listening. Scanning the room for a particular face, she saw the individual she had been waiting for. The one person Alanna needed to come to the auction now stood at the back of the room, accompanied by her estate manager. She was the sole reason Alanna had donated the *Angel Mirth* sketch.

What transpired next fascinated everyone. Alanna kept still

and waited for the first bid. It came from Will—a low and reasonable amount. The room quieted enough for Morrison to say, "We have an opening bid. Do I hear another?"

Alanna's eyes were not on Will. Instead, she stared through the crowd at the Duchess of Gordon.

"Twenty," the duchess's estate manager called out.

No one who knew Will expected him to bid again. But he did. "Twenty-five!" Will's voice was loud and confident.

The duchess craned her neck to see who was bidding against her. But Will had stepped behind a very large woman. The duchess exchanged looks with the estate manager. "Thirty pounds," came his bid. There was no other sound in the room until Will bid again. Back and forth the bidding proceeded, until Will matched a bid of fifty pounds.

"Make him show you the money!" a voice called from the crowd. Morrison stepped off the stage and made his way to Will. While everyone waited, Will produced a folded paper and handed it to Morrison, who read it silently. He nodded and handed it back. Returning to the stage, Morrison cried, "We have a bid of fifty pounds! Do I hear more?"

Outside, the daylight waned but no one left the hall. "One hundred pounds and not a penny more," the duchess exclaimed, much to everyone's surprise. "Let's get this over with so we can go home," she muttered to her estate manager.

"I have one hundred pounds. One hundred pounds, going once…"

"One hundred and ten pounds," Will shouted, his voice steady.

The duchess seethed.

"And where does a young ruin keeper get that kind of money?" the estate manager asked. "Has he shown you evidence of his funds?"

"He has," Morrison replied flatly.

"Fine, then. Let's be done. Two hundred pounds!" the duchess said. "Now bang the gavel."

Morrison pointed his gavel in Will's direction. Will shrugged. "Going once. Twice. Sold to the Duchess of Gordon!"

The duchess did not linger. She took the sketch and made for home. Only much later did the richest woman in Scotland discover the source of Will's funds to bid against her. Will had been bidding on behalf of an absent interested party—the duchess's friend and Alanna's benefactor, Robert Reid. The duchess could not find it in herself to begrudge Reid. His desire for the sketch was as legitimate as her own. She might have tolerated being outbid by Reid, but never by Will, no matter how attractive she found him. No. Never would she have let herself be outbid by a young workingman who, truth be told, she had once tried and failed to acquire.

47

No Iron in the Ground on a Friday

Alanna knelt next to her grandfather's bed and spoke softly in his ear.

"We did it, Grand-Dey. The Scientific Society owns the museum free and clear. It will not be long before the museum opens its doors."

Although her grandfather's eyes remained closed, a small smile visited his lips.

Will stood just inside the room. Morrison and Forsyth lingered quietly at the door. While Alanna talked, Will tried to find some familiar feature on the man in the bed. Possibly his nose or ears, but the rest of John Shanks seemed to have wasted away. Will no longer believed Shanks might one day return to the ruin with his shovel under one arm. But it was hard to believe this man would never tell him just one more story.

"Grand-Dey, can you hear me?" Alanna whispered.

Shanks nodded slowly.

"Will is here. We have something to ask you."

Will could tell by Alanna's face that she now doubted the wisdom of what they were about to do.

"Grand-Dey, Will has asked for my hand in marriage. Together we wish for your blessing." The old man did not react. "Easter will be here soon. After Easter we hope to be married."

Shanks lifted a shaky hand from the blankets and Alanna grasped it gently. Will stepped closer. The old man's lips twitched as though he might speak. There was a dry croak and a tiny clearing of the throat. "My girl," he managed. Swallowing with difficulty, he tried to fill his lungs. "Bless you. Both."

That night Alanna's dreams kept her restless. Wandering through a dense fog, she found her way to the museum. The doors opened of their own accord and inside she saw the first visitor. It was Grand-Dey! Dressed in his stocking cap and old coat, he floated through the galleries with his feet never touching the floor. He laughed silently at his reflection in the glass exhibit cases. His ancient face crinkled into a grin when he saw his own finds from the cathedral—the stone figures and fragments of sinners and saints carefully preserved. He stopped at a case containing his shovel and his silver snuffbox. He grinned as he touched his empty pocket where he had kept the precious thing. His smile became quizzical as he examined a tiny specimen under a glass dome. He turned to Alanna as though he had only just noticed she was there. "What is this?" he asked. She moved closer to see what was under the glass. But before she could explain Will's tiny carved creature, she woke with a startled gasp. Outside Alanna's window, the past rose up and shook itself loose. In the darkness an owl swooned, and history shuddered.

It did not matter that Shanks had never been a Catholic. In Elgin, ancient tradition still held firm. On the Friday of Holy Week before Easter, there could be no iron in the ground. No digging of graves nor burials. The funeral was hurried to Thursday. Even so, Isaac Forsyth held safe John Shanks's last will and testament. He assured the man's last wishes were adhered to, with one exception. The old ruin keeper insisted in his will that there be no tears at his funeral. Although Alanna did her best, she could not comply. John Shanks took nothing with him to his grave, save for a piece of Alanna's heart.

Shanks had long ago selected the site for his final resting place within the cathedral grounds. No one dared deny him the choice location for his earthly remains, though the plot rubbed shoulders with those of knights and dukes.

When the hour approached for the funeral service, most of the town came down the road. One last time the old ruin keeper ascended the steps and passed through the gates of the grand entrance he had rediscovered. The town's gas lights were lit, but the mourners still carried candles as they processed into the ruin. Breaking the silence at last, the mourners lifted their voices in song:

"Fast falls the eventide; the darkness deepens; Lord with me abide.

When other helpers fail, and comforts flee; help of the helpless, O abide with me.

Swift to its close, ebbs out life's little day; Earth's joys grow dim, its glories pass away.

Change and decay in all around I see—O Thou who changeth not, abide with me."

Weeks later, the *Inverness Courier* published a piece commemorating "the old cicerone," Elgin's Ruin Keeper. Citing John Shanks's enduring enthusiasm, the paper wrote of the man: "His unwearied zeal in clearing away the rubbish that encumbered the area of the Cathedral and obscured its architectural beauties, may be gathered from the fact that he removed with his shovel 2,866 barrowsful of earth and rubble, besides disclosing a flight of steps that led to the grand gateway of the edifice. Tombs and figures, which had long lain hid in obscurity, were unearthed and every monumental fragment of saints and holy men was carefully preserved. So faithfully did he discharge his duty as keeper of the ruins, that little now remains but to preserve what he accomplished."

Alanna was supposed to be deciding about her grandfather's headstone.

She had ignored Isaac's pleas for her attention to the matter. He sent his own modest suggestions for her consideration, but she had set them aside. Alanna could not find words to express her feelings. Her grandfather had meant many things to so many people in his long life. Whatever words she chose to chisel in stone, it would never be enough. To list them all would require a stone taller than any in the cemetery. Even higher than the Anderson monument—alleged to be the tallest in Scotland.

Isaac understood grief, but it did not excuse irresponsibility. "The stonecutter for the tombstone has grown impatient, dear child. He is anxious to finish his work and be paid. Promise me you will decide soon."

Alanna had never been good at dealing with the past. The future lent more to the imagination, with its own obstacles and open doors. The future might be anything she dreamed it could be. But like the rest of humanity, Alanna was powerless to manipulate the past. She set aside the matter of the headstone and turned her thoughts to marriage.

48

ALL THINGS GREAT AND SMALL

Will held the tiny carved creature close to his face, reexamining every detail.

Long ago he had memorized the feel of it—wings, snout, claws, feathers, scales, and tail. His good luck piece felt like a part of him. But that was about to end. Now that his creature was no longer a secret, it seemed impossible to think of the small carving as his alone. Ever since James Thompson stumbled upon the historical origins of Will's talisman. Now it had a history and an audience, which meant he would have to let the thing go.

Will rearranged the other items on the table before him. Each was precious in its own way. Brodie sat close, paying careful attention in case anything on the table might be edible. Will gently ordered the dog to lie down. Brodie gave a loud yawn and dropped his head onto his front paws. The dog reeked of dead fish and would need to be banished from the keeper's hut before Alanna arrived. She was coming to collect most of these precious items and take them to the museum.

Will carefully fingered a very old piece of correspondence with its wax seal long removed. It was folded and addressed, but the faded ink was impossible to read. A newer piece of paper was folded up with it, and on it Will recognized Alanna's handwriting. Next to the letter was an ancient-looking scrap of mud-stained buckskin. It was hand-punched with a few sets of holes, and the remnant of a rawhide lace threaded through. There was also the leather pouch with its broken piece of thong that once hung around Johnny Murray's neck. A tiny edge of ancient Murray Atholl plaid peeked out. Off to one side sat a stack of notebooks neatly tied with a length of black ribbon. The last item on the table was Will's most recent acquisition. An item he had never imagined owning. In his last will and testament John Shanks had bequeathed his handsome pocket watch to Will.

For the first time Will thought these objects might somehow fit together. He had acquired each of them here in Elgin. But he never had the emotional willpower to reflect on his possessions. It had been much easier to simply hide them all away. All except for his carved creature.

Now it seemed Will was at a crossroads. The museum's grand opening was less than a week away. The new curator had put out a call. He was looking for smaller items to fill one last case. A modest collection that might tell some part of Elgin's history not already represented in other displays. It was Alanna who thought Will might have the perfect compilation without even realizing it. When she presented him with her grandfather's watch, she suggested it might take the place of carrying the little carving in his pocket. Will had turned pale, too horrified by the thought to reply.

At last, there is a place to safekeep your beautiful carving for all to see, Alanna had told him. *You will no longer need to worry about it getting lost or stolen. And you will always have the tiny sketch of it in my locket, close to your heart.*

I will give it some thought, he had promised, and she had said no more.

Of course, she was right. He could visit the tiny creature whenever he wished. But the idea of putting his lifelong good luck piece in the museum felt more like she was suggesting he cut off his hand. How could it ever be the same? Looking at something behind glass was nothing like caressing its wings and holding it up to the light. He wanted to remind Alanna of her own experience, when she sketched the creature in the magnificent long light of the chapter house windows. The lighting in the new museum was impressive, but nothing like that.

Will closed his eyes. He tried to imagine his carved creature on display for others to admire. "I never should have shown it to James's historian friend," Will sighed.

It was the historian who had speculated about the tiny carving's history. How it most likely had a very long past, predating its time in Will's pocket by eight hundred years or more. The carving was at least as old as Elgin Cathedral. Or it might have been older, brought by ship from a country along the Mediterranean Sea. It could have been a good luck charm, a game piece, or a child's toy. It might have been carved by a medieval stonemason or an Etruscan artisan. The only certainty was that the tiny carving belonged in a museum. Or so the historian had said. "I believe it to be some sort of mythical creature, a combination of dragon, dog, and bird, perhaps."

Whether it once belonged to a bishop or a stonemason working in the cathedral, no one could ever be certain. But for most of Will's life, the tiny carving had belonged to him. It seemed a significant thing to be able to say you had owned something for most of your life. Or at least it had felt that way, until the historian made Will's period of ownership seem insignificant.

"You can do this," Will said aloud to himself. "It will still be yours." He imagined some small placard on the museum case: Donated by Will Clachan, Ruin Keeper.

Will picked up Shanks's pocket watch. The heft of the thing compared to the tiny carving made him shake his head. How could one ever replace the other? His life was changing. "For the good," he reminded himself. He would do this—for her and for them.

Will returned his attention to the other items on the table. Each held a piece of a story. The kind of stories John Shanks had loved.

How Will had come by the letter was easy to tell. Shanks had simply handed it to him. Why Shanks had given Will the letter was a more complicated question to answer. Long ago, after Will had struggled with Johnny to protect Alanna, he brought the odd-looking shoe to Shanks. The one Johnny had lost in their scuffle. "What do you make of this?" Will had asked the old shoemaker.

"Where did you get this?" Shanks had replied urgently, his expression a fusion of disbelief and curiosity. "In whose attic have you been rooting about?"

Will recalled how he had purposely remained vague in his answer. "I found it along the road. It seems like some odd piece of a shoe."

Shanks had turned the leather scrap in his hands as though it were sacred. "I did not know any of these still remained. Do you recall the story I told you some time ago—"

"Which one?" Will had asked.

"About the shoemakers of Elgin making shoes for the Pretender's men in the days before Culloden."

"Yes, sir. I do."

"Remember I said the shoemakers made seventy pairs of shoes in only a few days?"

"Aye. I remember."

"They needed to make shoes that did not require a custom fit, that had very little structure but would protect the men's feet."

Watching Shanks gently handle the dirty scrap of leather, Will had felt a sudden chill race through his core. "Are you saying—"

"Just like this," Shanks had pronounced each word carefully, never taking his eyes away from the object he was holding. "So, I must ask you again, Will. Exactly where did this come from?" Shanks had raised his eyes and looked hard in Will's face.

"As I said, sir. I found it in the mud, along the road between here and town. A few days ago, before All Hallows Eve."

Will still clearly recalled how he had stuffed the shoe in a pocket and forgotten about it in all the ensuing disasters on that horrid All Hallows Eve night.

Eventually, Shanks had taken Will back to his town house and had extracted an ancient letter from between the pages of a family Bible. Shanks had carefully unfolded it, so as not to damage the fragile paper. "This is the letter I told you about, Will. The one I had Forsyth purchase for me. The one that mentions the debt owed to the shoemakers of Elgin after they made seventy pairs of shoes for William Boyd's Jacobite regiment before battle at Culloden."

With great difficulty, because the ink was so faded, Shanks had read the letter to him. Will recalled how tiny flakes of paper crumbled into dust as Shanks carefully folded the letter. Shanks had assured Will, "Alanna is going to copy the words so we will still have them after the ink is faded away and the paper turns to dust. Then I shall give this letter to you. Put it with that shoe you found. If I am not mistaken, that shoe may be the only survivor from the seventy pairs."

"How—?"

Shanks had not let Will finish. "I might ask you the same. How can this be? A mystery without a certain resolution. But one thing is certain. On the morning after William Boyd wrote this letter, he was beheaded on Tower Hill."

49

A MUSEUM FOR ELGIN

An exciting idea came to Alanna as she daydreamed about wedding plans.

There was a custom she learned while living in Italy. On the way to church on a couple's wedding day there was often a ribbon-cutting ceremony. Cut by the father of the bride or the bride herself, it symbolized the start of a new life together. A joyful event she hoped to include in her own wedding day.

The recollection of a similar ceremony at a gallery opening in Florence shifted her thoughts to Elgin's soon-to-open museum. Alanna liked the idea of a beautiful ribbon strung across a door waiting to be opened. It might successfully erase the ugly memory of the chains that hung heavy on the museum doors until the bank was finally paid.

Installation of the museum's collections was nearly finished. People were anxious to see what was inside. If the fine weather persisted, Alanna was certain the free admission on opening day would draw a large crowd. A ribbon cutting would be a wonderful way to open the doors to the public. Alanna knew the perfect person to invite to do the honors. She wrote to the Duchess of Gordon. In her message Alanna did her best to convince the duchess there was no one better to officially open Elgin Museum. Along with her invitation to the ceremony, Alanna sent her sketch of the duchess. The one she carried to Elgin to give to Will on the duchess's behalf.

Although the Duchess of Gordon had never heard of a ribbon-cutting ceremony, she liked the idea, and quickly agreed to attend.

Elgin Museum teemed with volunteers.

No one was left idle under the direction of John Martin, the museum's curator. Brawny men wrestled the carved fragments from the ruin onto sturdy shelves. Others angled fossil displays to catch the natural light. With their delicate hands women petite and tall arranged antiquities inside the glass cases. Martin bustled about. He checked the beautifully hand-lettered signs to be certain they were affixed to the correct displays.

The curator had sought Will's opinion long before the specimens were moved from the ruin. "Give some thought to the stone carvings John Shanks treasured most," Martin had suggested. "The ones he fervently believed belonged in the museum. Keep in mind, nothing you remove from the cathedral grounds will change the significance of that historic place. It will forever be a museum unto itself."

Will appreciated the curator's perspective. The museum and the cathedral ruin would share a common purpose—to preserve Elgin's past in a way that might help people understand the present and think about the future.

Will and Alanna had sorted through the ruin's most treasured pieces. Not all their decisions were influenced by size and weight alone, although whatever they chose had to fit through the museum's doors. Compared to the ruin, the museum's space was small. But it offered protections the ruin did not—a safeguard from the elements and from theft.

Alanna made a list of items to go to the museum: the medieval glass fragments. The assortment of ancient keys, latches, and locks. Selections from the extensive collection of capitals, cornices, and pieces of ornamentation. All discovered by Shanks and Will while clearing the grand west portal. Shanks had displayed some of these pieces in the chapter house for visitors to examine. Many were breathtaking, but others grotesque, yet each meticulously carved. The details were often surprising. Carved figures that once topped the tall columns incorporated minute features that would have been impossible to see from below. Alanna's favorite was a tiny, wide-eyed mouse holding its own tail. Most she found unattractive, but her grandfather had cherished them all. One in particular—a mischievous monk laughingly exposing his detailed nether parts—had amused Shanks to no end. He had kept it covered with a cloth, and only revealed it to visitors whom he gauged would appreciate the humor. Alanna looked forward to ridding the chapter house of the nasty little monk. She and Will had personal reasons for wanting the chapter house cleared. Reasons that reached beyond the wishes of the late ruin keeper.

The day before the grand opening, John Martin invited Will and Alanna to tour the museum. "Come walk through before the crowds arrive tomorrow," the curator insisted. "It will be just the four of us in the museum, before we lock up for the night. I want you to see how lovely it all turned out."

"Four of us?" Will asked.

"Ah, yes. We finally hired a keeper. An old soul named William Ingram. Have you met him?"

"I cannot say that I have," Will replied.

"He was Isaac's selection. We cannot yet afford to pay for a keeper, but Ingram is willing to work in exchange for lodgings. He's moved into the two small rooms at the top of the tower."

"I see." Will grinned with a sidelong glance at Alanna. "Hopefully he's still spry enough to manage the stairs."

"I believe so," Martin replied, "though he is quite a character. And apparently a stickler for propriety."

Alanna and Will took their time exploring the museum. Together they peered into the display case given over to John Shanks's most memorable possessions. His shovel with its wooden handle worn to fit his hands. His keys to the ruin. The beautiful silver snuffbox presented to him by the town. And a stack of notebooks where Will had recorded the wheelbarrow loads of rubble removed from the ruin over the years. The couple had no words to express their feelings as they stared through the glass. Alanna could only sigh.

Will and Alanna strayed from one another as they moved through the museum reading descriptions and viewing displays. The museum was quiet, save for the new keeper repeatedly clearing his throat. The old man insisted on taking his post by the door.

The late daylight streamed through the high windows and reflected off the glass cases and white walls. It illuminated every corner of the museum. A design feature the young architect got right in his plans. Although Alanna had visited many museums in Italy, she had to admit Elgin's Museum was a small gem. She would be sure to graciously share that thought with Thomas Mackenzie.

Moving from one exhibit to the next, Will appreciated the work required to bring this museum to life. The cases held many historic documents and old maps pertaining to Elgin's past. There was Hugh Miller's fossil collection, samples of Pictish stone, and Shanks's favorite carved fragments from the ruin. Portraits and paintings featured Elgin's most important people and places. Although he found it impressive, there was something about the museum that bothered Will. He could not put his finger on it. Maybe it was a bit like looking at a bird in a cage—a thing in a place it did not truly belong. He would much prefer to discover a fossil along the shoreline and see Shanks's collection of carvings displayed in the ruin. But he would keep those thoughts to himself.

Lastly, Will stood before the case displaying his own contributions. The urge to look away was strong. His hand reached for his pocket that now contained a watch. Giving up his little creature was the right thing to do. Knowing just how rare and ancient it was, he felt some small relief. The carving was no longer his responsibility. Here it would be secured in a case, inside a locked museum with a keeper standing guard. His creature was about to be admired by any number of people. Not only tomorrow but for years to come. In a moment that felt like a lifetime, Will considered everything the creature had meant to him. And in that instant, he thought he might do anything just to touch its wings one more time.

"It truly is a lovely little thing," Alanna whispered over Will's shoulder, startling him. He had not heard her approach. "Time to go," she said.

Will nodded, but he did not move. In the morning, every important person in Moray would be here. The Duchess of Gordon would cut a bright blue ribbon and the doors to the museum would open to the public. Anyone with an ounce of curiosity would wait in line for their turn inside, eager to view the displays and learn about things they had never seen before. He considered the many people who helped make this museum something more than an old ruin keeper's dream. "Your grand-dey would have been pleased," Will said softly to Alanna.

"Good night!" Ingram ushered them out, impatient to lock up. "So I have it right sir—tomorrow morning the museum is free to everyone. But after that, it'll cost 'em six penny a head?"

"That's correct," Martin assured the new keeper.

"And who exactly do ye think might come back once they've been inside?" Ingram scratched his head.

"Good night, Ingram." Martin smiled. "We'll see you in the morning."

50

WISHING FOR CHURCH BELLS

Alanna intended to mourn for a year when her grandfather died.

But by the time the museum finally opened, Moray was deep into springtime. Alanna had forgotten the intensity of a Moray spring. A season bottled up, fermenting for months, waiting for the right moment to explode. In contrast, Italy's weather was glorious most of the year. By the end of her stay in Florence, Alanna had taken for granted the Mediterranean climate. But after a bitter cold Scottish winter, there was nothing like springtime in Elgin. A season when nature's gifts were embellished by longer and longer days. It heightened the senses—particularly for those in love.

More than ever, Alanna appreciated Will. Especially when he gazed at her with a look that was still boyhood smitten. From the moment Will placed the gold coin in Alanna's hand, he had been coy about not laying down with her. Not until after she agreed to marry him—and even then, he assured her, not until they were wed.

Alanna was unaware that Will was following the advice of Davina Hendry. "Remain virtuous until you wed her. It is your guarantee that she will not change her mind and go back to Italy," Davina had wisely counseled.

"I understand her need to mourn, and her respect for her grandfather," Will told Davina, "but I have no intention of spending another winter living alone in Elgin."

"Do as I say, and she will not last the month without setting a wedding date. Trust me, Will." Davina winked. "You are worth waiting for."

Alanna was surprised by Will's virtuous respect. His willpower became her newest challenge. One afternoon, as she was kissing him under a shower of apple tree petals, she suddenly realized now was the time to wed. In this month of Juno, the month Italians believed was the best time of year for a wedding.

When Alanna silently placed the gold coin into Will's sweaty palm, he happily agreed, kissing her fingers, her shoulder, her lips. There was no doubt they shared a sudden urgency to move on with their lives together.

"When?" Will asked, not letting her answer. "I'll go right now and give this coin to the smithy. It should not take long to make a band. We could be married as soon as the ring is ready." He took her hand and pulled her close.

"Soon, yes, soon." She let him kiss her again. "But first we must make plans."

"Not too many plans, I hope. I am weary of plans, Alanna."

But Alanna embraced planning a wedding, just as she had done with the bazaar and the museum. "There are people to invite," she began. "And I need a wedding dress—"

"Yes, of course," Will interrupted. "But you must promise me we will not take too long planning. I want to marry you now."

Alanna's eyes grew wide. Her smile broadened. "What would you think of returning with me to Florence after we marry?"

The joyful expression on Will's face disappeared.

"I think you would like it there, Will. I know how you prefer warmer weather."

"Alanna, I—" Will was stunned. But it was not difficult for him to imagine what she was thinking. She had seen a bigger world. And she had already spent part of her life with one ruin keeper. It was logical that she might be uncertain about spending the rest of her life in Elgin living with another one.

The sudden concern on Will's face frightened Alanna. She wanted nothing more than to take back her impulsive words.

Will stepped out of their embrace. "I see you are having second thoughts."

"I did not intend—"

"Someday we might travel to Italy together," Will offered, "but I cannot do that now. Elgin is still my home. I have family here. Friends here. And so do you."

Tears filled Alanna's eyes.

"Listen to me carefully, Alanna. There will come a time when I will be willing to travel with you to any destination you choose. But not now. Not when I am about to begin a better life here in Elgin as keeper of a magnificent cathedral ruin. A life I had hoped to share with you."

Alanna blushed at the selfishness of her request—for Will to give up his life in Elgin and move to Italy. A place where his only standing in Florence's English society would be an artist's husband. "How thoughtless of me," she said, as her dream of returning to Italy melted away.

"Maybe someday," Will whispered, taking Alanna in his arms again. "First, let me become someone here in Elgin." There were tears in Will's eyes as he hugged her close. Then all at once he took Alanna's arm and walked her purposefully in the direction of the ruin. It was no longer a lovers' stroll. "Come with me," Will said. "There's something I want you to see."

Inside the chapter house Will and Alanna stood catching their breath.

"What is it, Will?" She noticed he seemed suddenly shy.

"There is something I have been meaning to show you." He took her hand and kissed it. "Can you find the heart?" he asked.

Alanna looked at him curiously and then placed her hand on his chest.

"No. I mean the heart here in the chapter house. The image I once showed you on the walls."

Alanna hesitated—so much time had passed. She spun around twice scanning the walls until it came back to her. "Oh yes!" The look on her face reminded Will of the girl she had been the first time they stood here together. Alanna quickly bent down close to the worn image. "Here it is," she said excitedly. Then she quietly gasped. Neatly carved beneath the worn heart were three very small letters: WMC, followed by a plus sign. When she looked up Will was smiling. In his hand he held his unopened pocketknife.

"Are you ready to add your initials?" he asked.

"May we do this?" she whispered. "Won't someone mind?"

Will's eyes danced. "I have obtained permission from the keeper himself."

Alanna grinned. "The letters are so tiny you can barely see them."

"This is just for us," he told her. "We know it will always be here."

"What does the *M* stand for?"

"Michael. From my mother's side of the family. It was her father's name."

"William Michael Clachan," Alanna said softly.

"Alanna Maria Oglethorpe Shanks," Will replied. "Are you ready to pledge your troth? Once I carve your initials, it cannot be undone. It will be our unchangeable commitment to marry." He stared at her in a most serious way.

Alanna nodded. "I am ready."

It did not take long for Will to carve her initials next to his own. Kissing her, he whispered, "This will always be our sanctuary."

She bent down and ran her fingers over the letters. Tears came into her eyes. "We can marry as soon as you wish."

"Now?" he teased her.

"Not today, but very soon." The sun was streaming through the chapter house windows. "We could be married here if you wish. Here in the chapter house."

"I thought you had plans for a big church wedding," Will said.

"I do. I did. But now…" Suddenly Alanna was no longer sure what she wanted. "I suppose I never imagined a wedding without church bells," she confessed. "But I want a wedding dress. And I want your family and our friends with us. I want Robert to be present. We will have refreshments and some music."

Will was relieved she made no mention of wedding scenes in Walter Scott novels.

"It will be wonderful," Alanna said, taking Will's arm.

"Yes, it will," he agreed, and kissed her gently. "I only have one request."

"Anything," Alanna promised without hesitation.

"We marry on Midsummer's Eve. The longest day of the year."

"That's barely three weeks from now—"

"Yes. So you had best make your guest list and write to Robert

Reid immediately. We have no time to waste."

Once the happy couple shared their good news, everyone wanted to help.

Isaac insisted on seeing to the arrangements. "You will have enough to do," he assured Alanna.

"Just some refreshments for the reception and a bit of music," Alanna told him. "Morrison might help set up tables for cake and punch after the ceremony."

"I will take care of it, Alanna. Busy yourself with the rest of your plans."

"And we'll need invitations," Alanna continued.

"I've already seen to them," Isaac assured her. "You needn't worry. Focus on the ceremony and I will see to the rest. You are the bride, and your friends are your family."

"Thank you, Isaac. You are so kind."

"One more thing." Isaac looked away, blushing. "I have a wedding gift for you and Will. Before I have it delivered, I feel I should ask your permission."

"Permission for what?"

Isaac hesitated. "I wish Will were here," he mumbled softly.

"Did I hear my name?" Will stepped into the parlor grinning. "I have been moving furniture upstairs all morning," Will told Isaac. "After the wedding Alanna and I plan to use the large corner bedroom."

"It's been closed up for years," Alanna said to Isaac. "After my grandmother died, Grand-Dey could not sleep there alone. That's why he slept in the small room at the top of the stairs."

Isaac's face brightened. "How convenient! You see, I have a

wedding gift for you—a family heirloom. I was unsure where you planned to live when you wed."

"We have decided this will be our home." Will smiled. "On occasion I will still stay in the keeper's hut when need arises." Will had more plans in mind, but this was not the time to share them. The man was trying to give them a wedding gift.

"Perfect." Isaac sighed. "You see, my grandfather was a cabinetmaker. When he married my grandmother, he made her the most beautiful bed. A four-poster of solid oak inlaid with cherry and maple. It has been handed down through generations, but I have no one to pass it along to."

Alanna and Will smiled at one another but kept still.

"The bed is in storage. There is no room in my home big enough for it. My point is, I am an old bachelor with no living relations. I want the two of you to have the bed as a wedding gift. Assuming it will fit."

Will and Alanna exchanged a quick glance and smiled at their friend.

"What a lovely thing to do," Alanna said.

"It's very kind of you to think of us as family," Will added. "What say we go measure the room."

The church bells began to strike the hour. "Isaac and I will do that," Alanna replied. "You have an appointment to keep with the tailor."

"And when do you return to the seamstress?" Will inquired, unable to recall.

"Tomorrow afternoon." Alanna had discarded her first set of sketches for the elaborate dress of her dreams. Scaled back the design to something more reasonable for their wedding location. Time was of the essence with hardly two weeks before the summer solstice.

"Oh goodness," Isaac trilled, "and here I am keeping you."

"I would much prefer to stay and measure the room," Will mumbled.

Alanna touched Will's shoulder. "I have given the tailor instructions for your suit of wedding clothes. A blue frock coat and no uncomfortable collar. Go let the man take your measurements. It shouldn't take long."

Isaac slipped up the stairs, out of the conversation.

"Fancy clothes. A bit of a waste," Will mumbled.

"Not at all," Alanna assured him. "You will have plenty of use for them as keeper and shower of the cathedral ruin."

"Your grandfather never dressed up to show the ruin," Will pointed out.

"True. But then, you are not my grand-dey." She winked at him.

When Will returned from the tailor, he found Alanna in the parlor where the light was best. Her back was to him, and she was stitching. Bent over a billow of white fabric covering her lap, she did not notice he was there, but she had been thinking of him. There was no question he loved her more ardently than any man she had ever known. Equally important, Will needed her. In Florence, people loved her work, respected her talent, and complimented her beauty. But no one in Florence ever once needed her.

Will crept quietly to look over Alanna's shoulder. She was embroidering something onto the hem of a petticoat. He watched as she made the tiniest M with her stitches. He could see the W preceding it, but the rest was hidden by her sewing hand.

"What is that?" he asked softly, leaning over her shoulder.

"Are those—"

Alanna startled, surprised by his presence. "It is only a bit of good luck. You will see it soon enough but not now." She bunched the skirt out of sight, but not before Will saw the embroidered initials on the hem of the petticoat: *AMOS + WM* neatly stitched in deep blue thread.

51

Something Old, Something Blue

Seated on an old blanket trunk, up in the attic of the town house, Alanna wept.

A pair of shoes rested in her lap. They were a fine pair of sky-blue slippers, barely worn. Made of silk and kidskin, with soft satin ribbons. She had discovered them under her mother's wedding dress, carefully wrapped in muslin cloth. The shoes were lovely. There was no mistaking her grandfather's fine stitches. With a bit of cotton in the toes, they would fit her perfectly.

Alanna tried to control her tears. If she could have her parents and grandparents back again for only one day, it would be for her wedding. She knew they would be with her in spirit, but it wasn't the same as flesh and blood.

She had climbed up to the attic to search for blankets to fit the new bed. The discovery of her mother's wedding clothes was entirely unexpected. Her mother's dress was finer than any she could wish for. She would need to take up the hem and adjust the sleeves. Otherwise, all that was necessary was for Alanna to make the dress her own. It had a cinched waist and off-the-shoulder sleeves. The full skirt was trimmed in tiny embroidered bluebells and butter-flies, all in the palest pastels. The most delicate ribbons tied at the edge of each sleeve. From a small lace cap dangled little tails of silk and satin ribbons. They were meant to mix with the tendrils of a bride's hair, like a waterfall over her shoulders. Unlike in Italy, there was no need for a veil to cover her face.

She would have to send word to the seamstress. A change of plans. Only a few alterations would be required. The wedding dress sketches she had made and remade were destined for her portfo-lio. They would become an important part of her story. A story she hoped to one day tell her own children if the fates allowed.

Will and Alanna carefully chose the hour for their wedding cere-mony.

"For good luck the clock hands must be rising when we wed," Alanna explained to Will. With eighteen hours of daylight on the longest day of the year, there was no need to hurry. After the cere-mony and reception, the couple planned to return to the town house before sunset. What would happen after that required no plans.

Will was amazed by the size of the gathering in the chapter house. He had never seen his brothers and parents so well dressed. For the first time Will recognized his father as the successful master builder he had become. Both Da and Mam had gray in their hair now, but they still seemed young, especially today. Their smiles confirmed their blessings on his marriage to Alanna. His brothers Andrew and Ross were fast becoming young men. Secretly Will hoped to recruit Andrew to work with him in the ruin someday. Andrew was still the talker of the family. A natural storyteller who could charm even the sourest soul.

As the wedding guests arrived Will did not look at their faces. Instead, he searched for the faces only he could see on the walls inside the chapter house. With the souls of the ancients watching, he trembled from heart to heels.

Robert Reid proudly escorted Alanna. "I have never seen a lovelier bride," he told her. With no daughters of his own, it was a special day for him, as well.

Alanna carried a small nosegay of Scots bluebells and tiny white rosebuds. She was beautiful in her mother's wedding gown, and she wore the blue shoes made by her grandfather. She donned no jewelry. Nothing to compete with the ring that would soon be placed on her finger, made from a precious coin once belonging to her father. The spirit of her family felt ever-present.

Entering the ruin, Alanna could hear the sweet sounds of a string duet. Music students from the Free School were softly playing a processional. James Thompson had seen to the music as his gift to the bride and groom.

Outside the chapter house, Robert and Alanna were joined by Isaac. Both men had asked to present her for marriage on behalf of her late grandfather. Isaac was only slightly sad not to be chosen, but she assured him he could help "give her away." Together the two men walked the bride up the aisle created by the many guests. "Thankfully, the roles of the bride and groom are clearly established," Luke whispered jovially to Will as he stood proudly beside his brother.

Alanna beamed at the sight of the chapter house filled with family and friends. The size of Will's extended family made up for the handful of cousins on the bride's side. Alanna felt welcomed and adored.

The minister from Elgin's Congregational Church performed the simple ceremony. It was not the words she and Will repeated to one another that would remain forever in Alanna's heart. Instead, it was the warmth of Will's hands as he placed the ring on her finger. The strength of his arms as he held her and kissed her for the very first time as man and wife. And the sound of the three tiny bells he had given her to sew onto the waist of her dress, so she would have bells on her wedding day.

After the ceremony, Alanna's heart sank when she saw no evidence of a reception outside the chapter house. She turned to Isaac with a questioning look, doing her best to stay calm. All at once the peal of church bells began ringing out across the town.

Isaac smiled. "Follow me," he told Alanna. Accompanied by St. Giles church bells ceaselessly chiming, the wedding party and guests processed out of the ruin and into town. Everyone was laughing and talking, and curious about their destination. When they reached the Assembly Rooms, Isaac handed Alanna a pair of scissors. Then he nodded at the two youngest Clachan boys. They quickly took up their stations at the top of the steps and unfurled a white ribbon between them. Alanna laughed and joyfully cut the ribbon.

Inside the hall, the same ladies who successfully ran the charity bazaar had arranged the wedding reception. Isaac winked at Alanna. "I hired your experts. You did not truly believe I could do this all on my own, did you?"

Laughing, Alanna kissed Isaac on the cheek and made him blush.

Morrison had helped the ladies set up the reception, with Mrs. Hendry in charge of decorations. They stood together, off to one side. Mrs. Hendry was dressed plainly with a scarf on her head so as not to draw attention. She did not think Alanna would be glad of her presence, but she wanted to see Will on his wedding day.

After the wedding feast was beautifully presented, there was cake and punch, and toasts to the newlywed couple. Will quietly reminded Alanna not to drink too much punch, and secretly watered down both their drinks. "We will celebrate later," he said with a grin.

Alanna and Will exchanged wedding gifts, as was the custom. Will gave his bride a copy of Oliver Goldsmith's novel *The Vicar of Wakefield*. Forsyth had recommended the book as the perfect wedding gift. Will needed only to open the cover and read the first sentence: "I chose my wife, as she did her wedding gown, not for a fine glossy surface, but for such qualities as would wear well." A full-color frontispiece appeared at the start of the book entitled "Choosing the Wedding Gown."

Alanna's gift for Will brought tears to his eyes. A small landscape she had painted of his favorite view on the River Lossie. An osprey soared over the river, and Brodie could be seen playing at the water's edge.

Robert Reid also offered the couple "a small gift." He had arranged a honeymoon trip to Edinburgh and the use of his private coach for the journey. Will had never been to Edinburgh and the idea of visiting pleased him. Alanna, of course, was thrilled.

The massive bed made Will and Alanna feel like guests in their own room.

It was made up beautifully with the softest linens and pillows. The wood had been polished and the mattress plumped. Neither of them had yet slept in the bed. Its size was guaranteed to make a single person lonely. Yet here they were, about to do something together they had only dreamed of until now.

Alanna climbed gracefully onto the edge of the bed and placed her nosegay on the pillows. She let Will remove her shoes. He was slow and careful. He did not wish to damage family heirlooms. Alanna rested her cheek against the post at the foot of the bed, looking down at the top of her new husband's head. For the first time she noticed how his hair grew in a swirl pattern. Alanna imagined what else she was close to discovering about Will's body. She happily wiggled her toes, still sheathed in stockings.

Will shed his coat and shoes and sat beside her on the bed. "Anything else you wish to have help removing?" His smile was devilish but gentle.

"Not yet."

Will took her hand in his. Together they watched the celestial wonder of a lingering sunset. As a nearly full moon climbed into the sky, the sun glided slowly along the horizon. Will sighed. "This day has gone too quickly."

"The day is not yet over." Alanna leaned into his shoulder.

Will kissed her softly. Once, twice, three times. His patience surprised her.

"What was your favorite moment today?" she asked.

"This one," he answered without hesitation. "The one we are living right now. The present will always be my favorite moment with you, Alanna."

She touched the side of his face, puzzled by his answer. "And what of the future? There are sure to be moments of disappointment, pain, and sadness."

"My life with you will always be better than my life without you." Will stroked her hair and searched her face. "That will never change—no matter life's challenges or sorrows. Right now, though"—Will raised her hands to his lips and kissed her fingers—"I believe our moments together are about to become most memorable."

Alanna stretched out on the bed and sighed.

Will raised an eyebrow and grinned at her, reading her mind. He loosened his collar, unbuttoned his cuffs, and stretched out beside her. "And here we are again," Will said, a smile spread across his face. "Laying together."

Alanna laughed. "Except this time will be different."

"Oh yes. I can assure you." He began the process of unfastening sixteen tiny dress buttons.

For the rest of his life, Will would do his best to recall the many special moments of their wedding day. But he would never forget gently removing Alanna's silk stockings. Slowly rolling them down from the inside of her thighs. The tops of the stockings, high up her legs, were embroidered in her own hand with tiny butterflies and forget-me-nots. Their initials were stitched there, too. Will would forever suffer a delightful desire at the thought of those stockings.

When at last Will and Alanna lay together as man and wife, it was in full understanding of what was about to happen. Each brought a new awareness of the magic and joy of knowing one another completely. Wordlessly they offered new skills and experiences they had not possessed when last they met this way. The night was kind to them. A kindness destined to endure. A promise of future magic. New memories waiting to be made.

By the time the sun lifted over the treetops, Will was already wondering how would he keep his hands and lips from ceaselessly caressing his new bride on the long carriage ride to Edinburgh.

Will and Alanna were still abed when they heard urgent knocking at the front door.

Alanna had purposely given the cook and housekeeper the day

off. "I suppose I will have to get up," Will yawned as he reached for his shirt.

Alanna sighed. "Who could it be?" She slipped into a dressing gown. "I'll go see to our breakfast. Do not tarry long with whoever it is."

Will opened the door to find Morrison standing on the front step. He could not bring himself to look directly at Will. "I am sorely sorry to bother you, Will," he began.

"As am I," Will agreed, watching Morrison's neck turn red. "But here we are."

"I would not have disturbed, but Isaac insisted."

"What does the old bachelor want with me at this hour?" Will did not wish to be unkind, but his marriage bed was still warm.

"There's been a break-in at the museum. Forsyth and Martin thought you should come see."

"See what?" Will asked.

"Best if you hear for yourself what the old keeper has to say."

Will bit his tongue. He would stop asking questions and go to the museum. Find out what it was that could not wait, and then return quickly to his first day of married bliss. He sincerely hoped there would be more lovemaking squeezed in between their packing for Edinburgh. "Wait here," Will told Morrison. "I would ask you in, but Alanna is still—"

Morrison blushed and raised his hand. "Say no more."

When Will and Morrison arrived at the museum, John Martin, William Ingram, and Isaac Forsyth stood in the entryway. They thanked Will for coming.

"What's happened?" Will asked.

"It's a bit of a mystery," Isaac said.

"We thought you might have some idea," Martin added.

"Idea about what?" Will asked. "Please—start from the beginning."

"I was asleep upstairs in my rooms," Ingram said. "The museum was locked up tight for the night. I had done my rounds. Nothin' seemed amiss. Then I went to bed," the old watchman said, "with an ear out for any mischief."

Will wondered if the old man was referring to his deaf ear or his good one.

"The next thing I heard was the sound of glass breaking. I came runnin' down the stairs, but he was already gone. Whoever it was, the man moved fast. Then I came back inside to find what was broke." Ingram scratched his head, the wisps of hair still smashed flat from sleep. "I cannot make sense of it. The unbroken lock and the smashed glass case. But nothin' seemed to be missing."

Martin cleared his throat. "I arrived soon after. I was having trouble sleeping—the long days, you know. I have been through the entire museum to see what might have been stolen. At first, I thought the intruder had only broken a small glass case and nothing had been disturbed." The curator shot a sidelong look at the keeper. "But I was wrong. I believe whoever it was hid himself in the museum before closing. When he was certain all was quiet, he broke the case and took the one thing he came for. Then he let himself out the front door and ran off. Save for the one broken glass case, nothing else was disturbed."

Suddenly, Will understood why he was there. His knees went weak and his heart raced. He was certain someone had stolen his carved creature. "What was the one thing?" Will needed to know.

Everyone looked at the curator.

Martin chose not to share his true thoughts, especially in Will's presence. He had been relieved to discover the only item missing was an object that he himself had initially rejected from the collection. But Will had insisted. If the museum wanted his ancient little carving, they would have to take the piece of stained Murray plaid. Even though Martin maintained there was no evidence that the contents of the small leather pouch were Culloden artifacts. Martin believed the rotting scrap of stained tartan fabric had no place in Elgin Museum. Although many had heard the tale firsthand from the object's onetime owner, there was no proof it was a Culloden battlefield relic.

Martin looked at Will and said, "The only thing missing is the small leather pouch and the scrap of Culloden tartan."

Will stared hard at the keeper. "Did you manage to get a good look at the man?"

"Aye, I did. But I still cannot make sense of the break-in."

"Describe him to me, please," Will asked impatiently.

The old keeper squared his shoulders, as though what he was about to say might be important. "The man was very thin, but he had some muscles still. He was wearin' a dirty old kilt and a stained shirt. When I called out to him, he looked back at me. Were it not for the gas lights along the street, I might have thought he was a ghost."

A shiver chilled Will's spine.

"He had the body of a younger man, but when he turned, I saw his face was lined and wrinkled, his hair gone gray. There were scars on his arms, or maybe tattoos."

"Could you see the plaid of the kilt?" Will asked, already knowing the answer.

"Murray plaid, and ancient it was." The old keeper shook his head. "Barely a rag. He was clutchin' something in his hand, but I did not see what it was. I shouted at him, but he took off runnin' toward the trees."

Will was certain the thief was Johnny. He imagined his cousin, looking impossibly old for his age, still wearing the ancient Murray kilt. His hair graying, his face wrinkled. Running toward the wych elm grove with something small clutched in his hand.

"I am sorry for the loss, Will," John Martin said. "I know it was an important part of your collection."

"It was not mine to begin with. And if Ingram's description is accurate, the stolen item rightfully belongs to the man who took it."

"Johnny Murray," Morrison muttered. "I have never been able to puzzle out where Johnny goes after we see him. I cannot think where he disappears to."

I can, Will thought. The timing was right. Close to a solstice, a change in seasons, a near-full moon. Will still refused to believe in any of the old ways and tall tales, with this one exception.

"Are you sure the man was older than me?" Will asked the keeper. He wanted to be certain.

"Old enough to be your grand-dey."

"We will need to add a new lock, I think," Forsyth suggested.

Will shook his head. "I doubt we will ever see the likes of him again."

52

DISTINGUISHED VISITORS

Will stood on the steps of the ruin's grand entrance where visitors entered the grounds.

He stared down the road, waiting impatiently. The steps beneath his feet still stirred memories of pain and pride. He and Shanks had cleared a mountain of broken stone from this portal. But within another generation, he knew few would recall the landslide of rubble that had covered these steps for hundreds of years. That was the nature of being a ruin keeper instead of a builder.

To compose himself, Will shined the toes of his boots on the back of his pants legs. His clothes were new. His hair cut short and combed in place. He wore a gray coat, dark pants, and a cravat that he did not care for. The clothes were Alanna's doing.

"It makes you look respectable, like a gentleman," Alanna had tried to impress upon him.

"I am not a gentleman," he reminded her. "I am the keeper of Elgin Cathedral ruin." Although Will had performed the duties of shower and keeper for many months, the official transfer of Shanks's title, and some reasonable compensation, was a recent event. Over a year had passed since the death of John Shanks. It was a time of mourning and remembrance, joy and love.

Now Will stood waiting for important visitors. He resisted checking the time. The ruin had welcomed plenty of distinguished people, he reminded himself. He thought back to the widow Gordon and blushed. How young and innocent he had been when he and Shanks entertained the Scottish Works Committee, and when Robert Reid first came to visit. Will still enjoyed referring to Reid as the King's Remembrancer. In good humor Reid allowed it, seeing that Will was married to Reid's "goddaughter," as he now referred to Alanna.

Second only to John Shanks, Reid had changed Will's life—for better and for worse. Will laughed aloud at the thought of that phrase. He and Alanna had recited those same words when they wed. Now Reid was a family friend.

Will shook off the memories and focused on the soon-to-arrive visitors: Major Moray, Lady Baird, and their guests. Elgin's lord provost was expected to join Will on the steps, along with Forsyth and Alanna.

Will had toured many visitors through the ruin, but today was different. He felt it in his bones. His muscles twitched and his skin prickled with anticipation. This was the first time he would welcome a group of visitors as the official keeper and shower of Elgin Cathedral ruin.

At Forsyth's suggestion, Alanna would be joining the welcoming committee as granddaughter of the renowned John Shanks. Will understood the wisdom of Forsyth's suggestion, and he welcomed it. There were to be women in the tour group, and what better idea than to have a knowledgeable woman accompanying the tour.

The members of Elgin's small welcoming party gathered on the steps. Forsyth checked his watch. The lord provost fidgeted. Their guests were extremely behind schedule. A messenger had ridden ahead of the travelers to advise of their delay. Will was undaunted. He had given enough tours to know that important visitors were never on time. Although Will was always prompt. Throughout his life, there had been many things he could *not* be—but *on time* was not one of them.

Will joined Forsyth in checking the time. Mostly for the benefit of holding the pocket watch in his hand. It brought a soft smile to Alanna's face. She looked at him in a way that made him feel special, as only she could do.

Major Moray and Lady Baird were well-known across Scotland. While touring the northeast countryside, they had decided to stop to see the cathedral ruin. They would be passing through Elgin on their way from Inverness to Aberdeen with a stopover at Gordon Castle. And they were bringing guests. The major had sent correspondence to Elgin only the day before, asking for their visit to be kept as quiet as possible. Insisting on no more than a half dozen in the welcoming party. The purpose of their brief visit was to tour the cathedral ruin in the company of the resident expert.

The major's wishes were clear. There were to be no speeches, no presentations, no ceremony, and no crowd of citizens. Forsyth insisted town officials comply with the major's requests. Even though it meant disappointing a number of local worthies who would be displeased to learn they had been excluded.

The guests arrived in two coaches. The drivers' exquisite regalia matched the sparkling livery on the handsome Cleveland bays. There were four people in the major's party, not counting the servants. Major Moray stepped from the first coach and offered a hand to Lady Baird. She was wearing a handsome suit of emerald green traveling clothes, and a bonnet with matching satin ribbons. Lady Baird immediately opened her parasol. Together the couple greeted each member of the welcoming party. There were introductions, kind words, and the offering of punch, which was gladly received. The servants stood to one side. When the official greetings were completed, the major thanked the welcoming committee. He asked that their little group might take their tour with the keeper only.

"A tour is what we've come for," Major Moray said with a smile.

"And your guests?" Forsyth asked, gesturing toward the second coach.

"…will be fine, thank you." Major Moray was polite but firm in his reply.

"They will join us anon," Lady Baird assured Forsyth, patting his hand. "They have had a long journey, and they are a bit shy, you see."

"Of course." Forsyth nodded, unsure what more he might do. "If you are certain." He tried one last time to be gracious.

"Quite certain," the major replied.

The welcoming committee was surprised and slightly offended. They bowed graciously and departed, but not without a few backward glances. Only Will and Alanna remained behind.

The major and Lady Baird walked to the second carriage. The door was opened and out emerged a handsome young man with dark hair and blue eyes. He turned and offered his hand to a tiny young woman who stepped lightly to the ground. The major and Lady Baird bowed and curtsied. A parasol was quickly opened for the young woman.

"Would your guests care for some punch, Lady Baird?" Alanna asked politely. Without waiting for an answer, she offered a tray of filled glasses. A coach ride could be an impossibly hot venture this time of year, and few would turn down a drink upon arrival.

Without further ado, Major Moray introduced the couple to Will and Alanna. "These are our special guests, the Countess of Lancaster and Lord Karl Emanuel." Everyone nodded politely.

"I am Will Clachan, Elgin Cathedral's ruin keeper and guide. And this is my wife, Alanna. She is the granddaughter of the late John Shanks. A name that may be familiar to you. He was Elgin Cathedral's ruin keeper for many years. Together, we will take you on a brief tour. As you might imagine, Alanna is also an expert on the ruin."

There were pleasant smiles all around as they ascended the steps. Once through the portal, Will stopped. It was the spot where he liked to begin all tours, with a view of the cathedral yard stretching before them. He seldom bored visitors with too many facts, but he did like to start at the beginning. "The original Elgin Cathedral was established in 1224, on land granted by the Scottish King Alexander II. It was a great and grand Gothic cathedral, most likely designed, built, and decorated by Italian and French architects, sculptors, and artists. The manual labor was provided by local stonemasons, many of whom were descended from the Picts in this region."

"How interesting," the young lord said. Will noted a slight accent in his voice.

The countess added, "I recall once seeing a very old map of our country, with the land above what was once Hadrian's Wall identified as 'Pictland.'"

"Which, of course, eventually became Scotland," Major Moray added, bowing slightly toward the little woman.

"What I wish to show you next is the oldest item in the ruin, although it was never part of the original cathedral." Will led the group across the grounds to the Pictish Cross.

"What is this?" Lord Emanuel asked, moving closer for a better look.

"This is the Elgin Pictish Cross. Some call it a Pictish pillar. We do not know how old it is, but we know it predates recorded history in this region."

"Amazing! Is this a falconer?" Lord Emanuel asked.

"It appears to be." Will allowed his guests time to examine the details of the prehistoric stone. He answered their questions and, at Major Moray's prompting, shared the story of the stone's discovery.

"Captivating, isn't it?" the major beamed at his guests.

"At one time," Will continued, "Elgin Cathedral was considered the crowning glory of this region. It was called the Lantern of the North. This ruin remains fascinating because of what it once was. It was considered the ornament of the district, the glory of the kingdom, and the admiration of foreigners. As Chambers states in his book *The Pictures of Scotland*, 'It is an allowed fact that this was by far the most splendid ecclesiastical architecture in Scotland. Enough still remains to impress the solitary traveler with a sense of admiration mixed with astonishment.'"

Alanna enjoyed watching their guests' faces as Will recited this memorized text.

"Reading of these ancient cathedrals," Lord Emanuel said, "I am impressed by the design, the architecture, and the engineering required to build such a structure in mean times. The intelligence, skills, and artistry that were necessary."

Will nodded to his guest. "After the Wolf of Badenoch burned the Cathedral in 1390, much of the Gothic decoration was destroyed. But the Cathedral was slowly rebuilt to include a central tower that rose two hundred feet into the air." Everyone looked skyward, as they always did at this point in the tour. Imagination was a powerful device, and Will encouraged it in his storytelling.

The small group moved on, stopping next to see the colossal bishop statue. Standing beside it, the countess seemed little more than half its size.

"This bishop was one of four large statues that adorned the highest section of the central tower. It was made large enough to be seen from a great distance."

"What happened to the others?" Lady Baird asked.

"Likely they were destroyed when the tower collapsed. But we have found a rather large nose that may have belonged to one of the other statues."

As Will prepared to move the group toward the chapter house, he politely asked the major, "Have you visited the ruin previously, sir?"

"I have indeed." Major Moray turned to Alanna who was standing next to the countess. "My last visit was for the funeral of the Duke of Gordon. Rest his soul." The major turned to Alanna and said, "That was when I first met your dear grandfather." He paused and looked around. A brief moment of confusion crossed the major's face. "Where did you say the old ruin keeper was again? Is he not joining us today?"

Alanna and Will exchanged uncomfortable looks. Either the man was a bit deaf, or he had somehow misunderstood the earlier introductions. Without a hint of emotion in her voice, Alanna turned to the major, and explained, "Actually, sir, he is here. If you like, I can take you to him. He died a year ago last April. His grave is in the adjacent churchyard, not far from that of the Duke of Gordon."

Flustered, the major took Alanna's hand apologetically. "By all means, let us pay our respects."

Standing next to John Shanks's grave, Alanna gently patted the headstone.

"It says on his stone he removed 2,866 barrows full of earth and rubble from this place. Can that be true?" Lord Emanuel asked.

"So they say." Will's eyes danced as he smiled at Alanna. They did not linger at Shanks's grave. His headstone made clear all he had once been.

Lord Emanuel caught sight of the ancient knight's tomb. "Who is buried here?" he wished to know.

"This is the armored effigy of William de la Hay, Lord of Lochloy, who died in 1422. He was likely a member of the Knights Templar, exiled here from France."

"Fantastic!" the young lord said.

"Hay's tomb was rediscovered by my wee dog," Will chuckled.

"You have a dog?" the countess asked. "Is it nearby? I am missing my own little beast. I had to leave him at home this trip."

"Brodie has a life of his own, I'm afraid. Most likely he's napping by the river."

The countess nodded with a smile.

"I realize your time is short. The history of the cathedral is immense. But you cannot leave without seeing the octagonal chapter house." Will led the way, with Alanna and the countess walking together. Alanna admired the young woman's traveling clothes. Her turquoise corduroy skirts, an embroidered velvet jacket, a blue bonnet, and a cameo at her throat. The most delicate white gloves covered her hands. Her parasol matched her jacket. Even in Italy Alanna had not seen clothes so stunning.

"How long have you been married to the ruin keeper?" the countess asked Alanna.

"We were married last year. Not long after my grandfather died. The ceremony took place here in the chapter house."

The countess smiled. "My husband and I also married not long ago. The church where we were married was slightly larger." She grinned and placed her gloved hand to her lips. Lowering her voice she added, "I must say, we have handsome husbands."

Alanna smiled in agreement.

Will asked Alanna to talk about the chapter house. "She is our resident expert on this part of the ruin," Will explained. With some guests Alanna talked about discovering the angel carving in the roof, and how she sketched it in the company of the great architect Robert Reid. Today, their time was short—although she would have enjoyed telling the little countess about being hoisted up to the roofline. She sensed this was a woman who might appreciate such adventures.

Lord Emanuel looked around at the walls and up to the ceiling. "I know this place. I have seen a drawing of it. In London. An amazing sketch. A copy I'm sure. And now, I am here!"

"Do you recall whose sketch it was?" Will asked casually. Alanna caught Will's eye and gave him a stern look.

Lord Emanuel crimped his brow. "Hmm. I believe there were initials only. A-V-O- N, or A-M -O-S, or —"

"I am A.M.O.S." Alanna said quietly. "I believe the sketch you were looking at was mine, Lord Emanuel."

"My wife studied art in Florence before we were married," Will recited. He was accustomed to providing the details about Alanna's life, while she smiled quietly.

"My wife and I also have recently taken up sketching. Though we are but amateurs." Lord Emanuel smiled at the countess. "We can appreciate what is required to be as fine an artist as you." He nodded respectfully to Alanna.

"Thank you, sir," Alanna replied.

Major Moray was looking at his watch. "I am afraid we must be going. They are expecting us at Gordon Castle."

"Of course," Will said. "It was our pleasure to welcome you today." He bowed to Major Moray and Lady Baird, and to the young Countess of Lancaster and Lord Emanuel.

Back at the entrance, it was all Alanna could do not to stare at the magnificent coaches and horses. Something about the younger couple seemed mysterious. Perhaps they were distant relatives of the royal family. Will and Alanna stood respectfully as the guests prepared to depart. Will bowed, and Alanna curtsied in farewell.

"I will remember you," the tiny countess whispered to Will as he dipped his head to her proffered hand. "The young ruin keeper." She smiled.

Then the coachman bowed and offered the small woman his gloved hand. Assisting her into the coach he whispered, "Your Majesty."

EPILOGUE
SEPTEMBER 6, 1872
TIMEPIECE

Will was waiting for a train.

Making his way down the platform of the Highland Railway station, he resisted an impulse to check his watch. Dozens of people were busy greeting one another, and the assemblage was quickly growing. The happy anticipation in the air brought to mind a celebration with everyone dressed in fine clothes and fashionable hats.

The modest station house at the eastern edge of Elgin was among Scotland's oldest. Yet its brilliant white coat of paint with bright red trim was so fresh the fumes still lingered. Women along the platform reined in their voluminous skirts, fearful of brushing against newly painted walls. The white paint was a poor choice for the long-term. The soot from the trains would soon change the gleaming walls to a dingy gray. But this day left little room for future worries.

It was "a Queen's weather day" with a cloudless blue sky just as brilliant as Charles Dickens once defined it. The monarch possessed a reputation for always bringing fine weather on her official visits.

Even before the train appeared, Will was possessed by a child-like excitement. Silly for a man his age. The butterflies in his stomach preceded the far-off sound of chug and whistle and the advancing puffs of black smoke. Trains still fascinated Will. He was of a generation who could recall a time before they existed. Once, long ago, his father wished the world might stop changing so quickly. Instead, it now seemed to advance with a great haste. A ferocious speed. Even now, similar feelings existed among many of Elgin's population. Indeed, people of the old school believed life contained too much hurry and turmoil for the human frame. And yet, with the improvements of roads and the formation of railways, it seemed mankind was only progressing to a greater degree of speed.

Three decades ago in Elgin, the few coaches passing through the region were often half-empty of passengers. Hardly anyone left home. It was a rare thing for a person to travel to Edinburgh, and few Scotsmen had ever been to London. There were many in Elgin who lived long lives never venturing outside their native county. Now there seemed a constant movement. Even at remote railway stations, crowds of passengers anxiously waited to be carried to their respective destinations. Will wondered what his father might say if he were standing next to him now.

A train whistle interrupted Will's thought. He looked down the track, like everyone else on the platform. He was surprised to see there were people sitting on the rooftops of houses lining the railway bed.

"Please stand back!" the stationmaster directed, and the crowd obeyed. Handsome red ropes sectioned the platform. On one side, the citizenry of Elgin arranged themselves. Closer to the tracks, Elgin's provost, magistrates, and other officials were joined by the Duke of Richmond and the Earl of March. Banners rippled in the breeze. Several members of the deputation checked their watches. All were about the business of appearing most important.

Will hesitated between the two groups. It was a familiar dilemma. One of the magistrates motioned to him, wanting a word. It would have to wait. A sound far down the tracks caused everyone to look in that direction.

Will nodded to the magistrate before turning toward the larger group. It was an assemblage of the respectable classes from Elgin and the surrounding county. Alanna smiled at him from just beyond the ropes. His sons were there, too, wives on their arms. The excitement on each face so dear to him made his heart skip a beat. He slipped around the barrier where his family made room for him at the front of the crowd.

There were cheers of excitement as Her Majesty's special train came into view, arriving at the station as the bells of St. Giles struck two o'clock.

The beautiful state carriage was painted burgundy and cream and marked with the royal insignia. When the compartment opened, the Queen appeared at the door. She was attended by her Secretary of State, Earl Granville. Queen Victoria seemed in excellent spirits and much pleased with the appearance of the large assembly met to do her honor.

Women on the platform were not surprised to see the Queen still wearing widow's black. A sharp contrast to the fashion of patchwork colors displayed in the crowd.

The ceremony was brief. Elgin's lord provost presented the loyal address of the Elgin Town Council, and it was graciously received. Everyone seemed satisfied with the brief ceremony and gratified with seeing their benevolent sovereign among them. A reporter from the *Elgin Gazette* was present, and a photographic view was taken to preserve the scene for future generations.

As the Queen bid the lord provost farewell, she glanced past him where the townspeople were gathered. The Queen tilted her head and squinted. She motioned Granville to her side. He bent deferentially to hear her whispered instructions. To everyone's surprise, the earl escorted the Queen a few steps forward. Behind the red ropes the townspeople quietly gawked. The Queen waited while Granville moved to speak to Will.

"Her Majesty has asked you to approach. Please tell me your name and occupation so that I may introduce you."

Will felt his knees tremble before recovering sufficiently to bow and reply, "Yes, of course, Your Grace. My name is William Clachan. Her Majesty may remember me as the ruin keeper of Elgin Cathedral." Will followed behind Granville as he led the way to the tiny monarch.

As Will approached the Queen, he removed his hat and placed it under his arm. He did his best not to make eye contact with anyone and ignored the sudden flurry of whispers coming from both sides of the platform.

Will bowed deeply as the earl introduced him. Then he bent to kiss the gloved hand proffered by the Queen. With his eyes closed, a long-forgotten memory suddenly resurfaced: *Tell her when you bend to kiss her hand.*

"Your servant, my Queen." Will's voice was a bare whisper. He felt light-headed.

"I remember you." The tiny Queen smiled. "We met once before, many years ago."

"Yes, Your Majesty."

"You were the young ruin keeper. You gave my late husband and me a fascinating tour of the ancient cathedral ruin. It was many years ago. Still, I will always remember that day."

"As will I, Your Majesty."

The Queen leaned closer to whisper in Will's ear. "Like me, I see you have a few wrinkles around the eyes since we last met. And your hair is beginning to silver. Otherwise, you appear much the same to me. When I saw your lovely wife standing beside you there in the crowd, I knew I was not mistaken." The Queen nodded in Alanna's direction. "Such a lovely face. I recall you were both exceedingly kind to us that day."

"You are most gracious, my Queen." Will's heart pounded as he briefly raised his eyes. Queen Victoria was smiling at him.

Will bowed once more and stepped back. The Queen waved to her people. She and her retinue removed themselves into the carriage as quickly as they had descended. The royal train departed for the north amid the plaudits of the spectators.

Alanna hurried to Will's side followed by their children. Everyone was talking at once. Alanna reached for Will's hand. "How many people can say they have met the Queen of England, not once but twice in a lifetime!"

"Aye, it's true." Will nodded. Yet already the meeting was beginning to feel unreal to him. As though he had just awakened from a fanciful dream. He peered up the tracks in the direction the train departed.

Alanna smiled at him. "You amaze me, Will Clachan."

Will took his wife's hand. "She remembered you, Alanna."

"The Queen? Remembered me? Impossible."

"She said she recognized me only after she saw your lovely face in the crowd." Alanna appeared as though she might swoon. Will hugged her close, then held her at arm's length. "The Queen remembered us for one reason alone. She remembered us because of the ruin."

"It wasn't just the ruin, Will."

"You're right. There was something more." Will paused to

admire his brilliant wife, who knew his mind as well as her own. He had loved her longer than anyone in his life. "The Queen told me she remembered us for our kindness." Will gently touched Alanna's cheek. "But were it not for the once beautiful Elgin Cathedral…" Will's eyes danced.

"There would be no ruin," Alanna continued. "And without the ruin…"

"John Shanks would have never chosen me to be his assistant."

"And we would have never properly met."

"Even though I would have still loved you from afar." Will smiled.

Alanna hugged Will close.

This was their story, all of it true. Will would have never met and fallen in love with Alanna, married her, and fathered her children. Never become the ruin keeper. His life had been shaped by the cathedral ruin. And the man who chose him to be his assistant so many years ago. John Shanks, "the drouthy cobbler," keeper and watchman and peerless storyteller. This was the path of Will's life that twice led him to meet Queen Victoria.

"Shall we join the others?" Alanna asked, glancing toward the reception on the nearby lawn. "You look like you are in need of a dram."

"We will follow in a moment." Will guided Alanna gently to the far side of the station. He took her in his arms and kissed her softly.

"You will always be my knight, Will Clachan."

"And you, my lady." Once more Will bent to kiss Alanna. She closed her eyes, leaning into his embrace. Before their lips touched, she suddenly broke away. Her eyes flew open as she raised her fingers to her lips. A wide grin broke across her face. Her fingers lingered where Will's lips had been.

"What is it?" Will asked.

She reached for his face and ran her thumb gently over his lower lip. "The last place your lips touched before kissing mine was the hand of a Queen."

"Our Queen," he replied.

"Do you think you might ever meet her a third time?" Alanna's eyes sparkled.

"One never knows." Will grinned mischievously.

"Then I wish you both long lives so that such a thing might happen."

"You could invite her to tea," Will teased. They giggled together at the thought.

Alanna loved the way her husband's eyes crinkled when he laughed. He still retained his boyish charms, gray hairs notwithstanding. "More likely she might return one day, bringing a contingent from Balmoral to tour the ruin with her favorite ruin keeper," Alanna said.

"All those novels you've read, my dear, have left you with a vivid imagination."

Alanna laughed again, and he heard in her voice both the girl he first worshiped and the woman he now loved.

"Go join the others. I need one more moment."

"Don't be long." Alanna left Will standing alone on the platform, staring up the tracks. He did his best to form a solid memory. Something that might feel more real than dreamlike by morning. Will reached into his pocket and pulled out his watch. Long ago, the pocket watch had become his new touchstone, replacing his precious carved creature. He opened the watch but not to check the time. He ran his thumb gently over the words engraved inside the front case. Words he never tired of reading. They captured all that came before, and all that was yet to unfold.

We are the heirs of ages past
Whose lot is in the present cast.
We reap what others sowed.
The way we tread must yet be worn
By generations yet unborn
To whom our lives are owed.

—Henry Baker Tristram

He often caught himself reciting the Tristram quote, so dear to his heart. Yet Will rarely looked at the inscriptions inside the back of the watchcase. It was too much of a reminder of his own mortality. Someday, the watch would belong to a new ruin keeper. Until then, it remained his.

John Shanks ~ Keeper, Watchman & Shower of Elgin Cathedral
Will Clachan ~ The Ruin Keeper

Author's Note

The bishop's tomb young Will Clachan stumbled upon during his game of All Hide in the ruin remained undiscovered in the real world until the 1930s. Although John Shanks worked near it, the tomb of Bishop Archibald was encased within the walls of the presbytery, making it difficult to detect.

In 2016, following a £300,000 restoration effort, the seven-hundred-dred-year-old effigy of Bishop Archibald was returned to Elgin Cathedral. It is now on display, along with one hundred medieval carved stones—including that nasty little bare-bottomed monk.

Although Alanna Shanks and the Clachan family are products of this author's imagination, John Shanks is not. A notice of his death appeared in the *Inverness Courier* on April 28, 1841, crediting him with "…removing with his pickaxe and shovel, 2,866 barrow-fuls [sic] of earth, besides disclosing a flight of steps that led to the grand gateway of the edifice. Tombs and figures that had long lain hidden in obscurity were unearthed and every monumental frag-ment of saints and holy men was carefully preserved and placed in some appropriate situation. So faithfully did he discharge his duty as keeper of the ruins, that little now remains but to preserve what he accomplished."

The old ruin keeper is firmly embedded in Scottish history, along with Isaac Forsyth, Robert Reid, and the cathedral ruin they worked to preserve. Many more historical figures appear in *The Scottish Ruin Keeper*. Each with their own fascinating stories.

Elgin Cathedral claims the largest group of medieval memorials of any Scottish cathedral. Eighteen bishops were buried here. Although many of the canopy tombs have been lost, those that survive befit the high ambitions of the leading churchmen of Moray.

Queen Victoria's very brief stop at Elgin's railway station in September 1872 was reported in local newspapers and documented in a "photographic image" of the Queen's royal train, showing crowds of spectators lining the tracks and watching from rooftops.

Sources

Numerous antiquarian books proved valuable while writing *The Scottish Ruin Keeper*, and some appear in the story:

Annals of the Parish and Burgh of Elgin by Robert Young (1876)
Note: This unique book resides in the University of Guelph library in Ontario, Canada

The Complete Angler by Izaak Walton (1653)

Costume and Fashion by James Laver (1969)

Elgin: A Guide to Elgin Cathedral by John Shanks the Old Cicerone of Elgin Cathedral (1866)

Elgin Through Time by Jenny Main (2009)

A Feast of Scotland by Janet Warren (1979)

Ivanhoe by Sir Walter Scott (1819)

Kenilworth by Sir Walter Scott (1821)

The Picture of Scotland by Robert Chambers (1828)

Sketches of the Past and Present State of Moray by William Rhind (1839)

Theory of the Earth by James Hutton (1788)

The Vicar of Wakefield by Oliver Goldsmith (1766)

The Wolfe of Badenoch—a Historical Romance of the Fourteenth Century by Sir Thomas Dick Lauder (1827)

Acknowledgements

My thanks to Elgin Museum's kind volunteers who helped solve a few mysteries and provided facts and inspiration for this book.

I am most appreciative of time spent with Lynda Dean, a docent at Elgin Cathedral ruin who shares my fascination with "the drouthy cobbler," John Shanks. She kindly unlocked the door to the duke's palace for my unscheduled visit. We explored every floor of its dusty shell, chockablock with countless pieces of Elgin Cathedral. Tagged and cataloged by volunteers, it is a cache of history that can never be put back together again.

Many thanks to Cheryl Benton of The Three Tomatoes Publishing who enthusiastically supported this book project.

Most of all, I owe my patient husband, David Stewart White, a world of thanks. Without him this book would not exist. Far surpassing his tireless editorial, agent outreach, and technical skills, he has long been my British travel agent, and my personal driver. Scotland has over thirty-four thousand miles of roads, two-thirds of which are rural or unclassified. Over the life of this book project, we drove down more than half of them. David continues to assure me there is no "wrong side" of a single-track road.

About the Author

Deb Hosey White is the author of the novels *Pink Slips and Parting Gifts* and *Magic Numbers*. Deb is the coauthor of *Let's Take the Kids to London*, *Travels Beyond Downton Abbey*, *Portugal–A Tale of Small Cities*, and *Travels Beyond Outlander*. Her articles have appeared in the Washington Post, The Three Tomatoes e-zine and other publications.